THE WATCH LIST

IF YOU HAD THE LIST, WHAT WOULD YOU DO WITH IT?

JOSEPH MITCHAM

Joseph Mitcham

Acknowledgements

The storyline and text of this book is in better shape thanks to the inputs of Max, Neil, Michelle, Scott, James, Phil and especially Sue.

Support to the artistic elements of the project came from Stephen, Charaf, Jonathan and Nathan. Thank you all.

The views and opinions expressed are those of the author alone and should not be taken to represent those of Her Majesty's Government, MOD, HM Armed Forces or any government agency.

This book is dedicated to the members of **Op SPARTAN**.

STANDING TOGETHER, SIDE BY SIDE, ALWAYS SUPPORT, NEVER DIVIDE

Chapters

1

A day at the park

The usually quiet park is beginning to bustle. An hour before the event is to begin; people are gravitating towards the beautifully kept Pavillion Gardens Park on the west side of Birmingham City Centre. It is a glorious sunny day and Marie has been in desperate anticipation for weeks, looking forward to seeing her friend Coleen perform on the specially erected stage. Coleen's place in the final of a television talent show has generated ever-more public interest, making the usually modest open-air arts event an immensely popular draw.

This will be the first time that Marie has ever been to anything so exciting; she has rarely thought to ask her mum about doing anything that might have a cost implication. Since her parents had divorced, and her father disappeared from the scene six years ago, she had stopped asking for anything that she didn't consider essential.

As the car approaches what has become the unofficial drop-off point, on a broad stretch of footpath a hundred metres or so from the park gates, her eyeballs are on stalks, looking out at the crowds of hundreds of people - mostly young girls, all laughing and excited about the afternoon's entertainment.

Jenny is Marie's best friend and has been the driving force behind the outing. She is a lovely girl who has been lucky enough to have grandparents who have paid for her private education since she graduated into upper school four years ago. Marie and Coleen have remained her best friends, but Marie feels herself to be something of a legacy from Jenny's old life. Marie has not met Sal and Tanya before, friends from Jenny's new school, who have come along to see Coleen.

Marie sits in the front passenger seat, twirling a lock of her raven-black hair around her finger, alongside Mrs Simms; the other three girls are bouncing with excitement in the back of the big shiny new Volvo estate, also funded by Mrs Simms' parents. "I'm going to buy every kind of T-shirt they have. Will you be able to get Coleen to sign them for me?" Sal asks.

"I'm sure she will." Jenny says in a voice that Marie thinks sounds a bit too posh for her.

"Now listen to me girls." says Mrs Simms sternly - the four young ladies somehow take notice and listen in to her instructions, "The ticket email advises that no bags are to be taken in to the Gardens if at all possible, so make sure that your phones and purses are safe in your pockets. Use your money wisely and make sure that you get some water, it's a lovely sunny day – we don't want you getting sun-stroke and missing Coleen's performance now, do we?" She reaches back to pull Jenny's long blonde hair out from her collar.

"Mum, stop fussing." Jenny shrugs her off with teenage annoyance.

"Yes, tuck your mobile away then *Maria*." says Sal cruelly, knowing that Marie does not have a phone.

"Call me if you need me for anything, I'll be parked up somewhere nearby, I might even go and see what's on at the cinema, but I'll have my phone on okay?" Mrs Simms says increasing the volume of her voice as the girls jump from the car.

"Okay Mum, and thanks for driving, you're the best." Jenny blows her mother a kiss as she leads her friends off towards the park, joining the pavement as it begins to swell with people, many spilling out onto the road.

"Thanks Mrs Simms." the other three chime in chorus.

"Have a great time girls." The naturally concerned mother watches the girls hurry off to join the masses, ignoring mounting pressure from other parents in the cars behind her.

As the girls step onto the pathway they find themselves immediately in a long column of people with just over a hundred metres to go before the park entrance. "It was nowhere near this busy last year." says Tanya.

"Everyone's come to see Coleen." says Jenny.

"At least the weather's nice." says Marie, trying to put a positive spin on the lengthy wait that faces them.

"Yeah, great – let's all get sun-burnt and be swamped with thousands more people." Sal says with evermore sarcasm, as she yanks the hair bobble from her pony tail of fine, almost white blonde hair, freeing it to fall down as far as her waist.

The road is one long sweeping bend to the right with houses on both sides, up to where the Gardens' perimeter fence begins a little further down the road. The large trees just inside the Gardens overhang the fence and offer welcome shade to the crowd that has made it that far – the first landmark to aim for. The semi-detached houses all have beautiful gardens, full of flowers and small trees in blossom. There are expensive cars in the drives and nice looking people tending to their flowerbeds.

"Have you been to a proper concert before Maria? A real one I mean, not like this naff village thing." asks Sal spitefully.

"My name's Marie." she replies with contempt. "No, I've only seen them on the telly." Marie feels her esteem draining from her and hopes that it will survive the day, ignoring Sal who reels off a list of the bands and performers that she has seen. Marie has not become a fan of either of Jenny's new friends, though Tanya is much less of a bitch than Sal, and tends towards the condescending, rather than being just overtly nasty.

Sal is right though, it is a 'village thing'; the event has been organised by a community group for the past ten years, but has grown and grown, beyond the professional capabilities of the well-meaning committee, who are either unwilling or unable to give up their project to a more commercially minded and resourced organisation. This would have undoubtedly had additional costs for the event, and would likely mean that a ticket price would have had to be applied. There are no in-depth risk assessments in place, there are no security professionals - the security guards are husbands and sons of the committee ladies. The stage and sound guys are the only paid employees, and the most skilled and professional of anyone on site – even the first aiders are volunteers from St John Ambulance. The local Police Constable responsible for the area has been informed, but she has failed to grasp the scale of this year's event, so has not sought out any additional support, or insisted on additional security measures. To be fair; Coleen's success has caught everyone by surprise.

"You might even audition next year, mightn't you Marie?" Jenny changes the conversation in an attempt to defend her friend and get Marie on the front foot. Marie smiles nervously, but says nothing. "She wins all the karaoke competitions - she does a fantastic 'Time to say goodbye', don't you?" Jenny yearns for Marie to speak up for herself – she mentally wills her on to demonstrate to the girls the strength of personality that makes Marie, beyond any doubt, her true best friend.

Tanya looks at Marie with condescending sympathy, "That would be fun Marie; maybe we could form a girl group together?" she says sounding almost sincere - then she and Sal burst into a mock version of the song.

"Maybe I'll go solo." Marie jokes after hearing a few words.

The queue gradually ekes away, they make it to the end of the row of houses, and the start of the Gardens' perimeter fence – *shade at last,* Marie thinks to herself. She stands on her toes to see how far they have to go, she can see a banner for the event tied to the entry gates, and the top of a tall white van parked across the road from them – *once we get to the van we're in.*

The van gets ever-closer - only a few more minutes of prickly conversation to endure. Marie peers through the fence just before they reach the end of the queue and sees a small semi-circle of men dressed in white polo shirts and black trousers, conducting bag searches inside the gates - *this is what's causing of the bottleneck; the queue disappears after the searches.* "Move round to the right, those girls in front of us all have bags." Marie says, steering her group with her arm gestures as they pass under the old iron archway. The ancient gates, blistering and flaking layers of green paint and rust, channel the girls into the park. They raise their arms to show that they have no bags to search - the grumpy looking, middle-aged security man waves them through with a grunt.

Marie notices that the food and drink kiosks only have relatively small queues, and are mostly made up of adults. All of the girls and the occasional boy, are running straight along the main pathway towards the large common area where she assumes that the stage will be. "I'll get the water; you go ahead and save us some space in front of the stage." Jenny volunteers.

"I'll wait with you Jenny." says Marie, as more of a plea than a question.

"Text me when you catch us up and we'll wave for you." Sal says, as she and Tanya skip away following the steady but fast-flowing stream of fans.

"What's a whole school-full of them like?" Marie asks, kind of jokingly, but kind of seriously.

"I know; they're on another planet. You keep me sane Marie, honestly." Jenny turns to the lady serving at the kiosk, "Four bottles of water please."

Jenny is in a good place, she has what seems like the best of both worlds; having come from a humble background, but enjoying a six thousand pound per term education with all of the trimmings.

"How much do I owe you?" Marie asks.

"I'll get these ones." Jenny says tactfully, only too aware of Marie's financial situation.

"I'll get the next one then." Marie says with a smile, understanding exactly the nuance of Jenny's wording.

"Stuff that - we'll make Sal get the next ones; she's got enough money for five t-shirts." Jenny nudges Marie lovingly with an elbow to her ribs as they laugh together.

"My Uncle Ali has given me twenty quid, I was going to get something for my mum with it, you know, to say thank you for letting me come, and for everything that she's been through." says Marie.

"It's your sixteenth next week; I'm buying you a t-shirt. I'll get the same one for me too." Jenny wants Marie to enjoy herself and forget about the worries and woes of home.

The vendor plants down four bottles of water. Jenny hands her a pristine ten pound note in return.

The two girls enjoy each other's company and chat away as they walk in the shade beneath the giant oaks and enter the usually open space of the park, which is now swarming with people, the stage comes into view as they step off the path and onto the lush grass. The Gardens are spectacular, shrouded all around with a vivid multitude of green tree tops, encapsulating a bright mixture of colours of the burgeoning crowd; they look for the contrasted coupling of Sal's shiny light hair with Tanya's equally shiny brunette bunches.

"There they are." Jenny points to the front right of the rapidly filling open area, just a few yards from the stage. Sal and Tanya are jumping up and down like mechanical toys and waving back at them.

The animosity between the girls evaporates as they get into the mood to enjoy the entertainment. The party atmosphere is beginning to build; the DJ is doing a fine job and selecting some great tunes to get the crowd animated. The park fills to well beyond its safe capacity and not an inch of grass can be seen within two hundred metres of the stage. The first act is a dance troop of young girls, looking somewhat daunted by the crowd – their biggest gig before this had been leading a local carnival that had only attracted a couple of hundred people, they were now facing upwards of three thousand.

Soon enough, Coleen is walking onto the stage; she has the look of someone who is relaxed in her environment, despite being at the centre of attention, already a seasoned entertainer after a few short weeks of fame, about to perform to an audience that has now grown to over five thousand, all bellowing their support for her.

"Good afternoon everyone. Welcome to Pavillion Gardens. It's great being back here, where I'm from, playing for the people who got me where I am. This one's for you..."

The crowd erupts with louder cheers, as the first few bars of her new hit song play, and then goes quiet as she sings the opening line. The girls hug each other in the mass of people, looking up at Coleen, mouthing the words back at her, which they all know by heart. Coleen sees her two best friends and points back at them.

As Coleen sings the chorus for the second time, Marie senses a change in the atmosphere, a different kind of noise in the hubbub. She looks over her left shoulder and can see something is not right. She can see a refuse truck coming through the trees – *that shouldn't be there, they empty the bins when everyone's gone*. It makes no sense to her, but then suddenly she comes around to what is happening, and as the cheers turn to screams, she sees a tsunami of people begin to surge in her direction.

Coleen's voice trails off from the song as she becomes cognisant of what is going on - she screams into the microphone, "NOOOOOO." shrieking "RUN, EVERYBODY RUN." She breaks down into hysteric wailing, dropping the microphone as her personal security guard grabs her from behind and runs from the stage with her trailing like a rag doll. As the microphone hits the floor it sends a stark bang through the system, followed by a series of shrill, ear-piercing whistles of feedback, but no one's listening, it simply adds to the chaos and confusion in the melee of the horrific attack.

The truck thunders into the crowd, in a low gear to maximise its penetrating power – the engine roars, it scatters people and consumes them under its wheels. As they fight to get away, they knock each other over - as many people are trampled by each-other, as are caught by the preying vehicle. It rumbles on to the heart of the improvised arena, bouncing unpredictably as it rides up on top of people, then slips off of bodies – the wheels struggle for traction on the soft flesh of its victims and its momentum is eventually lost, but not before travelling over one hundred metres through the mass of people, before it eventually comes to a halt with mangled bodies stuck in its axles, with distorted and disjointed limbs hanging from under its wheel-arches.

The people who have survived unscathed are now running for the main exit. A lucky few have local knowledge and sprint for alternative escape routes from the grounds. A brave few, mostly adults, run to the screaming injured and lifeless dead or unconscious; those left in the wake of the instrument of devastation, and those scattered randomly as they fell in the crush, all around the park.

Marie finds herself on the ground, having survived the crush and stampede of people, she looks at her hand, she is still clasping a shred of Jenny's T-shirt sleeve – she never let go. She looks about her, there are bodies everywhere, some moving, others not. None are Jenny. She thinks for a second about what Sal and Tanya were wearing – *I don't care about those two* – Marie instantly regrets thinking such an awful thought, and emits a hushed, but involuntary sob to herself.

She gets to her feet and does her best to run towards the exit, having to pick her line through the bodies and others making their way to their feet. She passes the truck; as she desperately tries to envision the optimal path past it and beyond, she sees the driver's door open, and forces herself to push on, ignoring the pain that she has gradually become aware of in her left leg.

The driver jumps down from the cab. He wears half-bleached jeans and a black hoodie, and is carrying a large, rusty-coloured African Topanga knife in his right hand. The long slender, sinister-looking machete blade is narrow at the handle and gradually widens to give significant weight at the business end of its nearly forty centimetres of cutting edge. He stands firm and tall, shoulders rising up and head tilting back, his left hand grasps the rim of his hood and pulls it down slowly. His face gradually comes into view; Marie cannot take her eyes off of him, her face wrinkles and she cries in terror as she tries to get away. He has jet black hair, long, thick and shiny, falling down over his ears. He looks well-tanned and in his twenties, there is something perversely alluring about his calm, confident, but intensely focused expression as he surveys his hunting ground.

After analysing the scene, he slowly raises his blade high in the air and in an instant he comes alive, running with purpose towards those heading for the exit. He swipes his knife at those he gets close to, hacking into the backs and heads of the slow and already weakened, chopping them down to the floor. He moves like a crazy person, like a chimpanzee in a frenzy; he yelps and screams like an animal. A new wave of terror engulfs the already hysterical victims. He stalks the back of the pack like a sheepdog, or a predatory fish steering a shoal of prey. Racing for their lives, the remaining fans track the reverse route of the truck; they are fleeing through ground-zero, leaving the injured for dead, desperate to escape with their own lives.

The attacker rampages wildly, lashing out opportunistically, as he passes a woman on the ground administering first aid to a wounded young girl; he strikes her on the back of the neck, almost decapitating her – she falls flat on her face, on top of her patient - instantly dead. Another helper observes what is happening and bravely gets to his feet and charges the terrorist – he dives to tackle his assailant, but is seen too quickly; he is struck on the side of the head; swatted out of the air - he falls flat to the grass suffering horrendous facial injuries from the blade which remains embedded in his cheekbone, bisecting his ear and beyond into his hairline. His attacker wrenches the weapon free with an awful slurping noise as air is sucked into the vacuum left in its victim's skull.

As his pace is slowed the attacker has the opportunity to take stock of his progress, everyone that he can see who is able to move, is heading towards the main exit. The young girl, who the 'have-a-go hero' was tending to, cannot control her sobs. She tries to crawl away, but the killer steps forward quietly up alongside her and then silences her with a powerful and deadly blow from above to the side of the neck.

Adrenalin and flight instinct force Marie to ignore the pain and press on. She makes ground from the back of the pack and gives herself hope that she will escape the terrorist; she doesn't allow herself to slow until she passes out between the gates to what she hopes will be a safer area. Clear of the gates with a choice of directions to go, her chances of eluding the killer are already doubled. The main road is awash with screaming people, all trying to get as far away from the scene as they can, but the road is jammed by cars, wedged in in both directions by the weight of people. The main road is the obvious place for the people to run to and is swamped. A secondary wall of people, mostly parents, is coming the other way, somehow alerted to the incident and running to get back, already aware of what has happened. They are each inconsolable at the terrific horror of the situation. Their terror is compounded by the realisation that they do not know where their children or loved ones are, and whether or not they have been harmed.

Marie opts to push right, back the way she had come towards the drop-off point, but cannot find a way through. She screams; "He's coming, run." at the top of her voice. More people pile into the crowd, to be frustrated by the jam. She looks over her shoulder, back into the Gardens, she sees the black hoodie, she sees the flash of a blade – she trembles in fear, she cannot muster her voice to shout further warning. Then she sees something else, a flash of yellow from under the trees to the left – a Police Officer. The officer fires her Taser at the centre of the attacker's back. He drops to his knees, but she does not release her trigger.

As the chaos develops, a mobile phone, hard wired into a large improvised explosive device, in a van directly opposite the Gardens' gates, begins to ring…

Marie is overcome in an instant with the flash of intense light and heat, followed quickly by a deafening sonic boom and the immense blast wave, which brings with it the powerful physical impact of matter hitting her fully in the face. Her brain shuts down, unable to cope with the enormity, the pain and shock of what is happening. The detonation is huge, even for a vehicle-borne improvised explosive device - the force of the blast practically vaporises everyone within ten metres of the initiation. Anyone in the next ten metres of radius is ripped to pieces, from there on out the damage to individuals reduces at a merciful rate, as the poor souls nearest to the explosion act as shields and absorb the explosion's kinetic energy and metallic shrapnel released from the van and deliberately packed scrap metal shards. Never-the-less; those next closest are either killed or suffer incredible damage. Everyone in the vicinity is felled, blown off their feet, some sustaining serious injuries from being thrust against walls, railings, vehicles, and other people. Marie is blown back against others, who break her fall, as she breaks the fall of those in front of her.

The blast still echoing around the street, all else falls silent for an instant, then after a few eerie, but somehow peaceful seconds, murmurs and low moans can be heard by anyone with intact and functioning ear drums, then the crying begins as the first few people come around to what they have experienced, and are now beginning to comprehend.

2

Sensitive soldier

"I'm in the pub with the blokes from work; we're celebrating the end of the contract." Alex's mother is happy that he's doing well professionally, but at the same time concerned that he'll have nothing to move on to… and that he is out drinking again.

"Don't worry Mum, there's plenty out there for me and I'll be paid a stack for this job – I won't be crawling home any time soon." Alex had liked being at home, but he is not about to let his circumstances slide so far that he would need to resort to that. He also knows that his mum would love to have him home for a few weeks and hoped that she wasn't in too much of an emotional mood, or she'd be upset about him making light of it.

"Say hello to Tom from me and enjoy your holidays." Tom has been Alex's step-dad for almost as long as he can remember, though they'd never been close. "Oh, and don't piss my inheritance up the wall."

His mum is well used to his loose language, but detests it none-the-less. She pleads with him in a tone that communicates her frustration, and her knowledge that he isn't likely to take any notice of her anyway - "Just be careful tonight love, you never know what might happen in a place like that - have you seen the news about this terror attack in Birmingham?"

"Yes Mum, I know it's awful, but it's a million to one, and this place isn't much of a target." Alex has seen the headlines, but has not had much of a chance to look at the detail of the Gardens' bomb, and his teenage-legacy aversion to listening to what his mum says doesn't make him any more interested in it.

"Well, try not to drink too much anyway please."

Alex doesn't try to hide the fact that he feels patronised, but shows no anger; "I'm with a chilled-out bunch of blokes and will be going home before this place lights up, you don't have to be concerned Mum."

Alex runs his fingers along the back of the underside of the narrow green bench of the bus stop that he is using as shelter from the light rain, his forefinger meets with someone else's old chewing gum - he grimaces as his mum goes on, "I do worry, I always will – I'm your mother."

His mum's words are comforting as he looks about his surroundings, there are lots of people, but he has no real companionship. The street has taken on a murky haze as the sun sets and the warmth from the tarmac heats the raindrops back into the air as a vapour. The darkening atmosphere seems to have an accelerative effect on life, as people speed up to get home to their dry houses. As he ends the call, gets up and turns to walk back across the road, he thinks of his mum and has the faintest ache of guilt that he never spends more than two minutes talking to her.

The assembled group of colleagues he is heading back to are like-minded young men, but he can't really call any of them friends. They have worked together for a month, and he'd been with a couple of them on previous jobs, but has never made a serious effort to get to know any of them all that well. He would have swapped this night of celebratory drinks for a plate of his mum's 'spag bol' and a couple of pints in the Wagon and Horses with his old school mates in an instant – *maybe next week.*

The network fix that ended the contract had been stumbled over by Alex two weeks into their project and they had dragged it out for long enough to make a decent yield, (but not too long as to damage their collective reputation) and still trigger the completion clause payment. Richard, the project leader, had taken all of the credit for the work, but to be fair he'd promised to back-hand Alex an extra two grand in cash and told him that there'd definitely be more work for him if he wanted it. Richard is almost as technically gifted as Alex, but had decided to put himself into a leadership role in his own business and manage small trouble-shooting project teams for discrete, but highly complex computer network issues. Richard's current portfolio of customers includes the health service and military clients, but word is spreading further through the lucrative Civil Service contracting network and beyond.

Alex finds himself jumping through the obligatory social hoop of the evening to ensure that relationships are maintained for future work, and the venue and company is nice enough. The Claret is a well turned-out pub-come-wine bar in Hounslow that attracts a decent clientele of young and successful social and professional climbers; there won't be room to move by eight.

As he walks through the open doors of the pub he feels a change in his persona take effect the instant he smells the atmosphere and becomes enveloped by the beat of gentle, but modern trunk-funk – he is back in the room. The quality finish to the minimalistic oak fittings and the intricate duck egg green floral wallpaper gives the place a warm and comfortable feel. His eyes adjust to the subtle lighting as he takes in his surroundings and appreciates the quality of the décor. He stands off from the group; no one notices his return; being just above average height, average build and with unimaginatively cropped hair helped him to fit in as a natural part of the scene.

"Alex my old son, come 'ere and get this down your neck." Richard holds aloft a glass of god-knows-what and presents it to Alex like it's the Olympic torch. Alex sidles over between the nests of empty chairs to get to the group who have become gradually less sturdy over the course of the afternoon. As he takes the drink from Richard and necks a gulp of the sugary, alcohol-laced concoction, the next drinks are already being ordered, "Just Stella this time love." Richard pivots on his heels as he fulfils his duties as host and master of ceremonies. Alex palms off the drink to another of the less sober young men.

A big man, at six foot three, Richard is untoned and overweight, but exudes strength through his immense confidence and size. He begins his keynote address: "Now lads, thanks to this young man here," he pats Alex on the back, "you're all unemployed from today, but I want to thank each and every one of you for all of your hard work. You've proved that you can deliver on task, under pressure, and I'd work with any of you again." Richard is a showman when ordering fast food - when in full flow and lauding it up with an audience; he is as sickly sweet as the last cocktail.

"I've got a few jobs lined up and will be chatting to you all over the course of this evening and giving you a heads up - if you haven't already made plans?" There is a pause, no one else speaks; they are all hooked. This sounds interesting to Alex, who has the ability required to venture out on his own, and is as capable of doing as well for himself as Richard has, but he just cannot be bothered. He feels relaxed about his future, as a 29 year old free spirit; he has money to burn and no commitments to worry about, but never-the-less still has the need for a challenge.

The group naturally begins to disperse across the bar, some hover around it, queuing to speak to Richard, and others move swiftly to the pool table around the corner of the room. Alex hesitates to commit to joining any of the groups and ends up on his own, certainly not from a lack of popularity, more from a lack of effort on his part to join in. He puts twenty quid in the fruit machine and slowly sips his beer, anticipating his turn to receive counsel from Richard. As unbothered as he tells himself that he is, he still cannot wait to hear what Richard has to say, and he isn't going to be so alcohol enthused that he won't remember the details in the morning.

Richard is lapping up the attention and making the most of commanding the interest of his stable of young of engineers. The work that he has to offer is cutting-edge stuff which he knows will keep them chasing his coat-tails, but he is particularly excited about what he has for Alex; he is savouring it. The wait has taken its toll on Alex's funds and the slot has devoured his immediate resources just before he has managed to crack the machine's sequencing, which he is part-way through reading like the proverbial book. He makes for the door and the cash machine a few shops down. Richard immediately breaks conversation and calls out; "Alex, don't go, I need you mate." uncharacteristically unmeasured, Richard backtracks as he ditches Matt, a computer science graduate from Bristol. "I mean, you're not going are you? I've got something that I think will be a real challenge for you," Richard quickly makes his way over to intercept him, "and to be honest, it needs your clearances."

Alex had managed to keep hold of his elevated vetting status on leaving the Army by saying that he needed it for joining the part-timers – though that never was likely to happen. Alex had not been the stereotypical tough-guy soldier; he had barely managed to put up with the grotty conditions imposed during basic training, and had never even looked into completing an arduous course - not wanting to get his hands dirty, or any part of him dirty for that matter. Keeping fit appealed to him though, and he had become a physical training instructor. The Army offered him an easy route out of a dull existence of factory work and going nowhere. He had too much intelligence to be satisfied with a mundane life, but not enough get-up-and-go to make anything of himself, not on his own anyway. The Army offered opportunity in abundance and he'd quickly identified that life had not much else to offer him without having to put in a damn sight more effort than he was willing to expend.

Scoring highly on the aptitude tests, interviewing well, and with some strong exam results, Alex was offered his choice of any of the technical Corps jobs, with an option to go straight to officer commissioning. The Corps cap badge jobs had all looked fairly bland in the job descriptions, but he imagined that there must be more to them in real life. The recruiting Sergeant was from the Royal Corps of Signals, the Army's communications branch, and he mentioned that the basic 'scaly' operator skills would put him into a fifty thousand a year civilian job even if he only served his minimum time – this was an instant green light for Alex; his main motivation had always been money. To be fair to Alex, it wasn't really about money - money was just the only yard-stick for a kid from his kind of background to rate stability against. Whatever Alex did with his life; he wanted security. A family life wasn't on the cards in his mind, but a 'bought and paid for' house and a buffer in the bank was what he wanted for himself. He'd achieved that after making some good money on back-to-back tours in Afghanistan and some shrewd buying and selling of properties at the right times – it was all beer tokens from then on.

"What have you got for me Dickie?" Alex hopes that it will be military - he knows the system constructs inside out, they had clearly been built by the lowest quoting contractor - they would be an easy picking ground for him to enhance his reputation from.

"It's the Army Skynet 6 intranet platform, the new language developments that they've added into the old system weren't tested properly and it won't talk to some of the other intelligence systems, even their own." This had sounded like a nightmare to Richard, whose computer language skills aren't nearly as good as his infrastructure knowledge. Alex, on the other hand, knows roughly what will be required already and knows that it is seven day's work tops.

"How long are they giving us?"

Richard winces a little as he grinds out the words; "They need it done in ten days." Alex tries not to give it away, but he feels the grin coming. Richard goes on, "They're throwing money at this though, they need those networks talking, or else it's old school, cross-network working which is not good for slick intelligence work. This is a real threat, more so since this Birmingham thing, we have to get going on it from tomorrow."

Alex picks up the nearest pint, unsure of whether it is his, and not really caring, he looks over it as he raises it up level to his lips, "Right, sounds like this better be my last one for the evening - that is if plenty of this 'thrown money' is aimed in my direction?"

Richard lowers his forehead and grins at Alex, with a look on his face that says 'you're learning son'. "Of course, of course, it'll be double the rate of this last job," Richard says as quietly as he can get away with, "and you get to keep the replacement hardware." It is standard practice for military oversight teams to confiscate all computers and drives used in contracted system maintenance and fault-finding; the team would be permitted to purchase replacement items and claim back the money – healthy upgrades are a reliable benefit from this kind of work.

"That sounds great Dickie, but how about rounding it up to 20k? If it's just me on this, I've got a lot of responsibility to make you look good."

The skin on Richard's face is thin and prematurely ageing, not helped by his sedentary and otherwise unhealthy lifestyle, which make his facial expressions even easier to read; "You're a cheeky little Charlie." Richard says, breaking into a laugh.

Richard substitutes the word 'cunt' for 'Charlie' in all conversation after several accidental utterances in front of his kids. The substitution was only actually affected after his son had told his class teacher that he was 'a right cunt'. This had not gone down well with the nursery teacher, headmaster, or Richard's wife – the boy had only been three years old at the time.

"Will there be an early completion bonus on this one too?" Alex says with his tongue firmly in his cheek.

"Don't take the piss fella." The smile is still there. Alex's cheekiness lets him get away with a lot and endears him to almost everyone he meets.

"We'll see about that. Say goodbye to your buddies, get home for some rest, and I'll see you in the morning."

"Where and when?"

"It's Whitehall, Main Server Building; I'll send a car to the hotel at eight. Are you all right for clothes?" Richard doesn't like to think of his lads being uncomfortable, he wants them in optimal condition for work, but also doesn't want them turning up to work stinking.

"Yeah, I was expecting to be on the last job for at least a few more days yet."

"Bag up your laundry and I'll get Jen to square it away for you."

3

Angry man

Turning the key to his front door, Craig takes a cautionary look over his shoulder before entering. He has no reason to suspect that he is being watched, but vigilance and awareness have been drummed into him after more than two decades in the Army, he could never totally relax, even after a pint or four in the King's Head. His modest three-bed semi in Richmond, London is private, out of the way and perfectly placed for most work opportunities; it is also extremely convenient for the military mecca that is the Army vs Navy Rugby match every May. He walks down the well-decorated hallway, with walls filled with group photos of well-decorated men, and on to the kitchen. He flicks on the television and attacks the fridge. As he browses through packets of cooked meats and cheeses, he hears more news of the Birmingham incident that has fuelled the angry conversation at the pub all evening. The official death toll has been climbing all day and is now up to sixty-two. Craig has been shocked by the atrocity - this took some doing for a man of his considerable experience. He snatches a couple of spicy sausages from the middle shelf and slumps himself down at the kitchen table, his eighteen stone testing the wooden-framed chair to its limit. He further reflects on what has happened as he begins to eat. Having rapidly passed through emotions of surprise, furious anger and disgust earlier in the day, he is now experiencing a deep sadness, but with anger still bubbling through him. His mind turns again to vitriol, boiling again with rage as on screen, the Police site commander breaks down in tears whilst describing how the terrible acts had taken place.

The hostile vehicle attack and bombing is too much for Craig to accept. Battle weary from what have seemed like endless Special Forces tours of

Northern Ireland and various locations around the Middle East; he is fiercely patriotic and highly defensive of the freedom and way of life that he feels that he has helped to secure for the British people. Every little chip away at what he sees as the culture of his country has further enraged him throughout his life. This has been amplified since retiring from Service and having spent more time up close and personal with the civilian population.

From the revulsion that he had received when proudly displaying his George Cross flag on Saint's day, to the mispronunciation and slurring of words into 'indo-rapper' accents by the local kids - he feels that his freedoms are considered less important than those who have done nothing to earn the rights to theirs, and the fact that his combine-cockney patter is fairly far from being perfect Queen's English is an irony that he is blind to. Whilst watching the footage from earlier in the day of emergency services' personnel assisting the dazed and walking wounded, as the anchors go back over the number of dead which seems to have settled, he knows that the time has come to take action.

Craig has become something of a public figure from the TV role and persona that he had allowed to develop. Beasting minor celebrities through a mock Special Forces course had been a bit of fun to him, but the production company had lapped it up, and he was tipped for a broader set of prime-time presenter positions. The high profile military operations that he had been involved in had been used by the network to boost his notoriety and reputation, which had been crystallised by the way that he carried himself, and the way that he thrashed people, whilst at the same time looking out for them with respect and an inherent sense of a duty of care. His middle-aged spread and silvering hair gave him an air of approachability, and he had come to be regarded by many of the viewing public as a living legend, as he is by the servicemen and women who know him, or had even heard tales of his prowess. His social media following combines these audiences, and gives him great online power to wield.

The novelty of being a TV personality had quickly worn off for Craig, and he returned to some 'proper' private work, before finally retiring from practical jobs and taking a comfortable consultancy with an engineering firm that has interests in multiple developing, but dangerous areas of the world. Now on a six figure salary in return for very little in terms of tangible work – all that he has to do is provide some well-presented advice on force protection issues a few times a month, and make the odd appearance at high-level business meetings and functions, giving his employers enhanced credibility.

Spiralling into a fit of rage, as responsibility for the two-pronged attack is claimed; Craig storms into the lounge and snatches his laptop up from the coffee table. He lifts its lid as he climbs the stairs and heads into the third bedroom which has become a makeshift office. He snarls at himself to capture his composure and takes a few calming breaths. He places the computer on the desk, making sure that there is nothing over his shoulder, in view of the webcam, that could classify as a security breach, and opening a social media window, he clicks to initiate a live broadcast. Craig has no plan, no script or even the faintest idea of what he might say; he just wants to express his emotions to anyone that will listen.

"What the hell is going on in this Country?" Craig tries to remain calm and communicate what he is feeling, and what he believes the type of people that follow him are feeling too. "What sort of up toss-pot thinks that running over a group of kids in a bin lorry is going to make anyone support their cause, or even listen to them?" The broadcast's following steadily begins to creep up as it spreads virally through the linked networks of his fan-base. His profile for this kind of transmission is fully public and the exposure of his ramblings is growing exponentially. After ten minutes he is still exploring the inexplicably terrible acts that have happened just a few hours ago. Now fuelled by the online comments that audience members are posting to his broadcast, he attempts to dissect the reasoning of the perpetrators and how a lack of cohesive communities has allowed this to happen.

"No doubt we'll be hearing in the coming days and weeks about how this was an individual born in this country, with loyalties to some other country or religion, and how he was preyed upon to be radicalised – probably remotely, or from a British prison for fuck's sake." Craig is getting more upset, the more he thinks about the ambulances full of bodies and the eyewitnesses covered in blood and sobbing on camera to the eyes of the world. "What really pisses me off is the thought that in houses up and down this country, there are potential terrorists sitting in front of their televisions grinning from ear to ear at this 'success', and they're already thinking about how else to add to the nation's pain."

"Already known to the authorities - now there's a phrase we're all getting used to. If they're known about, then why the hell are they walking freely on the streets to commit such horrific acts?" The live broadcast audience is now up to 27,000 and still growing, but Craig has said all that he had wanted to say and is starting to repeat himself. "I don't know what the answer to this problem is, and I'm sure that the security services don't either. We're too politically correct to take any direct action through official channels; maybe we need a less formal approach?"

Craig's fifty-five thousand social media followers are stereotypically men, largely patriots, and the nucleus of people that really pay attention to him, and what he says, are either serving or ex-serving military. Many of those who had retired had found private security work abroad, joining what is colloquially known as '5 Para', after the three regular Para battalions, and fourth reserve battalion, the informal grouping of ex-elite and specially trained soldiers working in retirement is a significant resource controlled by six or so highly professional private security firms run predominantly by middle-grade ex-infantry officers. Craig loves staying in contact with guys like this and can easily while away entire evenings just engaging in the banter that inevitably leads on from whatever social commentary posts that he has made on his profile.

He is not so proud of the far right attention that his public image has attracted; he has kicked several users off of his page for expressing racist views or bigoted opinions. As much as he hates constricting people's freedom of speech; he will not allow others to hijack his voice, or promote their views, which are contrary to his own. As much as he has become bored with the public persona that he has developed, it is now his brand that secures his considerable income, and this must be protected.

Craig's vent is over, but there is no satisfaction that the physical power that he represents is not able to be brought to bear against the evil that has committed the Birmingham atrocity, or any of the characters living amongst the population who hate his way of life. He is frustrated by knowing that, at the right time, in the right place, he is capable of rubbing out any 'would be' terrorist with the minimum of fuss, and would take great pleasure in doing so. He regularly fantasises about such scenarios, finding himself in the middle of an unfolding terror plot as it plays out - he steps into the breech to do what is necessary. In his mind he savours that virtual moment while waiting tactically for the marauding gunman's magazine change, before charging him with the heaviest, hardest pre-selected piece of furniture or fire extinguisher that he has to hand. He challenges himself to invent solutions to situations where there is no improvised weaponry on offer, and has a portfolio of joint-crunching and down-right nasty hand-to-hand combat moves rehearsed in his mind that would make even a mixed martial artist wince. This is not the outlandish fantasy of a man without means; this is a reality waiting to happen and that might be the only way to relieve his frustration.

4

A fresh brief

At 08:00 sharp, a taxi pulls up to the hotel entrance; Alex is waiting, dressed smartly in shirt and trousers, carrying a tightly packed laptop bag. He's had a solid nine hours sleep after his early breakaway from the previous night's celebrations – clearly Richard hasn't; he is sitting in the near-side back seat of the black cab looking somewhat rough.

"Good morning, it must be a big job for you to get out of bed so early." Alex says as Richard pushes the door open, and then holds the folding seat down for him as he shuffles across to let Alex in.

"Tell me about it. All the other lads have at least a few days off, so I felt obliged to stick with it last night. I ended up leaving my credit card behind the bar at about one in the morning; I should have sacked it when you did." Richard looks every inch the fifty year old who has been trying to keep up with the boys.

"Have you seen the latest on Birmingham?" Alex asks.

"Bloody horrible Charlies, they need wiping out, scum like that." Richard is a family man and many of the victims are similar ages to his sons. "We need to get this job done, that'll be us doing our bit. The security services need to be joined up to fight this kind of war, and information is the vital ground." Richard's face twitches with anger – Alex is impressed by Richard's sentiment, and sarcastically so by his use of military phraseology.

"I'd maybe have sacked off coming in with you today if it hadn't been for seeing that on the news, but I definitely want you off on the right foot after that." The attack has clearly got to Richard, who is animating everything that he says with a shake of an open hand. "I've had a slight change of heart on the strategy for this one, no bollocksing about and stretching out the days if it goes well – I want this done and dusted as quickly as possible; if you need support just ask."

Alex pinches his lips together, and gives the slightest of bobbing nods with a furrowed brow. They know each other well enough to understand what is expected of one another, both are confident they will not be let down.

The taxi approaches a historical Government building, the towering architecture of stone pillars is impressive, but at the same time dirty; the masonry is thick with a carbonated coating of soot and it makes the beautiful old building feel somehow more ominous than its scale alone would warrant. They drive through the centre, and largest, of three grand archways into the building's internal courtyard and spin around to pull up to a doorway on the right side of the yard. They are out of sight of public gaze, though only a couple of hundred yards from one of the greatest tourist destinations on the planet.

Alex knows roughly where he is, owing to a brief spell on public duties, though the relevance or value of putting communications operators on this prestigious duty had not been immediately apparent to him at the time. Not that he would ever have complained; he'd had the time of his life - telling young impressionable tourists that you guard the Queen had been a keen aphrodisiac that had worked its magic on countless more-than-willing young ladies. The building is just off from Horse Guards Parade - if only he were going to get the chance to enjoy the sights.

As the vehicle draws to a halt, one of the two steel doors to their left, with opaque darkened glass, opens and an Intelligence Corps corporal in barrack dress uniform emerges from the brightly lit innards of the building. All three men in the cab pause to admire her turnout; her tailored light-beige shirt gathering tightly at the waist, held firm by her broad, colourful stable belt of green, grey and red, the belt covering the top of a heavy cotton brownish-green skirt that falls to just below the knee. Her hair is tightly gathered into a firmly pinned bun and is capped off by her starkly bright green beret. They quickly re-animate as she opens the nearside cab door. There is an awkward pause between greetings as Richard blocks Alex's exit whilst paying the driver. The young Non-Commissioned Officer waits patiently as Richard unfolds his considerable frame from the vehicle, making way for Alex - they compose themselves on the ancient and over-sized flag stones of the pavement.

"Good morning, Sirs, I'm Corporal Lucy Butler. If you'd like to come with me."

The two men follow Corporal Butler back through the door from which she has come. As their eyes adjust from the bright sunshine outside, to the different, but equally bright light inside, Corporal Butler is already collecting the access passes that she has had prepared for them. The reception area is a cold black and grey granite tiled room that has clearly suffered from budget cuts over the past few decades; infuriatingly minor repairs and maintenance has not been be tended to; cracks and chips adorn the well-worn surfaces of the floor and edges of the reception counter. "Please sign in your mobile phones and any other networked devices." says Corporal Butler. The reception work station is occupied by a well-dressed lady in her mid-fifties, full of smiles and aching to chat to the new-comers, but restraining herself to a quiet and polite; "Good morning". Richard and Alex each hand over a single mobile phone, the receptionist locks them away into a miniature cabinet and hands them locker keys in return.

Corporal Butler is running to a strict timeline and sets off left down the broad foyer, Richard and Alex follow on. Alex catches a glimpse of the receptionist's name tag and talks over his shoulder to her as they move off, "Thanks Marion, I'm Alex by the way, I'll be working here for a few days, I'll introduce myself properly later". He gives her a cheeky wink as he disappears around to the right, making Marion's day in an instant.

Catching up with the rest of the party, Alex nearly knocks into Richard as he rounds the corner. Corporal Butler presses the lift call button; she speaks with a hint of arrogance and without taking hers eyes off the changing floor number displayed on the square of black glass above the lift doors, "I'm your host while you are here and I will ensure that you have access to what you need and are properly resourced. I'll take you upstairs to the third floor, where you'll receive your formal brief from Lieutenant Colonel Tim Farrer, he's Lancashire Regiment, but well read into networks, so talk to him like a grown up please."

The steel doors open with an old-fashioned ping and they file in.

"Your passes." Corporal Butler hands Richard and Alex lanyards with 'accompanied guest' printed cards attached. "As you've been here before, I'll spare you the orientation and safety brief Mr Walker. Mr Gregory, I'll give it to you once we're up and running." Alex can feel Richard's smirk at Corporal Butler's choice of words and senses his craving for eye-contact behind Corporal Butler's back - Alex resists acknowledging it, for fear of jeopardising his credibility and assumed current status as a mature adult.

The lift door pings open; they exit and turn right, then immediately left onto the main corridor and the march is back on, straight to the far end of the building, passing several open doors to sparse open-plan offices, made less open-plan by the rigid desk partitions that give the occupants their own little worlds to operate from. There is a distinct lack of atmosphere, and even though they speak to no one and hear little conversation going on, they can tell that the place is wired and under pressure.

They find themselves outside an office door labelled 'Network Director'. "Wait one." Corporal Butler says to Alex and Richard before knocking on the door and walking straight in, closing the door behind her. Alex looks at Richard and raises his brow by way of questioning what is going on; Richard replies with a slight shrug of the shoulders.

After a brief moment; the door re-opens. "Come on in please gentlemen. This is Lieutenant Colonel Tim Farrer."

The Colonel is already on his feet as they enter the room. He bounds towards Richard. "Call me Tim, please chaps, I like to keep things informal with civilians. Good morning, good to see you again Richard." He shakes their hands in turn.

Richard smiles with a sparkle, "Hello again Tim."

Alex falls straight back into the habit of rank; "Good morning Colonel, I'm Alex Gregory." It is all that he can do not to call himself Sergeant; the military presence has brought back mixed, but mostly fond memories.

"So Richard, this is the guy that can crack our little issue?" Colonel Tim says standing directly in front of Alex, eyeing him up and down.

"We'll see Tim, but he's just smashed a job that we thought could take a couple of months, inside three weeks."

Alex masks his mild embarrassment and pride with a smile, and offers his initial thoughts on the project; "From what I've heard, Sir, it should be a simple language patch; it just depends on how complex and how different the languages are."

Colonel Tim's smile disappears, but doesn't quite make it to a frown. "Gentlemen, we need to get off on the right foot, and quickly, so forgive me for being curt." The Colonel looks squarely at Richard, having to look up slightly, despite being over six foot himself, "Alex should not have heard a word about this job until he was firmly behind the closed doors of this building - this is top secret gentlemen. This is beyond mere Information Act responsibilities or corporate confidentiality. Indiscretion on the subject matter of this piece of work is punishable by lengthy custodial sentence - are we clear on this?"

"Colonel, I'm sorry," Richard raises his hands in apology, "I gave Alex a partial brief on the fundamentals of the problem without any specific detail. Not a further word outside of these four walls, Sir, you have my word".

Colonel Tim pauses, staring Richard in the eye; he holds his gaze as he moves around the desk and sits down. "Right that's that put to bed, let's crack on. Please have a seat."

Richard gives a nod, underlined with a submissive, humbled, pinched-lipped smile to the officer, then looks across to Alex with an expression carrying remorse.

"As you say Alex, this looks like a cryptographic language problem between our new Skynet 6 system and the networks of our key intelligence partners - the languages involved are some of the most complex in the industry. Our contractor failed to predict conflicts, and to be honest neither they, nor we, carried out full live system tests prior to implementation, the operational cost of downtime was deemed too high. Hindsight is a wonderful thing, but the reality is, if you can resolve this in good time; it will just about have been a successful cost-saving measure."

Alex immediately identifies the debonair and svelte Colonel Tim as a 'flier'; seemingly very young to have made senior officer rank, and in a staff job that cannot be bluffed - however posh and well-connected he might be; he must be the real deal, a future General maybe. Either that or a future 'Dickie' - just the experience of his present role, backed up with his military rank and training, would make him highly valuable in corporate terms.

"What have I got to go on Colonel? Is anything getting through? Do you have a fault log?" Alex is prepared to work from scratch, but will take any head-start that he can get.

Colonel Tim picks up a thick, but flimsy cardboard folder in both hands. He shakes it as he explains – "We've captured everything, all of the reports are in here, as are any corrupted messages or data packets that have been received or transmitted; The Security Service has been very helpful as our priority 'distant end'. We don't expect you to leaf through this page by page, it's all digitally filed on the profile that Corporal Butler has set up for you on our system, she'll log you in once you get to your office. Standard search applications have been installed on your account, if you need others or need to import your own, just ask Lucy… Corporal Butler, that is." Richard thinks nothing of the slip of formality, but mentally it raises Alex's eyebrow.

Richard speaks to break what was becoming an uncomfortable pause in proceedings; "What hours will Alex be expected to work, Colonel?"

"Aargh", Colonel Tim's eyes flicker to Corporal Butler and back with uncertainty. He isn't a man who concerns himself with that level of detail, he naturally expects his people to work whatever hours they need to, in order to get things done.

Corporal Butler interjects; "This is a grown up environment Mr Walker - big-boys' rules. Mr Gregory will work as long as he can each day in a sustainable routine. He's no good to us if he's too tired to operate, so if that means going home at six, or having a nap mid-afternoon, then so be it. The urgency of this job means that if he is able to work twenty hours-a-day, then the support that he needs will be here for him."

"Quite Corporal Butler - well said. We want this squared away in the shortest possible order, and Alex is free to achieve that in the most efficient way that he can." The Colonel adds nothing of further value with his summary, but regains ownership of his meeting.

Alex has heard all that he needs to hear, everything else will come to him on the job. "Well if that's the brief complete Colonel, shouldn't we be getting moving?"

Colonel Tim jumps up from his seat with a sense of urgency. "Yes, Alex, let's not stand on ceremony. Corporal Butler, will you show this young man to his work station and see to it that he has what he needs." He makes his way around the table and shakes Richard's and Alex's hands as they rise from their seats.

"May I stay on for a quick chat Colonel?" Richard asks as Corporal Butler ushers Alex out into the corridor. Alex dawdles slowly out of the room, trying to catch the first few words of the conversation, but the door is firmly closed before he can hear anything of value.

Alex catches up with Corporal Butler who only makes it half way down the bright but grey corridor before she stops, turns back to face him and grabs the handle of an unlabelled door. "This is your office. The lifts are back there on the right, as you'll remember," Corporal Butler points back over her shoulder, "the toilets are opposite the lift, on the left, and there are fire escapes at each end of the building. Fire alarm tests are every Monday at 10:00, hopefully you'll only get to hear next week's."

Alex follows Corporal Butler into the room, a fairly generous space with two solid looking desks pushed back to back in the middle of it. The office is well lit, but has no natural light, nothing on the tatty, plain-weave papered walls. Apart from two expensive looking office chairs and a dirty-looking old telephone handset, the only other things in the room are two laptops - the only hint of modern working life in the room, one on each desk, one with its lid up and one with its lid down. "This is you." Corporal Butler points to the closed laptop on the near desk. She walks around to what is clearly going to be her domain, there is nothing to indicate that she has been working from this station up to this point other than the fact that the laptop lid is up; her desk is as clear as his.

"So we're going to be office mates then?" Alex takes his seat.

Corporal Butler looks at Alex with a dry smile, "Yes, we can't have you running up and down the corridor every time you have a question can we?"

"There's always Messenger." Alex jokes.

"Do you prefer to work in isolation?" Corporal Butler looks mildly concerned.

"No, I'm just kidding, I'm a 'people person', as long as you've got a sense of humour and can remind me what Army banter is like?"

Corporal Butler cracks a faint smirk – "Yes, I've got sense of humour, but I don't let it slow me down in work, especially when there's something this important to get done. Int Corps banter probably isn't up to what you'd hope for either."

"Well I'll work a lot faster if I'm relaxed, and if you're chilled out, then that'll be a whole lot faster."

Corporal Butler accepts this warmly, "I'm chilled, I just don't feel the need to waste time with unnecessary pleasantries."

Alex doubts the efficient young NCO's 'chilled credentials' and expects that this particular working relationship will require some effort to develop. He opens the lid of his laptop; "Right, let's get going. Do you have my login details please?"

Corporal Butler already has an envelope in her hand and slides it across the desk. "You'll need to change the temporary password immediately; your new one must be at least ten characters, alphanumeric - upper and lower case letters, with at least one special character. The strength tester will not allow formed words, so use your imagination."

There is only one source of inspiration in the room, *'C0rp0ra!Lu(y'* it is. Alex is starting to take a more than superficial liking to her - *I really hope that she's not banging the colonel!*

Alex logs on and is soon wading through screens of code and programmes. After carefully selecting the script programmes and applications that he will use for the language comparison, and defining the window sizes that he will need for each, he makes his order for what he will need, "Lucy, I'll need two nineteen inch monitors for each system that I'll be working on, a twenty-four inch screen for my own laptop too, and a switching panel to patch them all together."

"The screens aren't a problem; the IT office has a well-stocked store. What other systems do you mean?"

He looks at Lucy with a slight look of disappointment, "I'll need to have access to the languages that we're trying to establish with if I'm going to sort this."

"All of them?"

"Unless they are on common languages, yes." He pauses to think for a moment. "Maybe just the highest priority one today, but I'll need to check the others once I've cracked the first one – it'll be downhill all the way from there."

"That should be doable; we're using a direct login for some of the systems, from portable terminals downstairs at the moment. I'll square it away with Colonel Tim, but it might take an hour or two to clear it with the other agencies."

"Great, does this Skynet laptop and account have USB ports enabled with writing permissions? I'll need this and a memory device to transfer files to my laptop, ditto for the other systems."

Corporal Butler considers the questions for a few seconds, "I'll check, and make it happen if it isn't. I'll get the pen drive too, what size does it need to be?"

"It's not the size that counts; it's what I'll do with it..." Alex checks to see that Lucy is still smiling. "Seriously though, it will only be a few paragraphs of text at a time, so a gig will be plenty."

He looks at his screen and says dismissively; "Crack on then treacle, send your IT chap up here and I'll brief him on exactly what I need."

This request is met with a stony silence. It takes Alex a few seconds to notice something is wrong. He looks up to see Corporal Butler frozen with her eyes locked on him.

"What did you call me?" Lucy says austerely. There is no smile and Alex can feel that there is no cheeking his way out of this verbal faux pas.

"I'm sorry, I didn't mean any offence, just trying to keep it light." he begs, the faintest of grins emanating from the right corner of his mouth, which slowly creeps up his face as he senses that she is becoming disarmed, until his cheeks are pressing up against his eyeballs. "So while we're on the subject of what you do, and what you don't like to be called, are you happy with me calling you Lucy?"

"I get a whole lot worse than that - Lucy is fine, you're a civvy, so I wouldn't have expected anything else… but not treacle."

"Roger, clearly I'm fine with Alex, even as a 'stinking civvy' I don't expect you to call me Mr Gregory – no one calls me Mr Gregory, except maybe the magistrate."

"I know that's a joke; I've seen your security clearance report, but I'm still not going to laugh."

"And I thought you said Int Corps banter wasn't up to scratch." They both laugh. Alex feels lucky to have rescued the conversation. He tries again with his request; "Lucy, you make arrangements for the distant end systems and my hardware. I'll start setting up here and begin trying to locate the language passages that are most likely to be causing us problems." he says in an over-polite voice.

Lucy acknowledges this improved request with a cock of her head and a squinted smile. "Would you like anything else, a drink?"

Alex answers as he bends down to pull his laptop from its case, "Yes please, tea white one." Lucy disappears from the room at her usual speed. Alex plugs in his laptop, sets it on the desk beside the Skynet terminal and holds down the power button for a couple of seconds until it quietly purrs into life. As it boots up he begins to review the message failure reports and corrupted file packets that have been loaded onto his Skynet account. He creates his own working files to copy items of interest into. With an unexpected clatter, the door of the room bursts open behind him as a flustered woman laden with boxes crashes into the room.

"Where do you want these?" she says hurriedly, "Make your mind up quick." Before Alex can say a word, the woman drops them as carefully as she can on the floor in a heap to Alex's right – "Too late. Sorry. Hi I'm Carol; I'm Lucy's 'chap in IT'."

"Hi Carol, I'm Alex. Sorry, you took me a little by surprise. Great service though, I only asked for this stuff five minutes ago."

"No problem." Carol pulls a lanyard from the left breast pocket of her heavy duty work shirt, on the end of it dangles a chunky, rectangular metallic USB stick, "I've activated USB access on your Skynet account, there's your pen drive. It needs a password setting up at first use; follow the prompts on screen. It's 16 gigabyte."

Alex takes the lanyard and places the pen drive on the desk beside the Skynet terminal. "Thanks Carol, that's a bit of overkill for what I need, but it'll do the job perfectly."

"So you want paired screens for two systems to start with," Carol paints the configuration in the air with her right fore-finger as she speaks and then points at Alex's own laptop, "a bigger screen for this one in the middle, all running from a single switching keyboard and mouse?"

Alex nods; "Exactly."

"Well Lucy's in the kitchen by the lift, making you a brew if you want to take five while I put this lot together for you?"

"Thanks Carol, you're a star. Can I make one for you?"

"No, I'm good thanks, but I do appreciate the offer, I'll see you in a minute."

Alex heads down the corridor and finds the small kitchenette adjacent to the toilets. There is a sink and counter with a wall-mounted water boiler on the left and a small dining-room table and chairs on the right. It has received as much investment as the rest of the building, the fixtures and fittings, which whilst not particularly old, are particularly cheap – low quality surfaces and furniture, all held together with poorly applied mastic. Lucy is filling the second mug from the barrel tap direct from the boiler; she begins to chase the teabags around with a spoon, concentrating intently on this as she does

Joseph Mitcham

so. "You met Carol then?"

"Yes, she's lovely. She sent me down here while she sets everything up."

Lucy adds the sugar to Alex's tea then pours the milk into both mugs. "There you go." Lucy pushes one of the mugs vaguely in his direction across the work surface. The tea is extremely weak with lots of milk.

"Is this the 'negative brew theory' in action?" Alex asks.

"What do you mean?" Lucy retorts.

Alex has his cheeky smile on again; "You make brews so bad, that you never get asked to make them again – the negative brew theory."

"Are you saying you don't like my tea?" Lucy tries to look offended, but her sly glint gives her away.

Alex doesn't know quite what to say. "Well you'll have to let me make the next one and you can take notes."

Carol sweeps past the kitchen trying to balance the empty boxes, "All finished Alex, give it a test run and let me know if you have any dramas or need any more bits." And she is gone before either of them can thank her.

"It's a shame that all MoD employees aren't as efficient as her," Alex marvels, "we'd be unbeatable." Lucy nods in agreement.

"She certainly greases the cogs of this place."

"Right let's get to it then." Alex picks up his mug of terrible tea, turns right out of the door and heads back down the corridor.

Back in the office there is a growing estate of IT equipment, with Skynet running on the left pair of screens, Alex opens the subject files and programmes in windows across both of them. He is soon cutting segments of code onto the pen drive and importing them to his laptop for analysis using a number of different programmes and applications. He quickly becomes immersed in his work, and aside from a few expressions of excitement as he makes progress, he ceases communicating. Lucy is pleased that he seems to be working well, but is mildly put out that 'radio silence' has seemingly been imposed on the charm offensive. She subconsciously makes a few unsubtle movements and noises but Alex fails to notice.

Within an hour Alex has traced all of the problem sections of programming. He is starting to see patterns emerging. As he moves on to the corrupted message files Lucy breaks the silence; "How are you getting on?"

"It's looking good so far, I'm learning a lot from these files. Things should start to drop into place when I get the other agency hardware; I'm kind of working with one hand tied behind my back at the moment."

"You'll have it as soon as we get authority; our liaison officer is working on it." Lucy sounds annoyed in her tone of reply.

"I'm not having a dig at you; I'm just saying progress is good with what we have. Does your LO have an ETA?" Alex has slipped straight back into another military habit of reducing everything to initials.

"If you take an early lunch, we should have the first system or two ready for you when you get back."

"09:00 start, tea break, early lunch, I thought this job was going to be tough." Alex smirks.

"Enjoy it while it lasts Mr Gregory." Lucy smiles.

"I'll keep on with these broken messages and go for a walk once I've got my head around them. Where are you going for lunch?" Half hinting that he might like to join her.

"I've got a sandwich in the fridge; I've got things to catch up on while I'm not babysitting you."

"You could crack on with that now if you like; I'm fine here without you. I've got the clearances to be left on my own."

"No, it's not the clearance level; it's the 'eyes only' caveats on material in the rest of the building. If any of the other department heads get wind of you being here unescorted, Colonel Tim would be in big trouble, and I'd be sacked."

"Fair enough, don't want you getting sick of me on the first day."

"Oh it's too late for that." Lucy turns the knife of wit in Alex's guts.

"Ouch." Alex clutches his stomach mockingly simulating the body blow. "I'll be fine, there's a nice spot by the lake - I'll get some tourist food."

Head down again; Alex grafts through the files in rapid succession. The answers that he is looking for are locked within the meta-data of the messages - what he discovers complements his findings from the fault reports and builds naturally into the picture in his mind of what the solution will look like. The product from this analysis will be a series of potential language errors and incompatible protocols. He won't have a complete picture until he has sight of the other systems. He hits a wall in progress once he has been through all of the files and his eyes need a break. He lunges backwards, pushing himself up from the desk and announces; "I'm going to head out then. Good luck with the other systems, I'll not be able to do too much more until I've got at least one to be going on with."

Lucy gets up and walks with him to the lift, "We'd budgeted two days for you to get through that lot - you must be as good as Richard says you are." Lucy can't hide the fact that she is impressed. "That is unless you've done a half arsed job and not gained anything from the analysis?"

"We'll have to see won't we?" Alex is confident that he is on the right track. "I might need to go back and cross-check my findings, but your time budget for the project is in safe hands." Lucy stays in the lift as Alex walks out to reception. "I'll be back in half an hour." he calls over his shoulder as he disappears around the corner.

5

Arousing interests

Alex lies on the grass of St James's Park contemplating the weather, as wispy grey clouds morph and drift across the sky. The wind is strong and the movement seems unnaturally animated - *how can something as simple as air, water and heat create things so beautiful and diverse?* He ponders the vast array of climatic manifestations - *how can such simple elements combine to generate such force and spectacular extremes as lightning storms, hurricanes and tornadoes?* His thoughts spiral - he becomes cognisant of the parallels between the weather and human nature - *bodies of people with common beliefs can mix, overlap and converge in all kinds of ways and exist in beautiful harmony, as clouds layer and blend, but subtly different circumstances lead to electric explosion - Maybe it's just part of nature and it can't be prevented. The extremes of what is possible are explored by the tiniest minority of those who are capable. It's this facet of human nature that got us to the moon, and that got us into world wars - the polar opposite extremes of human capability and capacity. This is all getting too heavy for a Tuesday afternoon in the Park.*

He scrolls through his mobile phone newsfeed, thumbing up the screen to see a common feeling of shock, awe, and anger that is saturating his online social space. Considering that he has been exposed to all sorts of incidents, on screen in an ops room, if not in person, Alex is genuinely shocked by what happened in Birmingham. The deadened sentiment that he would normally meet such news with does not afford him the usual protection. The brazen rawness and savagery of the attack, and the group of young innocents that it had targeted, has a real affect him. He is overcome with a sense of vulnerability, not just for him, but his younger sister, his friends, the defenceless and unsuspecting hordes of people who should have no cause to fear.

Alex begins to look deeper into the aftermath of the Gardens incident; he feels himself demanding answers to how this has happened and he needs to know that something is being done to stop it from happening again. The search for someone to blame has led the media to begin analysing what the authorities had known about the existing threats. It has come to light that the authorities have a list of terror suspects - twenty-two thousand individuals who have been noted by the security services for reasons related to terror incidents or activity. The news coverage makes it clear that the list includes names of anyone that has been investigated or even named in any terror related enquiry. The list's net has been cast wide and the nucleus of actually threatening individuals is thought to be more like three hundred. Without them committing actual crimes worthy of incarceration, there is nothing that the authorities can do about these people, even watching them all is too expensive, so it is only a watch list in name – the majority of those people are not actually being watched – it is effectively just a list.

Further down the column of stories and posts, he spots a face that he recognises, someone he remembers. He replays the video that had been broadcast live the night before. The thick, but tainted cockney accent refreshes memories of the man further - Craig Medhurst from the television reality show that thrashes 'Z list' celebrities through military style training. But Alex knows Craig from before his TV days; he had served in support of his Special Forces unit on operations for a time. Despite knowing of Craig first-hand, he hadn't been able to endure his television show for more than ten minutes when he had happened across it during its first series – Alex is not a fan of reality TV, but is interested in what Craig might have to say about what has happened in Birmingham. Having seen enough, he rolls over on the grass and pushes himself up from his elbow, stands up and dusts himself off. His chalky grey chinos mask the dust from the dehydrated turf, but the sweat on his back has caused the sawdust-like debris to stick to his well-ironed white cotton shirt. He walks back across the green and over the road towards the gates of the Main Server Building. He cannot get the images of the Birmingham victims out of his head. He is invigorated to plough on with his work, but wishes that he were able to do something less passive.

He swipes himself back into the building, but that is as far as his 'escorted guest' pass gets him. He walks over to the reception desk and takes the opportunity to have a chat with the receptionist. "Hi Marion, I'm Alex. I'm sorry I didn't get much of a chance to say hello this morning, we were all in a bit of a rush."

"Oh that's fine Mr Gregory; it's lovely to have you with us."

Alex hands over his phone. "Call me Alex, please Marion, I'm only here on a short project, but I like to get to know everyone, and life's too short for titles and ranks." Alex puts on a mock officer voice; "The military tries to indoctrinate you, BUT YOU MUST RESIST."

Marion giggles as she passes Alex his locker key, "I don't think I'm quite indoctrinated yet, but it has only been eight years." Marion places ironic emphasis on the 'only'.

"That's a long time on one desk?"

"Well I was a training clerk for the first three years, then five years ago they put me on the desk in the mornings, Harry does afternoons most days, but he's at the doctor's today – he's supposed to be retired, but he works half days."

"I get it; a glamourous welcome in the mornings to greet important guests, it all makes sense." Alex says with a wink.

"Oh you're a smoothie, young man. You should focus your efforts on someone nearer your own age. Shall I call Lucy down to collect you?" says Marion with hardly a break between sentences.

He smiles uncharacteristically coyly, "Yes please Marion."

Marion picks up the phone from behind her hooded desk and dials the extension; "Hi Lucy, I have Mr Gregory at reception for you." As she replaces the handset she looks up at Alex with a warm smile, "She's one of the nice ones here, but she is a little stand-offish from most of the other staff."

"I'm having to tread carefully with her - I don't think that she's a fan of my brand of humour."

"You'll be fine Alex. I made your pass out for two weeks; I hope we see you here for longer."

Alex would be touched by this if it wasn't the exact kind of rapport that he was hoping to have with the receptionist. He isn't being subversive, nor does he have any kind of ulterior motive, he just likes to win people over. "That's kind of you to say Marion. As nice as you are, I've got to try and reduce that two weeks down to less than one, but I look forward to chatting to you for a few days at least." The lift pings and Alex pre-empts seeing Lucy emerge from around the corner. "I'll see you at home time if you're still here, or in the morning if not."

"Good afternoon Alex." she says as he turns to meet Lucy.

"How was lunch?" Lucy asks as they step back into the lift.

"I had a nice walk over to the park. Have you had any of the detail through on the Birmingham attack yet?"

Lucy pulls a deeply pained expression, "It's so awful. It's come as a huge shock to the community." she says, referring to the intelligence community.

"How long will it take them to figure out who it was? I take it the guy that they arrested isn't saying anything?" Alex has never been involved with intelligence operations in the UK and is interested to hear about how the investigation will work.

"They've confirmed the identity of the arrested attacker, but he's not naming his collaborators. He's claiming to be a warrior of the Middle East."

"That narrows it down."

"Police and The Security Service work together at the highest levels with input from GCHQ, they get the political steer from COBRA; the Cabinet Office Briefing…"

"I know what cobra is." Alex interrupts. He is in the dark, but doesn't want to be insulted.

"The Security Service will put a team together supported by the Police, analyse and exploit the human and material evidence that's immediately available, whilst simultaneously paper-sifting any known associates and likely suspects that they have on the system."

"And hope they get lucky?"

The lift pings onto the third floor. The conversation continues as they walk back to the office, "These types of attacks are designed and executed by glory hunters that want their names and their causes up in lights, it's usually a matter of hours not days before we have the names…"

"There's a 'but'?"

"…Unless they're planning a series of attacks."

"Seriously? I'd better get cracking on this network problem then." says Alex.

"To be honest; we're a small cog in the intelligence network. Military Intelligence played a big part in the process a decade ago, but since the Northern Ireland troubles pared down, we're seen as less relevant and less useful – realistically, that's totally true; we've a tenth of the resources we had at the height of the Provisional IRA's campaign."

Lucy gets to the office door first, opens it inwards, holding on to the handle to usher Alex in.

"You're keen" he says to her as he slumps down in his chair and swings neatly into place at his desk, as though he'd worked there for years. He is impressed to see that two new terminals have appeared, both notepad style laptops - one is already plumbed into the right hand set of screens. He logs back on to Skynet as they talk, "Which systems are they?"

Lucy's smug smile fades as she explains the assets - she points at the laptop already connected into the right hand side of Alex's set-up, "This one is FIL-B, it's The Security Service's system.

"MI-5?"

"The Security Service." Lucy tries to dissuade Alex from using its old name. "It has a higher level asset encryption than Skynet, so needs a longer password, and has to have this dongle plugged in whilst you login." Lucy thumbs a small USB device in his direction which is secured to her pass-holder by its own tether.

"And this one?" Alex gestures towards what is now the fourth laptop on his desk which is yet to be connected to anything.

"That's Kirwan, that's the Northern Ireland Office network, we use that a lot and that's produced most of the reports and corrupt messages, however FIL-B is our top priority."

"And I thought that I was going to get the afternoon off waiting for these." Alex cannot hide his surprise at the pace at which Lucy has turned this around.

"This is the highest priority task we've had during my time here. It should be Sergeant Ashton working on this - he's off this week, so they've given it to me to project manage. I won't waste a second when there's work to be done."

"So this is your chance to make a name for yourself then?"

"Nothing much happens here when everything's going right, it takes a crisis to show what you can do, and I'll leave here on promotion one way or another." From her attitude and glare Alex doesn't doubt it.

"Let's get me on to 'big FIL' then." Alex edges further around the desk to let Lucy in with the all-important dongle. Lucy switches on the terminal and plugs the neat little black plastic key into the side of it; a green LED comes flickering on immediately. Lucy punches in a six figure code to activate the machine, then removes the dongle, hands Alex a slip of paper and returns to her desk. "Once it's booted up use that to log on."

Alex enters his login, a generic multi user name that doesn't really mean anything to him, and then enters the temporary password. His Skynet password is long enough, so he uses that.

Once he is in, work routine follows the morning's pattern; his head is down and he is straight on the trail. In seconds he has windows into the system open and is hunting down sections of code corresponding to those that he has open on his left hand screens. "Can I get the USB ports working on this one please?" He looks up at Lucy hopefully.

"Pass me that piece of paper back." Lucy takes the login details and picks up the telephone handset. She dials five figures, and then looks straight at Alex as she speaks; "Hi Paul, it's Lucy, could you authorise USB access on a FIL-B account for me please?" Lucy listens for a few seconds maintaining eye contact with Alex, "It's for our contractor working on the compatibility issue - he needs to cut threads of language across for analysis... Thanks, its login ID ABtemp6680." Lucy flutters her eyelashes as she replaces the handset, expressing her self-pride in being able to satisfy seemingly tough requests on demand. "Give it two minutes and try it; if it doesn't work, restart the terminal."

"You're a star, thank you." Alex immediately carries on with his searches, not wanting to waste any more time. He carries on working for forty minutes until he has located all of the matching, or not quite matching threads to be paired with the corresponding Skynet coding. He plugs in the USB which works without any fuss, unlocks its window on the FIL-B screen, and then drags across the file of offending code sections into it.

As he moves the miniature drive over to his own laptop it occurs to Alex that his rapid progress coupled with a bit of luck in the close analysis, could spell an end to his time with Lucy within days, he has mixed emotions towards this thought. He inserts the pen drive into his laptop, copies across the file, and then opens his secret weapon - an analysis application that he has borrowed and improved upon. The programme is able to compare alternative sections of two different languages and identify elements that are likely to cause standard translator programmes difficulties.

Alex begins to run the sections through the app, a pattern emerges by the third tract, and it is all but confirmed in his mind by the fifth that he knows what the issue is and how to solve it. He wants a complete data set, and wants to ensure that there isn't more than a single issue, so he continues the analysis.

The app requires little attention and Alex's mind begins to wonder. He opens the network drive of the FIL-B system and explores some of the content – there are some interesting file headings. He can see that a file has been opened up on the Birmingham Gardens' incident; he can't help but have a look. Multiple files have already been compiled within it, but original documents are being created in the WiP file – *Work in Progress*. He finds a draft report and clicks on it to open; it is a template document and still has many empty headings. There is an overview of the incident and what has been found at the scene in gruesome detail; cataloguing deaths, injuries, items of evidence that have been recovered - this includes body parts of many individuals. Clustered at the bottom of the table are a number of fragments of what are suspected to be improvised explosive device parts, in the notes column beside these entries is written *"Fingerprint and DNA sampling will be cross-referenced with samples held on List Z actors."* List Z is hyperlinked - Alex is intrigued.

He clicks onto the hyperlink and a database document begins to open onto his screen. It takes a few seconds to appear - *this file must be huge.* The fields contain data on individuals that have been under investigation for terror-related offences – *the watch list?* He slides the side bar to the bottom of the table, there are 23,051 entries - each row is loaded with detail and has embedded documents and images stored within the database. He checks the file properties – the database is a nine gigabyte file.

"Alex, is everything all right?" Lucy senses a change in Alex's mood.

"Fine, fine… just a little surprised at my own genius." Alex changes the subject - what he has seen has really caught him by surprise.

"Just a little surprised?" Lucy asks.

"Yes, clearly I knew I was going to crack this, but I had thought that it was going to take a bit longer, we're looking good to be finished well ahead of time".

Alex begins to bring Lucy up to speed with what he has achieved; "I've found a major issue in the way that Skynet translates code from other languages. It's quite a fundamental programming error, but fortunately it appears to be one single big error, and not lots of little ones – that could've taken some serious time to rectify."

"You can fix it then?" Lucy is apprehensive and mildly excited all at the same time.

"I'll need to run through the rest of the data on big FIL, go through the same affected sections on Kirwan and any other systems you consider to be essential, and then once I've confirmed that it is a limited issue, I'll write a patch to correct the error."

"We need Skynet to be fully conversant with FIL-B, Kirwan and MILNET Secret. What are the timelines?"

Alex considers this carefully; his train of thought has been knocked by what he has seen on the old MI-5 system. He adds a healthy percentage on to what he believes is realistic; "Maybe eight hours to complete data analysis on three systems, then thirty-six hours of solid work to write a comprehensive patch."

"So finished by Sunday night?" Lucy seems to dismiss the difficulty of the work with her time estimate.

"It's Thursday afternoon," Alex says with exasperation. "I'm happy to smash out the analysis non-stop, but writing that patch will be a lick-out, book me in with Colonel Tim for Monday lunchtime, I'll be ready to go through the solution with him by then." Alex is already thinking that he isn't doing enough to manage Lucy's expectations.

"Great, he'll be delighted with that… if it works." Alex's face is a picture of dumbfoundedness. "Calm down, I'm only pulling your leg; I thought you'd acclimatised to Int Corps banter?

"It's dry I'll give you that, dry and savage." The smile comes back to Alex's face.

"I have faith in you, you've found the problem this quickly, I'm sure that you'll stay ahead of the curve. I'll go and update Colonel Tim now; you'll have made his afternoon. Deliver on Monday and you'll make his whole week." Alex sniggers silently inside, sparing the need to explain his childish mind.

"I'll give Dickie a call and let him know how we're getting on, too." he says as she walks past him.

"Cool, hit zero for an outside line." she says as she slips out through the doorway behind him.

Alex retrieves Dickie's number from an information file on his laptop and dials it.

"Hello, Richard speaking."

"Hi Dickie, it's Alex."

"How's it going? Making good progress?" Richard enquires curiously.

"It's going well, I've found the problem, just need to do some checks then get cracking on a patch, should be done Monday morning – I've already booked in with Colonel Tim for presentation at lunchtime."

"Fantastic. You'll be working through the weekend then." This isn't a question, and it certainly doesn't need answering. "Don't kill yourself; take rest when you need to."

"Roger, could you book a car to pick me up from here at 19:00 tonight, and pick up from the hotel at 07:00 in the morning please. I'd get the bus or tube, but I want to be as fresh as I can be."

"Of course, no problem."

"Same timings for the rest of the weekend, and Monday morning. I'll make my own way from here at the end of play on Monday."

"It's done. I'll pick you up myself on Monday; I'll be there for the presentation."

"Great, see you then."

Alex snaps back into action, continuing to analyse the FIL-B coding, but he cannot focus his mind away from List Z - he struggles to grasp how atrocities like Birmingham can happen when such intelligence exists. He wonders where on the list, if at all, the cell members might be and what level of priority they had been assigned. He wants the list. He isn't sure what for. Once the idea of taking a copy of the list has entered his head, there is no turning it off - like going to bed drunk having seeded the idea 'I'll run a half marathon tomorrow' – he'd done that before and regretted it - there is no changing of the plan, no matter how bad an idea it is; it is planted, it is set, and no matter how stupid it might be, he is going to achieve the aim.

Alex's mind runs wild, as he plans and schemes, developing methods of how he might take the database without being traced. He war-games potential plans in his head, trying to anticipate The Security Service's IT security systems and how he might be caught.

Alex decides that a pathway based on a VPN, virtual private network, between two systems offers a secure way to send the information from FIL-B to a destination terminal. Making a copy of the list in an encrypted file with an innocuous name on the FIL-B drive, hidden deep in the system files, would mask the file for its transfer; he'd then drop the file through the VPN wormhole, directly into an open window to a pen drive on a second laptop, so that the file never touches the sides.

His analysis of the three systems completes ten minutes before his car arrives. He has barely said a word to Lucy since he had found the list. He makes use of this time to re-establish his connection with her.

"So a working weekend for us both then? I hope I haven't spoiled your plans?" He asks.

"No, this weekend was written off when Skynet went live… and then died on its arse."

"Will there be many in here tomorrow then?"

"More than usual, the attack has generated a lot of work, the network issues have exacerbated that, so it will be pretty much like a standard week day. The civvies love the overtime, but the uniformed staff can live without the aggravation – but don't get a choice."

"Well I'm done for the evening; there are no signs of any new conflicts on any of the other systems, so it's a straight patch solution. Back in for 08:00 tomorrow, fresh as a daisy."

"I'll see you out then."

As much as Alex wants to engage with Lucy, his head is brimming with ideas about the list. A thousand questions he wants answers to regarding its content; who has sight of it, who manages it, the fine detail on how he will get it, what he will do with it once he has it – an endless spiral of thoughts.

Without even noticing, he's back in reception. "Alex, your locker key?"

"Sorry Marion, I was miles away." He hands his key over, "See you in the morning then."

"Actually I'm on in the afternoon tomorrow, Harry's no better - Liz will be on in the morning. See you then."

"Goodnight Marion. I've got you all day though right?" He looks at Lucy.

She doesn't bite; "Goodnight Mr Gregory;" she says wryly.

Alex gets into the waiting taxi, he makes minimal small talk with the cabby and stares out of the window all the way back to his hotel - his mind has not slowed down and his irritable train of thought moves on from the method of how to get the list, to what he might do with it once he has it. There is so much potential that he is again faced with a mental overload of what to consider first.

His mind dances between the possible uses for the list, groups that might be interested in getting hold of it, the security that will be needed to prevent it being traced to him. He starts seeing an outline of a plan that will match competent nemeses to those that pose the threat; he will need a single group or individual leader to take on the gauntlet offered by the list. It will take him until the early hours of the morning, in his sweat-soaked hotel bed linen, to come to terms with the fact that he doesn't even have the list yet. He must focus on executing the plan that he has developed to get it, before wasting any more time thinking any further forward.

6

Best laid plan

It is about to turn 06:00 on Monday morning, after a long weekend of work. The sunlight seeps into Alex's hotel bedroom through a small gap between the thick, heavy curtains. Alex's phone alarm sounds and vibrates from the bedside table, but he is already wide awake, he has been for a couple of minutes. He lays motionless thinking through his plan, rehearsing in his mind how today will go, as his phone buzzes across the table top, dancing to its own repetitive, monotonous tune. It eventually vibrates its way over the edge, bouncing and tumbling over the thick carpet. Alex snaps out of his trance and springs out of bed, retrieves and silences the phone, and gets straight into the shower.

The weekend has been full-on, but straight forward; he has completed the patch and just needs to run some confirmatory tests on it before he will be ready to present it to Colonel Tim. He has accomplished this even with the distraction of the list in his mind.

Alex completes his morning routine with more precision than is really necessary, even having a shave - not knowing where he might end the day. He takes care to attach a small innocuous key fob to his house keys, The keys had become a useful tool to help him smuggle a tiny USB device into the Ministry of Defence Main Server Building, it isn't until he does this that it occurs to him that he may actually make it home to his own bed this evening.

Clean, well-dressed and prepared for the day, he heads down to the hotel dining room for breakfast, and after his, now routine, coffee, orange juice and cereal, is ten minutes early for his cab. It is rare for Alex to be impatient to get to work, but he is excited and nervous about what the day has in store.

The taxi ride is quiet, traffic is as good as can be expected, but the journey still seems to take an eternity. As the vehicle passes through the busy streets of Central London, he stares out to the pavements to look at people and finds himself reviewing them individually - *is that one a potential terrorist? Or that one? Or the one with the ruck-sack? What are the chances?*

He gets out of the vehicle, as he has done for the previous four days, stepping from the cab to the pavement, up the heavily worn stone step into the Server Building. He looks up towards the reception desk, but something is not right – the shock of seeing a Ministry of Defence Policeman and a metal detector in what should be an empty foyer is like a punch to the sternum. He holds himself together and composes himself for pleasantries with Liz, whom he has met on the previous two days, but on whom he has failed to work his magic. One word repeats in his mind over and over again on loop - *abort, abort, abort.*

Alex slows down as much as he can to give himself vital seconds to think. "Good morning, how was the rest of your weekend Liz?" He throws the words out to defend himself from having to respond to any such small talk that she might fire at him.

He needn't have bothered; "Didn't do anything really." she answers, then looks at her screen without further engagement, she picks up her telephone handset and dials Lucy; "Corporal Butler, Mr Gregory has arrived."

It clicks in Alex's mind that this unforeseen barrier may not impact on the plan - would he get his keys back after the search? He diverts his attention to the Policeman; "Hi mate, I'm Alex. They've beefed up security this week?" He fishes for information with the guard as he empties his metallic items into a small tray on Liz's counter.

"Yes Sir, the threat level has been increased to 'severe' after the attack in Birmingham." The guard waves his arm at the new security equipment, "This is standard upgrade protocol for a category one MoD asset."

"So all leave is cancelled and overtime is back on right? Sorry what was your name?" Alex smiles and extends his hand out across the newly placed dividing table to the chap who is roughly the same age as him.

Alex's hand is accepted and shaken firmly. "Gary, Sir. Yeah, I'm lucky in that respect – no plans made for the next few days, and a baby to pay for; my missus would send me here with a camp-cot and wash-shave kit if she could."

Alex laughs as Liz takes his possessions and locks them all into one of the phone lockers – his laugh stalls, and his mind is back in a spiral as he walks through the metal detector. He racks his brains trying to invent a reason why he might need his house keys whilst in the confines of the building, but draws a blank. If there is going to be a solution to this setback, it will almost certainly involve Gary. Alex makes the most of the time he has; "So how old is your nipper then Gary?"

"She's eight months next week." Gary beams with pride.

"And clearly has her dad wrapped around her little finger?" Gary nods emphatically. "So how long have you been in the MoD-plod for Gary?" Alex asks in as a respectful a tone as he can manage, not wishing to appear condescending to the Ministry of Defence Policeman.

"Two years, I was Regular infantry with the Rifles before that, but after my second Afghan tour Cathy, my Wife, said it was either the Army or her." Gary's smile doesn't wane, if anything it grows a little stronger.

"It would seem that you made the right choice Gary. Here comes my babysitter." Alex raises his eyebrows in Lucy's direction, "really nice to meet you. It's my last day today, but please, call me Alex." He turns his back on Gary to take his locker key from Liz. "You keep smiling too, young lady." he says sarcastically to the apparently personality-devoid receptionist as he steps off to meet Lucy.

"You're not looking as pleased with yourself as I thought you might this morning, is everything all right?" says Lucy, as Alex strides towards her at the lift-lobby entrance.

"I'm fine, just a noisy night in the hotel; God only knows what they were doing to each other in the next room."

She ignores his attempt to make her blush. "So we're still on to present to Colonel Tim at 12:00 then?" Lucy is like a child at Christmas wanting her toys, with a non-too-subtle hint of impetuousness growing around her professional demeanour – Alex fears a foot-stomping tantrum should he say no to her.

"Yes, I've just got some final testing to do."

Employing a delaying tactic to buy himself some time to come up with a revised plan, or simply waiting until the threat level drops is not an option. He will drop his plans for the list if it means having a real-time effect on the intelligence network while there is a potentially live threat at large.

The conversation is all from Lucy on the way up to the office, as Alex considers the options left open to him. The whole weekend's conclusions from endlessly going over them are still clear in his mind, and he has ruled out the obvious solutions of transmitting over the internet or stealing the classified USB drive – both are eminently traceable and would inevitably lead back to him. He has to get a second unregistered USB device. As he enters the office and jacks himself into the networks, he scours his brain over to find a way to achieve his aim.

"I'll leave you to it then." says Lucy, writing him off as 'at work'.

An hour of sustained work passes by and finishing his first cup of tea by 08:30, Alex looks over his screens to Lucy; she is engrossed in her own work and doesn't become immediately aware of his gaze. Alex takes the moment, just a fraction of a second to appreciate her. Not a silky deep-brown hair out of place, every strand of it gathered into a large and perfectly round bun. The soft, beautiful facial features, full lips and light brown eyes belie her razor sharp mind. Her skin is smooth and tanned, *is that from holidays, operational tours, sunbeds or out of a bottle* he wonders. He does his best to mask his blush as she catches him staring, and bounces straight on with what he was going to say; "You've come a long way Corporal Butler; your brew-making skills are almost promotion-worthy." Having resigned himself to the idea of failure in his mission to obtain the list, he decides he might as well try and salvage a date with the attractive junior non-commissioned officer, who he has become gradually infatuated with. "You can add master brew maker to your list of accolades."

"I'd be nothing without you." Lucy answers.

"What have you got planned for after the presentation?" Alex ventures.

"Why, are you going to let me buy you lunch?" Lucy asks, still with a sarcastic slant in her voice.

"I might consider it." Alex is hopeful.

"I would have done, but I'm already pencilled in with the network team to get your patch into the system, sorry."

Alex masks his disappointment, "I'd be lucky to escape Dickie anyway, he'll be dragging me off for the next impossible mission, no doubt." As Alex nurses the second rejection that Lucy has inflicted on him, he starts to see opportunities lining up.

"What's Carol's extension? I need to receipt my laptop in to her for destruction."

"She's on 83364."

"Thanks, you couldn't make me another of those cracking cups of tea could you please? I promise it'll be the last one."

"Sure." Lucy waltzes around Alex and out of the room. Alex lurches for the phone and dials for Carol.

"IT, Carol speaking."

"Hi Carol, it's Alex. How are you?"

"Good thanks, but busy off my feet, what can I do for you?" Carol sounds out of breath.

"I'm finishing today, are you able to receipt in my equipment please?"

"I can Alex, when would be best for you?"

"Well if you are busy and you don't need me to be here, you could do it this afternoon? I'll leave it on my desk."

"That's perfect Alex; I won't get round to it before one this afternoon. You know that you have to leave your laptop and anything with a memory don't you?"

"Yes Carol, I'm aware of that." says Alex happily.

"Just get your firm to put receipts in for the replacements and we'll reimburse you, I'll sign it off - no problem."

"Will do Carol, and thanks for all your help this last few days."

"No problem, you take care." Carol sounds genuinely saddened that his time in the building is coming to an end.

"Bye Carol." Alex smiles to himself; Carol's efficiency is another obstacle to be discounted.

Lucy edges back into the office with two brimmed mugs of tea. Alex takes one of the mugs from her as she passes him. "How is the testing going?" She asks as she sits down.

"Complete and one hundred percent successful; pacing myself over the weekend has paid off. If I had been tired, there'd have been errors and conflicts, and it could have cost us another half day to sort out. There are a couple of specific things that need to be done on the upload - will your network people be in the meeting with Colonel Tim?"

"Yes, our two main guys will be there, Tom and Darren. They'll complete the upload this afternoon."

"Cool, I'll talk them through what needs doing, but will also leave them some written instructions too." Alex opens a blank text document and begins writing them up immediately.

Lucy takes a sip of tea, making a slight squint with her eyes as she does so.

"Even you don't like your tea." says Alex, looking up as he touch types. Lucy doesn't have a response.

"So what's next for you then?" Lucy asks, "Starting up your own tea-making consultancy?"

Alex is pleased that she is interested. "I'm thinking I'll take a few days off, maybe even a week or two."

"Holiday?"

"No, I might go over to see my dad in Northern Ireland, he's remarried over there, but it might just be nice to be in my own house for a few days. My mum and her fella are on holiday for the next week, so I'll get left alone, maybe see some civvy mates."

"You've got a place in your home town then?" Lucy seems to want to know more. Alex is feeling a little teased, having convinced himself that she isn't interested.

"Yes, I bought it a few years ago. Getting into property was the best advice my mum's ever given me. It's quite modest, but lots of boy toys."

"A proper bachelor pad then, fifty inch plasma screen no doubt?"

"Sixty-four inch, 3D ultra HD with surround sound." Alex laughs at himself.

"Prick." Lucy laughs too. "You're not one of those geeks that locks themselves away for hours on end, playing computer games and watching boxsets are you? My ex was a bit like that, that's most of the reason why he's an ex."

"No, I just like to chill in a minimalistic environment, with everything that I need to relax around me. It's nice to have quality surroundings, I've put a lot of work into getting my place comfortable - neat, but comfortable." Alex makes a mental note to hide his PlayStation should he ever get anywhere with this girl. "How long were you with him for?"

"It doesn't matter, he was a dick and I'm too busy with work for a relationship at the moment." Lucy looks at her hands and seems a little saddened.

"I didn't mean to upset you." It occurs to Alex that the subject needs changing; "I thought you were banging Colonel Tim."

Lucy is visibly shocked, immediately jolting upright in her chair; her hands slam palm-flat on the desk, with a look of astonishment on her face. The desired effect of changing the topic seems to have come off, but Alex wonders what fallout is about to be unleashed...

Lucy breaks into unbridled laughter, rocks forward in her seat, putting her face down into her hands. "What made you think that?" she laughs loudly, looking up at him through her fingers.

"Sorry, is it that ridiculous? He just seemed a bit over-familiar with you in the meeting on Thursday." The fact that Lucy finds the idea so absurd is relieving to him on two counts; firstly; he isn't in hot water with her for suggesting it, secondly; she isn't involved with someone else – at least not with the colonel.

Lucy gathers herself as her laughter eventually fades. "How men's funny little minds work - never ceases to amaze me! Unlike some cap-badges, the Intelligence Corps and some infantry cap-badges, such as the Colonel's, are quite relaxed in their inter-rank culture, particularly in grown-up environments like here at Main Server. We do, however manage to keep our hands off of one another."

Alex enjoys taking such risks; though he is not always necessarily consciously in control of when he takes them. Part of what makes him so likeable is his spontaneous nature, but it leaves him with a residual and constant feeling of precariousness; so many of the key turning points in his life story have been down to chances taken. Flukes of extreme luck and epic misfortune have railroaded him to where he has ended up. Aside from joining the Army, little seems to have been of his own free will. He had run his luck to the limit on occasions too numerous to count, taking outrageous risks and behaving appallingly - nothing malicious or spiteful, more over-exuberant fun and high jinks, usually alcohol fuelled and spurred on by his mates; he had been a typical forces rogue over his short career - he occasionally misses the environment in which he was able to comfortably play that role.

The telephone rings. "Corporal Butler speaking... Great thanks, I'll come down to meet him." Lucy replaces the handset. "Your colleague has arrived, bang on time. Are you ready to present to the Colonel?"

"Yes, I'm good to go. You go and get Dickie through the gates of Fort Knox, I'll finish up here."

As Lucy leaves, Alex sends the patch and accompanying notes to the Main Server's ICT mailbox. He then opens windows on the screens of FIL-B and Kirwan for a VPN pathway, favouring the Northern Ireland system for the destination host asset to his own laptop. He locates the Security Service system file folder in which he has discretely hidden a renamed copy of the list. He hasn't quite figured out what he might be going to do with them, but if the opportunity presents itself; he will be able to initialise a file transfer between the systems within thirty seconds, basically the time it will take him to enter his passwords. What the data rate of a transmission might be suddenly becomes a key factor, something that Alex has not considered – *the network connection here isn't too bad.*

As he thinks about testing the transfer rate, he hears Lucy and Dickie chatting in the corridor – he locks the screens down, tucks the official pen drive behind the FIL-B terminal, gets up from his chair, grabs his almost empty laptop bag from the under the desk and opens the door.

"Good morning young man, I hear you've been working your magic?" Dickie says with a smile.

"Job done, I might have done it quicker if the brews had been better." Alex looks at Lucy, waiting for her to bite, but she merely laughs him off.

"Shall we?" Lucy gestures with her arm towards Colonel Tim's office.

Colonel Tim is in an even more energetic mood than usual as he introduces everyone, "Alex and Richard this is Tom and Darren - they'll be introducing your patch to the system."

Alex feels a slight tension in the room as the group stands in anticipation of his solution. He has been aware that he has been fixing someone else's mistake, it isn't the mistake of either of these two guys, but it definitely feels like there are some egos at stake. "Good morning gents, I've done the easy bit, it's all on you now." Tom and Darren look at each other and almost seem to gulp for air.

Colonel Tim knows exactly what Alex is up to and smiles as they all take their seats loosely around the table, which isn't quite big enough for the six of them. "Alex, why don't you take us through the problem, your solution and what these guys need to do with it." says the Colonel.

"Yes Sir." Alex says with enthusiasm. "There was a small glitch in the standard interpreter-compiler step of Skynet's language programming. This didn't cause a problem on the system when operating in isolation, so wouldn't have been flagged on limited trials, but it caused big problems for interoperability. I have created a patch that will need to go to all servers and terminals, a full, timed, system re-boot will then be needed, but as soon as you've done that, the problem will be gone from the network."

"You can ensure success by programming a mandated, system-initiated update." Richard chips in.

Darren nods to himself, looking at the floor between his feet as he thinks about it, "I can do that, it was my bread and butter at Microsoft."

"Bonus." Alex grins, "There are a couple of specifics that you need to include in the executing file; I've detailed those in the email that I've sent to your mailbox. If you need any support, I'll be on my mobile for the rest of the day, I've left you the number in the covering email."

Alex has skated over the detail, partly because he has sent full instructions, but partly because his mind is battling to figure out a way of getting the list. He is conscious that he is leaving it late; he might be out of the building within in five minutes – maybe that is the key.

"Well Alex, you have certainly done a great job for us, hopefully we won't be in touch, well not for this issue, but maybe for others." Colonel Tim is looking directly at him.

"Yes Colonel," Dickie pipes up, "Alex is one of my best, but we have developed a bit of a golf bag of skills in the company, so anything you need, you just call me Tim, okay."

"Quite. Thank you very much for everything gentlemen." Colonel Tim gets to his feet; everyone else in the room follows his lead. The officer pushes his way past Tom, who hasn't said a word the whole time, and shakes Alex and Dickie's hands, then begins to usher them out of the office and into the corridor.

"We must get on with the implementation phase; I'm sure that you understand that time is of the essence. Corporal Butler will see you out. Goodbye chaps." Colonel Tim turns back into the room, as Lucy follows them out.

"I'll just be a minute, Sir." Lucy is already walking towards the lift. "Come on gents, I've got work to be getting on with."

Alex is hurt by her haste and tone. It seems as though the effort that he's put in with her has been expunged, in the way that she speaks in the same dry tone that she had done on day one. He contemplates that for a second, before deciding to get a grip of himself. He realises that if he had been observing the situation as a third party, he would have immediately identified that he is falling for the classic military female trap.

Corporal Butler is undeniably attractive, but no more so than ten other girls one might meet on a night out, or even on a walk down the high street. The fact that she is in a male dominated environment makes her rare - a scarcity within any given military domain, typically one attractive female to maybe twenty men; it becomes natural for the men to compete for her attention. Becoming momentarily cognisant of this brings him to a sharp conclusion – *snap out of it Alex.*

The three enter the lift. Alex's mind is one hundred percent back on task, the pieces of the puzzle are coming together; it is all going to be about timing.

As they turn into the lobby Alex is delighted to see two friendly faces on duty. "Good afternoon Marion, Gary." As they answer, Lucy senses that this might be a long goodbye that she doesn't have time for.

"Alex, I've got to go, but thanks for everything you've done." Lucy pinches her lips together to form an acquiescent, but dry smile.

"No worries, you've got my number if you need anything." Alex doesn't labour his comment and feels freer for it.

"Goodbye." She turns and heads back to the lift at her standard pace.

"Yeah, see ya Lucy." Dickie is clearly put out that he has been pretty much ignored.

"Bye Richard." she calls over her shoulder without breaking stride or looking around.

"Is that you finished then, Alex?" Marion asks as he sets off the metal detector, walking back through it with his locker key in hand.

Alex hands over the key as he answers; "Yes, I'm all done. It's been lovely being here and getting to meet you, but this guy's dragging me off for my next job… aren't you?" Alex looks at Dickie with an apprehensive smile.

"I'll drop you at the dole office." Dickie laughs.

Marion hands Alex back his phone and keys and takes his pass. "Oh, here's mine too." Dickie gives Marion his key and pass.

Alex turns to chat with the security guard while Marion retrieves Dickie's personal items.

"So is your daughter walking or anything yet Gary?"

"No, not quite, that's another four or five months off yet." Gary's smile shows that he finds Alex's ignorance about babies amusing. "I didn't know anything about kids this time last year either; it's a steep learning curve."

"When do they get teeth and start talking? I know literally nothing." Alex concedes.

Gary revels in being the font of all knowledge on this particular topic. "It all goes off around the one year mark; it's just potty training that takes a bit longer."

"Well you've got all that to look forward to Gary. I've probably got a few more years before I even have to start thinking about that sort of thing."

"Lucy blew you off then Alex?" Marion blurts out unexpectedly. All three of the men are surprised by the 'out of the blue' enquiry.

"You've really bought into the military banter haven't you Marion?" Alex replies. "To answer your question, I'd say 'crashed and burned' covers it."

Dickie steps in; "And on that note, I'm afraid we're going to have to make like Alex's pride; and disappear." In a jumble of laughter and goodbyes the two men turn to leave.

They walk the few steps to the exit, Dickie holds the door for Alex - but Alex has other ideas, he looks Dickie in the eye and says "Give me two minutes." Alex turns and runs back towards the reception desk. As he approaches at speed he waves his pen drive in his left hand and shouts "I've still got a memory stick." He thrusts his phone, keys and laptop bag onto the desk and bolts through the metal detector, setting it alarming for a second time.

Gary mobilises himself from his seat as though he intends to attempt to stop Alex, but Marion speaks up to allay his concerns; "It's okay Gary, he's left everything else here."

Alex isn't waiting around for permission and carries on his sprint to the lift lobby, but instead of pressing the button, he takes the stairs, through the door that faces on to the lift. He bounds up the steps three at a time to the third floor. He pauses to catch his breath and to compose himself before opening the door. As he peeks through the slightest of cracks he sees the lift doors are just closing, he creeps out and peers around the corner, down the corridor. He watches Lucy march towards the Colonel's office, but then she veers off centre of the corridor; she is returning to their office. Alex is in no-man's land, he holds his nerve, having no option but to wait it out. As he clings to the corner of the lift alcove he wills Lucy to emerge and head off to re-join the meeting with Colonel Tim. As he begins to consider possible contingencies, the lift motor roars into action, he watches the display change, 3, 2, 1, G, a brief pause, then 1, Alex can't wait any longer, he must get into cover, 2. As he is about to disappear into the stairwell, his office door opens and Lucy emerges, turns right, and is away down the corridor - he wills her to walk even faster than usual, 3. She opens the door to Colonel Tim's office as the lift doors ping behind him. Alex takes a deep breath and walks with confidence and purpose towards his former office. He makes it into the room without looking over his shoulder to see who is following from the lift, and locks the door behind him.

He pulls his tiny, illegal USB from his pocket as he slumps down into his chair. He enters his passwords and plugs the USB stick into Kirwan. He begins to feel his heart pound as the silence settles in the room and the tension grows in his head, as it begins to look as though the Irish system is going to fail to recognise the alien device. As sweat beads on his fore-head, a deeply satisfying tone omits from the Kirwan terminal to acknowledge acceptance of the minute memory drive. Alex turns to the FIL-B screen and drags the list file into the VPN portal window and sends it down the path profile to the memory stick address on Kirwan. Looking right, to the second screen in play, he sees the list register on the USB's memory. It is now a matter of seconds, hopefully not minutes, before the narrow rectangle fills solid blue to indicate the completion of the transfer. Each moment feels like an eternity, every noise from beyond the office door sounds like a security team coming for him; this is the definition of intense - his hands are well and truly in the till, this is a major criminal offence in progress. Alex resists the urge to try and hurry the transfer along by closing other processes, he just has to be patient, or risk disrupting the data flow, as painfully slow as it seems.

Three-quarters complete and Alex is dripping in sweat, voices in the corridor get louder and he convinces himself that they are heading his way. He looks around the room for potential cover - apart from the comedic options of under the table or behind the door, there is nowhere for him to hide. He is an instant from closing the VPN portals and aborting the transfer when the voices begin to subdue and the people pass on through the corridor. Finally the rectangle is full and the transfer window closes itself down – the file is now on his pen drive, he closes the VPN windows, ejects and removes the pen drive, and logs himself off the machines.

Jumping up from his seat, Alex composes himself behind the office door, he firmly places the pen drive in the back pocket of his trousers and puts his hands to his face, rubbing his forehead with his fingertips in a bid to clear his thoughts and disperse the cold sweat into his hair. He unlocks and opens the door sharply and strides towards the lift, his timing could not have been worse – a door on the opposite side of the corridor just ahead of him opens, and a robust looking Warrant Officer fills Alex's route to freedom, "Hello, who are you?" the Sergeant-Major asks, his warm smile quickly turning into a suspicious frown and instantly adopting an altogether more hostile posture as he notices the lack of a pass or an escort.

Alex stops in his tracks, he has no choice, his path is blocked. "I er…" his mind is overrun with half ideas, but none complete or attractive. He hears another door open behind him, Colonel Tim's door; he fears that the hot water that he is in is about to get hotter and deeper. As he looks over his shoulder he sees a friendly face emerge from the doorway, "Oh, hi Carol, there you are."

"Is everything all right Alex?" Carol asks.

The now grumpy Warrant Officer wants answers; "You know this man? Why hasn't he got a pass?"

"He's working for Colonel Tim, just finished today." From Carol's unusually negative and defensive tone it seems that she is not on good terms with this gentleman. "I'll take responsibility for him, I'm about to decommission his equipment."

Alex uses the time to think, "I'm sorry, I was just on my way out of the building and had handed my pass back, when I realised that I still had a classified USB on me, I was in such a panic to return it, that I just ran back up here to drop it off without thinking."

"Don't worry about it Alex." Carol turns to the Sergeant-Major; "I'll see him downstairs Mr Kinnair, there's no need for you to get in a flap." Carol doesn't wait for an acknowledgement; she pushes past the bemused Warrant Officer, shepherding Alex along with her towards the lift.

"Thanks Carol." Alex says quietly. As they reach the lift Alex can't help himself but ask; "So is there a little history between you and 'Mr Kinnair' there?"

Carol flinches a darting look at Alex as they step into the lift, as she considers her answer, but she pauses for a second to let the lift doors close. "Excuse my language, but that man is a wanker."

Alex would have probably laughed out loud if he were not still in such a state of nervous bewilderment. "He's upset you then?"

"You could say that." Alex fishes for more with his silent raised-eyebrow look towards Carol. "Let's just say that there was an interpersonal experience between us… at last year's Christmas party."

"Oh, say no more Carol, what happens at the Christmas party stays at the Christmas party." Alex finds himself in disbelief that his covert operation to steal the UK Terror Watch List has been rescued by the Sergeant-Major's sexual indiscretion with the IT lady.

The lift door opens on the ground floor, Alex sets off towards the reception desk, but Carol stands fast. "I'll head back up, you take care Alex."

"Bye Carol, and thanks again."

Alex is well-prepared to explain his actions to Gary and Marion, he has been over this simple conversation in his mind several times, but as soon as he catches sight of the metal detector he realises that he should be metal free at this point.

"I'm sorry about that, I'd completely forgotten about the encrypted pen drive that I'd been issued, I had to get it back to Lucy." Alex pleads.

Gary stands from his chair, "No worries, Sir, forget about it."

Alex hankers back and leans on the reception desk well back from the detector, almost beckoning Marion to join them in conversation at the secure end of her workspace.

"I got it sorted; I saw Carol and she squared me away." The conversation is not flowing from the receptionist or the guard, Alex senses that his abrupt actions have flustered them somewhat; an uncomfortable disruption to their usually quiet routines. As he scours his mind for how best to bring up his personal items, his phone begins to buzz.

"Oh, that's your phone Alex." Marion picks it up and hands it to him.

"It's Dickie calling from outside." Alex uses this as his cue to pass through the detector, which alarms as he does so. "Hi Dickie, I'm ten seconds away." He rings off, puts his phone in his pocket and gathers up his laptop bag and keys. "Thanks again for everything, I've got to run."

Alex joins Dickie in the waiting taxi. "What was all that about then?" Dickie asks.

"Oh I just had to hand back a classified pen drive; there would've been hell to pay if I'd have left the building with it."

"Quite, I don't want you losing your vetting, that's going to be vital for the next couple of jobs. Colonel Tim is spreading the word about our operation and I've got meetings lined up with a couple of the top level budget holders later this week. How's your schedule fixed for the next six months?"

The last thing that Alex has been thinking about is more work. The reality is that after two successive jobs where he'd smashed it out of the park, this would the ideal time to capitalise on his achievements, but he is beginning to see acting on the list as more and more of a vocational duty, rather than the whim that it had started out as. After taking this giant risk to steal the list; he owes it to himself to invest an appropriate amount of time and energy into at least exploring the options for using it - *I don't want to piss Dickie off too much, he might get the idea that he's paying me too much.* Alex considers his reply carefully. "I appreciate the opportunities Dickie, I really do, but I've got some personal business to take care of. I need a bit of time to get things sorted, and then I'll be back with a clear head, firing on all cylinders."

Dickie doesn't know where to start with his arguments to persuade Alex to change his mind. He looks back and forth several times, as though he is about to start to speak with each turn of the head, but then stalls. He does this at least four times before eventually siding with a damage limitation tact; "How long do you need?"

Alex is relieved. "A couple of weeks, maybe up to a month. If you get really stuck; I'm not going far." The bitter pill is delivered, Alex thinks it best to move the conversation on - it isn't likely to die there on its own.

"What's been going on in the outside world?" he asks. His life has been focused on the network solution and the list for the past four days and he has been blinkered to everything else.

"The fallout from the Birmingham incident is still carpeting the news channels, sixty-eight dead and nearly three hundred injured, nearly all kids; it's shaken the country."

"It's awful. Have they found out anything more on the group responsible for it?"

"The piece of shit who was arrested said that he was a soldier of the Middle East. The press reckon he was born in West Brom. They say that he was radicalised online. He'd got the instructions on how to plan the incident online, but they don't think that he was behind the bomb. The kicker, once again, is that he was known to the authorities – on the UK terror watch list. He hadn't done anything recently to warrant an arrest, so there was nothing the police would have been able to do about him. Unfortunately there's no sign of the bomb-maker or whoever initiated it – 'investigations are on-going' as they say."

Alex senses an opportunity to test a wider public opinion on what he might do with the list. Dickie is a civilian, never served in the forces, Alex wonders if his own thoughts are wide of the mark, he probes Dickie for a fresh perspective; "This terrorist, born in the UK and committed no crimes, no real crimes as such; what would you have done with him?"

"Huh." Dickie flicks a sideways glance towards Alex and looks straight back out through the taxi window into the hubbub of Putney and the kids filing back in through the school gates at the end of their lunch hour, "If there was even a sniff of him planning something like this; they should have dragged him out of his house and put him to sleep."

This is an emotive topic and the anger and immediacy of Birmingham is bound to be driving Dickie's thoughts, Alex needs an answer coated in a little context, "Serious? The police can't exactly do that can they?" he delves a little deeper.

Dickie eases around to look at Alex as he goes on; "There'd be plenty of takers to do it, no doubt. I'd publish their details, stick them on the dark web somewhere and put the word out.

Alex is tempted to let Dickie in on his secret, but that would be the population with the knowledge of it doubled before his escape from the crime scene is even complete. He'd gained an opinion, which is all that he had wanted. Alex breaks from conversation, feigning mild shock at Richard's answer with a frozen brow and a contemplative nodding of the head as he sits back in his seat.

7

Straight to the punch

Two days at home had been nice, but Alex had not been able to properly relax, all he could think about was the list. He now finds himself in another hotel, not far from the last, but vitally only a mile from the dwellings of Craig Medhurst.

Neatly placing his jeans and t-shirt back into his hold-all, Alex changes clothes into sports kit. As he pulls on his trainers his phone rings with a call from an unrecognised UK mobile number. He pauses for thought, then answers; "Hello."

"Mr Gregory?" Alex recognises the voice instantly.

"Yes."

"Do you know who this is Mr Gregory?"

"Lucy? Or should I say Corporal Butler?"

Lucy laughs, "Hi Alex."

"Don't tell me, Bill and Ben shagged up my patch and you need me to come back in and sort it out?"

"No the patch worked a treat; you'd have heard from me a lot sooner if there had been a drama there."

"So to what do I owe the pleasure? You want to take me out for that lunch you owe me?" Alex smirks to himself as he slouches back onto the bed.

"I was wondering about your little visit back up to the third floor on Monday?"

Though this question takes Alex somewhat by surprise, he immediately rolls out his mentally well-polished cover story; "Oh yes, the USB stick, I had completely forgotten about it, I caused a bit of a stir in reception, but I put it back in our... your office. I nearly got bounced by that grumpy Warrant Officer from across the corridor, but Carol rescued me." He rapidly tries to change the subject, "Did you know about their Christmas party incident?"

"Alex, I'm fairly sure that I saw the USB stick on your desk as we left the office for our meeting with Colonel Tim, I saw the lanyard dangling between our desks.

Alex's spine shudders; he can feel perspiration instantly boiling up all over his scalp. He should have had a contingency story planned, he hasn't, and he needs one right now. "I, er, I, well..."

"What were you up to Alex?"

Alex pulls himself together. Playing to Lucy's ego is a sure way out of this; "Well... I got to thinking, as I was about to get into that taxi, but I didn't want to leave without telling you how much I like you Lucy." Alex cringes as he says the words, bending his head over a full ninety degrees to his shoulder and scrunching up his face as he pauses for breath. "I ran back up the stairs and tried to catch you before you went back in with the Colonel and his boys, but I must have just missed you. I checked the office and you weren't there; it was then that I had the coming together with Mr Kinnair."

Lucy is silent for a few seconds, Alex tenses everything in hope that she'll buy his story - he'd never wanted to fall victim to humiliation so much. She goes for it; "Oh Alex, that's so sweet." Now maybe he can have some fun with the situation.

"Lucy, you're a special girl, and I don't mean window-licking special."

"Yeah, thanks for that Alex."

"You're great looking, you have a lovely personality - once you've cracked through that persona of yours that is. I could even cope with the fact that you're green-fleet." Green-fleet - a military variant of something, a term derived from the Army's green fleet of vehicles. "Are you sure I can't talk you into that lunch date?"

"With chat like that; hardly."

"Come on Lucy, I'm not after your hand in marriage, just lunch." There is silence. Even though he is only having fun with her, trying to distract her from investigating his escapade back into the Server Building, Alex senses receptiveness in her silence. His realisation of this comes too late to scupper his chances; he is on the front foot for once. He goes on with confidence, "You need to spend some time with me for your own sanity, who else can you have a laugh with like you do with me?" Lucy's silence continues. Alex considers his next move, it occurs to him that Lucy has made this call to him from a mobile number – presumably her own - has she engineered this situation hoping that he will ask her out again? This prompts Alex to become ever bolder, "Listen, I'm on a job a couple of tube stops away; I'll meet you at the War Memorial at the top of St James's Park, 12:30 on Friday." He doesn't wait for a response, not even an acknowledgement; he ends the call and puts his phone in the pouch pocket of his jogging top.

Alex leaves the hotel and heads roughly north-west, following his nose until he joins the trunk road. As he walks he considers what he is about to do; initiating contact with a man capable of exercising extreme violence onto a set of list-derived targets. Ethically, he is in unknown waters, having never been faced with such an issue of complexity and consequential weight. Still immature, Alex has not had a chance to appropriate a true value to life, and the enormity of his proposition, and its impacts, are still not properly registered in his psyche. His focus for the past seventy-two hours has been to conduct some basic analysis of the list and to seek out Craig. He has not had the time to fully process his ideas and formulate what he thinks should be the defined aims and objectives of the venture that he hopes to embark upon. He knows he should be putting more thought into the over-arching premise of the mission, but he is now distracted, again, by Lucy. In his mind it comes down to taking the list undetected, picking out the real bad guys, then getting the boiled down list to someone who has the capability and will to do something with it – something, but what this means; he is still not sure.

He had found Craig's online profile to be professionally managed, with few significant personal or geographical details that he could be traced by, as were his immediate family with the same surname, but the footprints of some of his associates were less careful. Through them he had tracked Craig down to Townsend's Boxing Gym in Richmond.

Kew Road gives a partially shielded view of the Gardens to the left of the path, another beautiful oasis of green in the sprawling City of London. Alex wonders if the concentration of people enjoying the flora would be enough to be considered a terror target - *possibly not*, though the same might have been said of some of the other recent targets of UK attacks. The fact that this thought has even crossed his mind annoys him. The attack in Birmingham and others like it had had their desired effect; insecurity is in his mind, his thought processes have been influenced, this is an assault on his freedom, regardless of how dismissive of the risk he might be. Alex turns left at the north east corner of the Gardens, then crosses the road and walks into the King's Head pub.

The pub is dark with old fashioned décor, there are a few elderly gents supping at pints in small, quiet groups, but his arrival causes no reaction or noticeable interest. "What can I get you, Sir?" asks the friendly barman, who appears to be in his early sixties.

"Good afternoon, I'll have a pint of lager please." Alex scans the bar area and the saloon that is just visible beyond it through the opposite side of the bar. "Nice place you've got here, do you have any live acts on?"

With a perplexed look, the barman answers; "Not really, my punters prefer quizzes and bingo I'm afraid." This is understandable to Alex, the place feels more like a working men's club or Royal British Legion than a pub. The barman hands him a thick looking beer in an old-style glass tankard.

"Proper pub, proper beer." says Alex with a nod. "My dad used to bring me to a gaff like this when I was a kid, I didn't appreciate it back then. What's your name?"

"Dave." Dave doesn't so much as ask Alex his name, as intimate that he'd like to know it with his face.

"Hi Dave, I'm Alex." Alex extends his free hand and shakes with Dave.

"Are you new to the area then Alex? Are you shopping for a new local?"

"No, I'm working in Richmond for a week or two. I like to enjoy a bit of local culture in my temporary workplaces, just thought I'd have a look in. I'm going to check out the boxing gym this evening."

"A lot of those lads drink in here; they come in for a drink after training. I sponsor their juniors for their outfits, gloves and stuff, have done for a few years now."

"That's great. So you're the landlord then Dave?"

"Yes, I took this place on twenty-five years ago and we're just about surviving. We've had some loyal customers and some special ones too." Dave points to a cluster of photo frames at the back of the adjoining saloon. Alex walks around the bar and through the partitioning door, through the hallway past the toilets and into the other bar. In typical London pub fashion, a proud collection of signed and framed photographs of famous patrons adorns the lavishly papered wall. There are stars from television and stage, old-school comedians, rock and pop stars. In the bottom right corner is a picture of Craig Medhurst.

"I know that guy; he's on that SAS selection show." says Alex, feigning surprise.

"What, Craig? Yes, he's one of our regulars; you'll probably meet him this evening at the boxing gym, unless he's off gallivanting around the Middle East."

"That's cool; he won't snap my head off for saying hello?"

"No, Craig's an approachable kind of chap, very friendly and encouraging to anyone who's interested in starting boxing. Just don't ask him too many questions about his work or personal life and you'll be all right."

"I won't, thanks Dave."

At ten minutes to six Alex sets down his half-drunk pint, sliding it across the bar towards Dave. "Thanks Dave, see you later." and walks out of the pub, turning right out of the door and on to the end of the street. Hand-railing the South Circular he heads north towards the river, he enters a modern sports complex. The boxing club is concealed in one of the huge arches under the South Circular road as it rises up before morphing into the Kew Bridge, he might have missed it if he hadn't seen a hooded young man heading that way. Alex pushes the door to the gym open and walks in to the sound of high tempo music and the salty aroma of sweat and leather.

The gym is brightly lit, but the alcoves, punch-bag frames, ring and dark matting seem to sap away the light and create a shadowy atmosphere. A group of furiously moving teenagers conducting all manner of drills suddenly seem to go limp as the coach calls time. They all begin to move in unison towards the front edge of the gym matting to pack up and go home. Concurrently, an older group of boxers are continuing to arrive and strip off their warm kit and prepare for an hours hard graft.

Alex waits patiently as the coach offers advice to his young fighters, "Nice work Danny, you just need to work at keeping your rear glove on your chin when you throw that jab – you're leaving yourself exposed every time you fire one out. Right lads, I'll see most of you on Saturday."

As the youngsters grunt their acknowledgements, Alex moves forward to introduce himself. "Hi, I'm Alex, is it okay to sit in and watch the next session?

"Hi Alex, I'm Jimmy, you can watch fella, are you wanting to join up?"

"I want to train, but don't want to be out of my depth if you know what I mean."

"There's a waiting list for this class that's about to start, can you do later? There's plenty of room at seven o'clock."

"No problem, is it the same routine?"

"Similar stuff, fairly relaxed format, the lads can mix it up and work on what they want. I'm on hand to work on specifics in the seniors' sessions. Some of the dedicated lads will do both hours back to back."

"Cool, is it okay to have a look around?"

"Fill your boots fella."

The gym is well equipped, but well worn, almost homely. He watches the session and is impressed by the standard of fitness and skill; he doesn't fancy joining in with this bunch from cold. As it approaches 19:00 more young men begin to arrive. Jimmy calls time bang on the hour; all fighters stop work and about twenty of the twenty-five or so boxers make their way to their kit bags. Conscious that he is lingering without real reason, Alex avoids eye contact with the coach, hoping to delay making further small-talk while he draws out time in the gym as he waits to see if Craig will turn up. As he succumbs to Jimmy's gaze, the door opens and Craig walks in, chatting to two other men. Without breaking conversation, Craig's presence commands the room – everyone seems alert to his arrival and the atmosphere seems to fill with energy.

"Have you seen enough then fella?" Jimmy asks.

"Are you doing any sparring in this session?" Alex asks.

"Maybe."

Craig drops his battered kitbag on the mat and walks over to Jimmy, giving him a firm handshake. "Evening Jimmy." Craig gives Alex a sideways look and continues; "New member Jimmy?"

"Possibly, depends if we pass inspection Craig. Young Alex has come for a bit of a look around."

Craig takes a proper look at Alex, who is delighted to see a spark of recognition in his eyes. "I know you, don't I? Alex... Alex, you're Signals aren't you?"

Alex smiles and holds off from introducing himself to see how much Craig can remember. "You were that clever little sod that squared away our Satcom in Musa Qala? When was that?" Craig stares up into the lights as he thinks back to himself, "Must have been 2005, 2006 maybe?

"Good to see you again Craig." Alex answers with a humble smile. "This is a fantastic place – you still keeping fit then?"

"Trying to – jockeying a desk more and more these days."

"It doesn't show much." says Alex, feinting a jab towards Craig's ample belly bulge.

"He's a cheeky little fucker." Craig laughs to Jimmy.

"Do you mind if I stick around for another session?" Alex says to Jimmy.

As Jimmy is about to answer, Craig steps forward and says with a jovial overtone; "A gym's a gym, this session's no different to the last. It's not a peep show; you can pay up and join in, or clear off Alex."

"You can't say fairer than that." says Jimmy with an appeasing smile.

"Fair one." Alex replies - and begins to take off his tracksuit.

Craig smiles at Jimmy; seemingly happy that he's motivated Alex to get involved. "What weight do you fight at?" Craig asks Alex.

"Did I fight at." Alex says, trying to manage the two men's expectations. "I used to sit comfortably in middleweight."

"Great category that, not too big to be slow, but heavy enough for some good power shots." says Jimmy.

"Some of the most entertaining fights ever fought were at middleweight." adds Craig.

The session starts with some basic footwork drills and skipping; it doesn't take Alex long to find his groove, he is soon bouncing up on his toes. He is in good condition, even though he has let himself slip from his own standards, he notices that Craig clearly has the power in his arms, but his movements are laboured, not helped by his flat feet.

As the group transition through some basic footwork and punch technique exercises, Alex proves his technical ability is up to speed with the others, he further impresses with his sharpness and skill on the bags and mitts as they progress to some more physical drills. "You're in good shape mate. Are you up to a few rounds with an old man?" Craig asks.

"I've not got a gum shield." Alex hopes that this excuse will keep him out of the ring.

"Let's work the body then." Craig says with a glint in his eye.

Alex knows that this is not likely to end well, but he is consoled with the knowledge that there is no greater way for two blokes to bond than exchanging blows and extracting a little blood from one another – a potentially painful way of achieving his immediate objective.

As Alex steps into the ring, Jimmy holds the cuff of one of the thick blue training gloves for him to push his hand into, once the fist is made inside the glove, Jimmy wraps the elasticated Velcro fastening around Alex's wrist to secure it. "Are you sure you want to do this?" Jimmy asks with concern, seeming to know that it is inevitably going to get out of hand.

"Yeah, I'll be fine." smiles Alex. He steps forward to meet Craig who is already dominating the centre of the ring.

"Two minutes, seconds out – box." Jimmy starts his watch.

Craig stays where he is, barely moving, just turning on his feet as Alex begins to circle him, keeping light on his toes as he orbits the big man. Alex tests Craig with a few light jabs, which barely touch Craig's guard.

"One minute." shouts Jimmy.

As the seconds tick by, Alex increases the pace, moving quicker in a clockwise direction and throwing more punches, but still keeping it light. Craig has taken his measure of Alex and sends his gloves out for a taster as Alex comes in for his next combination – Craig lands right and left hooks to Alex's kidneys. Alex is now on full alert and adjusts his defences accordingly.

"Time."

"Good round." says Craig as he retreats to his corner. Both men take a drink, Craig sucks in some huge breaths of air.

Jimmy looks at his watch – "Seconds out, round two, box."

Craig comes out fast, but Alex is already moving out of his way. His speed makes it difficult for the older heavier man to hit him, and Alex moves in and out tagging Craig at will. Half way through the round as Alex goes in for another raid on Craig's ribcage; Craig lunges forward to meet him and wraps him up with his long muscular arms, bullies him over to the nearest corner then delivers heavy left and right hooks to the ribs following up with an uppercut to the solar plexus, taking the wind momentarily from Alex.

"Take it easy Craig." Jimmy shouts from the gym floor. Craig retreats and walks around the ring.

"He's all right, aren't you Alex?"

Masking the discomfort, Alex holds a glove aloft and smiles to Jimmy, then holds both gloves up to Craig, signifying that he is ready to go again. This time Craig doesn't have to work to get Alex where he wants him, Alex meanders forward and the pair alternate in combinations, the punches much softer and under control… to begin with. The pace of each combination gets faster and the power of each punch increases. Working one another's defences harder and harder until Craig fails to stop one of Alex's hooks, Craig's next combination ends with an uppercut that slides up Alex's chest and goes through his chin, snapping his head back with a jolt. In the blink of an eye Alex finds himself on the canvas.

"Are you all right Alex?" Craig is on top of him and apologetic as Jimmy scrambles into the ring.

"Bloody hell Craig, he hasn't got a shield in."

"I'm fine Jimmy. No worries Craig." Alex checks the range of movement in his jaw in all directions, feeling it over with his still-gloved right hand. The tiny fragments of tooth chippings feel like sand in his mouth, but there doesn't seem to be any more serious damage.

Jimmy and Craig help Alex to his feet and out of the ring. "It's about time to sack it anyway, fancy a pint?" Craig asks.

"Or something stronger?" Alex replies. Jimmy returns to oversee the other boxers as Craig and Alex don their warm kit and head out into the warm evening air.

"I'm sorry about that Alex; I'm still a bit of an old brawler."

"Seriously Craig, don't worry about it, I expected much worse from my first time in the ring in a few years, especially with you."

"You did yourself proud, I only clattered you so hard cos I was on my chin-strap and getting frustrated - no malice intended. Where did you pick up your skills?"

"Inter-squadron boxing during my trade training course. The first thing I did when I got to a field unit was hound my troop boss to send me over to the gym – I was a PTI within a year, then got on the coaching courses."

The two men enter the King's Head almost side-by-side, Dave lights up on seeing them; "Good evening gents, have you had a good session?" He asks warmly.

"You could say that." Alex says with a pained smile.

"Yeah, you best get the lad a drink, I owe him one." Craig says with rather less pain in his smile."

The pub's usual elderly population is peppered with boxers from the first session finishing up a post workout drink, but Craig's arrival seems to spark some of them into ordering another round. More boxers from the second session come in as Dave serves up two pints.

"How's your chin mate?" one of them asks.

"It'll be sore tomorrow." says Alex modestly.

Craig passes Alex his drink and ushers him over to a corner table and they both take a seat.

"So what brings you to Richmond, Alex?"

Alex doesn't see any point in wasting time; he'd already made a good connection with Craig, so he decides to lay his cards on the table. "Well I've actually come down to London to meet you."

Craig's eyes flicker almost unnoticeably over towards Dave - "I'd gathered that much Alex, I'm not completely clueless. What is it that you want?" Craig's eyes are faintly suspicious and lock onto Alex's as though he is waiting to analyse his reply through body language alone.

"I saw your online transmission last week, the one from the night of the Birmingham attack."

Craig laughs a little to himself, "I was pretty fired up."

"It's got everyone angry, myself included. I wish that there was something that we could do about it. I wish that someone would be willing to take action." says Alex.

"There are plenty of blokes willing Alex, I'm one of them."

"Really? So if you got that watch list they're all talking about – you'd actually get off your arse and do something would you?" Alex asks in a goading manner.

"You're damn right I would."

Alex goes on in a hushed voice; "What if I gave it to you then? What would you do?" Now it is Alex watching Craig to see what his face might say. Craig's reaction is muddled, Alex can tell that he is transitioning between irritation at being questioned and realisation of what Alex might be telling him.

"Have you got it?" Craig gazes at Alex with an already impressed expression. Alex wants only to reveal enough to get Craig interested, and get him hooked into the venture, he does not want to be discussing the list in public, no matter how friendly the environment.

Alex goes on slowly and calmly, "Craig, I've got the list. You know the level of classification that we are talking about here; you know the conditions that we need to have in place to discuss it any further. If you meet me tomorrow at my hotel; we can have a serious chat about the potential for doing something with it." Alex maintains eye contact as he picks up his pint and takes a long deep gulp. Craig's eyes flicker as the questions build in his head, but he resists, knowing that Alex is right about the level of privacy needed to discuss such things. After a long pause he reneges and changes the subject.

"So what are you doing in Civvy Street? Apart from nicking classified documents." Craig asks with a refreshed voice.

"I'm working in IT solutions, it's good money and there's plenty of work. What have you been up to since your TV series ended?"

"That was just a bit of fun, I've been keeping the private security ticking over, but at the stage of career I'm at it doesn't take up much of my time." Craig looks troubled. "To be honest Alex, you've got my head buzzing; you've certainly got my interest. I'll be at your hotel tomorrow, but I'm knocking it on the head for tonight."

Alex nods, "See you 08:00 at the Holiday Inn on Lower Mortlake Road then?"

Craig gives the slightest of nods and walks out of the pub.

8

Question zero

Alex strides into the hotel dining room smartly dressed in a blazer, tie and chinos. He surveys the room to ensure that Craig has not arrived earlier than the standard military five minutes before, then walks over to the pristine servery and pours two coffees, confident that Craig will arrive certainly no later than 08:00. As he selects a secluded table, he sees Craig walking into the room. "Good morning Craig, milk and sugar?"

"Good morning Alex, yes please, NATO. How's the jaw feeling this morning?"

Alex ignores the question about his jaw, which he would've had to admit is still throbbing, and keeps his reply light; "What is NATO standard these days? It used to be white with two when I joined up, it was white and one by the time I left – is it a sweetener these days?"

"Always been white and two for me, cheers." Craig says as Alex adds in two heaped spoons of sugar.

Alex detects an air of apprehension about Craig – he senses that he is not interested in getting straight into the only topic on the agenda; would he want to know more about him before he would agree to work with him? Has he talked himself out of the idea of pursuing the list overnight? Alex feels that he has work to do to earn Craig's trust - he fires up the small talk;

"I slept like a log last night, the boxing really took it out of me." Alex can see that Craig has not had such a good night's sleep, he thinks about how his own mind had run in over-drive the first few days that he had known about the list. Would a man of Craig's experience and maturity have been as overly stimulated by it?

"Are you going to come training again? We'll take it easy on you."

"I'd like to, I've not done any consistent training since I became a civvy."

"Tell me about it, free-lance work is great, but you end up taking lots of work opportunities and never slot in enough time for fitness, or life even."

A mobile phone rings in Craig's pocket, "Excuse me I'm expecting this and have to take it." Craig holds the handset to his right ear. "Hi mate... yeah, send over." Craig listens intensely for a short while, eyeballing Alex throughout. "Cheers mate, see you for a pint, I owe you one." Craig immediately seems more relaxed.

"You've got my interest, if you've got what you say you've got, and it's detailed; I'd like to take a look at it and see if there's potential to do something with it. I presume that's why you've come to me?"

Alex smiles wryly, wanting to convey to Craig that it isn't necessarily the case that Craig will be calling all of the shots, or that the decision to proceed will be all his. "What I have is complete, and detailed enough to inform a significant action."

Craig takes a sip of his coffee before reacting. "There's a nasty bunch of people threaded through this country and a coordinated assault on the top echelon of would-be attackers might be the only way to solve the problem. If what you have details that element; then it'd be a travesty not to act. Achieving this on a country-wide scale is beyond security forces or armies, it's not within their capabilities or remit; it'll take a completely different approach.

"A limited problem, rather than overpowering endemic is what we have here, stopping it spreading might be achievable with the intelligence that you have, and a force that I could bring together." From the formed ideas that Craig has, and the pace at which the conversation has leapt; it is clear that he has put a lot of thought into the viability of such a plan, whether it was formed in the long hours of last night, or previously. "Let's skip breakfast and get down to business."

Alex leads Craig out of the dining room, back through the foyer and along a quiet corridor; this part of the hotel is decorated in moody shades of grey and has a more corporate feel to it. They enter one of the business suites on the right of the corridor; it is labelled with a printed sheet of A4 paper in a clip-shut frame, it reads 'Delta Communications'. Alex sets about making cups of tea with the supplies that have been left prepared for them, and launches into his ground rules before Craig is even in his seat on the far side of the large creamy table; "Wherever this conversation goes, we must have a clean cover story and everything that we do must fit into the narrative of that story, we must do nothing that will raise the suspicions of the authorities, and we must leave no traceable information from anyone or anything to do with it. Are you happy with that?"

Craig nods; "Of course."

Alex goes on; "Whatever we do with this information, just having taken it, or even being in possession of it, is plenty to have anyone involved put away. I'll come up with a security and information management policy once we've got a rough plan, but for the time being we just need a plausible story to hide behind, and a safe line of communication with each other." He lifts a metallic grey attaché case from under the table, places it in front of him and clicks it open. Alex takes out two smart mobile phones, still sealed in their packaging. "These are cheap and cheerful, but they can run a basic end-to-end encrypted voice and messaging application." Alex pulls two cardboard envelopes from the case, "These sims were bought for cash anonymously and have enough credit on them to keep us going for a good few months."

Craig mirrors Alex's actions as he opens the box and assembles the phone. Alex talks on in his 'instructor voice' concurrently; "I'd suggest for a cover story that I play the part of an IT security consultant offering a training package for you and your operators. I have the content and can create some bluff documentation to back this up – that should be good enough to cover us for five or six meetings and any number of group meetings with whoever you bring in for the project."

As the phones come to life, Alex moves the conversation back to communications; "Continue to use your own phone for everything that you normally would and for calls or messages to me that fit in with the cover story. Only use the new one for operational content, but keep it to the minimum necessary. Don't save any names, notes or anything else on it and you must memorise the menu route to the factory reset." Alex shows Craig through the screens, and then shows him where to download the encrypted messaging application. He enjoys helping Craig through the process - it reminds him of helping his dad get to grips with new bits of tech, as he had done throughout his teenage years. "Now we need to set passwords, twelve figures should do." Alex re-uses his Corporal Lucy sequence, and encourages Craig to make his as complex; "Start with words with a total of twelve letters in, then change some of the letters for numbers and special characters." Craig shields the screen from Alex's view — *at least he's taking it seriously*. "I have your number and will establish communications with you later."

"So is the list on there?" Craig points to Alex's laptop.

"Yes." Alex takes Craig's cue to give him the brief on the list's contents. He lifts the lid of his laptop and logs in, opening the list file; "The list has 23,051 entries, ranging from some seriously hard-core extremists with strings of convictions, to people that have evidentially done nothing more than know someone who has been investigated by the authorities on suspicion of terrorism related offences.

"Each entry contains detailed information on a single subject individual. There's too much data for one person, or even ten people to get through. I've done some preliminary analysis; it's relatively simple and efficient to filter it down."

Opening his encrypted notes on his personal phone, Alex gives Craig a rundown of how he has done this; "The list is in a simple database format, but has thousands of embedded files and notes built into it. It can be filtered by any combination of a number of these headings." Alex points out the frozen column headings on the top row.

"Some of these fields are irrelevant in assessing the threat posed, but others are key indicators. Those who have been recorded for their own actions, not purely for being an associate of a terror offender, cuts it down to 4267 straight away, removing those who have been successful on the Channel de-radicalisation programme reduces the list to 3532, discounting those with no form of physical evidence found on their person or premises brings it to 762, of those; 331 have committed multiple offences, filtering the remaining individuals assessed by the Security Service as high risk makes the final cut 178."

"What is MI-5's assessment based on?" Craig refers to The Security Service by its old name out of stubbornness to change – one of his defining characteristics.

"The definition of high risk isn't described anywhere in the file, some of the individuals are graded that way for no clear reason that the evidential content would support. I figure that it must be some sort of subjective analysis or susceptibility risk, at risk of radicalisation or something like that."

"What it comes down to Alex," Craig pauses for a mouthful of tea, "is that it's a judgement call on which of those on the list deserve to be marked, and which ones don't." Alex nods his head in reluctant agreement. "We must bring together a committee to oversee the selection of targets, based on your filters, and concurrently force-generate a team to execute the plan."

"Plan?" Alex raises an eyebrow at this jump in Craig's description of what lays ahead.

Craig smiles and shakes his head lightly, "That's a package of work in itself all right - it'll take some thinking about, but we'll need to have the target list first, else we won't be able to plan effectively."

"Establish a committee, target selection, mission planning, force generation, then execution." Alex summarises the skeletal basics of the project verbally, so both men are clear that they are in mutual agreement of the way forward.

Craig nods, but isn't satisfied to leave it there; "Clearly there'll be more to it than that; we'll have to think about security, finance, training, group communications, liaison, the full estimate.

"This isn't just a radical idea, if we manage it; it'll be historically significant. When else in history has a non-state actor holistically defeated such a threat to any nation's internal security?"

"When you say defeated, what do you mean exactly?" Alex feels perturbed.

"End the fuckers." Craig says dismissively. "What did you have in mind? Have a quiet word? See if we might persuade them to take their ideologies elsewhere?"

The penny begins to drop for Alex about what the bottom line will be in terms of physical manifestation of the mission of the ground. "When you spell it out like that I suppose it is the only line to take; we don't have a prison, our resources could never come close to the existing services in terms of long-term surveillance for interception."

"Think about it like this - what have you done with your life up until now? Joined the Army, left the Army, made a few quid? Well this is your chance son." Alex begins to see a new perspective as Craig goes on, "If we pull this mission off; you'll be the man that saved Britain from those that would do it harm from within." Alex looks solemnly at Craig as he senses his sincerity. "I've taken care of some serious business with the Regiment, made something of a name for myself, but it would pale into insignificance compared to this. This would be making a real tangible difference to the lives of the people of this country. We're giving them their full freedom back; no one's been able to do that in this country since World War Two." Alex has to agree with Craig's assessment of the magnitude of what they are contemplating.

"I've become kind of sick of hearing Servicemen and veterans, and even myself, talking about how we've 'fought for the freedoms of this country', but it's really come down to fighting for the price of oil and rights to trade; making life more comfortable, more than making it truly free. The argument that we ensure our security through defeating proxies and keeping precarious states balanced doesn't really wash with me, at best that's second order, and it would be of little consequence if we chinned it all off and concentrated on defending the homeland a little better."

"How do you justify being a part of those operations to yourself then? If you feel that you're involved in something that you don't really believe in?" Alex is keen to get an insight into Craig's motivation.

"I don't lose a lot of sleep about that, I don't think at a political level on a day-to-day basis, certainly didn't when I was on ops. The enemy that we face on the ground are no bunch of saints, and almost entirely have it coming, I'm very proud of rubbing out most of the bullying, torturing pieces of shit that I've had the duty to engage with."

"Wow, I never thought of it like that." The conversation is becoming an education for Alex.

"Whatever's going on in the world, there is always business for people in my line of work, there has to be. Every force needs a real-time training ground, look what started to happen to the patrolling skills of the Army once the troubles in Northern Ireland tailed off – they went to rat-shit. It was the same in the infantry for battle drills a few years after the Falklands. You can't sustain a high quality capability without real-time work experience, or even threat, for them to be going on with, never more so than in the SF community. We nearly lost the SAS after World War Two, but a visionary commanding officer grasped the nettle and re-roled the force for Oman - you'd be proud; he was a Signaller... and we've been in and out of the sandpit ever since."

Alex feels a little overwhelmed by Craig's stature and accomplishments, and feels the need to acknowledge it; "You've done so much with your career, you make me feel like a bit of a boy scout."

Craig is gracious, not at all magnanimous, and offers Alex encouragement; "You should not measure yourself by what others have achieved. Personal success must be measured against what is truly important to you. A lot of people forget that and find themselves chasing someone else's dreams. If you joined the Army to get out of the rat-race, see the world and shag some birds; then your military career was a great success by the sounds of it.

"Once you get to Sergeant in the infantry, you almost have to make a conscious decision to step back from a career path – the promotion pyramid gets so steep that you have to smash yourself to get further up the ladder. Loads of my mates that weren't interested in careers when we were juniors got sucked into the pace of life and carried on chasing the next promotion, when it wasn't really what they wanted – you couldn't tell them. They ended up stressed, depressed, divorced, or all three – I got the divorce myself.

Both men pause and take a sip of tea. Alex moves the conversation on; "So that's the list and my thoughts on which are the deserving members. What's next? Where do we go from here?"

Craig places his cup carefully back on the saucer, "Like I was saying; we need to form a nucleus, a core team. I've got two blokes that I work with all the time, have done for twenty years - in Service and on contract, they're perfect for this and will be bang up for it."

"How soon can they be available?"

"Can you book this room for all day tomorrow?"

Alex gleams a smile back at Craig, "Already have."

9

Taking the rough with the smooth

At 08:00 the next morning, Craig and Alex are already sitting enjoying a coffee together in the hotel dining room. "Mark and John will be joining us for breakfast at quarter past." says Craig.

Alex infers from the deliberate gap in their timings that Craig has something that he needs to say – he prompts the big man; "Is there anything that you want to talk about before they get here?"

"Nothing serious, I just thought I'd give you a heads up on the blokes. You'll be working closely with them for the next few weeks, so I thought I'd better give you a proper introduction."

"I'm looking forward to meeting them; they must be quality guys if you rate them so highly?"

"Yeah, they are. Mark's sweet as a nut; I think you'll get on really well with him. John though… he's a bit… well… fiery shall we say, just give him a wide berth." Craig takes a moment for a sip of coffee. "We tolerate him because he's so good at what he does, he'll take the jobs that others would prefer to avoid, and he's fiercely loyal."

"Right, I see." Alex thinks for a moment about how he feels about this, and how he should outwardly express himself with regard to those feelings, he goes on; "Craig, this gig is going to be hard enough as it is, I don't want to be put through it as an outsider by your blokes, that's the last thing I, or anyone else needs – I'd appreciate it if you keep John, or anyone else like him, on a tight leash please."

"I'm sure he'll be fine, just make sure you show him a good level of respect."

"I will Craig, but I'll not take any unnecessary shit either."

"I wouldn't expect you to; just let me know if he gives you any bother."

"Roger that." Alex begins to wonder what he is letting himself in for. He will need to find a way to establish a rapport and earn the respect of the wider team. The conversation isn't over; Craig's eyes give that much away.

"Alex, I know that you deserve respect, but you may need to lower your expectations on how you are treated. The kind of people that we need to bring in to execute our plan, are the roughest and toughest there are. These guys are totally respectful, but it takes a great deal to earn that respect in the first place. These guys will have served decades in and around each other, fought battles alongside each other, lost friends together. You cannot expect to slot straight in and rub shoulders with them as an equal, certainly not over the course of this mission. They'll respect you for your input, for your technical knowledge and ability, but it will take time for them to bond with you, and you're kidding yourself if you think they'll welcome you as an equal at all – not unless you decide to get your hands properly dirty."

Alex sulks a silent acknowledgement.

"I don't know if you'd planned to get in the ring with me last night, or if I rail-roaded you into it, but that was the best way to appeal to me - kudos to you if it was planned; you'll need to be as clever to win the respect of Mark, the others, and especially John.

"Do you want a top up mate?" Craig asks politely.

"Go on then, cheers." Alex hands Craig his cup and takes the few seconds alone to put his ego back together and into perspective.

As Craig walks back with brimming cups, he looks beyond Alex and across the room; "Good morning gents, just in time; it's my round."

"What, you got a new job as a waitress boss?" replies the taller of the two men, an aggressive looking man with a bony clean-shaven head – *John I'd guess.*

The two men, both clad in expensive looking outdoor gear, approach with vigour and embrace Craig in turn with manly affection and loud back-slaps. "Good to see you lads. This is Alex, he's the man with the proposal - we'll come on to that when we get behind closed doors." Craig pours the drinks while the men introduce themselves.

"Hi Alex, I'm Mark." Alex is greeted with a firm, but gentle handshake and a warm smile by the man with the friendlier expression on his boyish face, beaming from under his wavy brown hair. Though Mark is no taller, or noticeably thicker set that he, Alex senses the innate power in the man.

"Alex, John." is all that he gets from the second man. The handshake comes with a rock-like grip that doesn't shake at all, and is accompanied with a stern and searching stare that seems to be hunting out clues of untrustworthiness; Alex feels mildly violated by the experience. John, with his hawk-like features, is muscularly, but not heavily built. His height, at well over six feet, gives him a dominant presence. Alex is reminded of an evil looking Thai-fighter from one of his video games.

"Hi John, Mark. I'm looking forward to working with you both; Craig tells me that you're the best at what you do."

"Yeah we're mustard pal. So what is it exactly that you do fella?" John asks with unhindered candour.

Craig returns to the table with another two cups. "Let's not bore everyone in here with our business gents. Grab yourself some breakfast and take it through to the suite, Alex'll show you where."

The four men load their plates with all kinds of breakfast fare and make their way into the private room.

Leading the group from the dining room, out into the lobby and into the small business complex, Alex opens the door to the suite and makes his way round to the far side of the table, Mark joins him to his right, Craig sits nearest to the door with John on his right, they are evenly distributed around the table.

The three ex-UK Special Forces men enjoy their breakfasts whilst listening intently as Alex tells them, with almost zero specific detail, how he had come into possession of the list, and talks them through its contents, pausing every now and then to chew on a mouthful of bacon and egg.

"So we have the UK terror watch list, no one knows that it's been lifted, and we have free reign to go after these scum-bags then?" John asks, seeming to doubt that the proposition can be true.

Craig leans forward and into the discussion, "I've had a squizz, it looks genuine, there's too much detail in the document for it to be a spoof. Alex won't tell me exactly where or how he got it, but I know him from prior Service, and he checks out. Now I hope that I'm a good enough judge of character, that when I say I trust him, you will take that on its merit."

"If you say he's on the up and up; that's good enough for me boss." John gives the faintest of smiles to Alex. Mark nods his agreement.

"Thanks Craig. Look guys, I stumbled across this while I was working on a job and it took me by surprise. This whole Birmingham thing had me angry, and I took the document without really thinking it through, it just became a technical challenge for me. Now I've gone and done it, if there's anything to be done about some of these cretins, it'll take blokes like you to get it done."

Craig senses the interest of his lieutenants is peaking. "I want you two guys to form a committee for this project along with Alex and me. The four of us will formulate a plan of action, you two will lead on getting a country-wide team together, but the first thing to do is agree on what the target set is."

Mark seems to awaken from his slouch; "So there's over twenty-three thousand listed, nearly a hundred and eighty making a data-filtered provisional hit list, how many should make the final target sheet? Should we aim to take out every target on it, or do we tolerate a threat level commensurate with the capability that we can develop?"

Craig answers before Alex can muster his thoughts; "We'll have to see how recruiting goes and what the plan will entail. If we struggle to get operators on board, which I doubt, we would either have to come up with an execution model that lets operators take on multiple targets, or reduce the target set. I'd prefer the latter, as I'm favouring a coordinated, simultaneous strike to avoid us losing the element of surprise over any secondary targets."

"How many 'high risk' names are there on the list that don't appear in your final 178?" John asks.

Alex answers without hesitation; "53. I checked that, and looking at some of them; they're mostly high risk as recruiters, not real potential activists. That's consistent with what we're trying to achieve, the mandate that Craig and I have discussed is to eliminate the threat posed by those who would actively do us physical harm."

"Great, so we go through all this only to have the next wave of nutters down the list stepped forward and egged on by these known sparrow hawks?" John says with calm but snarling anger.

Craig responds; "We have to draw the line somewhere, and that line is at the feet of those that would do physical harm. We can argue the toss over going beyond that, but it's the right place to be for a number of reasons. It satisfies Alex's moral compass, it gives us a good realistic number of targets, and it'll leave a black hole in the national cohort of ripe activists that should give the country respite from terror attacks for the medium-term future. It might even make anyone planning on getting involved in any such activities reconsider." Craig sits back and takes a sip of coffee.

Alex backs Craig up with his views; "We're not saying that this method is faultless, not by any means, but it's a logical way of approaching it when there's so much data and so much of it is subjective. This information is time sensitive and needs to be acted on quickly – there's no time to be more in depth. There are a couple of sections of the list either side of the decision line that we will need to review and make the call on a case-by-case basis." Alex says with conviction. "We can go through some now if you like, I have twenty in mind – if you reach the same conclusions as me; then I think that all remaining target selections will be extant."

The men close in around Alex's laptop and watch with intense concentration as Alex goes on to explain the recorded histories of twenty individuals that none of the four men had ever met, but on whose future they may be determining, based on a few pieces of digital information.

"Wow, what a bunch." says Mark as they make the final call. "I'm impressed at the detail there is on each subject, it made most of the decisions straightforward."

"It's almost entirely religiously motived nutters." John says with little surprise in his voice.

"There are a lot of right-wing types in the lower order, but for one reason or another, none make it into our target set." Alex has done his homework.

"You're not on there are you John?" Craig laughs.

"Steady boss, don't even joke about it. I'm a patriot, not a bleedin' Nazi."

Resuming a serious tone, Craig continues the analysis; "There's a lot of rhetoric and fuss from the right-wingers, but they're all talk for the most of it. When they do eventually go hard boiled it's normally a first serious offence, and as much as a surprise to the groups that they're associated to as it is to the Feds. You're right Alex, it's mostly religious extremists, whether pure believers, fundamentalists, or the brainwashed. That also includes lunatics who are looking for any excuse to commit some sort of horror, and are just using religion as their justification."

"Isn't that all of them?" says Mark, not quite jokingly.

"There seems to be much more of a noticeable build up with those rooted in religion, whether through group encouragement, or preliminary activities. Perversion of religion, and preying on the weak through religion, are powerful tools of manipulation. The reliance of the weak-minded on having something to follow makes religious congregations fertile ground for predators of all kinds. You see it with paedophiles in the Church, fraudsters too – how common a term is 'embezzlement of Church funds'?" Craig asks rhetorically. "It's the same the world over, the weak need something to believe in and evil exploits it." Craig clearly has some deep personal views on religion, but no one feels the need to explore them just now.

"I need a piss, take five gents." Craig leaves the room.

A moment of uncomfortable silence without Craig in the room takes a few seconds to pass. Mark gets to his feet. "Pretty ballsy, swiping the list." he says with the tone of a question.

"Stupidity really, I just got the urge once I'd seen it; there's no going back when you get that sort of urge."

"Why'd you bring it to Craig?" John asks.

"I saw him ranting online and wondered if he'd put his money where his mouth is – looks like he will."

Mark sits down on the table adjacent to Alex on his right side at close quarters. John stands and walks slowly around the table towards Alex, talking as he moves; "You know we're serious blokes Alex - taking the list might have been a bit of a game for you, but doing something with it is anything but a fucking game – you do understand that don't you?" He doesn't wait for an answer. "Do you know what you're getting yourself into Alex? Getting us into?"

"I've thought long and hard about that." says Alex, hoping to negate the need for any pointless threats, but John seems intent on providing a show of force. He is now standing over Alex looking straight down at him from the left. Alex is boxed in with nowhere to go.

"Just by showing us that list, you've got us involved. If we commit to this, that will mean that there's no going back and that we're in this together – are you man enough to stand by that?"

Alex takes time to select his words carefully; the pause dignifies his answer and aids his chances of being taken seriously; "John, Mark, I spent two entire days thinking about nothing but the possible actions, their impacts and the consequences. I'm not taking this lightly, and I am committed. Whilst I know that you, Craig and anyone else that gets involved will take responsibility for their own actions, I will feel accountable for the risks that you take." Alex gets to his feet, getting uncomfortably close to John, who gives no ground. Alex looks both men in the eye in turn, "I'm up for this one hundred percent, and I'll do whatever I can to support, and keep secure, the blokes that are on the ground - doing the real work." Alex extends his right hand the short distance to John, almost jabbing him in the stomach. Just as Alex thinks that he is going to blank him, John takes his hand and holds it firm.

"I can work with that."

As John turns back towards his seat, Alex feels an incredibly firm slap on the back from Mark, "Me too fella." Mark takes Alex's hand and shakes it with gusto. Mark's physicality takes Alex back to his childhood; he'd not felt so physically dominated since wrestling with his father as a young boy. The sensation that it gives him is comforting, yet terrifying; he would be totally at the mercy of these men if he were to fall foul of them.

The door opens; Craig immediately senses the change of atmosphere in the room. "You boys been playing nice?"

"Getting to know each other boss - we're taking a shine to him." says John.

Alex picks up his laptop, walks over to a second, much smaller table in the corner of the room, sits down and plugs the laptop lead into a power socket. Mark and John are back in their seats.

Craig sits down at the table, everyone else awaits his lead.

The boss rubs the bristles underneath his bottom lip whilst clearing his mind, he then re-opens the discussion; "Well that's the targets boxed off, let's start talking force generation. Alex, as you'll be aware, the Armed Forces constantly haemorrhage personnel into society at a steady trickle; it's been an open tap with the military redundancies and changes to the pension system of late, and the network of physically potent individuals forms a well-structured layer amongst the people of the UK. The talented, most aggressive and skilled members of this layer find lucrative and gainful employment in dangerous private security contracts in some of the most troubled areas around the globe. That's where you find people like Mark and John here. This layer of society will form the basis of our recruiting ground, but even here there is a special type of person that we need – killers."

"So do we have an invitation list?" says John to smiles and disbelieving shakes of the head, "It's a serious question and we need a policy - who's in and who's out of scope for this mission?"

Mark enters the conversation, "Retired Forces, currently serving? SF… of course, Para Reg and the Royals should be okay, but even they have the odd bluffer, or shall I say those that you wouldn't want to rely on. Outside of that there's very little of this kind of experience, less convicted murderers."

Craig, along with John and Mark, is scouring his mental address book; each having flashes of images in their minds of some of their closest comrades in 'after action' states, bloodied and sweaty from battle.

"Aren't the Paras just pumped up infantry?" asks Alex.

"Careful sunshine." says John, trying his best not to bite fully.

Craig smiles at Alex's faux pas, "Every fighting force's badge has a streak of capable killers running through it, the Paras' streak is particularly broad - probably a company minus in each of the three battalions, those that go into the private game after they leave are usually of that ilk. Royals are similar, if they are the 'Rugby union brutes' of the Forces, then the Reg are the 'Rugby league thugs'; a bit less muscle, but more blood-thirsty and much more vicious."

"And to continue the Rugby analogy - definitely faster." says John.

"What is it that gives a bloke that quality?" Alex asks.

"Call it soldiery, call it savagery, call it professionalism, it's a single minded focus on getting the job done. Of course there's a sinister side to some of these characters, many enjoy inflicting violence, even killing, but they aren't generally evil people, most would consider themselves righteous and just."

"Are you righteous and just Craig?" Alex asks.

"Absolutely, knowing the difference between right and wrong is the only thing that keeps me sane. Lose that and you do become a murderous nutcase… like John."

"Cheers boss." John says sarcastically. The men all laugh together.

"Still-serving blokes won't be reliable, you know what it was like in the Regiment, they'd be off at a moment's notice and we'd have a hole in the

ORBAT." John refers to the 'order of battle', the human resources available to the mission.

Mark chips in; "Even the elite mobs could leave us in the lurch with operational tempo what it is these days, the only chance you've got are the few in staff or training jobs, and you know what sort of boy scouts you'll get from that."

Thinking back to what he had seen in the records at the Main Server Building, Alex has an idea; "What about The Security Service or the Secret Intelligence Service?"

"I've been considering that." Craig glances over in Alex's direction. "I've got a few contacts that I worked with in Afghanistan and on close protection here in the UK, I'm sure there'd be interest. They want this threat quashed as badly as we do." Craig looks thoughtful as he stares at his thumb and rubs the inside of his forefinger with it. "There is serious risk of compromise if we go down that road - every opportunity for them to get inside our group and record enough information to kill the job before it begins, or let us do it, then send us all down for life."

"Is that them off the cards then?" asks John, sounding as though he might like them to be.

"I'd propose a sectioning off, an air-gap partition in the mission. I'd be the only contact with them, similarly they'd only have a single lead – they would feed in workable operative locations through me, and I'd feedback targets and mission-specific details and orders to them, leaving things fairly loose, giving them a good level of mission command so that they are able to employ their particular way of getting things done." Craig smiles knowingly; he pauses and thinks back to dark times when he'd seen the 'men in suits', out of suits and in action.

"The working assumption would have to be that I'd be compromised and would have to be treated as such, that'd mean no direct contact with anyone." He takes reaction from the room. "Is it worth that disruption to the project for the gain in resources?" No-one looks comfortable with putting a barrier between the team and its leader.

Alex stands up; "What's the cut off for making the call?" He has something to offer with this type of planning, but needs more information to inform his thought processes; "How long would your spook friend need to get his people organised?"

Craig is pleasantly surprised by Alex's desire to contribute. "Hard to say, but these guys are well used to reacting on short notice. They'll have a similar, if flatter, recruiting challenge to us; I'd say that a few days would give them enough time to get their shit in a sock."

"How long do you think it'll take us to get a good idea on the success of our recruiting?"

"Three days tops," says John, "if we haven't done it by then, we won't."

"Then assuming that we will need a further few days preparation, orders, recces and so on – we can afford to give ourselves a head start for force generation, then make the call on bringing them in at that point."

"Yeah, that's a workable concept, nice one Alex." says Craig.

"Hardly rocket science is it?" John rocks back on his chair with arms firmly folded, clearly not impressed with the scowls that he is receiving from Craig and Mark for his remark.

Mark reignites the brain-storming session; "What about overseas players? There's some gleaming talent coming out of the Aussie SF, and Mossad would probably come over *en masse* for a sniff at this."

This is a curveball that Craig hasn't thought of, the complications and possibilities wash over him. He recalls the international combined arms' missions he had taken part in and how they had gone. They had never lasted long enough for him to establish firm friendships and can't think of one that he'd seen in action and that he'd stayed in touch with.

John isn't feeling any more positive; "Is it any of their business? Shouldn't we take care of our own dirty laundry?"

"I don't see that as an issue." says Mark, "This type of enemy is becoming a global problem, if I was living in Spain and there was a call to arms, I'd happily take part in it and wouldn't think any less of the Spanish for accepting my help." Mark's analogy brings nods of agreement from all, even John can relate to this perspective.

"I wouldn't rule it out. If there's talent to be had, if they can communicate clearly in English, and are a proper known quantity, then yeah, let's be having them. They'd need to be inconspicuous; any dodgy nationalities that might attract the wrong kind of attention might need to be vetoed." says Craig.

Alex looks thoughtful; "I guess that with all of these factors it comes down to context. This is highly subjective and to some extent it should be done on a case-by-case basis. The judgement should consider all of these things, but trust, physical capability and dependability are surely more important than the candidate's cap badge or nationality?"

"You're right Alex. There'll be a couple of red lines, but it'll be a judgement call by the handler." Craig points at Mark and John with a chopping arm, "Gut feel from blokes like you two is better than any filter we can put on their CVs." Mark and John both have the same look slowly come over their faces, a look of realisation of the pressure that this puts them under.

Mark gets up and begins to pour a round of brews, "How are we going to reach out to the boys we want?" He puts a nail into the elephant in the room, as he pours the first cup. The project's greatest challenge will be to reach out to one hundred and seventy-eight suitable operators, sharing news of this top secret information to individuals across the country, without being compromised by the security services.

"Well we're not putting adverts out or starting a Facebook page." Craig raises a laugh. "It'll all be about personal recommendations and direct networking. A shortlist of our own muckers will get us so far, but we will need to build out from this, this is where we incur risk, recommendations made by people outside of our immediate circle."

"We can use those secure mobile apps that the enemy have been using?" John thinks that he is onto something and starts to get excited as if he knows what he is talking about. "Everyone's using them and the Feds are blind to what's being said."

"I don't doubt that these means have a place in this project, and Alex is already on the case with that, but the act of recruitment has to be done face to face." Craig rubs the stiff stubble either side of his chin as he paces the room. "We'll need to carefully select handlers to work at top tier, that's us three and a few more." Craig bluntly excludes Alex. "This group will need to be representative across the relevant Services and ideally across the areas of target locations. How many do you think?" Craig asks.

The train of thought is developing; Craig's vision is coming together. "Like us three, these blokes will have served for prolonged periods as senior ranks, potentially in multiple squadrons or companies. Leadership quality and respect of the men are a must. We should all be capable of recruiting twenty to twenty-five bodies each, and be able to administrate and control ours teams, effectively troop commanders and troop sergeants rolled into one."

"Does that make you the CO then, eh boss?" John interjects with a smirk. Mark throws up a wobbly comedy salute, Alex doesn't know if he is supposed to laugh or not, but he is certainly starting to feel out of his depth and isn't even sure that he wants to know the operational detail of what is to be planned.

"We'll need to write down a list of who we're approaching and de-conflict each-other's nominal rolls." Operational record keeping has never been Craig's strong point and this part of the admin is not his forte. Alex sees where he might become useful.

"We will have to be very careful here guys. No-one should be writing anything down without making sure security is in place. This will be the easiest way for our mission to get compromised, all it'll take will be a page of notes or a list of names to be left in the wrong place and we're buggered." Alex is on firm ground and knows the topic inside out. "We need to select an information manager to keep track of everything and make sure that systems are in place to channel the project information where it needs to be, when it's needed, in the right format, and can only be accessed by those that we want to see or hear it." Alex is practically quoting from the government information management handbook.

"You're crypto trained aren't you Alex?" Asks Mark, "And you're a scaly-back too," Craig uses the nickname for the Royal Signals that references the battery acid burns that operators of early Army radios received to their backs, "pretty much self-selected." Craig turns to Alex with a raised eyebrow inviting him to take responsibility.

"I'll do it, no problem, I'll do it standing on my head, but you guys have to listen to me though." Everyone looks at John.

"What? I can do as I'm told, even by him." The room's reaction is mixed, John is amusing but mischievous; his failure to comply with operational security policy might have serious ramifications for them all. Craig identifies the need to stamp on this.

"Listen John, you want to start taking this seriously. Alex will direct all communications and you will fucking listen to him. If I am to be the Commanding Officer of this mission, then he has my authority, do you understand?"

John nods obediently; "Yes boss."

Alex takes a second laptop from his bag, places it on the table and opens it up. "Write your notes in here, put it straight into a spreadsheet if you can, this will be your operational record. You can all have the password, but Craig will keep the hardware with him." The three men gather around and begin to chat through their associates.

Alex listens, trying to keep track, as they discuss name after name of dark-sounding characters. The conversation disappears off topic at every turn to recount numerous funny or violent stories, but they mean nothing to Alex, he knows none of these people. He isn't missed from the conversation and he does not feel at a loss for not being a part of it. His mind is full of ideas; concepts of communication networks, of target and operative tracking. His thoughts roll over at a pace so fast that he cannot keep up with them - he starts taking notes on his laptop, conducts research on his phone and begins to construct a framework of secure systems.

Eventually the three warrior-types run out of ideas, their phone and social media contact lists ravaged, and there is a moment of quiet in the room. "We've got nearly 120 names here," says Mark, who has been manning the keyboard, "that's bloody good going".

"The next step is to cream off our top six handler-level assets and work with them to recruit these and the rest." says Craig, "What's the best means to do that by Alex?" Craig asks pointedly, trying to bring Alex back into play.

"The working cover story is that my IT security training packages are bringing groups of you guys together here, or wherever we need to be. Get on to your prospective handlers and tell them that Craig would very much like them to attend a course and get them down here in the next day or two.

If you have encrypted messaging to them, use that, if not it's fine to send in clear as long as you stick to the cover story. I'd suggest meeting them individually prior to the main get-together in case it's not for them." This is one of the pieces of the puzzle that Alex has already run through in his mind, it comes naturally to talk about it, and he sounds like a well-versed expert.

"I reckon we've got twelve blokes worthy of handler spots, of those we might be lucky to get six down here for tomorrow." says Craig.

"I know two who are local, straight off the bat boss." says John keenly.

"Sounds promising - let's go for that. Tomorrow, late start, give them all a chance to get down here if they're traveling, say 11:00." says Craig.

Alex looks at his watch; twenty to twelve. "Guys, these are your operational phones." Alex passes them a handset and briefs them on their use, exactly as he had done with Craig. "If you spend the next couple of hours getting hold of your handlers on your personal phones using unclassified messages based on the cover story, I'll meet you back here at 14:00."

"Where are you going?" John asks.

"I've got a line of intelligence to pursue, could be useful."

10

Difficult mouthful

Alex's light embellishment of being only 'a couple of tube stops away' from the Server Building is more like fifteen. This excursion requires him to invest over two hours of his planning time. He justifies this to himself by including Lucy as a valid intelligence source who may have further utility, and that he can think in transit. He considers that having Lucy on the team will be a significant advantage, as some of the targets are under surveillance - some of the watch list members are actually being watched, and the list's detail becomes less accurate by the day. Alex needs to know when they are being watched, and when they are not. Lucy might provide vital access to surveillance patterns, and no end of other existing and new intelligence. His motivation is not to use her; her intelligence value is simply his justification for pursuing her. He has no confidence in his ability to talk her into helping him, but that is a moot point, a flaw in the argument for him taking the time out to meet her, a flaw that he is subconsciously willing to ignore.

He jumps off the train at Embankment, walks past the theatre and then heads west, along Northumberland Avenue, avoiding the Server Building, and the potential for bumping into Lucy in an untimely manner. As he walks, he begins to feel a different kind of nervousness come over him, he has not had confirmation from Lucy that she'll turn up; it will be no surprise at all if she doesn't, but if she does, well that would be a watershed moment in their relationship. It will be, that is, if it is to be real - *What if she is baiting me? What if her team has found out about the list?* His unescorted trip back into the building might have initiated an investigation that would not have needed to be too thorough to discover his actions - *get a grip*, he tells himself - *she's not even going to be there.*

The roundabout at the end of the road is jammed with cabs and open-top buses, the pavements are at choking point with pedestrians - *am I being followed?* He considers a lap of the roundabout, but then realises that counter-surveillance efforts would be a waste of time - *if they are on to me, they will know where I am going.* He takes the second exit onto The Mall. The cityscape and park are bustling with people dressed for summer and sightseeing; at least he stands a chance of escaping any attempted apprehension on foot in the cover of the crowd.

As he gains a view of the proposed meeting spot he looks at the time on his phone. It is exactly 12:30 as he steps onto the darker block paving that surrounds the monument. There is no immediate sign of Lucy, he methodically analyses everyone in sight, checking that he isn't being watched. Every brunette head that bobs into view he hopes is Lucy's, but one after another it is not - *how am I going to look if she does turn up? I'll look pathetic standing here waiting for her.* He steps off to walk back towards the roundabout, not really sure what his plan is, but as he does, Lucy calls to him from behind the monument.

"I wondered how long you'd wait." she says. Alex is relieved, excited, astounded and almost at a loss for what to do next. Like a dog chasing a car down the street, he has no clue what to do once he's caught her. "I thought it'd be longer than four minutes if I'm honest."

Alex laughs politely. "I wasn't sure that you even got a chance to register the invite. Like I said, I'm just round the corner and it was no trouble to stop by on the off chance."

"Well I wasn't going to pass up an opportunity to buy you that lunch, I'm getting a lot of credit for managing the Skynet solution; I'll probably owe my third stripe to you."

"You managed me perfectly Lucy, that's what being a good Senior Non-Commissioned Officer is all about - if you get it, you'll have earned it. Now are you going to treat me or what?"

"Come on." Lucy beckons Alex towards the food kiosk just into the green of the park. "This place is well-known for its coffee – it's where all the locals come." They walk over to the concession; "Two white Americanos and two baguettes, please." Lucy says, as she helps herself to the sandwiches from the rack. She pays the vendor and hands Alex a beef and horseradish baguette. "So what is your latest challenge then?" she asks him.

"I'm working on a private security initiative, a bit controversial, but there are some good ideas."

The few sets of white-painted iron furniture are all occupied, so they walk further into the park to find some space on the grass to sit down.

"The park is beautiful. Do you come down here much?" Alex asks.

"I'm too busy at work and I live in High Wycombe, so I'm not around at the weekends. It's lovely to have half an hour to take it all in. There are so many people from all over the world, from all walks of life."

"It's nice when people can get along in peace." Alex looks around to check that they are out of ear-shot of anyone else. "Has any more progress been made into finding the rest of the Birmingham Gardens cell?"

"Not yet, just a lot of dead ends at the moment."

"This kind of case must be frustrating, especially when so much was known about the one they caught?"

"Yes, but our hands are tied. Unfortunately there's no crystal ball – we can't predict which of the identified risks will go on to be realised." Lucy says with a look of disdain.

"It's a shame that decisions can't be made on the balance of probability in these situations." Alex says with slight trepidation that he might be extending too far too soon.

"Could you imagine?" Lucy says with a level of excitement, "Being able to step out of a life of accountability and put an end to some of these scum bags. The best we can hope for is hitting that sweet-spot of catching one of them in the act, about to do something horrendous; it'd be open season - there'd be no holding back, not if it were up to me."

"Double tap – no messing." Alex interjects, raising his hands up to an imaginary rifle to pull an imaginary trigger, feigning some mild humour.

Lucy continues; "But those are just fantasies; even with the best intelligence, it's like a needle in a haystack, and when it does happen - it's an overpowering arrest, governed by strict human rights law."

"So you think they should get to spend some quality time with some people with less accountability then?"

"Hell yeah, all sorts can happen in self-defence."

"You'd put them out of the picture for good?"

Lucy just smiles and looks out across the park.

Alex knows that she wants to end the conversation here, but he sees his chance to reach out to her. "You would though, wouldn't you?" He presses her as firmly as he dare without wanting to venture into entrapment territory.

"Oh come on Alex, anyone serving would. A fanatic that wants to murder innocent people - it's the collective fantasy - getting hold of one of those pieces of shit and putting them out of their misery."

There it is, laid bare; she has the desire, the hatred of the target set, but does she have the will to make the jump to bringing it into reality? Might she be persuaded? Alex pauses for a mouthful of sandwich, then changes tack. "How long have you had your place in High Wycombe?"

"I've had it for five years now, I bought it with some money I had in trust from my dad. It's the girly version of your place; bachelorette pad, lots of comforts, lots of pink, I love it."

"Big screen TV? Wired for sound?"

"The sound system's good, I brought it back from a tour of Germany a couple of turns of the handle back, but no giant screen. Music's important to me, it helps me unwind and relax.

"Do you have your own 'in-crowd' in High Wycombe?"

"Not really, a few civvy friends from the neighbourhood, but no-one really close." She takes a sip of her coffee. "What do you do to chill out?" Lucy asks Alex as he takes a big mouthful of baguette. "Sorry." she laughs as he covers his mouth with his hand and tries to chew through the thick crust and generously thick slab of beef.

After taking an embarrassingly long time to swallow his mouthful, Alex answers; "I like a movie, a few beers with some friends, just monging out on my sofa. My folks and old school mates keep me grounded and relieve the stress that people like you put me under." They both laugh. "You said you had trust fund money from your dad? I take it he's not around anymore?"

"He died in Service with the RAF on Special Duties in Northern Ireland, he was killed in a massacre - he was in a pub, off duty at the time."

"Really, would I have heard of him?" Alex racks the section of his brain that stores snippets of military history for incidents involving anyone called Butler.

"He wasn't listed in the dead and his death was never acknowledged in the press at the time, his presence as military would have blown a huge operation. The mission eventually collared a super-violent node of paramilitaries."

"Wow, that's rough that he never got public recognition for his sacrifice."

"Knowing that he contributed to taking those terrorists off the street is worth more to his memory than any plaque or public recognition. He was awarded a posthumous Distinguished Service Cross; he was one of the first Non-Commissioned ranks to get it."

"Is he why you joined the Army?"

"I was less than a year old, I didn't even know him."

"No, but the fact that he'd served, did what he did, what happened to him; the way he died - that must have had some influence over your life choices?"

"I don't think so, I always wanted adventure and the Army was a natural choice. My uncles were all in the Forces; my mum constantly regaled me with tails of how great Service life was as I was growing up. I did a couple of years as a ski instructor in Italy after university, and then I joined up."

"How did you end up in intelligence?"

"It wasn't a conscious choice; I had good qualifications, but didn't want to Commission, so they kind of steered me towards it. It was Intelligence or Signals, and your Corps sounded like 'major boring shit' - no offense."

"None taken, I realised I wasn't that interested in green comms fairly soon after joining, I just wanted to be doing sports and getting amongst the computer side of it. Did you keep up the skiing?"

"Yeah, I get away on a few training camps and the Army and Tri-Service competitions every year."

"Sweet, I did the same with kayaking."

"Why did you join?" Lucy asks as she takes a bite of her baguette. She seems to be relaxing into Alex's company.

"Nothing better to do, adventure, I just didn't want to get stale and live my life in one place. Everyone laughs at how shit it is while they're serving, but there's no better life."

"What about now? Are you sorry that you left?"

"No, I got what I wanted out of it. I'm into another gear now, I get a different type of satisfaction from the work I'm doing now. Like with the job I did for you, I'd never get let loose with that in a uniform, but put me in civvies and away I go. It's weird how the Army will trust you with a rifle, will trust you to make life and death decisions on the ground, but won't trust you to do anything else remotely specialist that they haven't trained you on specifically."

"How deep is the satisfaction you feel in your work though? Solving complex problems and challenging yourself is one thing, but does it stand up to the feeling that you get from uniformed service?"

"I know what you mean, it does feel like there's something missing, I think that's what I'm chasing with this new project."

"What is it? You said it was some sort of private security business?"

"Well it's a private group being set up to eradicate the UK mainland terror threat."

"Wow, quite a mission."

"Yes, the group plans to identify the nastiest elements of society and remove the threat."

"How's it going to do that?"

Alex decides there and then to go for it; "execute a pre-emptive strike." He looks up from his sandwich to read Lucy's reaction.

"What?" she says with a mix of surprise, confusion and disgust. "Suspects - unconvicted suspects? Under who's sanction? What department could possibly order such a thing?"

"There is no sanction, there is no authority, it's an entirely private venture."

"Alex, I don't understand, you mean it's criminal?"

"That depends on your perspective."

"No Alex, taking out suspects - that's judge, jury and executioner, that's pretty far from legal. I can't believe what you're telling me."

"How can it be right that these people can roam the streets, plot horrendous atrocities like Birmingham, and we just let it happen?"

"We have to trust in the security services to get it right; they stop a Birmingham happening nine times out of ten."

"They shouldn't have to Lucy, but the fact that one in ten gets through is enough to warrant action. If the top tier of activists were to be removed, think about how much money could be better spent on health, social care, housing. The removal of a couple of hundred low-lives would save many hundreds from becoming victims, and save thousands more through better use of the money."

"That's not how life works Alex."

"It's not, not in this ultra-liberal world - can't you sense everyone getting sick of it? Aren't you sick of it? God I'm starting to sound like John."

"Who?"

"It doesn't matter. But can't you see how we've become so wrapped up in people's rights for everything, we insist on everyone's freedom to do what they want; we give away our right to safety."

"What then? Lynch mobs?"

"Not lynch mobs, well-informed professional operators working on official intelligence to surgically remove clearly defined threats. On a balance of fairness of the winners and losers, isn't that a better set of outcomes? Two hundred less bad guys, god-knows how many more good guys get to stay alive, not get maimed, don't lose loved ones? It's your collective fantasy come true."

Lucy has a look of frustration; she does not have an argument immediately to mind.

"What do you think your father was doing in Northern Ireland? Gathering evidence, collating it all to bring the bad guys to a court of law? I'd assert - not so. That was a dirty and bloody war over there, but it was what was needed to be done."

"Is that why you wanted to see me? You want to drag me into this?"

"No Lucy, I wanted to see you for a release from it, not to involve you. I didn't intend to tell you about it, certainly not today anyway. We have more intelligence than we can handle at the moment."

"But you might need more?"

"Possibly."

"And I'd be a potential source?"

"Yes, I suppose... no... I don't know. That's not why I'm here; I just wanted to see you."

"I wanted to see you Alex, but I'm not so sure now, what have you got yourself into?"

"I believe in it Lucy. I'm not a nutter, or a psychopath, I just want to redress the balance, make people feel safe, give them back their freedom of security. I know it's not an ideal solution, but it's a better solution to the terror situation than putting our fingers in our ears and feeling good about ourselves, that we've respected the rights of people that hate the way of life in this country."

"So where is your team getting its intelligence from?"

Alex had hoped that this question would not come, but it has. He doesn't want to lie to Lucy, but there are multiple reasons why telling her the truth is not a good idea.

"I got it from a previous job."

"You stole it?" Lucy pauses, it doesn't take her long to figure out how many organisations there are that hold that kind of information, and how many of them that Alex has had access to while working on the Skynet issue. "You stole it from me?"

"Not from you, from The Security Service, I took their UK terror watch list."

"Whilst working on my hardware, under my supervision? Alex, what have you done? You'll go to prison for this… I'll go to prison for this."

"I didn't want to drag you into this, I'm sorry. The Birmingham thing affected me, I was upset by it. When I saw the list just there in front of me on my screen, it was like it was meant to be. I decided to take it; it didn't seem like such a big deal, just a small file transfer."

"Is that what all that fuss was about with the pen drive?"

"Yes, I hadn't planned on Gary and his metal detector." Alex made it funny, Lucy almost laughs. Alex feels that things aren't completely at a loss, maybe Lucy likes him more than she is letting on, and maybe she is more sympathetic to his chosen mission than he thought she might be. He carries on his attempt to persuade her; "You know that if all of these high threat individuals and cells were connected together in a conventional way, part of a formed organisation, like the Taliban, or the PKK, there'd be no concern about going after them. Why should it be any different, just because they are in isolation from each other? It's a new enemy model that our Forces haven't evolved to keep up with, the cumulative body of terror activists have the combined effect of a network or group, worse if anything, even if it isn't one – it should be treated as one, if not by government agencies, by some other group."

"Alex, you're preaching to the converted, I'm as frustrated as you are, but what you've done is highly illegal, and if you're actually going to do something about it; very dangerous."

"I know Lucy; I can live with the guilt of stealing the list and I've enlisted the help of some of the most capable people in the world to take care of the operational end of business, so I'm not too worried about anything going wrong." Alex looks thoughtfully at his hands as he plays with a blade of grass between his fingers, "but I'm still coming to terms with the guilt that I might feel for being responsible for the deaths of so many people."

"The watch list is over twenty thousand names, I'm guessing that you've slimmed that down somewhat?"

Alex explains the filtering process, the final selection that he had been through with the committee, and the nature of the individuals left on the final cut of the target list.

"I could let you read the files of any of the remaining 178 and you'd agree that they deserve to die." Alex says confidently.

Lucy says nothing for a while, she sips her coffee and eats her lunch whilst looking at the people, the park, the lake, seeming to be soaking up life in general. The whole place is alive, there is a joyous atmosphere of fun; it feels as though everyone has come together to celebrate being alive and to enjoy human company, though Lucy and Alex are no longer contributing to it. Alex feels as though he might not be there, that he is day-dreaming of being in Lucy's presence. He feels unsure of whether he should be worried that she has ceased interacting with him, or whether he should be pleased that she is able to relax in his presence and enjoy the park with him in silence. As his mind bounces between trying to continue to talk her round, or dismissing the conversation as theoretical, she leans towards him, turns her head towards his ear and whispers quietly, "I want in."

11

Safe keeping

The tube journey back to Richmond is a mental workout for Alex as he attempts to think through the potential and possibilities that Lucy's involvement in the project might open up. Not just for the project, but for him personally; he is excited that Lucy's interest must be founded at some level with him. Although for notably different reasons this time, Alex finds himself distracted from the task in hand by the presence of Lucy.

The next part of the plan, which is unfolding much faster than he has anticipated, is to solidify an information management policy – with five people already in the know, and who knows how many others being invited to the next meeting, this should have been fully established by now. Alex has been trained by the Army to have a full understanding of computer systems and network security, but it is his recently acquired commercial knowledge that will serve him best in this task. The military have taught him about protecting discrete systems and the processes of distributing items of hardware that contained classified content, but this was all done under armed protection and well behind friendly lines, in his experience at least. Alex needs to keep every aspect of this project's information entirely out of the public space and come up with a method of transmitting information between nearly two hundred people without raising suspicion or triggering an investigation. There must be a constant air-gap between the key sensitive information and wired systems; it must never be left unencrypted, or be issued in any more detail that immediately required.

'A secret is something that you only tell one person at a time' was one of Alex's favourite sayings. Keeping a closed loop is exceedingly difficult once word begins to spread and the risk of the dilution of security procedures increases. The key to success is to ensure that everyone accepted into the loop appreciates and respects the secrecy, and respects the rules that keep the secret a secret. Craig's buy-in is assured; Alex will need to wield that afforded authority like a sword, and back it up with a clear message of the stark consequences that await anyone who fails to play by the rules.

Alex walks back into the business suite at 13:55 to find it empty - *is this a good sign? Have they completed their task and gone for lunch, or have they thinned out for good?* The laptop is still on the desk, on, but locked. As he pours himself a coffee from one of the thermal flasks, he hears voices approaching through the door – they sound jovial. The door bursts open.

"Good afternoon young man." says Mark "I'll have one of those please."

"Me too."

"Me three."

"Expensive round." Alex says as he lines up the cups. He passes the first cup to Craig.

"Cheers Alex. We've had a productive lunch; we've got six handlers coming here tomorrow for a 10:00 start."

"Excellent, I've been fairly busy myself."

"Your intelligence source? How did that go?" John asks.

"Great. We've got a new team member, currently serving in a sector of Government security services, connected to all networks that we could possibly need access to. I can't say much more than that."

"Impressive, is he an old Army connection?" Mark asks.

"It's better for everyone that you don't know, there's no need. In the same way that I don't need to know your people on the ground; the less we all know, the safer it is for everyone."

"I make you right Alex, I don't want to know." says Craig.

"That brings me nicely onto the information security policy." says Alex.

John and Mark both spontaneously lie back in their chairs and simulate snoring.

"Knock it off fellas, this is serious." says Craig.

Alex continues, "We have to consider every communication, every contact we have. Would we have made each one if we weren't on this project? What possible explanation should we have for it? Everything must be covered off with a plausible story or be on covert communications." There is an air of discontent in the room.

"Look, we're not children; we know more about OPSEC than you'll ever know." Mark's comment brings indications of agreement from the other two.

"And I don't doubt that Mark, you guys are the experts in that, but that is OPSEC, operational security, this needs to be 'everything-SEC', your whole life and everything you do. Perfect example; Craig, you called a friend to have me checked out, to do a review of my military career on the military system?"

"Yes Alex, that's OPSEC, making sure you aren't some mole or nutter."

Alex smiles. "Yes, but now someone out there knows that you have an interest in me. There is a record on the Army system that my file has been searched for and accessed, the person that did the search can be identified. It won't take Sherlock Holmes to marry up the time of the search with the phone calls made from that office, giving a datalink from me to you."

"You're fucking paranoid mate." says John.

"Paranoid about leaving this sort of trail, five, even two years ago - maybe, but with the data-mining techniques that the combined security services are getting into now, we won't even have to be suspects before a super-computer algorithm can piece together our entire careless team."

Almost like a primed audience member Craig throws it back to him, "So how do we escape it then Alex?"

"The cover story has to be in place and maintained to justify our connections. What we have is a great start and might even see us through to the end of recruitment; from there we could be onto one hundred percent operational communications, unless there's a need to bring anyone together again after that. All of our meetings are dressed up as IT Security training sessions." Alex takes three envelopes from his attaché case and hands them out. "Bring these to all meetings - it's course material; you get brownie points for reading them, you might even learn something." Mark opens his envelope and flicks through the handouts and booklet. Alex goes on; "I'll bring these and operational phones for all new team members that you recruit to your meetings, either here or regionally.

"We need enough messaging and call traffic on our personal devices to make the cover story plausible, and everything else relating to the actual operation stays on the operational network, so we arrange meetings based on the cover story using personal phones. You will need to let me know how many people you're bringing online, where and when so that we can source appropriate numbers of devices and get them distributed. If that's not logistically possible; I can train the handlers to buy and set up handsets so that they're untraceable.

"Each player on the operational network will have an alpha-numerical call-sign so that names cannot be matched to digital profiles should we be compromised. Each handler will have a messaging group for their team on the encrypted application and will manage their group's information through that. Craig and I will be included in all groups for monitoring purposes. I will create a super group with everyone in for all-informed messaging; we'll also have a command group for us and the handlers."

"Why do you need to be on the tactical nets Alex?" John asks.

"I'm the comms guy John. I'm the fun police; I need to know that the networks are being used appropriately. Is there a problem with that?" Alex looks straight at John for a second, and then takes a sideways glance at Craig to check that he still has his support – Craig is glaring firmly at John.

"No problem Alex." says John.

"I'm also going to be managing real-time intelligence and reporting, so will need to see what's going on.

"Once we have everyone online and inducted, the information network will be in place and target information will then be distributed by me to handlers, they will then send on target packs to their individual operatives. Digital target packs will be named to match the corresponding operative. Any questions will be dealt with through direct messaging between operatives and their handlers. Any discreet meetings that are required, but don't fit the cover story, can be arranged on the operational network. Such meetings must be attended covertly, and personal mobiles are not to be carried to those meetings. Personal mobiles must not be taken to any operational activity; they are an easy way to place the carrier. All operational mobiles will be properly destroyed immediately after mission completion – instructions to follow."

John's face has a troubled look on it, and has done since Alex had mentioned the constraints on the passage of information. "Something wrong John?" Alex asks.

"Between us three and the six other handlers, that's about twenty operatives and targets each. That's a lot."

Alex hasn't considered the workload; he has been focussed on the methods of communication. He looks across to Craig.

Craig doesn't look concerned. "I've been thinking about this since we came up with the handler shortlist. It's not an issue. We'll nominate area second in commands and the handlers will work in pairs. They'll share the workload and double up as clean up teams."

"So right away we add another nine blokes onto the recruiting target then?" says Mark.

"Yes, but it'll be well worth the investment" Craig replies dismissively.

"While we're talking about investments;" Alex says sheepishly, "can we discuss the financing of the project please?"

There is a moment of consideration and looking at one another. All of the men in the room have lived entire service and private careers without needing to worry about where funding was coming from; everything had always been provided for them. "There's no quartermaster with an unlimited Special Forces budget on this project, everything has to be paid for. I've got some cash and I've paid up for all of our phones and very happy to pay my own hotel and travel, but nearly two hundred phones is going to be a bit of an ask for me to cover."

There is a chorus of sympathetic responses, led by Craig. "Don't be silly Alex, we'll all pay our share, I'm sure that anyone that we recruit will be more than happy to cough up too. You just let us know what we owe."

"Thanks guys, that's a bit of a relief. The phones and credit are fairly cheap. It's getting them without being traced that's proving tricky, but I've sorted an illicit credit card and email account, and I've got my eye on a derelict property to have the remaining bulk of phones delivered to."

"Can't you just chin off paying the credit card if it's a spoof identification?" John asks with a grin.

"I could do, but there's a risk of sparking a line of investigation that we can live without for fairly small beans each." says Alex.

"Fair one." says John.

"I'll book us a bigger room and source another six phones for tomorrow." says Alex as he picks up his attaché case and heads for the door. "See you all back here for breakfast with some more new friends."

"Alex." Craig pulls on his arm as he attempts to make his exit. "No one's gonna believe this cover story if I don't take you out for a pint to thank you for your work. Meet us in the King's Head at eight tonight… unless you've got plans?"

"Sure, see you there."

12

A pint

Alex walks into the Kings Head right on 20:00. Craig is standing at the bar sipping the top off a freshly poured pint. Before he can get it out of his mouth, Dave is already laying on the hospitality; "Good evening Alex, what can I get you?"

"I'll have what Craig's having please, Dave."

Dave begins pouring as Craig wipes his top lip dry with the back of his left hand. "I've been coming here for years. You can't beat a good local."

"It's nice to be in a place with so much history and character." Alex replies. The landlord hands Alex his drink.

"Cheers Dave, put it on my tab." Craig says as he leads Alex across to the same table they'd sat at two nights before.

"So Alex, are you happy?"

Alex isn't sure where this question is coming from. "Yeah… I'm happy. Is there something in particular that I should be happy about?"

"Lighten up Alex, I just want to know if you're happy with how things are going, the plan, the people… the targets?"

"It all seems to be going great so far. I didn't think it would take off this quickly. I only met you forty-eight hours ago and we're already three layers deep into the planning."

"Like you said Alex, the information you've brought us is time sensitive and we have to act fast.

"Are you sure you're up to this mentally, Alex? There's no shame in walking away and leaving us to it you know mate; we've got plenty of communications experts in our network."

"No way." Alex says, not quite convincingly. "I know that this project is what I want. Every time I see footage of the Birmingham victims, those poor kids - no, this needs to happen and I'll be proud to be a part of it."

"It does Alex, and it will, but that's not what I asked, I asked if you were up to it. There's no shame if you're not. I've seen the toughest of guys crumble mentally when their hearts are not completely in something as challenging as this."

"You don't think I'm up to it?"

"Listen Alex, it doesn't matter what I think, there's no way I can judge, it's for you to decide."

"Can't a man of your experience tell who's got the minerals and who hasn't?"

"All I know is that you're untested in that way Alex. Even if you'd been through the mill like me and my boys, that's still no guarantee." Craig looks into his pint glass thoughtfully.

"You've been caught by surprise before then?"

Craig lowers his voice further, "Listen, I've seen some of the worst action encountered by my former regiment, which by definition, is about the worst that anyone anywhere could have been exposed to, so I have difficulty in understanding why others, including some of my closest comrades, have succumbed to mental health dramas, PTSD and all that. I don't pretend to understand it and I don't judge, not anymore."

"That sounds like a hard lesson learned?" Alex says whilst trying to make eye contact, but Craig is solemn, with his head down firmly over his pint.

"I saw it first hand when my best mate committed suicide shortly after leaving the service."

"Oh Craig, I'm sorry."

My best mate, Gaz, flung himself down the stairwell in his swanky flat, leaving himself hanging a couple of feet off the floor in his living-room. The cleaner found him the next day."

"And you never saw it coming?"

"I'd known him forever. We met on soldier selection at Pirbright and we went through every stage of our careers together – purely by chance at first, but we became tight in the Anglians and decided to give selection a go together; we made sure that we'd follow the same path - we were like brothers… more than brothers. He was an emotional kind of guy on a different level to me; he'd cry like a baby after every kill – a lot of tears. The years took their toll, forcing him from service before his time, and compounded with the shock of civvy street, it all became too much."

"Jesus." Alex doesn't know what else to say.

"I've done some serious soul-searching whilst mourning Gaz, but without tears. I just find myself zoning out thinking about him, and his situation, from time to time. As much as mourning my friend, I've had my own internal struggle to come to terms with." Alex becomes conscious that Craig's reassuring pep talk is turning into his own counselling session – he is unsure of what to do or say, but carries on listening intently.

"Is there something wrong with me? Why do I feel nothing about the things I've seen, done or been exposed to? I have this creeping feeling that there is something deeply wrong with me and that it could spill out at any moment, like it's in the post and there's nothing I can do about it. I know myself as an openly emotional person in other ways, I'd get a wobbly chin from a heated exchange in the NAAFI, or a lump in the throat watching DIY SOS, but the dead or dying on the battlefield, even my own men – not a flicker. Something is definitely amiss and there surely must be some sort of mental deficit to be repaid."

Alex tries to respond with feeling; "I've not seen anything like what you've seen. One of my mates was killed on tour, but I wasn't there. Another guy I knew from basic training was killed in a vehicle accident on the area, but things like that happen, they don't really affect you that badly. I can't begin to imagine losing close mates the way that you have. To be honest I don't know what affect our project will have on me. All I know is that I want to be a part of it and that I'm willing to take the consequences of our actions."

"That's honourable Alex, but you keep thinking about it."

The two men turn to their pints for a moment of silence. Alex tries to put his experience in perspective with Craig's, and struggles to fathom how he must be feeling - the torment that he must wrestle with every night before he goes to sleep. He thinks of how he might cope with the guilt that he may feel for the executed targets, and whether the saving of lives that he expects to achieve from this mission can provide sufficient recompense.

Mark taps Craig on the shoulder, "Another drink chaps?"

"My round." says John. "All right Dave, same again for Craig and Alex please, and another two. Can I offer you one?"

"Very kind John." Dave replies as he begins pouring.

Mark sits down next to Alex, "Not interrupting are we?"

"No Mark, we're just talking over what kind of a head-case you need to be for a project like ours." says Craig.

"Defo need a screw loose - we're all qualified." Mark says intimating that he excludes Alex from his declaration.

John places the drinks on the table, his huge hands engulfing the four pint tankards. "War's a job that needs doing." John takes a seat next to Craig, "If the elected government of the day saw fit to send us in to do a job, then there's nothing on my conscience. The blokes with me all had a choice, they could've been working in McDonalds if they didn't fancy it – bang, get it done and get home in time for tea and medals. I never lost any sleep over it - never will.

"Okay, there's no Government sending us in for this one, but bloody hell, the targets of this mission have it coming more than most that I've taken down." says Craig.

"John's right to a point." Mark agrees, "If you can cut off your emotions and see it in such black and white terms like that, then there's no problem, but we all know that it's just not possible for everyone to do that. I certainly can't. I'm constantly thinking back about jobs I've done, targets I've hit, people I've lost, but I don't let it get me down, I see the positives; I'm still here, living a good life in honour of the fallen. I can't say I lose much sleep over thinking about scumbags I've slotted, mind."

"Bad guys are bad guys." says Craig, "The worst thing I've had to deal with was a strike on a building in Iraq; we'd been taking sniper fire from this place for hours, we had no cover to make an approach, no other routes in, so we called in some fast air. They put a five hundred pounder down on it – went right in, straight through one of the windows – there was nothing left of it. I went forward to conduct a battle damage assessment and we found a whole family, kids and everything, all fucking dead."

"You don't need that." John says sympathetically.

"That's what gets a lot of soldiers - the collateral damage."

"Well that's not going to be an issue for this mission, unless something goes seriously tits up." says Mark.

"So you're all fairly comfortable with taking on these targets without any ethical concerns at all then?" Alex asks.

The three Special Forces men look dismissive as though they'd never really considered that there might be anything to consider. Mark is the first to respond "Alex, we understand that this might be tough for you, but wiping out bad guys is what we do."

"Gents," Craig says addressing John and Mark, "when you came in I was chatting to Alex about his position in the team. He's keen as mustard to be a part of this, but we need to give him some support until he gets his head around it properly."

"'Course." says John.

"No worries Alex." says Mark with a supportive smile.

"Cheers guys, I'm sure I'll be fine. It's just kind of hit home over the last day or so that this is unsanctioned, not ordered by any form of authority. As John mentioned, that's what can take the heat off your conscience, but as we've all agreed, the target selection is defensible and action is warranted."

Craig is at the other end of the soldier spectrum to Alex; old school in his attitudes and believes that the Army should not have evolved with the perceived weaknesses of 'modern soldiers' - it is lost on him that his seniors had the same reservations about his generation. He sees the value in tolerating Alex's reticence to embracing a fully aggressive attitude, as he feels that this trait of conservatism may be useful to the mission.

"So where do you plan on being when it all goes down Alex?" asks John.

"I don't know John, I haven't really thought about it. Maybe my hotel room, maybe back home, or maybe somewhere with an alibi."

"Why don't you come out on the ground with one of our clean-up teams? You could come with me. You'd be plenty far back enough from the action, but still feel a part of it?"

"No you're all right John, I'll need to be set up in front of my computer with my phone should anyone need information on their targets."

"Let's not get talking in too much detail here, fellas." Craig says quietly.

John refuses to let Alex off completely; "It's not your fault, Alex. You've been brought up in the wrong conditions for this end of the wedge, like most of the kids these days, that's why Hereford has trouble recruiting. I remember when I was a kid - the bullying was brutal, and whilst no one enjoyed it, it prepared us for life, it made us tough and resilient. Kids grow up these days having never faced a challenge or had to fight for anything. It's all very nice for them, but it doesn't help them face real situations. I don't think I would have joined the Paras if I hadn't been bullied a bit at school."

Craig cuts the topic off - "Have we had any word from our colleagues? Are they all on their way?"

Joseph Mitcham

"A couple are well on their way; two will be arriving tonight and staying in the hotel, the others will all be here in the morning, all due in by train in good time for the meet." says John confidently.

"Is Mike getting here tonight?" Mark asks.

"Yeah, but late."

"It'll be good to see him; it'll be like old times with the three of us."

"What are you, the musketeers?" Craig ribs the pair of them.

"Yeah, the slap-stick version though, unfortunately our soldiering skills never helped us out when we were on the piss." says John, looking far more relaxed than Alex had seen him looking before. "Remember that time we fell asleep pissed on the bus on our way back to your folks' house?" he says gesturing to Mark.

"I remember the gashed wrist from climbing over the barbed wire fence to get out of the bus depot - nearly set me back in training."

"You were such a bell-end."

"You still are."

"Yeah cheers for that." They both laugh at themselves.

"You can't beat the banter." says Craig, enjoying the lads' recollection of times past.

"The best bit about leave was coming back to barracks to hear the stories of what the blokes had been up to." says John.

"You're not wrong mate." says Mark, all four men raise their glasses and take a swig of beer.

"Well, we better be ready for them; let's call it a night men." All four of them pick up their drinks and down what they've got left in their glasses; Craig and John clunk their glasses down simultaneously and arise from the table together. Alex and Mark are a little slower to do so and follow on towards the door.

126

"Don't you worry, Alex, you do whatever you're comfortable with mate. The more comfortable you are; the better you can look after us."

"Thanks Mark, see you in the morning." Mark pats Alex on the back as he passes him on the way to the door and sets off to catch up with John and Craig.

Alex walks slowly south towards the hotel. He tries to imagine that he is a Special Forces operative with a back catalogue of confirmed kills - how differently would he see this challenge? He considers the looks on his new friends' faces when he had asked them about their ethical concerns; their lack of apprehension was predictable if he had thought about it, but still left him feeling cold. *How will I get myself into such a frame of mind? How will I shut down my feelings? Will I lose my innocence? Become someone new? Will my soul be ruined? Will I be haunted by the experience forever? Is the fact that I am facing such mental anguish a sign that the mission is based on flawed premises? Is the whole concept morally and ethically corrupt?* He might have walked across the whole of London thinking about his mess of emotions and still not have made any sense of them or come to a conclusion. The proverbial train has very much left the station; Alex now has to decide if he wants to stay on, as it rapidly begins to accelerate.

13

Roll for a role

Breakfast had been a long drawn out series of warm greetings and manly hugs, the handler selection process seemed to have drawn out a friendly bunch. Though politely introduced, Alex had been firmly side-lined by all-comers, which he was not offended at; his expectations had been successfully managed by Craig, and he expected nothing less of a reunion on such a scale of soldiers with such deep-rooted and interwoven histories. He'd sloped off to prepare the conference room, making sure that there were enough, but not too many chairs around the table, and that the refreshments had arrived and were well-stocked.

Alex delivered the list overview brief to the full cohort of handlers much the same as he had given to Mark and John, and Craig before them. Craig then explained the concept of the mission and the proposed structure, strategically led by the committee, operationally commanded by the handlers and tactically actioned by the operatives, he explains his vision of a coordinated strike against the refined list of targets.

"So what do you think fellas? Are you in?" Craig asks pointedly.

"You're damn right I'm in." Don, a stout, bearded man, slightly older than all the others, says enthusiastically. Hearing nothing else immediately from the others, he looks around the table at his peers.

"Oh yes," says Cliff, "this has got 'me' written all over it." Cliff is a wall of muscle and the most fearsome looking of all the men in the room. Easily six feet four, the man from Leicester has aggression etched on his face.

The group of prospective handlers is unanimous with successive acknowledgements of their commitment to the project.

"So when does it all go down?" Mike asks from the far end of the table, slouched back in his chair, his tufty black hair pointing in all directions, as do his nose and ears, which have suffered from the rigours of international-level judo competition spanning two decades. He is another Hereford man, having graduated up to Special Forces from 2 PARA, and is clearly a tight friend of John's; they have been side-by-side, thick as thieves, from the moment that Mike arrived.

"We're planning a D-Day in a little less than two weeks, as soon as we can get it together." Alex answers, beating Craig to the punch.

Craig looks across to Alex sternly as though he feels that his toes have been stepped on. Alex gets the message loud and clear that Craig sees this as his time to be the focal point.

"We've done a partial estimate on what needs to be done and how long it will take." The 'estimate' being the systematic analysis process military planners at all levels use. "You guys are the next step, and we're certainly on track with that – thank you all again for getting here so quickly." Craig has been quick to praise and thank the handlers at every opportunity; Alex wonders if Craig is always so positive with his men, or if the lack of financial or contractual hold over them means that he has to be so nice.

"Recruitment of operatives will be the most time consuming stage of the mission, and again the responsibility for managing that efficiently will fall largely to you blokes. The type of guys we're looking for are your best mates, your reliable blokes, your experienced and bloodied fighters. The Committee, that's Alex, Mark, John and me, have discussed the criteria and we agree that it has to be a character judgement that we will trust you to make."

"I must know forty blokes that would be up for this." says Don.

"Yes Don mate, we all do, the only thing is that twenty-five of the forty blokes that you know are twenty-five of the forty blokes that I know, probably more." says Mark. "What we need to do is have a brain dump of all our potential candidates, select those that we think are suitable, and then decide who's best placed to approach each of them. Then we go on a recruitment drive around the country."

Don is a chatty, friendly man. He had been quite a poor performer in military intelligence before getting a taste for fitness and action, and had never looked back after transferring into the Paras, and then onwards to Hereford. He is clearly well respected within the group.

Craig takes up the narrative; "Once we've hit the recruitment target, we'll split the operatives into regional teams under the nine of us, and then allocate troops to task. You'll need to select a second in command to help out locally, but let's not get ahead of ourselves. There's no point thinking any further until we've looked at the feasibility of force generation."

Mark opens the operational laptop and sets it on the table in front on him, "Right, I'll scribe."

Alex has little more to do than to keep the brews flowing; he takes brief opportunities to acquaint himself with the new members of the team and finds none of them as hard to get on with as John, but none of them as easy to get on with as Mark.

The list of candidates grows through the morning as the handlers systematically go through the names of recently serving soldiers from the Services' toughest units, squadron by squadron, company by company, then on to sweep through remaining contacts that they have made in the world of private security. Each name receives differing levels of response, all getting at least a low grumble of agreement, some initiating rapturous jeers of jubilation at the identification of another significant player.

"What about Andy Freeman, he got a citation in Kosovo - slotted a couple of bad lads who were terrorising a village." says Mike.

"Yeah top bloke, I did my Stripies' course with him, mega bloke." agrees John.

Mark interjects; "He's an absolute fruit bat."

"Does he get bonus points for that?" asks John with a laugh.

"No, he's properly tapped - those lads he offed in Kosovo were just the start of it; he went seriously off the rails, ended up sectioned and medically discharged."

Craig looks troubled. "It's a good job you knew that Mark, we have to be very careful and do our research."

"What if we get it wrong, what if we bring in someone that has a background we've not heard about, or has some other flaw that the recruiters somehow don't know about? How do we deal with those we need to take off the project?" asks Mike.

"We will have to tread carefully; put anyone's nose out of joint; and we could end up with a security problem." says John.

"It'll be a Committee issue, well most of the Committee." says Craig, "Mark, John and I will take responsibility, nothing a good talking to and a look in the eye won't sort out."

They break for lunch with nearly three hundred good names on the spreadsheet, all with phone numbers and varying levels of detail on current location and the names of the handlers who might be best placed to make the approach. Each candidate has been given a score out of a hundred for suitability and the final act is to re-order the names from most to least suitable.

"They're a canny bunch." says Don.

"You could pull off a major coup with that lot." adds John.

"Can we go into business after this? Taking over small countries and selling them on." Mike's idea fetches a laugh from the others, but to be fair; it has been done before, and by far less capable groups.

"All right fellas, be that as it may, the less we have to do with each other after this the better, for a while anyway. There are more pressing matters ahead of us. We need to look at how we split the targets into regional groups." says Craig. Alex has inconspicuously connected his laptop to the room's projector; he fires it into life to display a map of the United Kingdom peppered with red cross-hairs. "These are the targets by location. As you can see they are mostly well clustered with main centres of gravity being London, Birmingham and Manchester."

Craig pauses for a moment to let the image sink in, for the reality of the situation to wash over the handlers. Alex takes the moment to look at his part of the world - none in Peterborough, one in Luton, four around Leicester. In the grand scheme of things; five potential bad guys within a 50 mile radius of where he lives doesn't seem too much of a threat. Then he looks at his current location - nearly eighty threats within twenty miles; he doesn't feel quite so safe anymore.

"London and Birmingham are riddled." says Don.

"Yes, there'll be three handler teams in London and two in Birmingham, all other teams will have operators dispersed over a pretty wide area, and one of you is going to have to cover all of Scotland and most of the North of England." says Alex.

"What's going on with Northern Ireland? We all know that that should be speckled with targets?" asks Spence, a slender man with shrew-like features, jet-black hair and so much covert experience from the provinces that he has developed a full accent that he's not been able or willing to shake off.

"The watch list would seem to be strictly mainland, there must be a separate list for the Provinces, and thank our stars for that – I wouldn't want to get involved over there. We all know what sort of a nightmare it is, not to mention the number of agencies' operations we'd be stepping all over – best left well alone." says Craig.

"Okay, so what's our MO going to be?" Don asks.

"I'm not sure." says Craig, "We need to decide what message we're sending, if any, and how that's going to be best delivered."

Alex senses a suitable moment to contribute. "The annual homicide rate is about six hundred, so it's not going to go unnoticed as a significant event if the kills are overt in nature. Another option is to completely mask the deaths as naturally caused; there are half a million of those a year, that'd take a little longer to come to light, but you can't just knock off the top few percent of the UK terror watch list without one agency or another noticing." says Alex, his research having paid off and bringing him some credibility with the handlers.

"Don't we want to send a strong message? Achieve some sort of deterrent?" asks Mike.

"We do, but it's a double edged sword. It could create a backlash, or act as a motivator to the religious nuts, or any other group who registers it as an attack on them. The last thing that we want to do is to stimulate more terror attacks, that's the opposite of what we are trying to achieve." says Alex. There is an atmosphere of frustration in the room, but the lack of comments suggests that everyone sees the logic. Alex continues, "If we decide not to use the opportunity to send a message and go fully covert, then I suppose we do not need to get this all done on one night and we can reduce the need for so many operatives."

Craig stirs in his thoughts, "There definitely needs to be a message." He pauses for further thought, everyone in the room sensing that this is a key moment of consideration. They sit in total silence.

Craig continues, "So keeping it synchronised, but going fully covert and making the deaths look natural would result in a deterrent eventually, which would have the bonus of giving our operatives time to extricate, and for any evidence at the scenes to be significantly compromised or even destroyed – that sounds like a great option."

"I'd rather we hammered them with a big fuck off tablet; good an' messy, that'd be a proper deterrent." says John.

"That'd be like an act of war and would certainly have unwanted repercussions. The discreet option is subtle and would have a mysterious, maybe even sinister air about it - it'd put the willies up anyone thinking about trying anything." says Craig.

"So, a quiet option, what's that going to involve?" Mike asks.

"Injection of a naturally occurring or quickly deteriorating toxin - an insulin overdose is the classic - easy to get hold of, easy to explain possession of, not checked for on your standard post-mortem." says Don.

"What kind of intelligence were you in Don?" John asks. The room brightens with laughter.

"I like that; we'll give it a bit more thought." says Craig.

"Whether overt or covert, we should consider a media release, telling everyone why we've done it and what we stand for, just so that there are no bad assumptions and to stop any other bunch of Charlies hijacking it for some political or nationalist reason." says Alex. "It needs to be a concise message, clarifying the motive and aim of the mission, something like '178 individuals that posed a threat to the security of the UK have been neutralised permanently by a group individuals with no agenda other than to keep the general population of this country safe' or words to that effect."

"There needs to be a warning in there too." says John, "How about adding 'similar culls of terror suspects may follow'."

"That starts to sound a bit 'hill-billy,'" says Craig. "What Alex said stands on its own merit; keeping it simple is best. Anyway, let's draw a line under that conversation for now. Let's carve up this list of potential operatives between us."

Alex slowly stands up from the table, hovering, waiting for Craig to notice, "I'll leave you to it if you don't mind, I'll go and sort your phones out." He walks out of the room which immediately bursts into a furore of chatter. He smiles to himself at the thought of them arguing about which of their mates they will be contacting, like a bunch of big school kids picking football teams.

Walking out of the front door of the hotel and turning right, Alex takes his personal mobile phone from his pocket and dials Lucy's office number, getting ringtone.

"Hello, Corporal Butler speaking."

"Hi Lucy, it's Alex."

"Christ, Alex, why are you calling me on these means?"

"Lucy, relax, I'm calling from an app - it's not traceable."

"Even so… what do you want?"

"I just wanted to know if you're still up for a part in my new venture."

Lucy hesitates; "I've been thinking about that… a lot."

"And?"

"I think I might need more convincing."

"Really? What can I do to persuade you?"

"Lunch was nice, maybe dinner would be nicer?"

"That sounds good to me. Dickie paid me for your job this morning so I can afford to take you somewhere nice."

"How nice?"

"Let me surprise you."

14

Clouded conscience

Back in the room the list of potential operatives has been divvied up with additional names in reserve in every area. There is a strong air of confidence that even with absences and disinterest, there should not be any issues with manning the mission.

Alex walks around the table, he hands each new handler an operational phone and talks them through the set-up process. As the men set their passwords and download the encrypted messaging app, Craig reopens the methodology conversation; "So as I said earlier, I like the idea of a covert execution and Don's insulin idea sounds like the way to go."

"Can that be done in the victim's sleep without waking them up?" asks one of the handlers that Alex has yet to hear speak. He has been quiet in the corner, not seeming to know any of the others that well, but seems close to Craig.

"If done with care, Duncs." Don responds.

"You'd probably want a back-up plan though." says Mark.

"What, a mallet?" John suggests.

"How easy is it to get hold of untraced?" asks Duncs.

"Mallets? Easy, most DIY shops have them." John laughs at his own joke.

"Hardi-fucking-ha - insulin you pillock!" Duncs' stern face breaks into a broad smile, the skin over his cheekbones tightening and his forehead wrinkling as he laughs to himself and rubs the fingertips of his right hand through his receding, loosely curling grey hair, as if he has finally woken himself up into the discussion.

"I have a friendly doctor, I can sort that. We'd need to look at the logistics - how much of a dose we'd need for it to be guaranteed fatal, how long it can be out of the fridge for, what the legalities of carrying it are - we need some detail." says Craig.

"It's fine out of the fridge for most of the day, you'd need a shot of about five millilitres for it to be fatal, so a couple of litres would be enough." says Mike.

"Are you diabetic, Mike?" Craig asks.

"Yeah, I got diagnosed a year or so ago, it's a pain in the arse."

"That might put you into a quartermaster role; you've got the perfect excuse to be carrying it. If between us we can get together the required amount, then you can distribute it out to the blokes. Can you complete the research and get us the specifics?"

"I can do that, I'm up for the QM bit too, as long as I'm back in place with my region in plenty of time before the off."

"Sweet." says Craig.

Alex suddenly begins to feel uneasy. The project so far has been a lot like pushing on open doors; nothing has yet seemed like hard work, everything has fallen into place without too much effort. It is all happening at such a pace that he has not slowed down; he has busied himself seeing if it can be done, and has not properly taken the time to consider whether it should be done – Craig's words and support now somehow don't seem to cover the lethal injection of 178 souls. He stands up to address the room; "Look guys, I know I'm the one that brought the list to you, but this has all happened a little bit too fast for me to get my head around. Killing is second nature for you fellas, but I feel like we need to make sure that we are in the right place morally. Shouldn't we at least have a bit of a discussion about the ethics of this mission concept?" An awkward feeling comes over Alex the instant that he finishes speaking. He sits back down.

The room falls silent; the handlers aren't sure whether to take Alex seriously or if his statement is a joke. John shakes his head as everyone else looks at each other. Craig is the first to speak; "Our Alex here, he's quite the sensitive soldier."

"Fucking choir boy." says John.

"All right John, enough." Craig snaps back at him.

Alex continues; "Isn't it worth a conversation? Even if it's just to put things into context. You guys are used to following your orders in far off countries, wiping out proper legitimate enemy – this is something completely different, the targets are un-convicted civilians, mostly UK citizens. They may be radicals or extremists, but in doing this we put ourselves on the spectrum of extremism; we are at the limit at the opposite end.

"Everyone has a view on how these Charlies should be dealt with, but we are taking an extreme view on what should be done. We are the counterpoint to what they're about, maybe it's right that there is one, but then maybe it's not."

Cliff responds to Alex directly with a chopping hand; "It might not be legal, but this mission is based on the populist spirit of the country right now. You cannot vote for a party that would back this, but imagine how popular it would be if you could."

"The last time you could vote for such an option, six million Jews were murdered - 75 million soldiers and civilians died." Alex replies with a hint of venom.

Cliff continues; "Let's not allow populism to become confused with nationalism, this is not a racist, bigoted pack of hyenas looking to ethnically cleanse or discriminate against a particular group or race – that's what the media will want to brand it as without even analysing it, and that's why we certainly do need a press release. This is purely a movement against a bunch of people, not defined by a race or religion, just by the fact that they want to hurt our public, whatever their reasons or motivation."

Mark makes an observation; "You see how quickly a discussion about a list of named threats turns into a discussion about race and discrimination? This is exactly how populism gets twisted into racism, nationalism, fascism – people have become blinkered by the sensationalism of the media."

"There's no race filter on Alex's list." says John.

Don lifts his head and waggles a finger lightly in the air as he talks; "What we're doing is definitely with the will of the people. The PC brigade have built up and protected the rights of people that wish to do us harm - they can say what they like, do what they want, but everyone's had enough. How far would you get in Saudi Arabia or the Emirates, subverting their way of life and plotting against it like that?" he asks rhetorically, "Not very far at all, that's how far."

"Eliminating a threat is all we want to do Craig, stuff the politics." says John.

"You can't ignore the politics John," says Alex, "you're a mug if you think you can. If you haven't thought about the politics; you should. The fallout and repercussions of this mission have to be considered. It would be irresponsible to think that there won't be knock on effects, and that we wouldn't be accountable for them.

Don carries on from where he left off; "The politically correct bandwagon is well and truly mobilised, everyone's jumping on it. It's a political tool for attacking anyone that says anything remotely controversial. It's the source of the current underlying public anger; boiling the piss of people who see it for what it is, and it'll build up to a massive backlash – you mark my words. It's happening in the States, it's happening in Germany, Italy, countries all over Europe - look at the rise of hate crime against minorities and immigrants, something needs to release the pressure, something big, something like this mission."

Mike manages to interject; "I'm with you Don, political correctness is prompting a reaction from the right, and not just the far right – it's turning so many people off that it's re-zeroing the centre on traditionally right wing opinion."

"I had this black mate a few tours back," says John, "when I did a spell in the Middle East on a mentoring job. We did everything together and had everything in common, he was a fantastic bloke, we should've had a proper 'bro-mance' going on, but it didn't happen like that. I was constantly scared of offending him, always being over-nice, always nervous of saying the wrong thing. The way it's become natural these days to be offended by every little thing makes it impossible to relax with people, it makes it tough to connect with people - you can't be yourself anymore".

"Maybe he just thought you were a cunt, John?" Blakey suggests, sending the room into raucous laughter.

"John – being 'over-nice', I wonder what that's like!" says Don with a smile.

"Yeah cheers for that… tossers. Seriously though, it's a guilt-trip put on us by the liberal media. They make me want to vomit in disgust." John says with spittle spraying from his mouth, "Their pretentiousness, insidiousness, their over-correctness - I want to throttle every one of them and get us back to a normal way of living our lives. Fuck knows how society has let itself become so wretched."

"The public's moral compass has gone to cock, everyone's been conditioned into taking offence at everything, so there's no reality to what is actually offensive to people anymore. It's become a total dichotomy between the left and the right with the voice of the people shouted down and lost in the middle." says Craig.

"Did they teach you some new words on that TV show boss?" Mike asks, as more laughter fills the room.

Craig laughs too, but continues; "It used to be the left fighting for the freedoms of everyone, they've got so preoccupied with defending the rights of minorities, they forgotten about the rights of the majority, putting the demands of the few over the freedoms of the many."

It's a paradox – there's a word for you." says John, "The rights to freedom pitted against the right to security – for some reason the right to security doesn't get a look in these days.

Mike nods his agreement, "You're right John. This type of conflict doesn't just affect security and freedom though – it's rotting away at all of society; look at the welfare state - the liberals want everyone to be equal, everything to be 'fair', but that's toss. It's a market economy, you work hard and do well; you get paid, a safety net's a safety net, but a free living is for the birds.

Good working people don't want to put up with it any more, that's why people aren't fighting the erosion of the welfare system - the lefty-types are getting a good stiff ignoring."

John grunts in frustration; "For fuck's sake fellas, we're getting a bit off topic here – there's plenty to talk about on the simple matter of the target set. The trouble is that most terror activists in the UK can't be deported, as they're passport holders; they can't be locked up, certainly not for long enough, until they act or at least try to act. Even if they could be locked up, how much would that cost? There's nothing that can be done until they commit their murders, and even then dying is part of what most of them want out of it.

Craig jumps in; "In Afghanistan, Iraq, any number of places, we've had people in the cross-hairs with less evidence against them than this lot, and not hesitated to turn them into a fine pink mist. That was sanctioned, that was backed by government, but that was also on far off shores where the direct threat wasn't to our own people. Why should we not act here, where we really care about what actions these scumbags might take?"

Alex has heard many of these arguments before in Craig's ranting broadcast; he's talking to a room of formed ideas and established beliefs – and is resigned to not making any difference to their opinions. He throws a question to the room; "How do you feel about what is going on in the States right now? The neo-Nazis and white supremacists are using extremist tactics not dissimilar to those that our targets are using – how do we feel about that?"

"It's wrong, clearly. You don't think I'm one of them do you?" Craig has no idea what Alex is getting at.

"But if the far right in this country upped their game here - would you go after them like we're planning on going after this group of targets here and now?"

Craig sees Alex's angle and a confused state engulfs him, "Sure we would, if there were any on the list; we'd be taking them down."

"So if the balance of the race relationship were the other way round, would we be so strongly motivated to step in?"

"That's different and you know it you weaselling little fuck." John gets to his feet - hackles up.

"Whatever their colour or creed, everyone on that list is defending their culture, their way of life, with whatever warped perspective they have, but they're trying to preserve what they've got." says Alex apologetically, "Is wiping them off the face of the earth the solution? Or should we find a better way?"

John is seething and spitting again; "Fuck that, that shit's failed – that's why we are here, that's why you brought us that list. There's not much watching going on; it's a nominal roll of mother-fuckers that are pissing on this country and planning on attacking its people indiscriminately – they've had their chance, they've got to go. It's all well and good you pontificating like a fucking snowflake, you won't even be getting your hands dirty, Alex, you leave the worrying and burdened consciences to us."

"You're all making interesting points, John, you really are, and I agree with most of what you're saying in principle, but when you say what we're planning to do out loud it sounds wrong… maybe I am just being carried along by the PC culture?" says Alex. He is feeling the heat, and mindful that he has brought together a formidable force, with an extremely aggressive perspective, Alex knows that he will need to tread carefully if he is to get his point across without risking taking some serious damage. "Look, it's not like I'm on their side, or want them to be able to get away with anything, it's just that this plan has developed into a serious step up."

Craig eyeballs Alex with a measuring look on his face, he stands up and leans on the table with both hands; "Look Alex, I understand your fear, you're not the same kind of animal that we are. As we near the moment, this plan will feel ever-more savage and I've got no doubt that one or two of our operatives might even consider bottling it. You can relax, we all know what we are doing and you can melt away."

Alex remains seated, deliberately emphasising his submissive posture. "This all comes back to me guys. There's no plan without the list. It's all on my conscience even if I don't lift another finger and no one ever traces anything back to me."

"Your conscience is clear fella; the names on your list are of dogs, not humans. We've done due diligence, we've checked them out, they all mean to do harm."

Craig addresses the team of handlers directly; "We are not like them. We are not indiscriminate. We will focus on defined enemy as identified by evidence. We will not recruit our force by perversion of the facts, collusion or coercion. The consequences of what we will do will be made clear, and all will understand the potential sacrifice that they sign up to. We are not racists, we will not tolerate racism, we are single minded in pursuing threat, and threat alone. The values and standards that we learned by heart and held dear in the Forces remain with us. We are not a bunch of hicks, or a baying mob; we are a skilled force of professionally trained men that will not tolerate a threat to the way of life that we have all served to protect."

John turns his head to Mark; "Put that bloody thing down Mark, this is important."

Looking up from his phone Mark announces; "There's been another one." with a combination of anger and upset in his voice.

Everyone turns to Mark. "What, another what?" Craig asks with some urgency.

"There's been a hostile vehicle attack in Kotka, Finland. Early reporting yet, but there are already two confirmed dead. There's some amateur footage online and it looks like there are bodies all over the place. The driver was slotted by the cops as he got out of his truck by the sounds of it."

The room falls silent; the men all look at each other, almost in turn. Alex waits for someone else to say something; he can almost hear the cogs of thought moving in the other men's heads.

Craig finally breaks the silence; "End of conversation then, the plan is a go. Alex's concerns are duly noted, but we will not let that happen again here."

John sparks into life, "Right fellas, make your contacts, select your second in commands, and give me a call to arrange regional orders groups once you have your respective forces in place." John looks across to Alex as he goes on; "Remember, use the cover story to arrange initial meetings and to invite them to the briefing. From there we go operational comms with issued phones, which Alex will bring along to the orders sessions."

Alex feels disappointment that he has failed to settle his apprehension and effectively communicate the concern he holds about the objectives of the mission being disproportionate to the threat in reality. As the room empties, he imagines the handlers dispersing around the country like flames fanning out in all directions from a forest fire in swirling winds – *I've lit the blue touch paper*. He finds himself staring at the carpet in a room empty but for him and Craig.

"Are you all right Alex?"

"Huh? Yes, I'm fine."

"That was brave of you to lead that conversation; you did well, it really made the guys think."

"I didn't change anyone's mind though, did I?"

"Did you expect to? Did you want to? Do you really believe that continuing on this mission is the wrong thing to do?"

"No, don't know, and no, I suppose."

"So you've got to ask yourself what your problem with it is, son. Is it fear, mental fear, physical fear?"

"I guess I'm just a little conflict averse - the thought of initiating such an action, causing so much pain, destroying families, it doesn't sit well."

"Don't think of the targets' families, think of the families of the victims that won't become victims."

"Mmmm." sighs Alex unconvinced.

"The trick is to immerse yourself in conflict, don't try and dodge it or avoid it. Sense it coming, anticipate it and enjoy it. Like a boxer getting into the ring, you have to relax into it. If there's a hint of fear about you; it will either eat you up from within, or be exploited by the enemy and you will suffer. You have to be comfortable with things not going your way, whether getting into a blazing argument with John, taking a beating, or putting your life on the line; soak it up and know you're alive. Once you've mastered that and shed your fear, you can take that anywhere, in the ring, on the street, on the battlefield.

"So you don't get scared ever?" Alex asks doubtfully.

"I'm not saying that you don't have fear on the ground, but for me, it's a different perspective, there's more a fear that I'll let my men down, make a mistake, or lead them into trouble.

"My biggest fear on this project is that we get compromised, and get found out by the authorities before we strike, more so than if we get found out after the act. That's why I'm so keen for you to stay on the mission – I know how good you are, I know that you can keep us protected.

"So are you staying with us?"

Alex, now leaning forward in his own lap staring into the floor, turns his head to the right, looking up at Craig, "Hundred percent."

15

Light relief

Alex knocks on the door firmly, but not too firmly – *don't over-think every little thing*. He waits patiently admiring the neat minimalistic front garden and strong modern lines of the two-bedroomed semi. A young couple smile a silent hello as they pass him by. Eventually the door opens, Lucy is almost unrecognisable in civilian clothing, she has clearly made an effort, but in a subtly casual way. Alex battles in his mind over whether to compliment her on her appearance, not knowing how that might go down.

"You look even better out of your clothes… sorry; I mean uniform… in civvies I mean."

"Wow Alex, your chat gets better and better." she replies as she locks the door behind her. "You don't brush up too badly yourself."

Alex smirks, mixing his embarrassment with his gratitude for the compliment. "It's a lovely house, I can see why you're happy here." He turns and walks towards the waiting taxi, beckoning Lucy to follow.

"Thanks, living in the block with the Guards doesn't bear thinking about. So where are we going?"

Alex opens the taxi door and helps her in, "Just into Marlow, I thought we'd get dropped at the top end of the village and take a short walk to a nice little restaurant." Alex closes the taxi door and gets in the other side.

"How's work?" Alex hates to ask, but it is the easiest thing to talk about. He hopes to be able to get to know her a little better once conversation starts flowing.

"It's fine, everything's bobbing along, the new system is running great and is making things a lot more efficient than they were, so we're starting to get more done. I might even be able to take some leave over the next week or two."

"That's great. When are the Corporal to Sergeant promotion board results out?

"Three days."

"Fingers crossed, how do you think you'll do?"

"It would have been extremely likely if your job was a few months ago, but that missed the reporting period."

"Shame."

"Yeah, shame. We'll probably both be in prison by the time the next board results are out!" They both laugh at each other mutely, then look at the back of the driver's head, realising that they should probably end the current line of conversation.

"Have you managed to have any time off since you finished at Horse Guards?"

"Not really, my new project has kept me busy. I've met lots of interesting people. It's a different kind of work from what I'm used to, I'm having to hone my people skills a bit to persuade and influence my new colleagues."

"How's that working out? Your 'smooth-talking' must be doing wonders." Lucy laughs and playfully nudges his arm with her elbow.

"I'm doing all right, the plan's coming together, and the team is forming up nicely, though I am the black sheep of the group."

The taxi pulls up in Marlow at the end of Wycombe Road. Alex pays the driver, gets out, and joins Lucy on the pavement.

"Let me guess – The Purple Bouquet?" Lucy enquires.

"I thought you wanted a surprise?" Alex smiles.

"Really?" Lucy says with genuine excitement. "That's my favourite restaurant, have you been stalking me?"

"No, I must just be lucky. It certainly looks nice anyway, stars and everything. Are you sure you don't want to go somewhere different, for a change?"

"No, I love it, it's beautiful, lovely people and the food is excellent. You've got to have the seafood pancakes, they're to die for."

As they begin the short walk south along the quiet suburban road with houses tight up to the pavement, Alex uses the narrow walk-way as an excuse to move closer to Lucy and brushes his hand against hers, fishing to see if he can get her to take his hand; she drifts away from him slightly.

"How long have you been single for?" she asks him.

Alex laughs coyly, "Properly single for a good while."

"How long?"

Alex has to think for a second, "Three years since my last real relationship."

"What happened?"

"The Army; I got posted and she didn't want me enough to leave her home town, and I didn't want her enough to put myself through the weekend commute or 'commit big'. I wasn't getting home to Peterborough enough as it was."

"Fair one."

"What about you? How long ago was your serial video-game junky?"

"Charlie? That was over a year ago. He was sweet, nice personality, good job, professionally successful, but he didn't have much else going on. He had no ambition or get-up and go – I couldn't accuse you of that."

Alex grins inwardly, *Is she considering my qualities in the context of 'boyfriend?',* and feels a surge of pleasure spiral through him.

They walk on in silence for a few minutes. It is comfortable and Alex feels an air of conscious relaxation, more so than he has done in a long time. He is confident that Lucy is feeling fairly content, but has no idea what his chances are of taking things further, and is enjoying the thrill of trying to find out.

"Here we are." Alex opens the door making way for Lucy to enter; the head waiter welcomes her like an old friend and shows them to their table in a secluded corner of the restaurant. Alex beats the waiter to the punch in pulling out Lucy's chair; she smiles at the two men, finding their chivalrous rivalry amusing. Her chair backs onto the rear of the room. Alex takes his seat with his back to the entrance of the small room which has another two small, unoccupied tables.

The waiter attempts to hand Lucy a pair of menus. "Your menus." She doesn't raise her hand to accept them. "The specials are...", but that's as far as he gets.

"Can we have a bottle of the 2016 Merlot, seafood pancakes to start, and the fillet steak, medium rare, with peppercorn sauce - you do want peppercorn don't you?" She doesn't even pause for Alex to answer, "Oh and a jug of tap water and two glasses please." She looks at the menus as if to emphasise their redundancy.

The waiter laughs quietly; "Well, some women just know what they want." he offers to Alex.

"And what I want too." says Alex, smiling with a glint of embarrassment as he raises a palm to the menus to confirm that he will not be challenging the order.

The room is dimly lit, homely, warm and aesthetically beautiful. The table is intimately sized and rectangular, covered with a fine white cotton cloth. The cutlery and accoutrements are high quality and laid out in perfect symmetry. Alex cannot find fault with the establishment, the atmosphere, or the mildly pushy company.

"I based my dining room on this restaurant, it's so lovely."

"You don't mess around do you, Lucy?"

"Well, I figured you'd have had enough of the small-talk and would want to get on to the main agenda point. Having him," she tips a nod in the direction of the waiter's exit, "backwards and forwards to the table isn't commensurate with the conversation that we'll be having."

"You're amazing." he says, as though a little awe-struck, "I do want to talk to you about the project, but I also want to relax and enjoy your company, have a nice normal night out for a change."

"We can do that, but don't go getting all heavy on me though."

Alex smiles outwardly, but inside he knows that he has a habit of becoming a little needy, and has scared off a number of potential girlfriends by taking things too fast - *play it cool*. The waiter comes to the rescue, placing the water and glasses on the table, and then pours the wine.

"So how is your new mission progressing?" Lucy says as the waiter retreats back to the kitchen.

Alex feels relief at the change of topic. "Unbelievably well actually, we've assigned handlers to regions and areas. Operative recruitment is in progress. Now I need to start preparing the individual target packs and any other relevant intelligence I can muster."

"I can help with that, if that's what you were alluding to. I've been thinking about what I might be able to contribute."

"Really?"

"I might be able to get surveillance patterns on relevant targets from the counter-terror units."

"That'd be really useful, one less thing for the guys to worry about."

"Give me your list of targets and I'll have it for you by the end of tomorrow."

Alex feels his pupils constrict, the hair stand up on the back of his neck, and icy pin-pricks needling his forehead - *is this the honey-trap moment? Does she plan to turn me in once she has the evidence against me? Or is she really going to turn for me? Can I trust her? Would I trust her if she weren't so hot?* His silence speaks volumes to Lucy.

"You do trust me, don't you Alex?"

He needs to rescue himself from his predicament and quickly, a stall in conversation here and failure to show good faith would be detrimental to his chances with Lucy and for her further involvement with the project. "Of course I do, I just get twitchy when I think about moving this data around." He smiles at her and looks into her deep brown eyes, hoping that she might do more to earn his trust before the night is over.

"You were saying that you're the black sheep of the team. Who are the other guys? I'm guessing there are no other girls playing?"

"No, no other girls, just a bunch of hairy-arsed warrior-types. They're mostly ex-Special Forces, almost exclusively now working intermittently on overseas security contracts. Most of them see me as a complete outsider. Some of them are easy to get on with, but others are real arseholes; I tried having a conversation about ethics and morals with them this afternoon - they looked at me like a cow looking at a wrist watch."

Lucy laughs sharply as she drinks from her glass of water, spluttering and splashing Alex. "Sorry, that was funny." she says as she wipes her chin dry with the crisp white napkin. "I can imagine that was a short conversation?"

"We actually talked through a lot of the issues that I have with the mission. Some of them seem to have trouble isolating the threat and the necessary politics from the unnecessary politics - hate, prejudice, nationalism, you know, the obvious."

"It's an easily blurred line to be fair. As long as *you* know why *you're* doing it, you don't need to worry. I take it you'll be handling the public face of the mission?"

"Yeah, I'll be taking care of that - we'll have a clear message."

"But you have some issues with the ethics of your own mission - is that going to be a problem for you? In the long-term I mean?"

"I don't think so; now that I've had a chance to talk it through a bit, spend some time thinking about it and reconciling the pros and cons; it sits a little easier with me. How do you feel about it?" Alex wants a second rational opinion, but also wants Lucy to take the opportunity to convince him that she is on the up and up.

"You've got to look at the possible outcomes of going ahead against aborting. If you look at previous successful attackers and see where they would have featured in your target list, you'll be able to assess what the likelihood is that your strike will be hitting at least some of the right targets. Based on the assumption that you take out a good proportion of future perpetrators, you can calculate where the balance of lives saved will be. To be honest, and in my own opinion, the value of an innocent life is worth more than that of a serious terror suspect, so even if you're not potentially saving more lives, you're saving more of the right lives."

"That's an interesting perspective."

"The spirit in which we're doing this is for the greater good; you shouldn't feel guilty at all." Lucy looks Alex straight in the eyes with a warm smile. She leans forward slightly and reaches out, placing her hand on his. Alex is reassured, both that his mission is founded on a defensible, legitimate and ethical basis, and that Lucy is properly on board. He figures that he'll have a credible case for entrapment if she isn't.

"So you're still keen to be involved then?"

"In for a penny, in for a pound - I'm complicit already; I might as well help to ensure its success."

"What level of detail can you provide?"

"I can access the Regional Counter Terrorism Intelligence Units' systems via FIL-B; I can obtain full details of surveillance activity that may be in place against any or all of your targets. I'll be able to get numbers of officers assigned, number of hours per day, shift patterns, operational task orders which will tell us whether the surveillance is on static watch only - just on residences, or full tracking. There might even be some intelligence updates on activity recorded since you took your cut from the list."

"Are you happy with how to do that without being traced?"

"Well you're the expert there, but I had thought that I'd lift an 'un-signed for' terminal and log on with one of our unnamed operational crisis accounts and pop the data onto a disposable USB."

"Good option, are you sure you can get that done without being caught?"

"It should be straightforward. The laptops are stored in Carol's room which is empty and unsecured most of the day. I still have access to our office where I can work alone. The metal detector and guard have gone now, so I won't have the issues that you had with removing the device from the building." Alex laughs at the memory of his haphazard effort to get a copy of the list out of the Server Building.

"When do you think you'll have that?"

"Monday."

"Perfect. We're hoping to have the operatives in place by the end of next week, that'll give me a few days to sort out target packs with what I have from the list and whatever you can add."

"I can help with the packs if you like, I'll go in to work on Monday, get what we need and book the rest of the week off. Can I bring it to you?"

"Great." Alex slides an operational phone across the table. "Use this for any communications with me relating to the mission; in fact our little cover story doesn't apply to you, so you'd best use this for all communications with me from now on." Alex points to the operational handset, "I've pre-programmed it with the encrypted app we're using for the mission so use voice and messaging through that. You'll need to set a password." Lucy sets the password and as she slips the phone into her purse the waiter arrives with the first course.

"Smells delicious." Alex says as he cuts into the moist, cheese sauce-covered pancake, revealing a medley of succulent seafood. He takes a bite.

"I told you – to die for." Lucy smiles energetically at Alex's expression of delight.

With the essential topic of discussion covered, and Alex's belief in Lucy's commitment to the mission assured, the conversation drifts off into a congenial flow of Army life reminiscences and the pair's likes and dislikes. Happily for Alex; there is a lot of commonality. Their convivial chat continues until the taxi pulls up to the neat little semi.

Lucy grasps the taxi door handle with her right hand and turns to her left to face Alex. "I've had a lovely night thank you, but I'm not going to invite you in."

"Are you a third date kind of girl?"

"I don't live by stupid rules, I know what I want and when I want it; I'll keep you posted." She kisses him lightly on the cheek and gets out of the car, giving him a big smile as she pushes the door closed before turning and walking up the short garden path.

"I feel your pain there, brother. Where to?" asks the driver.

"Train station please."

16

Home truths

Alex dials and gets an answer on the third ring; "Hi Craig, how did the rest of the weekend go?"

"Hi Alex, yeah good, good; recruiting is well on track, the handlers are rattling through their contacts. We've been lucky as it goes; the private security market is in a bit of a trough at the moment, so a lot of the guys are back home."

"Where are you?" Alex asks.

"I'm in Reading, meeting up with one of my lads."

"What's the take-up been like?"

"Great, we're telling them enough to get them hooked, but not enough to make it clear what the mission's about just yet. We've had around ninety percent say that they'll come to the regional orders groups. We should be good to go for those from Thursday and have a good load of spare blokes left at the bottom of our nominal roll as a reserve. A few odd jobs have come up since I did my estimate, so they'll come in handy"

"Mega, I'll have the target packs ready by then."

"Sweet. How did it go with your potential intelligence source?"

"Great, she's up for it; she's on her way here now, bringing us a breakdown of targets under surveillance by The Security Service."

"She? You little snake, you didn't tell me you were chasing after a femme, and she's coming to your gaff? Does she know what she's letting herself in for?" Alex can hear Craig chuckling to himself, in just the same way that his dad would laugh at his own jokes.

"You're supposed to be impressed at the extra intelligence Craig, not taking the piss."

"Sorry Alex, you're right, that's very impressive."

The door intercom bleeps. "That's her now. Let me know the order you want to do the briefings in and I'll meet you at the first one on Thursday. Send me a venue and timings."

"Okay fella, will do. Don't do anything I wouldn't do."

"Hi, I'll buzz you up." Alex clicks the door release, then opens his door and begins to walk down the stairs to the ground floor, but stops as Lucy comes into view from under the edge of the first floor landing.

Dressed for comfort in a hoodie, jeans and trainers, she still looks acutely attractive. "You found it then."

"Yes, I think I even picked out your parking space; I got some glares from the neighbours as I pulled in."

"They're all friendly enough."

"You've worked your magic on them too no doubt?"

Alex scores himself mental points at her use of the 'too', assuming that this means that his magic has worked on her. "No doubt at all." He smiles.

Having thought that being on home territory would give him confidence, he suddenly feels a wave of vulnerability hit him as he welcomes her into his little world. "Come in." He shows her into his flat. "Well, do you have any breaking news?" he asks.

Lucy's smile breaks into a huge grin – "I got it – you're now looking at Sergeant-to-be Butler."

"Fantastic, congratulations." Alex goes in for a big hug, which starts well, but then turns somewhat awkward midway through. They release each other like inexperienced teenagers. "Do you want a brew?" Alex asks.

"If you're making, how could I refuse?"

Alex fills the kettle and prepares the mugs. "How did yesterday go? Did you find much worth risking your career for?"

Lucy laughs almost mournfully, but pulls a neat little pen drive from the back pocket of her jeans. "I found several useful logs and registers of surveillance, there are some great map overlays showing where operations are active on the ground. All of this will help us to prevent our operators encountering friendly forces. There's more work required to understand all of the data and it needs to be applied to your target packs – this could be a couple of days work for us."

Alex turns to Lucy and leans back on his pristine black granite work surface, "Best get cracking then; I've got a spare laptop for you. We'll do the first couple of packs together to get some consistency, and then we'll split them between us and motor through." He pours the hot water, stirs the tea for an almost precise thirty seconds, switching between cups with the spoon, ensuring evenly brewed tea, "It's a science." he says, as he pours the milk.

Lucy swipes her mug of beautifully crafted tea from the work top and walks out of the kitchen and into Alex's large living-room. "You weren't joking about that television."

"No." Alex smiles and places his tea onto a stainless steel coaster, hoping that she won't notice the PlayStation-shaped clean spot in the dust on the glass table beneath the television.

"Oh sorry." says Lucy as she picks up her mug and replaces it on a coaster.

"Don't worry about it." says Alex as he pulls two notebook laptops from the shelf under the coffee table. Sitting down on the sofa beside Lucy, Alex opens and switches on the first laptop and hands it to Lucy, then opens the second. "May I have that pen drive please Sergeant Butler?"

"Yes Mr Gregory," she replies maintaining the spontaneous 'business-like' role-play, "though I don't get to wear my third stripe until I'm posted."

Alex copies the new intelligence files into a folder on his laptop, then plugs the drive in to Lucy's terminal, enters her password and completes an identical file transfer.

"I've created individual folders for each target, then extracted all relevant information on them from the watch list and placed it in their folders. I've reformatted the information into smartphone friendly images and texts. We'll send these files out via the handlers who will match their operatives to the target packs – the target pack folders are already separated into regional folders. They will issue the packs to operatives using the operator and target call signs that I've assigned them, meaning that they can maintain separation and will not know who is tackling which target – once the operational phones are destroyed, there will be no record or memory of who acted on each target, only the individual operatives will know who they were assigned to, and the handlers might retain some limited memory locally."

"That's clever." Lucy remarks.

"It doesn't leave much room for error." Alex acknowledges.

"What do you mean?"

"Well, everything will be a little unsighted."

"It makes no difference, the guys on the ground will get it done; if they need support, they can contact their handlers – have some faith and try not to be such a control freak." Lucy is just the reality check that Alex needs, a real breath of fresh air in what has become an introverted little 'mission world' building itself inside his mind.

"Say what you really mean Lucy." Alex jokes. "Let's have a look at what you've found."

"It's quite raw."

"Roger that. Let's start from the top then."

Alex and Lucy begin their trawl of the new data; some is easily matched, Lucy having labelled it with the relevant target names. Other larger documents have information on several targets embedded within them, but searching by name makes the data sift quick and simple. They work methodically through the first region, which alphabetically is Birmingham East. They quickly reach the end of this first set of files, having identified only two targets that are currently under limited active watch out of the twenty in the folder.

"Last one in this region - Zafir Abdulaziz." says Alex.

"He rings a bell." says Lucy, as she types the name into the search tool, "There's something juicy on him, I picked up on it yesterday. Here look, West Midlands Counter Terrorism Unit received signal intelligence from GCHQ that Zafir has made and received several calls to known activists in London on Sunday just before lunchtime. Surveillance was on by that evening and he was photographed meeting up with several other known 'bad lads', none of them on your list, but also present at the meeting was an unknown bearded Caucasian, some sort of convert weirdo." Lucy opens several images of the meeting on the screen. "The West Midlands CTU assess that the risk of Zafir being involved in a terror plot is worth investigating further – he's got a team on him, daylight hours only."

"Wow, this is frightening. We've been through one ninth of the list - they are all credible threats, but only three out of twenty are being watched at all." Alex has fear in his voice. "How do the counter terror officers cope with this as their day job? It's stressing me out just knowing what little we've found out so far."

"Yeah - bit scary, but don't get hooked up on physical surveillance as the be all and end all of keeping tabs on them; informant networks, data analytics, online and telecom footprints all combine to provide a pretty good picture, as we see with our Zafir here. It doesn't take much to trigger an appropriate response when the conditions dictate."

Alex and Lucy continue through the folders, preferring to work together; completing target packs on the 39 list members who are resident in

Birmingham in time for a slightly late lunch. They put down their laptops and move to the kitchen.

"Fish finger sandwich all right?" Alex asks.

"Hmmm, as long as you've got vinegar?"

Alex gives a nod, "Of course." He switches on the oven and takes a large box of fish fingers from the freezer.

"Your staple diet?"

"No, I normally make an effort, but always have some of these in stock for when I'm not going to be home much."

"I know what you mean. Even when I'm in normal London routine, I still throw out more fresh food than I eat – too tired to make something proper, and end up taking the easy option out of the freezer."

"Don't worry, I've been to the shops and got some decent stuff in for tonight."

Lucy smiles, but doesn't ask what he's going to make for her. "Do you ever feel lonely Alex?"

The question takes Alex by surprise; he hasn't detected the seriousness coming from Lucy before she asks. "And you didn't want me getting all heavy?"

"I know, but I get the feeling that we're living similar lives, alone in our little worlds, with no one much to share them with."

Alex speaks as he butters the bread, "I do feel lonely sometimes, kind of, but I'm happy in my loneliness, content enough for now. You could say I'm living the dream in lots of ways, plenty of money, no debts, no strings, but I often find myself wanting to share things with someone else."

"Share what? Your life?" She asks.

"No, not necessarily the whole relationship thing, but to have someone to talk to, to tell about my day, what I'm up to, to sound things out with." Alex says almost in a day-dream.

Lucy looks at her bare ring finger; "That's the sweet spot. What you're describing there is what's at the heart of a good relationship. I've not had that, not in a meaningful way. I've never wanted to rush home, or anywhere else, and tell a particular someone my news, only my mum and she doesn't really count."

"I'm more extrovert than you, I tell my news to anyone who'll listen - I'm not fussy." Alex says with a grin.

"Yeah, but what about the important stuff? What about your secrets and worries?"

Alex pauses to consider his reality, what are his true feelings towards his solitary existence. "The stuff I can't share, I bottle up and those thoughts stay whizzing around in my head. This project is overloading my brain, it's constantly chuntering away, cycling through the issues and my concerns, it's like there's no off switch."

"I'm here Alex; you can talk to me about it."

"I know… thanks Lucy. You've contributed a lot with the data you've brought, but I'm more appreciative of having someone to talk to about it."

"Someone that's not a trained killer you mean?"

"Well, exactly. I don't know if I'd cope without someone like you around. It's not just the release and the sharing of the thing, but you're switched on and 'in the know' enough to give me a mental slap around the face and keep me on track." Alex puts the butter knife in the sink, turns about and leans back on the work surface to face Lucy.

"You need to be strong to get through this. I'm with you all the way. If you need to talk, or vent or scream and shout – I'm here Alex."

He looks down at her hand as it comes to rest on his, he gazes upwards and into her eyes as she moves in towards him, closer and closer, until their lips come together. Alex presses gently into the kiss, but with restraint, not wanting to make more of this than it might be, and as he fears, it is over in but a second. Lucy breaks off with a lurch and looks Alex in the eyes.

"Come on, let's crack some more of the packs while lunch is cooking." she says in tones of embarrassment and self-consciousness.

Lucy turns and strides back to the living room, leaving Alex in a daze - *does she want me? Is she setting me up for a fall? Is she just trying to make sure that I go through with this? Just ignore her flirting for now.* Alex follows on and resumes his position on the sofa as if nothing has happened, playing it as cool as he can. "Next up is 'East', basically the whole eastern side of England from Luton to Leeds and everything in between - Twenty more bad lads."

The pair develops a slick routine, scooping up details of intelligence on each of the targets, building on the picture painted by each pack. Breaking only for Alex to make and retrieve the fish finger sandwiches, they quickly work through the three sectors of London, North West England, South and save Scotland for the home strait. Scotland also includes targets from some of the North East of England, but even with those, it is the smallest of the folders – a nice short burst to finish on.

"What's for tea then?" Lucy asks.

"So you're staying are you? I thought you might want to head back as we got through them so quickly?" Alex plays it as cool as he dare.

"After that delicious lunch, I'm having trouble containing myself to see what you're preparing for us this evening. Do you mind if I take a shower while you get it going?"

"No, you fill your boots. The bathroom is there on the left. I'll get you a towel."

"Thanks."

Alex manages to conceal his sense of joy that Lucy is going to be staying longer than is absolutely necessary.

By the time Lucy has had her shower and changed, Alex has plated up and is about to uncork a nice light Sauvignon Blanc.

"Have you got any beers?"

"Yes, is San Miguel okay?" Alex puts the wine back in the fridge and provisionally grabs the necks of two beers.

"A bit poncey, but it'll do. What are we eating?"

"Well it's a bit poncey, but this little quinoa dish is delicious; chorizo, peppers, onion, lentils, topped off with crushed almonds, feta and a few leaves of coriander."

"The butcher's sold out of steak then?" Mildly bemused, Alex rolls with Lucy's playful teasing.

They pick up their plates and bottles and move into the lounge, a music channel on TV sets a comfortable and relaxed atmosphere.

"So you're a hundred percent up for this then?" Alex asks.

"What, quinoa? Yeah, I'll try anything once." Lucy smiles at her own joke.

"You know what I mean. I never thought in a hundred years you'd go for it, I can't believe I even let on to you. Now you seem more determined than me to make it happen."

Lucy takes a long and deliberate swig of her beer, locking Alex's gaze as she does so. "I'm pretty right wing Alex, always have been since I was old enough to understand what happened to my dad. You were right about my reasons for joining the Army – I want to hold people to account, kill the bad guys, expend my energy in a meaningful way. I'm pretty disillusioned with the Army, have been since 2016 sitting in Lashkar Gah for six months doing sweet F.A. while the blokes were out getting blown to pieces, or even in camp getting shot up by the people we were trying to help." She takes another long sup of her beer, almost finishing it.

"Public sector justice can be slow in coming." says Alex.

"Here's to privatisation." Lucy holds up her bottle, Alex gently clinks his against it in ironical jest.

"What you're offering, Alex, is a unique opportunity to make a tangible difference, a chance to take down some actual bad guys."

"It's certainly that." Alex half rolls his eyes.

"Don't do that Alex, don't doubt the value of this plan; you shouldn't be in any doubt after seeing the contents of those files. You need to 'man up', get a grip of yourself and see this for what it is, what you saw it as when you took the list. Don't let yourself crumble to what's been made the fashionable view – keep your perspective, remember the bottom line outcomes we talked about."

They both swig, Lucy's bottle drops down first empty, Alex's soon follows. "You're right - of course you're right; fewer bad guys equals more good guys – simple maths."

"This is good."

"What, me getting focussed?"

"The quinoa, but that too."

"Would you like another beer?"

"Yes please."

Alex brings two more beers from the kitchen and hands one to Lucy. "I'll call the others in the morning and tell them we're ready when they are. They should have everyone in place by the end of play tomorrow and I'll be meeting the rest of the Committee in each of the nine hubs for Orders groups from Thursday. Recces will be out on the ground across the country before the weekend is out, and we could have a D-Day as early as Wednesday or Thursday next week."

Alex has shed his downbeat tone; he is beginning to sound like a soldier, like a leader. This has an instant effect on Lucy who now looks at him as though inspired. She reaches out and grasps his hand. "That's more like it." She pulls him down towards her, threads her other hand under his arm and cups the back of his head. Alex stumbles clumsily down on top of her, but she is not perturbed. She kisses him forcefully and envelopes him, wrapping her legs around his waist. Alex decides not to let her take charge. He puts a firm hand on her neck and slides it up the side of her face and around through her hair, he dominates the embrace and manoeuvres her around so that they are lying on the sofa. Alex's assertive forcefulness has Lucy unlocked. As he slides his hand under her shirt, feeling the soft skin of her body, pushing straight under her bra and firmly squeezing her breast, she gasps in ecstasy. She pulls at his shirt until it comes up over his head. Alex leans back momentarily to throw it to one side. Lucy looks up at him with wild eyes, "I want you inside me right now."

17

Community engagement

Alex pushes, but not hard enough, on the front door of the Hodge Hill Community Centre. He leans in with his shoulder on the dusty, heavy old security door and it gradually gives in to him with an ear piercing screech. He enters the bleak and desolate hall, an old converted church, abandoned by the faithful and resurrected by a group of well-meaning local residents.

Closing the door behind him with a further energetic shove; he calls out, "HELLO, ANYONE HERE?"

A door opens at the distant end of the hall, "You're early." Craig calls back at him, "Good to see you, Alex son. What have you been up to?"

"I cracked the target packs with the help of my contact." Alex says as he strides down the length of the hall towards Craig, who greets him with a firm handshake and pat on the back. "They're good to go and way better than what we had from the list content alone."

"Good, good."

"I've spent the last few days procuring mobile phones and pre-programming caller groups and call-signs into them so that they can just be handed over to the operatives."

"Great stuff. We've been busy too; we're recruited to one hundred percent, so the spooks option is ruled out."

"Excellent, I didn't fancy that much, to be honest."

"No, I don't think any of us did really."

"So we're delivering orders today to the Hodge Hill twenty?" says Alex.

"Yes, they'll be fairly generic instructions obviously, we'll set the modus operandi for them, but they'll all be working to the individual circumstances of whatever you've got for them in their target packs."

"Shit gets real." says Alex.

"You're not wrong. This being the first session, we'll ask for feedback and make any necessary adjustments for the other regions. How are you feeling about the whole thing now?"

"Better, much better actually, my intelligence source has given me the shot in the arm that I needed."

"Really? She sounds like quite a girl?"

"She's that all right."

'SCREEEEECH' the main entrance door opens again, "Oye oye fellas." John struts in closely followed by Mark and Mike.

"Good morning gents." says Craig, "The caretaker let me in, I thought you'd be here by now."

"Sorry boss, I picked up these two on the way across from Wolverhampton, traffic was rammed."

"No worries, let's get this room in order. Someone get the brews on – tell me you brought brew kit?"

"I'm on it boss." Mark grabs the van keys from Mike and about-turns.

The next fifteen minutes are spent transforming the hollow shell of the old church into a fully decked out briefing room. The small portable water boiler is almost hot enough in the back room kitchenette, as Mark and Alex standby to pour.

"So John's leading up this region?" Alex asks.

"Yes, Mike's got the other half of Birmingham, I'm taking a share of London along with Craig and Don." says Mark.

"We're doing Mike's lot this afternoon, then moving up to the North West for this evening. We'll travel to Glasgow tonight ready for Spence's boys tomorrow first thing."

"Busy day."

"Tomorrow will be busier; we've got Scotland, East Coast, London and South to nail."

"I hope that van's supercharged?"

"We'll be fine – the London lads are all meeting in the same non-central location, and the South group will meet not too far away. You'll be balls deep in your intelligence source by 22:00."

Alex flashes a surprised look at Mark, "What do you know about that?"

Mark laughs, "Craig was telling us that you were pumping someone for information."

"It's not like that."

"No, I'm sure that it's true love Alex."

Alex laughs, Mark laughs back. "It's a mutually beneficial relationship all-round… apart from the whole 'destroying her career' part that is."

"And the rest of your lives in prison part, don't forget that."

Alex and Mark walk back into the hall carrying brews for Craig, Mike and John. The operatives have begun to arrive. "There's tea and coffee next door guys, help yourselves." Mark says loudly above the hubbub of welcomes and gleeful reunion.

As some of the newcomers drift towards the brew room, the main door opens again - the noise draws everyone's eyes for a second, but Alex's remain fixed on the latest arrival. Not sure whether he can be certain, not sure if there can be any doubt, Alex trusts his memory and instinct and confirms in his mind what he had immediately suspected – *He's the Charlie from Lucy's meeting photos.*

"Are you okay Alex?" Mike asks.

"Huh? Yeah, yeah fine. Craig, Mark, John, could I have a quick word - out by the van please." They each look at one another with vague concern. "Sure." says Craig. They walk out of the tatty door and into the street.

Two more operatives are arriving and approach Craig with open arms, but Craig forestalls them; "Gents, great to see you, but I'll catch up with you inside in just a minute."

"Right-o Craig."

"Get yourself a cuppa, we'll be in shortly."

The four men are alone in the otherwise deserted street. Alex has the attention of the Committee members. "What have you told these potential operatives John? How much do they know about the mission?" Craig and Mark look surprised at the question, John is taken aback.

"Nothing, just that there's a chance to have a snipe at some terror suspects, I gave each of them the brief on the cover story to get them here, and that's it. Why?"

"One of your blokes has been seen by the West Midlands Counter Terrorism Unit talking to one of the targets. It looks as though he's been radicalised."

"You're kidding me? That's bollocks… which one?" John asks.

"The last fella in, the one with the big ginger beard."

"Tony, Tony Blunt?" says John. "Fuck off."

"It's real. I've seen photos of him meeting with some serious people; one of them is a top target from this region."

"I don't believe it." says John.

"There's damage limitation to be done, and right now." says Alex. "If he doesn't know anything; he can't do us any harm, as long as we get him firmly out of the picture. If he doesn't know what we know about him, hopefully he'll just walk away if we make it clear to him that his services are not required. You guys need to play it cool, get him outside for a chat, run the drill as we've discussed." says Alex.

"Who the fuck do you think you're talking to Alex, you little cunt."

"I've just saved your bacon John, get it sorted; you can apologise and thank me later." Alex heads back into the hall at speed, not sure if he's taken a liberty with John, and certainly not wanting to incur his full wraith.

Alex walks over to the large table with fifteen or so men congregated around it, some seated in the lines of chairs, others standing in small groups. Tony is on the periphery, skulking on his own, sipping tea from a disposable cup. Alex tries his best not to look at him, but can't help himself. Tony's fashionably long beard hadn't marked him out as different to the others in the room, many are sporting operational beards that they have grown while overseas, some of their better halves have let them keep them, most haven't.

"So you're the man who's worth making the effort to meet?" says a voice to Alex's right, he turns to greet the stranger. This man stands out from the others as not looking even slightly intimidating. Just shorter than Alex, slightly broader shoulders, but a kind face that does not have the toughened, weathered features of the others in the room.

"Maybe - I'm Alex, sorry, who are you?" Alex raises his hand to the smiling man.

"Jez."

"Are you another Hereford man Jez?"

"No, I knew Craig in the Anglians, he was my Section Commander. I only did eight years, I got into the private game early – never looked back. I've worked with Craig on several contracts in Iraq and Afghanistan; he had been working for me before he got his current contract. He came and saw me personally to invite me to this 'training'."

The doors of the hall open with another loud creek. Mark walks directly over to Tony, says a few words to him; Tony nods faintly and follows Mark back outside.

"So what is the juice that makes this trip worth the squeeze?" Jez asks.

"I don't want to steal Craig's sandwiches, he'll be briefing in detail shortly, but I've uncovered an opportunity that gives us a shot at taking down some serious bad dudes." Alex thinks that Craig has clearly been more discreet than John with his invitations, his stature exercising more influence than John's sparkling personality.

"I like the sound of that. As you say, let's not spoil the surprise. I thought it was going to be some sort of major anti-climax. Are you getting involved yourself?"

"Me? What on the ground? No, I'm a tech-geek."

"You're not interested in seeing what goes on? What the front line is all about?"

"I've had a brush or two with that in Afghan, but I'm not keen to get involved."

"If this is what it sounds like, I'll be jumping at the chance to get back into the action – I've been a desk jockey in the ops room for far too long. Not even the ops room any more really, the negotiating table or board room these days."

"I get a little square-eyed in front of screens all day, but nipping out for a run or a walk around the park sorts me out – I don't feel the need to go and plug someone." Alex says with smile.

"The action is the drug for some blokes. You try and wean yourself off it as you grow up, but I'm like an old junky, and you're putting me in the pharmacy here. Have a think about it anyway and if you decide that you want to hit the ground; drop me a line – I'll look after you."

"Thanks Jez, but I'll be fine sitting in with my computer."

The door thrusts open, bending backwards against its hinges. John thunders in, followed by Craig and Mark.

"Job done, he's gone." John says sternly as he brushes past Alex and heads to the brew room. Alex notices that John is clasping his hands together and can see that his knuckles are badly scuffed.

Alex looks at Craig as he approaches with a questioning eye, Craig grimaces; "We'll discuss it after orders. Let's get everyone settled down and focus on what's to come.

"GENTLEMEN, PLEASE TAKE A SEAT, THE BRIEFING IS ABOUT TO BEGIN." The men react quickly and assemble in the chairs. Craig stands before them, Alex, John and Mark sit off to the left flank.

"Gentlemen, welcome and thank you for your prompt response to our call for support. I'll cut straight to the chase. You'll have all heard of the UK terror watch list, some of you are probably on it." Craig rouses a rumble of laughter from the audience – a reliable joke recycled. "We've managed to get hold of a copy, and I can tell you that it doesn't make for pleasant reading. I've seen some damning evidence in my time on operations, but this demonstrates a poisoned vein running through this country that needs to be leached." There is a stir of emotion evident from the operators, some emitting anger, others, with the inside track on what the briefing is about, exuding confirmatory glee.

Craig goes into detail describing the contents of the list and how it has been filtered and trimmed to distil the worst of the worst, and shows on the large projector screen the distribution of the targets across the country.

That's your 'situation - enemy forces'. In terms of friendly forces, that's us. Alex, John, Mark and I form the Mission Committee, all of us, less Alex, are also regional handlers along with those other five hoods." Craig points to the right flank of the audience – Mike tips a nod and waves his hand across the others. "Mike there is also acting as Quartermaster."

"The rest of you in this room are invited to be the task force for Birmingham East. If you commit to this mission, you'll individually be assigned a target and will neutralise them on these orders. Your region handler is John." John raises his hand and nods. "If this mission is not for you, please take your leave now, you'll be debriefed on your way out and thanked for your time."

Silence fills the room as the concept is digested.

"So you've got a list of suspects and we're going to go round and kill them all?" One of the younger men asks from the front row.

"Yes Tom, there are 178 in total, twenty in Hodge Hill and the surrounding area. Each of you will seek out, monitor, and then kill one of the targets, I can't make it any clearer than that. This enemy set is collectively a greater threat to this country than any organisation or state actor that we've ever gone after overseas - consider that, but also consider that this is a voluntary job, without sanction, without the protections of the MoD. It's unpaid, in fact you'll be asked to contribute a few quid to the cause. No pressure, no arm-twisting – you've got to want to do this, not for the Queen this time, but certainly for the country."

The room reverts to silence momentarily. "Can I have two?" a voice from the centre of the crowd calls out. Laughter brings the hall back to life.

"No Jez, don't be greedy. So you're all in then?" Another, but more positive silence – "Good, so that's the task organisation covered."

The other handlers smile at one another, clearly pleased with the level of commitment and the job well done in selecting the right people – *they may not be so smug once everyone knows about Tony,* Alex thinks to himself.

"So the detail on the enemy is specific, there is no overview of organisation, there is no command structure, there is no standardisation of what to expect. In fact this entire set of orders is something entirely different from anything I've ever had to pull together." There are sighs of appreciation around the room. "You'll each receive a target pack of specific intelligence detailing your target, the environment, friendly forces operating in relation to the target, and anything else relevant that we have on them. What I hope to convey here," Craig points to the floor beneath his feet with both forefingers, "is the generic stuff, the context of the operation and what is expected of you.

"There are eight other regions, each with fifteen to twenty-three operatives acting on their own individual targets; each region has an assigned handler leading coordination.

"Now, the ground. Clearly with 178 individuals, all living separately at addresses all over the mainland, this paragraph of the orders lacks detail, and you'll be finding out for yourselves about the operational environment during your reconnaissance. Of the twenty targets in this region, six live alone, seven live with friends or house-share, and seven live in a family home, more on this in the 'actions on'." Alex feels his stomach churn as he thinks about operatives disturbing families and causing the worst kind of collateral damage.

"Your mission – to covertly destroy a specified target, as defined in your target pack, in order to neutralise the threat posed, by them, to the UK public. I say again; to covertly destroy a specified target, as defined in your target pack, in order to neutralise the threat posed, by them, to the UK public.

"Concept of operations - after a period of reconnaissance, all of you, as individuals in isolation, will conduct a coordinated strike; this will be consistent across all regions, ensuring that the element of surprise is maintained across the national target set. The strike will be delivered in the form of a lethal dose of insulin under cover of darkness; a night strike will maximise the presence of sleeping targets.

"Scheme of manoeuvre – from this location," Craig again points to the ground beneath his feet, "you will deploy back to wherever you came from, this evening you'll be sent your target packs via the phone that you will be issued. You are to study the target details as supplied, then deploy on reconnaissance. Make good use of your recce time, and don't cut corners – you need to obtain maximum information through observation and search. The primary aims for this phase of the operation are to establish the pattern of life, and to become familiar with your target's accommodation – I know that a weekend and two week days is not a lot to go on, but it's all the time we can spare.

"Start wide – identify any local surveillance systems and avoid them at all costs especially on routes to and from the target's location. Gain access to the property, whether vacated or while the occupants are asleep should there be people home twenty-four hours. You know what you're looking for; best concealed access-egress routes, easiest methods of entry, and contingencies for both, alarm systems, pets – heaven forbid dogs. Conduct physical checks for hide locations for laying up in, potential improvised weapons for if it should all go tits up.

"Search for any actual weapons that the target may have, especially in the bedroom – if they can be innocuously moved out of reach of the sleeping target without raising suspicions, then do so. Also do your best to find any evidence of the target's routine; diaries, calendars, club memberships. Give yourself the best head start you can, think about what you might wish you'd have known – put yourself in the situation; war-game everything you can possibly imagine going wrong. Practice routes through the accommodation, not just from the primary entry point to target bedside – think where else you might need to get to in the pitch black of night.

"If you're happy with the recce of the accommodation, you are free to spend any residual time tracking your target's movements, but don't take any risks of being compromised.

"On the night of the strike, you will infiltrate your respective target's accommodation, either before or after they have bedded down – that'll be your decision based on your recce findings. Once the time window opens and your target is asleep, the insulin dose is to be administered. You'll be issued ten millilitres, five should be plenty."

"Boss, I've tried putting a needle in someone before – there's no way I'll manage that without waking the target up."

"Don't you worry Marco, there's a plan for that, just you wait my old son."

"Sorry boss."

"As well as the insulin and syringe, you'll also be issued a small tube of anaesthetic cream, you will squeeze a small blob of it onto the area of skin to be injected – arm, leg, hand, neck anywhere really, give the cream three to five minutes to take effect – if you've got the time; use it, then administer the insulin as gently as you can.

"You will then extricate from the accommodation, leaving no sign of your presence. Once well clear of the premises, send a brief report stating mission accomplished – keep them short and sweet; once you've had an acknowledgement, dispose of the operational mobile. You will also need to forensically dispose of your outer layer of clothing. From there, recover to wherever you need to be to re-join your usual pattern of life. And that's it – if you've done it right, there'll be no come-backs and the UK will be about a hundred and fifty bad guys lighter, given an expected fifteen to twenty percent failure rate.

"Key timings – now pay attention, this isn't to be written down anywhere, so you'll need to remember this backwards.

"Deploy on recces - no later than 20:00 hours, Sunday eleventh of June.

"Recces complete by 12:00 hours, Tuesday thirteenth of June.

"Recce reports, by exception, in to handlers no later than 13:00 hours, also on the thirteenth – if you have no issues, concerns, or new intelligence relative to other potential targets – we don't want to hear from you.

"The green for go order will be given 18:00 hours, Tuesday thirteenth of June.

"H-Hour is set for 02:00 hours, Wednesday fourteenth June.

"All operatives are to be clear of target locations no later than 06:00 that morning.

"I know that's sparse, it's deliberately loose – you need to have latitude and have the space to make things work for whatever situation you find yourself in. Your target might be fast asleep by 22:00, on their own, with the door left open. Equally they might be a raver, up until two, partying with six flatmates. The long and the short of it is – whatever it takes to get the job done and get out of dodge by 06:00, you're free to do it. Your main effort is a covert kill."

"Actions on." Craig raises his voice noticeably to signify the importance of this section of the orders, "Now here's where I do have some clear guidance to offer, and I do expect you to follow it to the letter, especially under a contact situation."

"It's all about the 'actions on'." John whispers with gratuitous satisfaction. Alex isn't an expert on formal orders, but he does recall that John is quite right – it is all about the actions on - he remembers one of his old troop commanders telling him how the art of the orders process is ensuring that the troops know, without a shadow of a doubt, what to do in any given situation, they must know the actions to take, it must kick in like auto-pilot.

"Yes John." Craig says, slightly grumpy at being interrupted without reason. "Actions on security services' present – we've identified where Counter-terror Police and The Security Service have over-watch where we can, but be aware that our information is only as good as our last update. If it's detailed in your target pack, then identify the teams and give them a wide berth, use your first twenty-four hours to map them and figure out how you will get past them, then use the second day to get the information you need without being compromised by them or the target. We've assigned 'watched' targets to operatives with skillsets compatible with achieving this. The rest of you will need to remain vigilant and not go rushing straight into the target area.

"Actions on target not present – if you've been on the recce location for more than twelve hours without sight or gaining an insight into where the target is – report in via John and we'll do our best to locate the target through a third-party intelligence source." Craig winks at Alex, "Aside from that, just use your initiative to find them – it's inevitable on this timescale that we're going to miss a few of these characters. If there's still no joy - maintain eyes on the target's accommodation all the way through to 02:00 hours on Wednesday morning, then draw stumps and return to where you would normally be. If we don't hit a positive yield from recces of sixty percent, then we'll review and revise by 15:00 on Tuesday – we may opt to extend the recce period by twenty-four hours, or abort until a later date – so all of you keep an eye on your operational mobiles regardless of how things are going.

"Actions on awoken target – whether awoken in their bed or if they're up and about in the accommodation upon entry – you must have considered a back-up plan for achieving your mission with a conscious target. Minimal disturbance, noise and site contamination are priorities – so whatever method you select, make sure that it fits that bill. I'd recommend hammer or garrotte, but think about traceability.

"Actions on awoken family member, members, or other third parties – if pre-seen; let them go back to bed and delay the strike within timelines. If interrupted during insulin administration, the chances are that it's going to go noisy, so attack third parties with non-lethal force – knock them out clean if possible, then finish the target by whatever means necessary as before. If you're discovered once the dose is administered – then just have it on your toes, collateral damage is to be minimised.

"Actions on insulin delivery failure – as with awoken target, use a secondary means – it will need to be completely silent if the target is in the marital bed – so bladed weapon is probably best in that situation.

"Actions on injury or debilitation – if you get in a scrap, have a fall, or otherwise get injured and can't get clear of the target accommodation under your own steam; message John on your operational means. He, or a support team, will be with you as quickly as they can to remedy the situation. In this area, none of you are more than ten minutes away from John and his quick reaction force.

"Actions on site contamination – If you leak blood on the target location, you'll need to do a good job of cleaning up, check out cleaning supplies during your recces and sort out any minor compromises on your own. If things go seriously badly – consider torching the gaff if safe to do so, otherwise call for a clean-up team through John.

"So in summary, go from here, learn what you can about your target with the data we'll provide, then deploy on the ground by Sunday evening, find out what you need to know, and then conduct your own estimate on how to crack your particular nut. All being well you'll infiltrate the target's accommodation and make the kill in the early hours of Wednesday morning; make like Elvis and leave the building, report in, destroy your handset, get back to your life and forget this ever happened. Are there any questions at this stage?" The men all know better than to ask anything silly, and that there is a whole lot more information to come still. "Okay, Mike, take us through service support please.

Craig moves to the back of the room as Mike begins going into the details of logistics; "Dress for the recce period is to be inconspicuous and in-keeping with the community within which you find yourself operating in – anticipate this, if you misjudge it, don't be afraid to withdraw and get changed if it helps to avoid potential compromise. For close target recce and strike phases; you are to dress in dark clothing, ensuring cuffs and trouser legs are sealed, and gloves are worn. Don't wear issued boots, probably worth investing in some shit common ones you can just throw away afterwards. You're to travel light into contact with the maximum of a small day sack.

Specialist equipment and stores will include insulin, syringe and anaesthetic gel. You will be issued these by dead letter drop – make sure that you identify a drop location and report it in to John early in your recce. As Craig's mentioned, you will all need a secondary weapon system, be that hammer, garrotte, knife, silenced pistol, whatever you like and whatever you can get your hands on, ideally organic to the target location – you're all resourceful blokes. Keep it to 'quiet and humane'; less mess the better.

"For the destruction of outer-layer clothing, you will need a half litre of accelerant. I'll give you bottles of white spirit, but to ensure that the phones get done properly, I'll be issuing you two hundred millilitres of high concentration sulphuric acid and a small, shallow glass bowl.

"The medical plan is largely self-help, so take a small first aid kit if you feel the need to - a civilian-type field dressing as a minimum; we've got those to give out. John has identified friendly medics who will be on call to assist you, ideally meeting up with you well away from the target location – send details of the injury, rendezvous and expected time of arrival via operational mobiles using the text app or voice means. You are to each write your blood group on the back of your wrist just up from where your watch would be.

"Everything that we're providing has been sourced safely and cannot be traced. If you require anything else, sort yourselves out locally, and if it's anything out of the ordinary, make sure that it cannot be traced back to you – take the necessary precautions. Take a cash float out on the ground with you of two to three hundred quid, if you need more – give John a call.

"Transport – you are not to use your own wheels for this operation; if you've got a distance to travel to your target location use public transport, or park over half a mile away and walk in, raise no suspicions, don't block anyone's drive or be noticed for any other reason. Each handler has access to a vehicle for support – again, cleanly sourced and untraceable." Mike looks towards Craig, signalling the end of his brief.

Craig remains in his chair, "Alex, Command and Signal please."

Alex stands and moves in front of the troops, unsure of himself and not confident that the operatives will take any notice of what he is about to say. He locks eyes with Craig as his pause extends into the silence. Craig gives him the faintest of willing nods, raising both of his eyebrows enthusiastically.

"Command and Signal – Craig is mission commander, Mark is first alternate mission commander, John is second. I am the operational communications manager and watch-keeper. John is also your regional handler and is your primary point of contact for all matters.

"As Craig mentioned, recce reports are only required by exception. We don't expect to hear from you unless you find something useful to other parts of the mission, or if you are unable to locate your target. Otherwise, the next time we want to hear from you is those mission complete messages. All of your messages ghost to my phone, Craig's too.

"Operational security – you are not to use any names in your messaging, your messaging and call profiles are coded, you are all 'O' – operative, 'BE' – Birmingham East, then the number of your target, one to twenty. Your targets will have matching codenames beginning with 'T'; so OBE1 will be targeting TBE1. John has assigned you each to your targets. This method keeps everything clean and untraceable, I don't even know most of your names, and John isn't clever enough to remember who's tackling who!" Alex brings a cheer of laughter to the room, he flicks his eyes towards John who mutters under his breath, but seems to take the joke in good spirit. "So you will know who you've taken down, but no one else will, not from the communications alone. As long as you properly destroy all forensic traces on your operational handset, follow all of Mike's guidance on equipment and that which I'm about to go through – you should be bullet-proof.

"You will need to do your homework on public and private CCTV in your areas of operation and either avoid, or conceal yourself when transiting through these systems' arcs of view. You must not take your personal mobile phones, or any other device that can be tracked via the mobile networks. You are not to write anything down anywhere other than on your operational mobile. Leave your wallets and all forms of identification at home, including credit cards and bank cards, as Mike said: have plenty of cash on you for clean transactions.

"Your operational mobiles will serve as a synchronised authority on the time, so we won't bother with setting our watches. Are there any questions?"

Craig's orders had been unusual and missed a lot of the detail that trained soldiers learn to expect, but had still managed to bring the mission to life. This had put everyone at ease in terms of what is expected of them, but simultaneously made crystal clear what the acts committed on H-hour will involve. Alex is moved by this, not so much by the effect on the targets, but what Craig has covered. Some of these targets will be seriously tooled up, and whilst hopefully completely unsuspecting of the mission and its premise, they may be vigilant and be expecting something at some time. The operatives may be walking into anything, given the gap between recces and the hits – all of this is compounded in Alex's mind with the near compromise of Tony Blunt.

The next thirty minutes are spent issuing kit; Alex distributes phones to their correct recipients and takes the operatives, in small groups, through the password setting and general use of the operational smartphones.

Craig dismisses the operatives; "Go to it men, remember, not a word of this to anyone." The men start moving out of the building in a buzz of chatter.

Alex approaches the boss, "Craig, I'm not going to be able to get the target packs out and make it around this tour of regions, I need to be on my laptop in a good environment, or else it could go badly – I don't want to make any mistakes."

"So what, you're not going to be about to issue the rest of the mobiles? You did a great job on delivering command and signal for me." Craig has a look of disappointment on his face, almost a scowl.

"I'm sorry Craig, but Mark knows the score with the phones – he can do what I've just done, that's simple compared to the target pack distribution, and anyone can reel off the opsec guidance."

"I know it's no show-stopper Alex, but I really wanted to have the Committee together for these orders groups."

"Thanks Craig, it's nice to feel part of the team, but I need to get this target pack thing done right. I'll see you on the other side of the recces once the reports start coming in. I'll meet you in London."

"Okay, let's get the Committee in for a bit of a de-brief." The two men walk together towards the brew room, sweeping up Mark and John away from some of their old friends on the way.

Craig has one thing on his mind and flies straight into business – "What does this Tony bloke know exactly, John, how much did you tell him? Does he know about the list?"

"Well yeah, I did mention it."

"In detail? What exactly did you tell him John?"

"I told him that we had the UK terror watch list - that we'd picked out the worst couple of hundred bad guys and were going to wipe them out. I can't believe this, he was one of the legends of the second battalion, are you sure you've got your facts right Alex?"

Craig ignores John's question and presses on; "What was his reaction?"

"He was interested right away, quietly enthusiastic. He had lots of questions come to think of it, but I didn't have any answers. He wanted to know if there were many targets local to here and if I had names."

"Fuck me John... we should've taken him out of the game." says Craig through gritted teeth. "This needs follow-up. John, you put two of your reserve blokes onto him tonight, I want to know who he's talking to and what his agenda is, more importantly – what threat is he to this mission."

"Roger that boss."

"Right, let's forget about that for now. Alex is off for the rest of the regional briefings – he needs peace and quiet to get the target information out to the operators as directed by regional leads. Mark – you'll pick up command and signal in the orders groups and the issue of phones – make sure you get a full handover from him before we leave."

"Yes boss." Mark acknowledges with a wink to Alex.

"Are we done? I'm going to take a shit." John walks out of the room. Mark follows without saying a word.

This is the quiet moment that Alex has been waiting for to ask something that has been bothering him. "Craig, how do you feel about the possibility of something going wrong on one or more of these targets?" Alex is sheepish with his question and hopes he has phrased it delicately enough.

Craig looks relaxed. Alex expands his question, "I mean, is that something that you consciously prepare for when they launch, or do you just hope that all goes well?"

Craig looks thoughtfully at Alex as though he really cares about what he is about to say. He pours a jug of water into the boiler and begins his reply as he starts the search for clean mugs, "Alex, I could brush this off and just say 'don't be a fanny, man up and get on with it, we're SF'. That's the end result of this conversation, but there's more to it than that, and I want you to understand that while we live harsher lives than you, blokes like me are not emotionless machines; we are actually sensory beings, more than you could ever know.

"Servicemen fall into two types as far as I'm concerned, there are those that have a desire to kill and those that don't. You are the latter - I am the former. That doesn't make either of us better or worse than each other, but it sets us apart as far as I am concerned when it comes to the question that you have asked."

Alex appreciates the consideration that Craig has clearly invested in his answer so far. Maybe he has given it before to some other 'non-ferocious' serviceman. Alex is intrigued to see where it is going.

Craig continues; "I've lost four men that I'd consider as close friends from active service, one of them was on a mission that I'd planned and led into the field. These experiences were tough, but more for my personal loss of a friend rather than feeling bad that they'd died. Do you understand that? Do you see the nuance?"

Alex thinks through the wording of Craig's sentences. "So you miss them, but aren't bothered by the fact that they've died?"

"In a way, but the key thing is that they were volunteers to be there, they had an option. At Special Forces level you're the gambler who has consciously agreed to be at the table. If you get taken down, then that's what you've bet against. It's always sad to lose a mate, but at the end of the day, we all had the option.

"I've felt deeply saddened and regretful about soldiers dying, but only when it's been some poor sod that either joined up thinking that they'd never see real action, (this is the category that you'd fall into), or those who came from deprived backgrounds, who only joined up out of a lack of other options. This second group includes those who are well up for getting into the action, but basically had no other choice in life." Alex bobs his head with an understanding nod. This is a revelation for him; he has never seen this complexity to life and death, and a whole lot more of Service life begins to make sense to him in an instant.

"It's very sad when someone loses their life when they never wanted to put it on the line - they had greater priorities than fighting, and never got to achieve those things, whatever they were - they die incomplete. If me, or John, or Mark die tomorrow, it will only be sad if it's not fighting – it's what we've lived for."

Alex tries to comprehend Craig's answer as the big man pours two 'not quite hot enough' cups of tea. "How do you see this mission, is it like any other Army or private operation to you?" Alex asks.

"No, no this is a different kind of responsibility. Given missions, no matter how gruesome or clinically merciless, are decisions made by someone else. This is different; this is my call.

18

Surprise surprise

"So the rest of the Committee are touring the country right now?" Lucy asks with intrigue, rolling the brim of her wine glass along the line of her bottom lip.

"Yeah." Alex says nonchalantly without looking up from his laptop screen. "We did the first orders group at Hodge Hill, I jumped ship, and the rest of them have gone off on a clockwise circuit of the UK They'll be finished in London this time tomorrow."

"Do you need a hand with sending the packs?"

Alex is intently focused on completing the target pack transmission. "No thanks, I've just about finished the second half of Birmingham. I won't send Manchester until I've had confirmation that all of the operatives have accepted the mission. Whatever could we do until then?" Alex says with a smile, closing down the laptop lid, rolling around to Lucy, who carefully places her glass on her bedside table. They kiss with anticipatory vigour and begin tearing each other's clothes off.

Soon enough Alex is taking a leak in Lucy's small en-suite bathroom as she pulls the bed clothes straight. "I FORGOT TO MENTION." he shouts through to her.

"What." she peers around the bathroom door.

"I've got some intelligence for you."

"Oh?"

"Remember the bearded white guy in one of your pack updates, the one photographed with one of the targets and some other hoods in London?"

"Yes."

"His name is Tony Blunt; he's ex-Para Reg."

"How do you know that?"

"He turned up as a potential operator at Hodge Hill. Once I told them, they took him outside and gave him a good kicking."

"Holy shit Alex, that's fucked up."

"I don't think they hurt him too badly."

"Stuff him, I mean it's fucked up that there's been a major compromise." Lucy's face contorts with anger. "What the hell were they thinking recruiting someone like that?"

"I know - it's bad. John's put a couple of guys on him; they should have nipped it in the bud."

"That might not be good enough Alex. What if he's shared what he knows before going to the meeting, or what about the other intelligence he'll have gained just from being in that room before John's men catch up with him? Have you had any updates on this from John?"

"No, I'll message him now."

By the next evening the target packs are all issued and Alex arrives at his own front door. A desperately needed pit stop for fresh clothes and a taste of reality – he has longed for his own bed, even if it doesn't have Lucy in it.

It is still light, with a low, bright sun. Alex turns the key in the lock, but something is not right, he can't quite put a finger on what exactly. He drops his laptop bag just inside the front door and walks through to the living room. He experiences an instant of confusion as he feels and hears the polythene sheeting under his feet. Confusion is usurped by petrifying fear. Before he can escape his frozen state, his ears are shocked by a deafening crunch as the front door is smashed out of its frame, crashes sideways, jamming awkwardly into the bathroom doorway, and a fraction of a second later a blur of a figure rushes at him. Alex is already off balance and the flying assailant hits him hard from the side with a cosh under the arm which he raises in defence. His attacker bundles into Alex, unable to stop on the polythene sheet and tackles him over the end of the sofa. Alex rolls on top of him and hooks him straight into an arm lock. "WHO THE FUCK ARE YOU?" he screams at him. As the words leave his mouth, Alex becomes acutely aware that the assailant is not alone, but too late – another swinging bar comes at him, but with his arms tied up with the first attacker's, he has no protection. He bites down and braces himself for a direct hit.

Feeling the cold metal surface strike, almost in slow motion, Alex feels his consciousness rattle around inside his head, he desperately tries to hang on to it. He loses focus, but is aware that he has lost his grip on the man beneath him. He makes futile attempts to grab at him, but his coordination and strength have deserted him, and he falls down beside the first assailant. Eyes now closed, Alex feels boots and bars raining down on him, his head injury mercifully numbing the pain. He clenches every muscle in his body and rolls left to right doing his best to avoid the worst of the blows where he can, but as the punishment endures, he is able to make less of an effort, as he goes limp.

The two men drag Alex to his feet and throw him back onto his armchair. His senses returning, Alex takes some deep breaths, sharp pain reverberates around his rib cage, probably a couple broken, but he feels as though he has been lucky so far, certainly no other bones broken. "Who are you, what do you want?" he asks.

The men stand before Alex, they look at one another; the taller of them gives the other a nod. Taking this as instruction he begins searching Alex's flat. The taller man steps back, interlocks the fingers of both hands together in front of him, and bows his head towards Alex. "Mr Gregory, my colleague and I are from an interest group. We're interested in something that you have, a list."

"So you're friends of Tony Blunt?" Alex asks, trying to get himself as near to being on the front foot as he can. The tall man looks sternly at him, but says nothing in response to the question. Alex thinks that he may have found a chink in the armour. "You know The Security Service has footage of you talking to him? You know that they're on to you?"

"I don't think so, I've never met Mr Blunt, but I understand that he has been very helpful to us."

Alex is more distracted by the shorter man rifling through his things than he should be. The only thing that they want is in the bag by the front door, there is no other copy of the list in the house, but his obsessiveness for neatness means that he cannot resist paying attention to the disruption that the poorly conducted search is doing to the rest of the room. "I don't have the list, and even if I did, you're too late, the information is out there – it's beyond me to call it back."

"You misunderstand our intent Mr Gregory, we don't want to know who you are targeting - we want the rest of the list. Can you imagine a better, more fertile ground to recruit from? You go ahead and martyr a couple of hundred, already-tainted brothers. You will be doing half of our job for us; we'll reach out to the twenty thousand remaining warriors-in-waiting. They are the prize and they are the soldiers of our future. With this much angry young blood, we will bring a real war to this country.

"You are in a game of chess, Mr Gregory; you have fallen into a trap beyond your comprehension. How foolish you thought us for our strategies of isolated incidents and hopeless charges into death. Our bigger picture is beyond your field of vision."

The shorter man, completing his search of the living room, looks to his associate for guidance; the taller man nods towards the kitchen door. The searcher walks around Alex and heads for the doorway behind him.

"So the list, do you have it, or should we ask Ms Butler."

As Alex begins to snarl a response, he hears a squelching thud from behind him and the searcher is sent tumbling over his left shoulder. Alex is half pushed, but half rolls forward towards the taller assailant, who waves his cosh and strikes Alex on the back of the head on his way down to the floor. Just before his eyes close he catches a glimpse of a third figure in a shiny

black jacket moving with force and meaning towards the tall aggressor –
John?

Alex wakes from his brief sleep peacefully, the bright light from the window
stopping him from opening his eyes immediately, his mouth and nose are
filled with a warm taste which reminds him of a good, full-bodied red wine,
a rich, deep filling aroma. As he takes a full breath to appreciate it, it dawns
on him that he has not been drinking wine; in an instant he remembers his
last moments of consciousness, someone coming to his rescue, and the
beginnings of the physical battle – but not the end of it. His deep breath
initiates a hacking cough, ejecting a substantial clot of blood from his lungs
and trachea out into his hands.

"Nice. I'll get you a towel." John says from the doorway of Alex's bedroom.

"John, what are you doing here?" Alex says weakly, as he gets to his knees
with slow shuddering movements.

"You can thank me if you like."

Alex surveys the carnage in his living room. "I'm sorry, of course… thank
you John." As much as Alex detests John, the words are not begrudged, he
is truly thankful; he would have been dead for sure without him there, but
would his attackers have been there at all without John's lack-lustre
screening of potential operatives?

"That's more like it. Now be a good lad and put the kettle on, I'll start
sorting this pair of Charlies out."

Alex turns towards the kitchen, and as he does, he notices John placing a
spool of rope and a warehouse knife on the floor next to the edge of the
polythene. Alex thinks to himself as he fills the kettle; '*the polythene was on the
floor before the attackers came, one of them slipped on it; he wasn't expecting it to be there,
and why would they be searching the flat if they'd been in here already? Where has John
got all the other kit from?*'

Alex makes the tea and staggers back into the living room as John ties a
third rope around the second polythene-covered body.

"We'll get this pair in the van in the dead hours, set your alarm for 03:00." Alex hands John his tea. He notices the blood on both their hands against the white porcelain."

"How did they die?" Alex asks, slowly bringing his mug to his lips.

John points to the taller man, "I clubbed that one in, he put up a bit of a fight, but after the first good knock it was straightforward enough. Him," John points to the shorter of the two plastic parcels, "He never came round after the first whack I gave him coming out of the kitchen – I just snapped his neck with a boot, to save leaking any more blood than necessary."

"Yeah, handy that polythene being down on the floor." Alex says, watching John intently for a reaction. "What were you doing here John?"

John stares back at Alex. The pair try to read each other, their eyes flickering over each other's faces. Finally John speaks; "Listen Alex, you've been pissing me off since we met. I was angry as hell about Blunt, and you talking to me the way you did had me raging. I came here to put the shits up you good and proper, to put you in your place, and if you'd not toed the line – I probably would've killed you myself. Is that what you wanted to hear?"

"You are nuts - you are absolutely fucking nuts, John. So do you still want to kill me then?"

John laughs, "Things all kind of drop into perspective when you're faced with a real enemy. We're on the same side – just stop making me look a Charlie and we'll get on great."

"Bloody hell John, I can just about cope with this because of the concussion." Alex tries to straighten out what has happened in his head. "Fuck it – let's start again." Alex extends his arm, John reciprocates and they shake hands.

"Have you reported in to Craig?"

"Not yet, he'll go mental. We've not turned anything up on Tony Blunt yet either – it's like he disappeared off the face of the earth."

"That's not good. Whatever this organisation is that these people are working with, it's not just a bunch of idiots, if they're connected to Tony

Blunt – that's evidence of a real network. I'll message my intelligence contact and ask her to look further into it."

Two incinerated bodies, 90 miles in a transit van, and after extensive counter surveillance manoeuvres, John and Alex re-convene with the rest of the Committee for breakfast in a quiet, but friendly, café ten minutes' walk south of Craig's house. Alex recognises an additional face at the table.

"Good morning gents, you've had an interesting night then?" Craig asks rhetorically. "You've met Jez haven't you Alex? He joined us for the rest of the orders groups, helping out Mark filling in for you."

"Yes, we chatted at Hodge Hill. Hi Jez."

"Hi Alex, the offer's still there if you fancy helping me out with my recce, it looks like my target will be quite interesting."

"I've had enough action in the last twenty-four hours to last me a lifetime thanks Jez."

"Yes, so what were you doing in Alex's flat then John?" Craig asks almost matter-of-factly, "You were supposed to be looking for Blunt."

"Look, it doesn't matter what I went round there for, I saved his life and took out a serious pair of players who knew about our mission – they were there for the list – I think you're missing the point here, Craig. The point is that there's an enemy organisation out there that we know nothing about, and they seem to know plenty about us."

"Would that be because of Tony Blunt?" Craig retorts with a snarling degree of anger. "These people don't work in big groups of sprawling networks; this will be a large cell at best, maybe just four or five blokes who stumbled into this information, and they've got nothing."

Alex interjects, "Normally I'd agree Craig, but like I said when I identified Blunt at Hodge Hill - he had been photographed with at least one of our targets and several other individuals in some sort of planning meeting just days ago. It might have been our bad luck that he made it to our orders group, but I certainly wouldn't dismiss this as a lucky few." John acknowledges Alex's acceptance of it being the group's bad luck, and not just his mistake, with an appreciative nod. Alex goes on; "The way those two functioned and behaved in my flat, they were a couple of cogs in a bigger machine, there was just something about them that read like they were part of something coordinated, a proper organisation."

"What did your guys find out from Blunt, John?" Craig asks.

"Nothing, it's like he vanished straight from the orders group."

"And you didn't think to mention this John?" Craig's anger builds further towards John, but he holds himself together and pauses for thought.

Mark plonks his mug of tea down on the table, "So what's your suggestion Alex? What's our strategy here?" Alex doesn't immediately have an answer. He begins to think about what the enemy know, *'what might they be doing or planning to do right now?'* "They don't have the list, they don't know what we know, and they don't necessarily want to stop us. We don't abort, we don't delay, and we go on with caution and vigilance." Alex impresses himself with his own sense of leadership and direction, but continues to think; *'If their aim is to obtain the list – how would they be going about looking for me? How had they found me in the first place? How did they find my flat? Was I identified and searched out? Was I followed from Hodge Hill?'*

"Lucy, fuck, LUCY."

Alex jumps to his feet in a blind panic and pulls out his operational mobile. He racks his brains as he sets the voice application dialling, *'How careful was I on my way to her place on Thursday night? Could I have been followed? Surely I would have noticed?'* Then he remembers the threat they made before he was knocked out – his panic spirals.

"Who's Lucy?" says John.

"His intelligence source." says Mark.

The phone rings and rings, and eventually rings off. Alex looks at his colleagues in desperation, but they seem to fail to understand the situation, or just don't seem to care. He turns to walk out of the café.

"Where are you going Alex?" Craig asks.

"My intelligence source – I've compromised her, I've got to go."

"And do what? Recover her body? Search her empty house? Whatever they've done, if anything, there'll be nothing there for you."

"What if she's been taken? What if there's a note?"

"What if it's an ambush, Alex?" Mark asks.

Craig reasons with Alex; "If it's a kidnapping, they'll be asking for the list, or that the mission be aborted. We can't give it to them, and we're beyond aborting now – it isn't going to happen. If you go there, you'll be wasting your time and you'll be jeopardising the mission."

Alex can't hold himself together, he is falling apart. He has found someone perfect in every way and all indications are that she's been taken from him. This terror is compounded by the fact that he has caused it to happen – he has got her involved with the mission, he has led the perpetrators to her house.

"I've got to go, Craig; I'll be no use to you here, not now. If I'm needed, I'll be on operational means, I just need ten minutes at her house. I'll be back for tomorrow."

"I'll go with him, we'll take Jez. You trust Jez, right Alex?" says John.

Alex looks back at him, "I trust both of you John." Alex turns his gaze to Craig with a begging expression, no words are needed.

"Go on then. I swear to God I'm going bloody soft."

"Thanks Craig, I won't let you down."

"Just go easy, don't go crashing in and whatever happens, keep it contained and keep it clean."

"I'll make sure of that boss." says John, "Jez is on the ball; we'll take care of whatever's waiting for him."

19

Learning experience

Alex remains seated in his plush first-class leather seat as the train pulls into at High Wycombe station. As the carriage empties, he takes a deep breath, anticipating an eventful afternoon which will hopefully culminate with him being reunited with Lucy. Leaving it as late as he dare; he gets to his feet, walks to the door and steps down onto the platform.

He heads slowly down the concourse, analysing everyone he sees whilst trying his best to remain inconspicuous. He slips his ticket into the barrier and walks on through the station and out of the main entrance. He strides briskly through the exit, hugging the corner to the right, onto the main road. His delay in leaving the train ensures that the rush of people has passed and the path is quiet. He heads over the railway bridge and turns immediately right again - following the train track east towards Lucy's house, which is a further mile and a half's walk.

As he follows Totteridge Road he has a clear view of any pedestrian traffic that might be following him. He keeps his eye on the bridge over his right shoulder. At about fifty metres beyond the bridge he allows himself another glance – he sees two figures followed by a third coming across the bridge, all three dressed in similarly dark clothing, the lead pair turn onto his road and appear to increase their pace. *Where the hell are John and Jez?*

Alex tries to remain calm; he continues to walk at normal speed, allowing the pair to gain on him. By the time he reaches the mild bend to the right they are within twenty metres of him, the third has dropped back ten metres from them. Alex matches their pace as he passes the end of Queen Street; as he does so, a white van lurches out of the junction, the driver has a balaclava over his face – Alex is frozen to the pavement with fear.

Alex is surprised and relieved as the van whizzes past him and screeches to a halt adjacent to his tailing pair. The side door slides back with a roar and a masked figure jumps out and strikes the nearer of the pair around the side of the head, dropping him instantly. As the second one draws back a fist to retaliate, he is felled from behind with a stamp to the right calf by the now-masked man who had been trailing them - *Not one of theirs, but one of ours.* The masked attackers bundle the two bodies into the back of the van, throwing them hard against the internal offside wall panel, and jump in as the driver wheel spins in reverse, back into the Queen Street junction, then spins round alongside Alex, pulling off his mask; it's John – "Get in". Alex runs around the front of the van and climbs into the open passenger door, which shuts itself with the movement of the van, as it jolts forward and heads off down the road.

The interrogation is already underway before Alex straightens himself in his seat. "WHERE'S THE GIRL?" Batons whip down onto the two bodies as they writhe on the floor, their wrists bound behind their backs with heavy duty cable ties. "WHERE'S THE GIRL?"

The two men squirm and yelp, they cry out, but they do not speak. "WHO'S WAITING FOR US AT HER HOUSE?" Still the men say nothing. The first interrogator searches the men; he passes forward two mobile phones to Alex.

"They're fingerprint authorised." Alex calls back to them.

John turns to him from the driver's seat; "Do you want the fingertips?" He asks in a macabre tone.

"No, just unlock it for now please." says Alex passing the first handset back.

"STAY STILL." The handset comes back unlocked.

"This phone's only dialled one number in the last two days." Alex notes the handset's number and the dialled number into his operational handset. He checks the phone for communications apps, finding a recent message stream. "There's been plenty of text chatter with the dialled number and a third number – I'd guess that's his mate's." The text is harrowing for Alex to read, it provides clues of the planning of how they were to take Lucy and acknowledges success of that mission, but gives no detail of where she might be or what condition she might be in. Alex bounces over into the back of the van, the two interrogators back off, one of them hands Alex a baton.

"WHERE IS SHE, WHAT HAVE YOU DONE TO HER?" Alex lets fire with all of his energy, beating both men to their bodies and legs; despite his anger he cannot bring himself to hit their heads. The explosive outbursts sap him of energy, he soon collapses onto his knees between them with tears of anger and fear on his cheeks. He rubs his eyes with his sleeve, brushing the baton across his chest. As he opens his eyes he sees the man on the floor to his right looking up at him with a sadistic smile on his face.

Alex loses control immediately; "YOU FUCKING MOTHER FUCKER." He launches an assault on the skull of the man, blow after thunderous blow hammering down; blood quickly begins to flow and then splash. At this point the nearer interrogator steps in, perfectly timed between blows, and wraps his arms around Alex, preventing him from inflicting further damage to the body of the now obviously dead man.

"That's enough." Alex recognises the voice as Jez.

"You're next if you don't start talking." the second interrogator says, exploiting Alex's action. Alex realises that the second interrogator is Mark. The comic book romance around the mission evaporates in an instant. The stark reality of what this task means to the people involved hits like a hammer blow to Alex's chest, which resonates through his body, his thoughts cease to make sense, he loses focus on what is happening as though slipping away from reality, everything feels numb and distant. Alex just wants to curl up on the floor of the van, and for the whole situation to go away; he wishes that he had never even heard of the watch list.

The practicalities of the blood slowly trickling towards him and the fact that he is slumped over dead and living members of an enemy force awaken him from this trance. Hauling himself to his feet, he grabs the second phone from the front seat, opens it using the thumb print of the remaining, living captive – who puts up no resistance, either too scared, or resigned to the fact that all intelligence of use has already been gained from his colleague's handset. Alex busies himself with the phone, and the pattern of its movements soon become clear.

The van pulls off the road into a farm complex. The sliding door opens before the van has stopped, Mark jumps out, walks across the farmyard and enters a large galvanised steel barn by a side door. He is out of sight for just a few seconds, then returns to the vehicle. "All clear, get the live one first." Jez and Mark each hook an arm of the bound and now gagged captive and drag him off into the farm building.

"Are you all right Alex?" John looks intently at him, with what appears to be genuine concern.

"Fine... just murdered somebody... but fine." Both men look over their shoulders at the lifeless body.

"It's not as bad as you think is it? Can you live with it when it's so well deserved?"

"You're sick John, I've said it before, and I'll probably say it again, you're fucking sick."

Mark returns to the back of the van. "Get yourself round here, Alex; I'm not clearing up your mess on my own." Alex doesn't know if he is joking at first, but based on what needs to be done, he feels he has no choice but to take responsibility. Together they wrap the polythene sheet around the body, tucking the ends over the head and the feet before rolling him up laterally – *this is how I make wraps for my lunch*. Jez pulls some rope from a spool tied to the back of John's headrest and cuts three lengths, each a couple of metres long. "Tie off with bows, not knots – he'll not be in here for long." Mark jumps down from the van and turns around, with focussed effort he drags the body to the edge of the van's floor-pan and wrenches it over his shoulder.

"Do you need a hand?" Alex asks.

"No, I'm fine, leave this bit to me. You help John."

"Let's get the van turned around." says John, as he walks around to the near side of the transit.

Having had the polythene wrap on the floor makes this a quick operation. Only a few spots of blood are present on the white paint of the wall panels. The surfaces wipe clean easily with industrial sized wet-wipe cloths which John tugs from a bucket sized container at the back of the van. Alex notices small speckles of blood on his own clothes, it is barely noticeable – he scrubs at it impatiently, wanting rid of it from his person.

Once all traces of blood are removed from the van, they place all of the waste into a bin bag. The two then re-line the floor with a fresh sheet of polythene. As they jump down from the van, they are mildly startled to see Mark perched on the low wall of the cow shed adjacent to the vehicle.

"What did you do with him?"

"It's a farm Alex, there's a good few ways to get rid of a body in a place like this, don't concern yourself." says John.

"What if someone finds the remains?"

Mark jumps down from the wall, "Look Alex, we're not muppets you know; we're not 'special' cos we lick the minibus windows. We didn't leave the café this morning, rent a van from Hertz and drive down here for a joy ride. We've been non-stop in the planning and preparation for any such eventuality of this operation since we were tasked, until the minute you got off that train. It may have been short notice, but we don't muck about. Where do you think all of this equipment came from?" he says pointing out the roll of polythene, the maps and other items that Alex is yet to notice. "The owner of this farm is friendly; he has connections to the Forces and will go a long way to help us, and the van is clean as far as records go. Special Forces training is more than just being physically capable, it's about being one step ahead of the game, that's why we win."

Alex takes a proper look around inside the back of the van; it is fitted out with all kinds of useful stores and supplies, gorilla boxes with all manner of tapes, tools, lights, weapons, spare clothes. His respect for these men grows even further, as does his confidence that they will succeed in finding Lucy – his only hope is that she is alive and unharmed.

"Have you got anything out of the other one yet?" asks John as Jez returns from the Barn.

"No. I've left him hanging for a little while; don't let me forget about him, for fuck's sake."

Alex is having difficulty matching Jez as he sees him here in this farmyard, a seemingly callous torturer, with the 'nice guy' Jez whom he had met in Hodge Hill. He finds this unnerving – maybe Jez too is feeling unnerved after Alex's episode in the back of the van… but then maybe Jez isn't the type of guy to get unnerved.

"It doesn't matter; we've got enough from this phone to find the handler, assuming that's where Lucy is." says Alex, "I've tracked the geo-data history of one of the phones and it looks like they're using an old school building, it's local - can we go now?" he asks John.

"I'd say time is of the essence; if he doesn't hear from his boys soon, he might get twitchy. The limited communications on their network indicate they're operating in isolation from any broader team, but we'll still need to be careful. It'd be better if we could wait until dark o'clock." says Mark.

"She might be dead by then. I could send a holding message from one of the handsets, but that's risky, I really think we should go now." says Alex.

What's the location?" John asks.

"It's a school complex, only about seven or eight clicks south-east of here, just east of Wycombe." Alex shows John the area of ground on a map from the van, John locates the buildings on a satellite image on his phone, "They look like old buildings behind a newer school; they're possibly derelict."

John scrutinises both images to try to build as much of a picture of the ground in his head as he can. "There are three approaches that look like they've got good cover; north-east for vehicle entry and walk in through the school, up from the south along the garden wall, and south-west around the outside of what looks like a perimeter wall. Have you done close target recces before Alex?" John asks.

"Once or twice, I've normally got a rifle though."

"I'll find you a stick mate." John laughs to himself. "If you see anything or find anyone, you just sit tight and let us know."

"What's the communications plan?" Alex asks.

"That's your ball-park fella." John replies.

"We can't be texting, entering passwords every other minute – not workable. I have a few sets of earphones that came with the operational phones in my bag; we'll use them and keep an open group voice call going using the messaging app voice facility."

"Great. I'll drive and stay in the van, I'll be on call for pick-up and quick reaction, Alex - you can do the walk in from there and act as a diversion if necessary when the guys are on their final approach. Jez and Mark will come in from the south." John points out the routes with the nib of his pen on the phone screen.

This is real-time quick battle orders that Alex has only ever practiced on exercises. "Alex, you stay on that corner until you get the order from Mark." Alex assesses that his stop-short position is no more than sixty metres away from the target building.

Mark takes the briefing on from John; "Alex, you wait on that corner and keep low, Jez and I will move in as far as we can without being seen; if it's quiet, we'll go straight in, find the girl and neutralise any hostiles."

"I'm more than happy to get amongst it. Can't I move in too?"

Mark and Jez look to John, who looks with a troubled expression back at Alex. "Alex, that's admirable mate, but what would you do if you came up against one of the targets? What about a target with a knife?" He points a finger towards Jez and Mark; "These blokes are trained, they know exactly how to disarm, disable and put to sleep a target of any size, shape or strength. What would you do?" John picks up a plastic water bottle from inside the door of the van, he wields it high in the air and moves aggressively towards Alex, he thrusts the bottle down towards Alex's head. Alex spins around taking a double handed grip of John's right wrist and throws himself, with a twist, towards the ground, pushing through John, landing on top of him, he continues with rolling momentum across John's chest and draws his elbow down hard and fast towards the Hereford man's left temple, stopping just before making contact. All four men freeze, John in temporary shock at Alex's impressive response. Mark and Jez are both stunned. Alex is petrified at what retribution he might be about to get back from John.

A few seconds pass before the atmosphere is cut by John, who feigns a fearful grimace; "You're in." He drops the bottle, simulating his submission. Alex rolls himself up, trying not to put too much downward pressure on John's chest. Jez offers him a hand and hauls him to his feet, Mark does likewise for John.

"Who's going to babysit our man here?" Alex asks.

"He'll be in the ground Alex, don't you worry yourself about him." says John.

"Seriously? Do we have to?"

Jez places a hand on Alex's shoulder, "There's no arguing with these guys, there's no negotiation; we can guard him in a barn forever, or put him out of his misery - this Charlie is probably more dangerous than the worst on our target list; he's a high-level activist, part of an organised formation and not even on our radar – that makes him too dangerous to leave dangling… as it were."

Jez and Mark make final preparations from the van, putting a few sets of 'plasti-cuff' cable ties in the pockets of their black combat trouser pockets and placing their heavy wooden batons in the back pockets of the front seats, Jez turns to Alex; "You want one? You're pretty handy with 'em."

Alex feels a tingle of shame; he catches a flash of the pummelled head of his victim in his mind's eye. He overcomes the guilt as he thinks about Lucy and what predicament she might be in – "Go on then." he replies.

The van rolls up slowly to the entrance of the school complex. "Oh bollocks," says John half under his breath to himself, "the school's only having a bloody open day isn't it." he says to Alex. The grounds of the school are full of cars, and parents and children are bustling around. He follows the intended route; the school estate is well-kept and the buildings look newly built. They drive past the front of the main building and reception area, and round towards the car park, behind which are the old abandoned buildings. The car park is full and busy with pedestrians, young families making their way to and from the new buildings. "We're getting danger-close now; this is way nearer than I ever wanted the van to be." He speaks into his phone mic; "Fellas, this is John, can you hear me?"

"Loud and clear." Mark acknowledges.

"Change of plan. Where we just dropped you will now be the emergency rendezvous, if you need me I'll be coming in on foot, I'll drop Alex here as planned and return to that location."

John describes what is going on for Alex; "The large grey building directly to our front – that's the target building. Look slightly right, you'll see a large greenhouse amongst the trees – say seen if seen."

"Seen."

"That greenhouse is next to the tennis court where we dropped Mark and Jez. You know where you're going to meet me once this is done?"

"Yes, got it." says Alex confidently.

"Right get out and make yourself inconspicuous, you'll hear me give the order to the boys to move in once I'm back round there. Are you getting this Mark? Jez?"

"Roger."

"Roger."

Alex needs no further invitation, he opens the door and jumps out of the van, John instantly reverses round in an arc and sets off back to Hammersley Lane, behind the school complex from where the lads are making their approach.

Alex feels a sudden sense of vulnerability and isolation. He gets into cover as best he can, crouching down behind parked cars. He edges his way towards the building; by the time he gets behind the last car in the row he is less than twenty metres from it. He settles in place, knowing that John cannot be far away from position.

John's voice fills Alex's ear; "Okay men, I'm in position. Final comms check."

"Jez, okay."

"Mark okay."

"Alex okay."

"All okay. Right, Jez, Mark, get across the line of departure."

Alex watches intently for any sign of movement, but the building blocks all visibility to the south. He considers moving across to the other side of the car park, but that might be his diversion spent.

"Hello Alex, this is Mark."

"Send over."

"We're as near as we can get, just open ground between us and the target building. Can you make your presence known and we'll go in."

"Roger, moving now." Alex is unsure of what sort of distraction he could possibly make – he isn't at the planned range to make a laboured approach, he is practically on top of the target location. He stands up tall and wanders out from between the cars and edges towards the building, dragging his feet and scuffing lose stones across the floor. He hears the echoes of a crunch from the back of the building, he decides that he is not going to wait for the 'all clear' and runs at the double-doors in front of him, raising a sharp front kick to the right hand door. It gives way easily and he pushes through into the building. He runs through the empty shells of rooms to see Jez lying on the floor and Mark standing with his arms raised trying to calm Lucy down from a frenzied rage, as she waves a length of steel picket like a baseball bat at him.

"LUCY." Alex shouts as he runs towards her.

Lucy turns to him. "Alex?" She drops the bar of metal and throws her arms around him. "You came for me."

"Of course I did. What have you done to Jez?"

She turns her head to look apologetically at the man struggling to lift himself into a comfortable seated position. "I thought that he was one of them. You know that there are three of them?"

Mark speaks into his mic, "John, are you there? We've got her, she's okay. No further hostiles expected."

"Roger, good news. Get clear of the building and get back to my location."

Alex releases Lucy, sensing that she feels safe and doesn't wish to be mollycoddled. "We've got two of them; we got your location from their phones. They're gone now."

"What happened to him?" Mark asks pointing to a body lying in the corner of the room with a jacket over its head and chest.

"I twatted him with that bar." Lucy says calmly, already seeming to have returned to her usual composed self.

"They had me tied to that radiator, with bloody string for crying out loud – I saw that strip of metal in the corner of the room and decided that I was going to attempt an escape as soon as a chance presented itself. The other two left a couple of hours ago, but it took a while for him," she points at the cooling body, "to relax and leave the room – that's when I untied myself and grabbed the bar. I waited for him to come back; when he did, I knew that I had to at least knock him out, so I didn't hold back. The edge of the metal went right into his skull, it made an awful noise, and he went down like a sack of spuds. I was just figuring out the best way to make my escape, then I saw these two coming round the corner," she waves a hand at Jez and Mark, "I thought it was the other two coming back."

"Fair play love, you did the business on me." says Jez, who has made it to his feet, but is clutching his left arm to his chest.

"I'm so sorry, are you okay?"

"I'll be fine."

"Lucy, this is Jez, he's one of the Birmingham operators. This is Mark; he's on the Committee and is a regional handler for part of London. Gents, this is Lucy, she's been a huge help to our mission."

"Yeah, okay Alex, I just want to go home. Can I go home?" Alex looks to Mark for an operationally astute answer. Lucy looks from Alex to Mark.

"We've not been to your place yet; we do need to go there and see if there's any trace of these guys; though it's not likely that there are any others, they might have left clues. Let's get back to the van and talk to John.

Joseph Mitcham

20

Grey sheep

"Thanks for coming back to London with me; I couldn't be on my own tonight," Lucy says rolling over in the super-king size bed, as Alex walks out of the ridiculously large wet room, "and thank you for booking such a super, gorgeous room for us."

"It's the least I could do; it was my fault that they found you."

"Don't be hard on yourself, even the Hereford boys were surprised that Blunt managed to have you tracked so quickly, these aren't the kind of clowns that we usually have to deal with."

"Do you think you'll be able to find anything out about them?"

"I've got nothing to go on really; if we could have got photos of them, I could've tried facial recognition. All I can do is search for reports of any structured networks that might have been noted and flagged. It should be fairly simple to find anything we have - suspected enablers and directors of terror activity are well documented and well signposted once we get to know about them. I'll go into work tomorrow and run some searches, make some calls."

"I've arranged to meet Craig just round the corner from the Server Building tomorrow morning, so I won't be far away." Alex jumps onto the bed and puts his still-dripping wet arm around Lucy; she doesn't mind at all and hugs him tightly. Alex senses that she might still be too traumatised for too much physical attention just yet. "I've said that I'll go to Birmingham and help Jez with his recce – I think his arm is a bit more injured than he's letting on; do you want to come?"

"I'll think about it. I'll let you know tomorrow afternoon. Shall we meet for lunch at Horse Guards?"

"The same spot?" Alex asks. Lucy doesn't reply, just relaxes her hug, pulls away to look him in the eyes and then pulls him back in for a deep sensual kiss.

Sunday morning, and a glorious day, the streets are full of tourists. Alex kisses Lucy goodbye as she heads for the office and checks again that no one is following them. He watches her disappear under the archway and into the safe ground of the Ministry of Defence property. He nods to Mark, who has shadowed them since they left the hotel, and is now standing watching from the other side of the street. He walks over to meet Alex, "Let's go and find Craig." The pair walk through St James's Park, past Victoria Monument and along Constitution Hill to the café where Craig sits waiting with John – he stands to greet Alex with a friendly handshake that pulls him in for a manly hug and pat on the back.

"How are you son? You've had a rough week?"

"You could say that."

"And Lucy; is she okay?"

"She's unbelievable. After what she's been through, most people would be in pieces, but she's strong, and as keen as ever to help us – she's in at work now trying to track down this 'Interest Group' bunch."

"Talking of tracking things – how did you track her down to the school? Are you tracking any of us like that?" Craig asks with a suspicious overtone.

Alex feels instantly deflated as Craig's supportive sentiment evaporates, and he is now, again, apparently under suspicion. "No. I'm not interested in tracking you. The less I know about what you get up to the better. I downloaded a tracking application onto the enemy handset to find the location from the phones' historical geo-data - you can all check your phones now for apps if you want – there's none there." This insinuation from Craig acts as a stark reminder to Alex that he is still not a fully trusted member of the team; he is still the outsider. The events of the past two days have brought him closer to Mark and Jez, and to his amazement, John, but Craig has been missing from all of this.

"Are you okay Craig?" Mark asks, clearly surprised by his overt and unsympathetic questioning of Alex.

"Yeah, yeah, I'm fine Mark. Sorry Alex, I'm a little out of sorts. I'm feeling a little paranoid after the Tony Blunt thing, and if I'm honest; a little jealous about not being in the thick of things with you blokes – even Lucy's getting more action than me." The men laugh faintly, the ice is again broken, but an air of concern still lingers across the group.

Craig's head continues to quietly boil. He is frustrated, he is tetchy, but it isn't with Alex - Craig knows that. He has enjoyed being back amongst the guys who have been at the coalface, only now, more than ever, he is a step back, he is now in the past tense when talking about the action; he is no longer a part of it. This had been a large, but subconscious part of the reason he'd left the Service; it was painful not to be amongst the action. The adrenalin rush of contact with the enemy is what his breed of men live for, without consciously wishing for trouble, they crave the madness and 'danger to life' that action brings. Controlled to a point by regimented training and bound by efficiently planned and delivered orders, special and elite force operations administer the natural drug that gives a perfectly clean high which, whilst having no chemical side effects, can do as much psychological damage as any street poison, to those to whom intense violence does not come absolutely naturally to.

Like the injured rugby player retired from the field, to watch or to be around the sport hurts intensely when unable to participate, and it gives an interminably painful ache that gnaws from within. This ache is what many retired soldiers cannot live with and it either drives them to distraction, or they end up working abroad looking for a fix. In his brief daydream, Craig ponders - *how many ex-squaddies hitting the bottle are trying to forget the terrible things they've seen, and how many are just mourning the loss of their favoured lifestyle?*

Craig fears the look that all veterans fear from currently serving men, the look which asks 'who the hell is this old has-been?' Craig has a partial antidote to this; his legendary status within the Forces and the emboldened personality that his television exploits have personified ensure that everyone knows who he is and what he has done. The very fact that he has seemingly single-handedly raised a force to defeat the hidden enemy is evidence enough that he is a man to be respected. Respected or not, Craig can sense the blood on the hands of the other men in the room, and is envious of their youthfulness and active status.

Coming around to himself, Craig takes a slurp of his tea and plonks the cup firmly into its saucer. "So, what do we know about these characters? What have we learned?"

Mark gives a hopeless wave of his hand, "Their operational security is pretty faultless, they carried no form of identification, and their phones had no contacts saved and no personal information or content on them – similar to our own operational phone set-up. They had no vehicles that we could find; we've got nothing to go on."

"But they openly admit to not wanting to stop us, or warn the targets? They just want the residual list for recruiting purposes?"

"It's pretty cold, and difficult to believe, but that's what I got from them. They thought they were about to finish me off - why would they bother making it up?" asks Alex.

Craig shakes his head. "You had a classic James Bond escape there Alex. He analyses what they know aloud; "So in operational terms, we've taken five members of their group out of the game, and we have no idea about how many more there might, or might not be. We know that Tony Blunt has knowledge of us and our mission, possibly others in his network, but we don't know if his network is one and the same as this group, or if they have merely fed into it – it may or may not feedback the other way."

Alex adds his thoughts on the situation; "The missing link might be the target that Blunt was photographed with. You didn't tell him about how we knew about him when you de-briefed him at Hodge Hill did you?"

"No."

"No."

"No." come the answers from John, Mark and Craig, in that order.

"Then hopefully that target has not been compromised." says Alex.

"And that target needs some special attention." says John. "Good job I assigned him to Jez." He says with content satisfaction.

"I was debating about whether I'd get myself involved on the ground," says Alex, "Jez's injury made it more likely, but if it means helping to put the nails in the coffin of one of the bastards that went after Lucy – I'm there."

Craig continues; "From what we know of their intent, there's no risk to the mission, we just need to keep extra special care of the list. Clearly we can't dismiss additional risk to the blokes on the ground; we don't know what else we don't know. We need to put out an all-stations message telling everyone to be extra vigilant, but as far as I'm concerned - we go ahead with caution. What say you?"

"In like Flynn." John says without hesitation.

"Absolutely." says Alex. There is a short pause for Mark to give his opinion…

"The concept of them getting organised and developing networks only makes me want to do this more. I only hope we don't start an all-out war."

Craig looks up at Mark; "It might yet take a war. Let's hope that it doesn't come to that."

21

Game on

Sunday, 07:30, Lucy is in the shower and Alex is about to open the hotel room door to head down for breakfast alone – there comes a faint knock. Alex's heart skips a beat. He doesn't alert Lucy, but looks through the peephole and sees to his relief that it's Jez, who slightly unusually but not unexpectedly, is dressed in a navy blue boiler suit.

"Morning Jez, what have you come as?"

"Good morning Alex. Put this on." Jez throws a neatly folded boiler suit, matching his own, onto the bed. "We're going to use the classic 'gas man' disguise. Very easy to give it the old 'there've been reports of a gas leak; we have to check it out'. Never fails - no one wants to be at risk from a gas blast."

"Very clever." says Alex.

"I didn't bother sending you a kit list, it's not like you can go home and get anything, and the less time you spend on the street the better. I've got almost everything else you'll need in the van, including a fake British Gas ID. How's Lucy?"

"I'm fine thanks Jez." says Lucy, emerging from the bathroom in a plush white robe. "How's your arm?"

"Fine, still a bit sore, so I'm glad to have your fella helping me out. Is there any update to the target pack?" He asks both Alex and Lucy, not really knowing who might be best placed to answer.

"I've got all the detail Jez. Lucy doesn't know which operatives have which targets. It's safer for everyone that way."

"He hasn't even told you which target we're on?" Jez asks Lucy.

"No, he's rigid on that. He thinks that's how Craig wants it."

Alex almost snaps back at Lucy; "It is. All you need to know is the call signs." Calming himself, he pulls on the boiler suit. Looking up from his struggle with his new outfit, he spells out to Jez the simplicity of the intelligence update service that Lucy is providing. "Lucy's using those terminals," Alex pulls his left shoulder into the suit and points to the pile of laptops on the coffee table, "to search for anything that crops up under any of the target names – I've installed programmes on the relevant intelligence systems that will alert her to any new information. Lucy matches the intelligence report to the codename against the subject target, then messages the report to the matching operative call sign – having your names involved would just complicate the system, and compromise you all should even one of the operational handsets be discovered unlocked."

"Fair one." says Jez, "I've got everything you'll need with me, just bring a change of clothes – nothing flash, just jeans, t-shirt and underwear."

Alex stands, straightening the collar line of his outfit and turns to Lucy; "You stay here until it's over; go to town on room service. He kisses her, then looks at her tentatively, "I'll see you when it's done." he says to her solemnly. He grabs his clothes, picks up a small laptop bag from beside the bed and follows Jez out of the room.

"So, Zafir Abdulaziz, what is he up to on a bright Sunday morning?" Jez asks philosophically. It is just past ten, they have made good time from London after a swift breakfast.

"He's not particularly keen on going to the Mosque unless it suits him, so he's not likely to be at Morning Prayer according to the target pack." says

Alex.

"Morning prayer would have been hours ago." says Jez, "next one will be noon."

"Apart from that, there's not much more to go on. We've got more detail on his weekday routine, but there doesn't seem to be much of a pattern for weekends, and Ramadan puts a further skew on what we already know." says Alex.

"Ramadan's a double edged sword for us. Assuming that he's participating in typical celebrations and rituals - his routine will be altered from what's on record, but he'll be more docile and easier to dispose of once we've got him pinpointed. He's more likely to be at prayer or staying away with friends or family. He's also much more likely to have house guests, even if he's not a proper God-botherer."

"Really?" Alex asks somewhat surprised. He has difficulty imagining the target as anything other than a single-minded, religiously fanatical terrorist.

"Are you a proper Christian? Go to church every Sunday? Missed it especially this morning did you?"

"Not exactly."

"But you still go to your folks at Christmas, or go out celebrating with friends and colleagues during the silly season?" Jez asks, knowing that he need not wait for an answer. "Why would people of other religions be any different?"

"Fair one."

"Any of our operatives worth their salt will be all over this if they have Muslim targets; it'll be one of the first things they'll have considered when conducting their estimates. Hopefully we can get into his property without too much drama and find a calendar with his plans on it; otherwise it could prove a little tricky and require a little more ingenuity."

Alex dreads to think what that might translate to in terms of actions on the ground. "So what's the plan?"

Jez half mumbles as he concentrates on his route, "His flat is above a chip shop, I've identified an unoccupied flat across the street from it – we'll gain access to it from the rear and set up watch for at least the next twenty-four hours. We'll need to identify whether the spooks' surveillance team used the same location, they may return if there is any change in situation.

"See this patch of wasteland ahead on the left?" says Jez. Alex squints under the sun visor and can see the unkempt area of scrub. "His flat is the first one on the first floor of that row beyond it." Jez subtly points with a single finger without releasing his hand from the steering wheel.

"I thought we weren't supposed to bring vehicles in this close?"

"Relax, the situation dictates; we'll be in totally dead ground, and in the guise of gas men - have you ever seen gas men walk more than a few yards with their equipment?"

Alex isn't convinced that they should be going against the big man's direction, but can't imagine the vehicle's presence causing a huge problem, so lets it go.

Almost as soon as Alex positively identifies the flat, Jez takes a right turn and heads north away from it. "We're just going around the block and will arrive at our stakeout from Shetland Road, keeping us out of line of sight."

After a couple more left turns the white van heads south down Shetland Road and takes a final tight left into an alley. Jez coasts into a tailor-made parking spot directly behind and parallel with their stakeout building in the rough-looking courtyard. "Wait here." says Jez.

Alex hears the rear door of the van open, Jez picking something up, and the door close. He sees the reflection of Jez in the driver's wing mirror gliding across the narrow gap between the back of the van and the next vehicle, then all is quiet for a minute: he waits in anticipation. Jez's reflection reappears in the mirror as he returns. The rear door opens again and Jez calls through to Alex, "Let's rock and roll fella."

Alex climbs from the van and meets Jez at the back doors where Jez hands him a baseball cap and a pair of contact gloves, "Put those on and don't take them off unless you really need to." Jez then lifts out a large rubber-coated duffel bag, hands it to Alex and grabs a second one for himself. They enter the building taking the steps immediately to their left up onto a small landing; their door is off to the right. "Home sweet home." says Jez with a smile, as he pushes open the latched door.

The flat is a compact unit; from the hallway, which is barely big enough for the two men and their bags, there is a small toilet and bathroom to the right and equally small kitchen to the left. Through the door to the front is the living room-come-bedroom with large windows facing out onto Merville Road.

"Right, first things first, you've got pretty much everything that I've got, less the watch kit and sleeping system – they're shared between us, oh and a few bits of recce kit. There's no hard routine, so there's a towel and limited toiletries, but we're not getting too comfortable, and there are no kit explosions – everything must stay in the bag and we must be able to leave here without a trace in less than thirty seconds, got it?"

"Got it."

Jez is already setting up a tripod and long lens camera. "Get round and check this place out for resources, it's not quite semi-furnished, but we might get lucky with some bits and bobs. The bed's a bonus for a start."

Alex explores the confines of the flat and reports back to Jez; "We've got power, water, and a few knives and forks in one of the kitchen drawers."

"Great, get the brews on." Jez throws a travel kettle to Alex. As he walks to the kitchenette he opens the lid to find two plastic cups stuffed with teabags and sachets of milk and sugar. It hasn't escaped Alex's notice that the warrior-types that he has encountered on this mission are never far from a brew and that brew kit is abnormally high up on the priority list of equipment – it is too clichéd to mention, certainly until the small talk begins to dry up.

"How's it looking over there?" Alex asks as he returns to the bedroom with the cups of tea.

"Not much of a choice for routes in or out." Jez replies, without looking around. "It looks like a straight staircase up the left-hand side of the chip shop into a bedsit flat; it won't be dissimilar in layout to this place, but without the external landing."

"Low complexity, it'll be easy to search." Alex offers.

"Yeah, but nowhere much to lay up. There doesn't appear to be anyone in at the moment, curtains are drawn." Jez takes a slow slurp of his tea and puts his eyes back to the optics, "Let's get comfy. How long do you want the watch stints to be?"

"Two hours?" suggests Alex.

"Yeah that's doable, I'm not sure that there's going to be much to see. I'll take the first watch, call it from eleven."

Alex checks his watch; it's 10:53 – *a bonus seven minutes scored off shift*. He sits down on the bed, leans against the wall where the headboard might have been, and takes a drink of his tea. "So what is there of practical use in the target pack?" Alex asks.

"Well he's being looked at mainly for his extremist and political views, he's been reported on several occasions for hate preaching within the community, and he's got previous convictions for violent crimes. Most cases were dropped due to victims not wanting to press charges, but he was convicted of one two years ago when Police were involved and he punched an officer: he got a six month suspended sentence for that." Alex is impressed that Jez is able to recount the notes from Zafir's file with a good level of accuracy and detail.

Alex revisits the files on his operational handset – "He was found in possession of bladed weapons during one of his arrests, and on searching his flat, they found extremist materials from banned groups."

"Bear the bladed weapon thing in mind if you ever come up against him, though you're pretty handy when it comes to knife defence." Jez looks back at him with a smile, a clear reference to the way Alex had tackled John with his water bottle.

Alex continues; "More recently he's been detected in communication with known terrorism activists, and notably has been seen at a physical meeting with an emerging group in London, which also included our friend Tony

Blunt. That was an incidental discovery – that wasn't picked up by a team tracking him specifically. His own surveillance reports are limited, but suggest that he is in the flat most nights. He doesn't seem to have a regular job, but is out on the street daily, meeting with people, socialising, nothing else tangibly untoward. Physical surveillance hasn't provided much on him, so that's probably why they stopped it. They're getting more from tracking his online activity."

"That might be in the process of changing though, since he's been seen with that group. We'll have to keep our eyes peeled for friendly forces – Special Branch and The Security Service."

Jez's first watch passes by with nothing serious to report. Alex's first stint is similarly quiet. "Am I back on?" Jez says, glancing at his watch as he flings himself up from the mattress.

"Yeah, that's two hours of my life I won't get back. I'm starving; shall I nip out and get us some food?"

"You sort yourself out - I'll go after this watch for a leg stretch; it's good to take in a bit of the local geography. Take off your suit and put on the baseball cap. Don't do anything stupid and don't get too friendly with anyone."

"Roger, see you in ten." says Alex as he pulls himself free of the boiler suit.

Alex walks down the stairs, out of the building and out of the courtyard, turning left onto Shetland Road. He tries not to stare at the target building which comes into view as he nears the main road. He glances up to his left at Zafir's flat as he crosses the bottom of the street, and then continues on the same heading across the main road. As he steps onto the footpath he notices that the next turning is immediately in front of him onto Newland Road – he decides to follow it to get a view of the rear of the property.

Alex meanders slowly past the end of the row of shops to find an open delivery courtyard, similar to the one behind his building, which gives a clear view of the back of the row of shops and flats above them. The shops at Zafir's end of the building complex have been extended at the rear and conjoin with the buildings of this street at the far side of the courtyard.

Zafir's flat can just about be seen, but there is nothing note-worthy, there are no doors, and only small windows – no potential access points. He almost comes to a halt as he tries to gather more information and identify potential routes up to the flat from the rear, and he suddenly becomes conscious of how conspicuous his behaviour is, as a man walking his dog on the other side of the road glares at him overtly. He resumes his walk away from the flat, and then quickly falters again outside the next building as the flat begins to slip from view.

He finds himself outside a Mosque, nothing spectacular architecturally, just another part of an estate terrace, but the entrance way has been modified to reflect the grandeur of the building's use - the door is open. Alex notices fresh graffiti on the wall to the left of the door; a mop bucket and scrubbing brush on the wet ground beneath it shows someone's futile attempt to remove it. As he hesitates about whether to continue or turnabout, he is greeted by a man in the doorway who is midway through replacing his footwear, a pair of highly polished brogues, "Assalam alaikum." the man says in a quiet, nervous voice.

"Ah… hello, ah… walaikum assalam." Alex says, recounting some of the only words he can ever remember in Arabic.

"Can I help you? Are you here to pray, or to meet someone?" the man enquires with growing confidence.

"No, err… I'm just interested to see what's going on." Alex can't think of what else to say.

"Oh, well, may I welcome you on behalf of our humble Mosque. My name's Ali Talib."

"Hi Ali, I'm Alex. That's terrible." says Alex pointing to the graffiti.

"Yes, that's why my welcome was a little less outgoing than it might usually be. Everyone here is on tenterhooks since that terrible atrocity at the Gardens; we have all been praying for the victims and their families."

"Yes, it's terrible; did you know any of the victims?"

"Yes, my niece was very badly hurt. Little Marie, she and her mother, my sister come here regularly; she was hit by the bomb blast."

"Oh, that's terrible."

"She is recovering well, but all of the friends she was with were either trampled in the rush to escape or killed by the bomb."

"That's awful."

"Come; let me introduce you to our Imam." Ali doesn't wait for an answer, he kicks off the shoe that he has half put back on and sets off, leading Alex through the foyer and along a short corridor to a large office, the door of which is wide open. Alex pulls off his shoes and follows him. Ali is talking to Alex, but he isn't listening, he is focused on the raised voice coming from the office at the end of the corridor.

"NO ZAFIR I WILL NOT TOLERATE YOUR PRESENCE IN THIS HOUSE OF ALLAH, I WILL NOT HAVE YOU POISONING OUR YOUNG MINDS WITH YOUR THOUGHTS OF EVIL. Now go please, until you have come to your senses."

Just as Ali finishes what he is saying, he realises that the Imam is busy. A young man with a raised hood covering his brow bursts through the doorway and strides past angrily; his head is down and he ignores Ali and Alex. Alex sees enough of his face to recognise him as the man from the target pack.

22

Gas inspection

"Where the fuck've you been?" Jez asks in a not too concerned manner.

"I've just seen our target." replies Alex trying to mask his excitement and self-satisfaction at achieving a major intelligence coup.

"Me too, he went into the flat about twenty-five minutes ago."

"He must have come straight home from the Mosque."

"What Mosque." Jez asks seeming slightly annoyed that he is out of the picture, and that Alex seems to have risked a serious breach in operational security.

"I couldn't find a shop, but I found a Mosque. I was having a nosey at the back side of Zafir's flat and got invited in - I couldn't say no."

"So what? You went in for tea and biscuits?"

"Basically... yes. As I was taken through to meet the Imam, our man came steaming out of the office on the back of an argument."

"Did he clock you?"

"No, he was raging - he wasn't taking any notice of me. I didn't want to be too pushy, but I got some good intel on him. He's been thrown out of the Mosque for his extreme views. The Imam meets with him still, trying to talk him round. He's refused the de-radicalisation programme; they're on the verge of calling in the Police as he's getting out of hand."

"Sounds like our mission might be just in time for him. Did you get anything we can use on him?"

"He's been traveling to meet at another Mosque on Mondays, likely he's made friends with some like-minded individuals, it could be where he was photographed. He's going early this week for celebrations, so leaving tonight. We can expect him home late tomorrow, maybe Tuesday morning."

"So tonight's the night for getting into the flat, dark o'clock – say 03:00."

"Sounds good, I'll keep watch over you from here."

"Will you hell as like – you're coming with me." says Jez with a half-smile, but still making it clear that he is deadly serious.

Alex pauses to consider whether he really wants to be that involved – he doesn't. He starts to formulate excuses; "Is that wise?" he ventures. "It's kind of all our eggs in one basket, don't you think, having us both over there together?"

"On the contrary Alex, it gives us twice the fighting force on the spot, should anyone interrupt us. There's no need to preserve an egg – if there's a compromise, there'll be no second chances, there's no need to keep your powder dry. More importantly, it gives us both the first-hand knowledge of the ground in detail. If anything happens to me, then you're fully in the picture and ready to go, having you on the CTR is an insurance policy."

Alex gives up arguing - his aversion to participating countered by his excitement at the prospect of it. The buzz he had received from sneaking around farm complexes on training estates, when he was serving, was one of the most memorable things that he's done in the training environment - avoiding fake enemy and trying to gather intelligence on them. They were just colleagues in scruffy old pattern uniform, it had been like some sort of over-age game of hide and seek, but it was a real thrill.

"Here we go, we've got movement." Jez says, as Alex begins to put his boiler suit back on.

"Zafir?" Alex asks.

"Roger, he's closing the door, he's got a blue sports bag with him and it looks well packed. He's changed clothes since he came home, dark green long sleeved top with a round-neck collar, dark blue jeans and black trainers."

"Shall I follow him?" Alex asks speculatively.

"No, we know where he's off to tonight, it's just more risk of getting compromised."

Jez and Alex both watch through the manky old net curtains as Zafir looks left and right before closing his front door, then spinning away from it and setting off east, to their left as they watch. "I thought he'd have headed west towards the city station." says Alex.

"That's over four miles away; he'll be getting a bus or a lift. There's been a number fourteen bus coming past here, heading into the city every five minutes or so. My bet is that there's a stop just out of sight and he'll be on the next one."

Four minutes later, a double-decker bus rumbles past - both men's eyes dart around the inside of its lumbering shell as it trundles across their field of view. "There he is, "says Jez, "just sitting down on the near side, about four seats back." Jez's lower viewpoint and the optics of the camera offer him a much clearer view. "We're lucky he's sitting this side, we wouldn't have seen him otherwise."

Alex is soon back on watch. Both men sit in their overalls, Alex behind the camera and Jez on the bed. "Is there any need to maintain this watch? We know where he is, and we know he's not coming back for over a day."

"We're strangers here, Alex, we need to know what goes on - there's a lot to be learned about the routine of the environment, patterns of life, regular movements. I want plenty of detail in that log book, and I want you to read everything that I've written in it too."

The time ticks by, shifts come and go, Alex starts to pick up on what Jez means about patterns of life; the regularity of the buses is an obvious example, alternating five and eight minute gaps between them, but with some irregularities, maybe momentarily late due to traffic fluctuations now and then. The traffic comes and goes in pulses set by the traffic lights. The rate of pedestrian flow peaks and troughs through the hours, the type of person walking by seems to vary too, though he doubts that this is a reliable pattern. This is Sunday, it would be different on a weekday – he will learn more of relevance tomorrow, but hopefully they'll have learned a lot more in the dark hours by then.

At 02:50 Alex wakes Jez with a nudge on the right elbow. He groans into consciousness, but is up on his feet and ready for action in a few seconds. "Remember we're looking for any clues to pattern of life, hiding places, alternative methods of entry, and any potential weapons. We're in and out in silence, no white light, and we leave no discernible trace of our being there – got it?"

"Got it." Alex says confidently.

"There's a red filtered head torch in your bag, don't put it on until we're in, you'll look daft. I've got a few bits and bobs in here." Jez holds up a small tool bag. "Nothing out of step with our 'gas man' cover story. You follow me close, and keep watch while I gain entry. If the lock gives me a problem – you stand back from me and make small talk with me if anyone passes, act natural, as if we're there with a kosher job to do."

"Roger." Alex immediately gets into a minor panic about what sort of banter gas men might have - *the 'trying to shag his sister wind-up' - I'll go with that.*

"Let's go." And with that; Jez is off out of the door, along the landing, down the stairs at a brisk pace, but in total silence. Through the parking area at the back of the building, onto the bottom of Shetland Road - it is deadly silent, no people, no cars. Across Merville Road, Jez doesn't head directly to the door, he takes a line that makes it look as though they are heading south towards the Mosque, but as he nears the junction he turns acutely, but almost naturally, to follow the line of the shopfronts, brushing past them, still no traffic, still no pedestrians, no twitching curtains, nothing.

As they reach the door Jez pulls a fine-gauge Allen key and a piece of wire from his pocket and sets to work on picking the lock - *a standard six pin Yale*. Alex's ears prick up as he hears people approaching from the east - distant, but loud and rowdy; Jez flashes him a look that says 'standby' - *three clicks down*.

Alex considers the options; "Should we abort? It'll only cost us five minutes." he whispers.

"Give me a second." Jez wiggles the Allen key gently left and right, in the top of the lock barrel and as he rakes the wire downwards across the pins, another pin clicks into place - *four*.

The approaching party is singing, some sort of football chant or rugby choir practice. They are getting closer, Alex can hear the detail in the sound evermore refining, ever louder - probably four of five individuals, maybe twenty metres away. He resists the urge to look around the slim amount of cover offered by the overgrown hedge that protrudes around the corner of the building from the wasteland to his left.

"Come on you bastard." Jez says under his breath as he hears and feels click five.

"Jez, let's cut and run, we'll be back in five minutes."

"Wait, I've got it."

The last click isn't forthcoming, Jez rakes the pins with more and more frustration and aggression, the shouting and laughing gets louder and louder, it feels as though they are almost becoming a part of the group of noisy louts.

"Jez, let's go."

Click – "We're in." He twists the Allen key arm and falls into the open doorway, pulling his tools from the lock as he goes. Alex is right behind him and is closing the door as he pushes through, thrusting it shut, sacrificing his balance for getting the door closed as quietly as he can. He trips on Jez's feet and his weight sends both of them over, landing softly but awkwardly on the surprisingly effeminate and very clean, deep-pile cream carpet of the stairs.

Both men have felt the pressure and are breathing heavily. Alex is on edge; he's visibly shaking and has broken into a cold sweat. He wipes his brow under the brim of his baseball cap.

"We've got to stop meeting like this." says Jez, looking up at Alex, barely visible in the darkness. He wraps his arms around Alex's shoulders for a mock hug. He quickly releases him, "Get up, you Charlie."

In one way Alex is glad that Jez is able to keep his cool, but in another, he is greatly displeased that he had let such an unnecessary situation like that develop. He reins in his annoyance and decides that it is best kept for an after-action debrief back at the stakeout, rather than creating friction whilst on target.

Alex hauls himself up, and then feels for Jez's hand, which he takes and pulls him up. "We've got the place to ourselves, let's take our time and get this right." Jez says, reviving Alex's confidence in him. Jez pulls out his head torch and switches it on, then pulls it over the top of his head. Most of the lens is covered in black tape and a finely tuned beam of soft red light illuminates a section of bare wall. Alex dons his too.

As Jez leads the way up the stairs, Alex notices that the walls are freshly painted in a plain pale colour, indeterminable in the red light, possibly magnolia – it reminds him of Army accommodation and he feels as though he's in the house of a squaddie mate on the married patch rather than in the home of a 'bad-boy' terrorist.

The staircase brings them to the back left of the main room of the flat as they have been viewing it from across the street. Jez opens the door at the top of the stairs; the room is now at right angles to the orientation they are used to seeing. It is a modest sized bedroom with two doors to their left on the back wall, there is a standard-sized double bed in front of them, with the headboard hard up against the distant wall. Jez prevents Alex from entering any further with a raised finger and opens the door to his immediate left.

Alex surveys the room while he waits momentarily for Jez. The room is dominated by the unusual desktop to his right, beyond the end of the bed, underneath the window, which they had tried to catch glimpses though the previous day. The desk is decorated with items one would not expect to find in a bedroom, particularly not in such a neat and tidy bedroom. The standout items are a soldering iron, a large eyeglass mounted on a stand, and complementing lamp, *'What's he doing with those?'*

Jez is back in the room in seconds, "Clear." he whispers, as he moves straight for the second door a metre further along the wall. He barely steps inside, "Clear - that's just the bathroom. There's a kitchen through there." he says, pointing back to the first door. That is all the de-brief that he gives, nothing more is needed at this stage.

The pair gravitate towards the desk, moving around the end of the bed and stand together over it, taking in the information it has to offer. "I'll start here; you get amongst the cupboards and drawers." Jez says, viewing the desktop with intrigue. Alex turns to the tall wardrobe to his right, which is set back into the alcove naturally created by the void of space above the stairs. He opens the doors to find nothing unusual, well-pressed shirts and trousers hanging from the rail in some form of logical order, neatly folded clothes in cubby-hole shelves, a clean pair of shoes, and several pairs of trainers and more casual footwear.

Jez bends down and checks under the desk, "Bingo." he says as he gently pulls out a large rugged plastic toolbox.

"What have you got?" Alex asks, peering over his own shoulder to see.

"Hopefully our secondary means of neutralisation." he says as he pops the clips open and lifts the lid of the box. Alex is distracted from his search; he is interested to see what Jez has in mind. The top tray is full of different types and scale of grips, pliers and forceps, a number of blades from Stanley knife to scalpel, sets of miniature screwdrivers and a neat set of Allen keys in a tiny wallet, all perfectly tidily packed as the confines of the small workspace, and a neat and tidy mind would demand. Jez slowly lifts the top tray from its seating within the body of the toolbox - Alex catches sight of something not quite right.

"STOP." he shouts as loudly as he dare. Jez freezes in place and slowly turns his head to look at Alex. "There's a wire under the tray." Alex says almost apologetically, "It's probably nothing, might just be a scrap... sorry."

"Let's check it out, here you take this." Jez gestures with his eyebrows towards the tray. Alex takes a step and then kneels adjacent to Jez and takes the tray from him with a hand at each end, being very careful not to lift it any further than Jez already has. Jez sprawls out on the floor along the full length of the bed, taking care not to let his feet stray underneath it; who knows what other tricks might await them if the place is booby-trapped? He re-takes control of the tray and angles it upwards so that he is able to see underneath it. "Move your right hand onto the centre handle." Jez instructs. Alex does so in a careful movement, Jez taking the weight of the tray during the manoeuvre. Jez has a clear view of the underside of the tray - he makes a sound between a grunt and a heavy sigh, not a sound Alex can remember hearing before, but he immediately knows it is not good news. "A definite deliberately attached wire, let's see what it's attached to. He shuffles his left elbow up under his shoulder, and raising his head up a few inches, cranes his neck up, and peers into the toolbox. A few seconds of analysis pass. Alex fixates on Jez's facial expressions, the worrying look of surprise quickly disperses, and is first replaced with one of puzzlement, and then what Alex hopes is relief.

"What's the verdict?" Alex asks.

"Well the bad news is that it is an explosive device."

"And the good news?"

"Well to say it's rudimental would be an understatement." and with that Jez lifts himself back up onto his knees, takes the tray out of Alex's hands and rotates it through 180 degrees to the right, so that it is now in front of the box. "You see how it's attached here," Jez points to the top of the wire, and then moves his finger down it to where it connects to a ring, "and acts as the pull for this old grenade." The grenade pin has been pulled out to its very tip. Jez hands the tray back to Alex and carefully presses the pin back in by a couple of millimetres. "You see what he's done here?" he asks Alex, pointing to two 600ml cola bottles filled with a liquid that clearly is not Coca-Cola.

Alex gives the faintest of shakes of the head, "What?"

"That'll be some sort of accelerant, most likely petrol. If the grenade goes off, this place will be an instant firestorm. Not meant to kill, but to act as a warning to him not to return."

Jez assesses the other contents of the box; "Perfect." he says, gently liberating a claw hammer from the main compartment of the toolbox. "This too." he says as he grasps the handle of a broad chisel, with a blade nearly three centimetres across. He takes the tray from Alex and replaces it in the box, clips the lid back into place and replaces the toolbox in its spot underneath the desk.

Both men get to their feet, Jez hands the hammer to Alex, then points at the toolbox; "Now this little device offers us an option, Alex." Jez says scratching at the stubble under his nose with the end of the chisel. "We could reposition it somewhere in here and have it do our job for us." Alex is interested by the idea and begins to think through practicalities, just as Jez begins to talk them through. "There's a selection of possible sites, behind the door, under the bed, in the toilet cistern, to name the obvious ones, but there are two major problems with such a plan - what do you think, Alex?" He puts the question to Alex like a teacher to a student, giving Alex a strange feeling of being some kind of 'assassin's apprentice'. His immediate thought comes from his limited experience of grenades on the range; "Lethality" he says with a good level of certainty.

"Correct, grenades don't have a great kill radius; the charge in them is small. A well-placed grenade would guarantee serious injury, but not one hundred percent certainty of a kill, which is what we need. What else?"

"What if he checks the toolbox before initiating it - he'll be on to us." Alex guesses.

"Yeah, that'd be a consideration, good thinking, but what if the next person into this flat isn't him?" Alex glances at Jez and raises his eyebrows questioningly. "What if his mum pops round with his ironing or his best mate nips round to borrow something? We'll have caused collateral damage that is to be avoided at all costs, and he'd be on to us."

"If his mate pops round for a chisel - that'll be his problem." Alex says with a grin, Jez chuckles.

"So we'll firmly discount that option - and bear booby traps in mind for the rest of our search." Jez gets back to work looking through the neatly stacked piles of paper on the desk.

Alex looks at the hammer in his right hand, he bounces it up and down into his left palm - he feels the dead weight of its head and notes its extremely top-heavy balance, he firmly caresses its head with his thumb, feeling its unapologetic density, its totally solid constitution. The tool brings back memories of his late grandfather's garage workshop, where he spent hours bashing at things, doing damage to things that he was trying to make or fix, doing damage to his fingers and thumbs, even shins and toes when mishandling a hammer, bouncing it off the concrete floor when putting together makeshift crossbows or some other construction that his elders wouldn't approve of. The unforgiving nature of the claw hammer makes Alex fear it. This inanimate object, even in his own possession, feels nasty and dangerous. Fleetingly haunted by news reports of pensioners attacked in their own homes with the humble claw hammer, images flash in his mind's eye of smashed old faces, black and blue, of broken eye sockets and cheekbones – they give him a cold shudder. He places the hammer on the bed and moves on from his search of the wardrobe to the chest of drawers the other side of the desk as Jez moves out of his way and heads into the kitchen.

Alex quickly discounts the bottom two drawers, finding only clothes - nothing stashed amongst them. He carefully sifts the contents of the top drawer which is neatly sectioned, separating underwear and socks into compartments, leaving a quarter of the space for trinkets, aftershaves, receipts and bits and bobs. At the back of the space are four assorted types of cheap mobile phone handsets and a polythene bag containing ten sim cards. He begins switching the handsets on in turn to check for any useful information.

"Anything interesting?" Jez asks as he returns to the bedroom.

"Just some phones. Anything in there?"

"Lots of knives and a calendar… and some schematics of Pavillion Gardens."

"You're shitting me - seriously?"

"Serious."

"Bloody hell." Alex is stunned for a second. "This Charlie's definitely got to die." It takes a few more seconds for Alex's mind to move on. "What about the calendar? Does it tell us anything useful?"

"It's well populated and looks well-kept - it points towards him being at home Tuesday night."

"Great." Alex acknowledges the new information, which formalises that the hit will be on in little over forty-eight hours, and leaves him with an eerie feeling of cold resignation.

"I'll check the bathroom." Jez says as he moves to search the final room.

Alex sets back to work on the phones, but finds nothing of value. He hears Jez moving around in the bathroom, making some interesting noises, and goes to investigate. "What are you doing?" Alex asks Jez, who is sitting on the floor pulling at the side of the bath unit.

"There's a load of dead space under baths, it's a standard stash location for para-military quartermasters, drug dealers, smugglers, anyone else with something worth hiding."

The top edge of the creamy plastic panel finally pops out of its groove and drops forward. Standing over Jez, Alex lifts it up and out of the bottom runner, and places it on its end up against the wall. As he turns back towards the bath, he realises that they have found something worth finding, purely from the look on Jez's face. His eyes adjusting to the dark space under the tub, he takes a few seconds to identify wires, batteries, switches, and what he assumes is plastic explosive, six chunks each the size of slab of butter - component parts required to construct an improvised explosive device, the only missing part - a container, which could be anything.

"Shit the bed!" exclaims Jez, having digested what lies before him, while Alex is still trying to take it in. "This Charlie is on your list for good reason."

"What are we going to do? We can't just leave all this here. What if he decides to use it?"

"He won't; there are no plans for a future target. It stands to reason that if the plans for Birmingham are here, there'd be plans for the next one too."

"Maybe, but we can't be sure. What if he's planning it on the trip that he's on right now?"

"Then he'll need a window of time earmarked to execute it, and there's nothing marked on his calendar before tomorrow night."

Alex follows through the logic of Jez's argument. "Okay, we leave it here then."

"It's not even up for debate Alex; it's not an option to remove it - that would compromise us and the mission – end of."

"Okay, okay. Let's get this back in." Alex passes the panel back to Jez. "What's left to do?"

Jez concentrates on clicking the panel back into place without causing any damage to the paint along the bottom skirting board. "Final confirmation of what we've learned." Jez says, brushing past Alex and heading back into the bedroom. "We have no real places to hide up, so that's breach entry as we did tonight – nice and easy, and shouldn't be heard from up here. We have a claw hammer and a selection of knives in the kitchen as back-up weapons, there is a booby-trapped toolbox in here, a shit-stack of explosives in there," he says pointing to the bathroom, "and we have his diary, and evidence that he is *the*, or is one of *the* Birmingham bombers."

"Not a bad night's work. So what are we going to do with the hammer, won't moving that be a potential compromise too?"

"Well, initially I thought that'd be low risk - what are the chances that he'll need a hammer over the course of a couple of days? But as a serious technical actor, the chances are that he might be tinkering, and that he is the type of guy to notice a missing hammer, even if he doesn't need it specifically." Jez rubs the dark stubble on his chin and neck as he ponders the risk. "We should put it back, even if it means that we resort to a kitchen knife as a secondary, the risk of a bit of mess is better than the risk of blowing the mission."

"Agreed."

"Wait here a second." Jez opens the door to the stairway and walks down slowly to the front door. Alex takes the moment to send a message to Craig and Lucy detailing the new intelligence on Zafir. Jez steps back into the room. "Third and eighth steps creak." He then walks into the kitchen, checking the floorboards along the way. He checks the door for creaks and its balance for any tendency to move on its own, then walks back to the side of the bed. "So into the room, into the kitchen, take the wide blade carving knife and slip it into the map pocket. Around the bed and onto one knee up against the bedside table and administer blobs of anaesthetic gel onto the target's skin. Give it five minutes to take effect, remaining ready to go with the knife at all times, then syringe out and stick it in him. Knife back in the draw, back down the stairs, not forgetting steps eight and three, and then back to the van. Job done."

"Not back to the flat?"

"No, the flat will be packed up and we'll be having it on our toes."

23

Double-bubble

Alex wakes up with a dribble of saliva running from the right corner of his mouth, and an aching back, it's 07:21. He has slept on the floor for some reason and is mildly annoyed to see the bed empty to his right. "Good morning." Jez says without looking round from the window seat.

"You didn't wake me up?"

"Nah, pointless. I stayed up last night for long enough to reassure myself about overnight traffic, and then I had a kip for a couple of hours. I only got up fifteen minutes ago myself. Stick the kettle on will you."

Alex pulls himself up from the floor and staggers stiffly through into the kitchen, fills the kettle and plugs it back in. He checks his phone - "There's a lot of overnight traffic from the operators." he calls through to Jez.

"Like what?"

"Some good intelligence, looks like a couple of cells might have been identified."

"Anything relevant to us?"

"There's evidence of terror target reconnaissance in Coventry, that's possibly in our guy's area of operations. Hopefully it'll be academic after tomorrow night." Alex stirs the tea and takes it through to Jez.

"Cheers. What else have you got?"

"A few 'target not present' messages."

"Not enough to risk an abort?"

"No, seven, that's less than five percent so far. There might be a further blip tomorrow afternoon when the recce reports are officially due in, but some of these seven might have turned up by then." Alex continues scrolling through the most recent messages: "Craig's acknowledged our report. He's happy with how things are going so far, just some work to do finding support for some of the London operators – there are some complex jobs in the capital."

"At least he'll have something to keep him busy. It's going to be a slow day today; so maximum concentration - don't switch off. Grip your admin too, get yourself squared away and get all the sleep you can when you're off shift, we need to be rested for tomorrow night."

"Roger."

The day creeps past at a snail's pace, nothing happening at the target flat or on the messaging front. Alex can't sleep when off shift, not during the daylight, he lies on the bed fidgeting, he makes brews, he checks his phone over and over again. When he is off shift; he wants to be on, and when he is on, he wants to be off. He craves change, and movement, any kind of action to relieve his boredom.

15:45 – as he lies on his back he starts to calculate how many more shifts he has. *Seventy-five minutes left of Jez's current shift, then a further thirty-four hours until H-Hour, that's seventeen and a half two hour shifts, nine of them are mine - I'll be off shift before the op.* He sees that Jez is reacting to something - "What is it?"

Jez snaps some shots on the camera, which he is pointing to his left of arc. "Two chaps coming our way from the east, possibly just off that bus," Alex is on his feet in a second, "one of them looks like our target. Confirmed –

Zafir's on the far side, he's carrying the same bag he left with yesterday. His pal's carrying a heavy-looking black duffel bag." Jez and Alex continue to observe in silence, repeated camera exposures are the only sound in the room. The two men approach the flat door, Zafir inserts the key, turns it and they go in.

"The new fella seems to be the dominant character, more senior in demeanour, what do you think?"

"This is big, Alex, if this other guy sticks around it could make things very complicated for us. Do you recognise him from any of the other target packs?"

"No. Send me over the best of those images and I'll get it to Lucy for analysis. I'll have to tell her that it is Zafir that we're on."

Within a minute a high resolution image has made its way to the Main Server Building in London and is being compared to millions of images on several databases. Alex's mobile handset vibrates; he smiles as he sees the encoded caller ID, then slides to accept the call.

"That was quick." he says into the handset.

"I don't mess about." says Lucy.

"Did you get a result?"

"Yes, interesting, and consistent – your man is on The Security Service's image list of 'persons of interest', no name; just his image – he's yet to be identified. This guy has been present at some of a series of meetings attended by some known terror suspects. The meetings have sparked interest because of the number of players attending, but also some of the unknown attendees appear to be senior people, but still unknown. Your target has been present at two of the three that we have been aware of so far."

"How do they know that these unknowns are senior if they don't even know their names?"

"Observed respect, compliments paid, expensive tastes, lavishly looked after - it's straight-forward to tell an individual's standing from body language alone. The agents wouldn't even need to be in close to tell that much."

"Fair one. How many delegates are there at these meetings?"

"Up to twelve including known actors, but there seems to be a hub of four unknown leaders."

"What is The Security Service doing about it?"

"It's a single agent on it at the moment, she's still investigating the purpose of the meetings, and is trying to get extra resource to enhance surveillance on the known actors, and initiate it on the unknowns."

"Should we expect any extra company here? We've not seen anyone so far."

"Not right now. I should be able to get you twelve hours' notice if she manages to get it."

"Cool. How's the rest of the intelligence picture shaping up outside of that?"

"Active I'd say. There's a definite vibe in the community, like there's more going on than usual, not something I can put my finger on though."

"Do you think we've been compromised?"

"No, I think if there had been a catastrophic compromise; there'd be a whole lot more going on. This is something more worrying, it's like this emerging group is sending waves out through the underworld."

"This stinks of what those Charlies were telling me when they came for a copy of the list. Could they be preparing for a counter-surge?"

"It's hard to say until more investigation is done."

"Should we consider aborting?" Alex asks. Jez throws him a look of disdain.

"No, we've got these bastards on the radar now; if anything we add them to the list." Alex is taken aback by Lucy's aggressive assessment of the situation, but is equally reassured by it.

"Let me know if you get any updates."

"I'll keep you posted."

Alex can still feel the heat in Jez's face from his displeasure at the mere mention of an abort. He isn't sure whether he should address it or let it pass. He doesn't get the option...

"What were you talking about 'abort'?"

Alex doesn't want to ruin his relationship with Jez, but feels that he has to make his point. "The whole point of this mission is to reduce the threat to the UK public, not start a civil war – that's the exact opposite outcome."

"That's not going to happen."

"Lucy agrees with you. She thinks that we should wait for The Security Service to identify the leaders and then add them to our list."

"That's more like it."

"She says that Zafir's friend might be a part of an organisation that's bringing things together. It looks like we might be able to add him to the plan if he sticks around."

"It gets better and better."

Contemplating the implications of the existence of a secret organisation passes the time for Alex. His own efforts have already killed one of their henchmen, now it seems that he has more to do – classic mission creep.

With his mind occupied, Alex's next shift is soon upon him, and then the next, and onwards – time is on the move again, it will soon become a ground rush towards a time for action, and he knows it.

It is Tuesday morning. The sun is rising and already warming the clear blue sky. The shutters are up at the back of Henderson's Butchers and there are collections to be made, as well as the usual deliveries.

Mike had busied himself procuring enough insulin and syringes to resource the mission, it hadn't taken him long, as he had a well-established, friendly source, and no questions had been asked.

Similarly when it came to a base location; Eddie Henderson had stepped up. Eddie was in Mike's platoon for basic training; they were roommates and went on to 1 PARA together. Good with knives, but not so good at soldiering, Eddie failed SAS selection, became disheartened, and left the Paras to become a butcher. He was Mike's first port of call when he needed a place with a large freezer, which wouldn't become suspicious with a few vans out the back. Eddie's shop in Eccles is the perfect place.

Mike has recruited a courier for each of the regions with the help of the other handlers. His small delivery force is due to meet him at the butcher's over the course of the morning. Mike has brought nine large cool-bags, 180 small brown paper bags and 180 half-sized plastic sandwich boxes, the type that seal on each edge with a snapping clip. Eddie has offered up all the ice that Mike will need and given free access to his crusher.

Ronny is the first to arrive at 06:00 hours in his small, white, and nondescript Citroen van, destination - Birmingham East.

"Morning Ronny, you found it all right then?" Mike says as Ronny gets out of the van.

"Yeah, fine, I hope the drop-offs are as easy, I need to be in work for lunchtime."

"Won't be a problem, I've done you a route card, but don't leave it lying around now, will you?"

"'Course not."

"Have you changed the plates on the van?"

"'Course I 'ave. I ain't been out than long Mike; I'm still on the ball."

"I know Ronny, I know, I just want to be sure that we do this properly."

"Roger that."

"Come and give me a hand packing up."

The two men enter the back of the butcher's, turning immediately left into a large, bright cutting room. Mike's cool-bags are piled on top of a large stainless steel table in the centre of the room; he grabs one and pulls it out of its thin polythene wrapper, and opens it out so that it stands on the table as a self-supporting cuboid with the lid flapping down at the rear.

"Start filling those boxes with ice will you, please Ronny?" Mike says as he takes a large bag of ice cubes from an industrial sized chest freezer to his left and empties them into the top of the heavy-looking ice crusher, which rumbles into action automatically.

Mike opens the fridge to the left of the freezer and takes out a small, plain white cardboard box and places it on the table; he then grabs a handful of syringes in sterile sachets from a carrier bag on the sideboard and places them next to the small cardboard box on the table. Ronny has already put four sandwich boxes filled with crushed ice to the right of Mike's work-space.

Mike carefully opens the top flap of the cardboard box and rips it off, exposing the perfectly round and uniform, sterile sealed containers in their five neat rows of ten. He pinches the neck of the top left vial between his rough, worn forefinger and thumb, and extracts it from the box. "Now this is the fiddly bit." he says to Ronny.

The vials are vacuum sealed and the syringes are brand new, so will be stiff at best.

"The way to do it, I'm told, is to use a second needle to release the vacuum." Mike pushes a letting needle into the first virginal bung. He takes a syringe, removes it from its packing, then forces on a wide gauge drawing needle and pushes it in beside the first, using the body of the syringe to drive it through the rubber, being careful not to bend the fine strand of steel. Once inserted, he holds the vial and the business end of the syringe together in the palm of his right hand, and then pulls gently on the plunger until the liquid reaches the 10ml graticule marked on the syringe's cylindrical body. He pulls the needle free of the vial and then, with controlled force, he plucks off the drawing needle from the syringe and replaces it with a finer, sharper administering needle, still in its plastic sheath.

"Aren't you going to tap it and squeeze the air bubbles out?" Ronny asks, as Mike places the filled syringe into the first container of ice.

"No, I don't think that we need to worry about that." Mike says dismissively. "I told you it was fiddly; I might need your help with this."

Ronny quickly fills the remaining boxes with ice then begins to help Mike with the syringes.

Two bent needles, a broken vial, and half an hour later, the twentieth syringe is filled and packed. "My hands will be in tatters after a hundred or so of them,' says Mike.

"Tres Airborne." Ronny laughs, "Could you be any more of a fanny?" The men laugh together.

Mike scoops a thick layer of ice into the bottom of the cool-bag and presses it flat, then lays the boxes in rows of four, packing more ice around the edges as he completes each row, until all twenty boxes are tightly packed. Mike zips the lid closed and places a carrier bag with twenty small tubes of anaesthetic gel and twenty small brown paper bags on top of it. "Are you happy?"

"Yes Mike, I'll give you a bell if I can't find any of them." Ronny grabs the carrier bag, picks up the cool-bag and walks out to his van. A second van pulls into the parking area as he starts the engine. Mike smiles and waves Ronny off – *running like clockwork.*

Alex takes over watch at 09:00. "Zafir left the flat at 07:20 and came back at 07:28 with a small bag of shopping." Jez tells him. Alex keeps an eye on his operational mobile, keeping track of what is happening on the ground across the country - by his count there are currently eight 'target not seen' issues live; he will know the full picture by 15:00 today.

The seconds are trickling by, every minute feels like an hour. Alex checks the time; 10:05. Having looked out to the flat across the street for yet another hour, Alex feels his eyes are playing tricks on him. The mesh of the net curtains at Zafir's window seems alive with shadows and shimmers, *is it movement from within, or merely tricks of the light reflecting on the window?* He questions himself - the sun is rising in the sky behind him to the right, the shadows have long since dropped, making the bright daylight unbroken. Alex's eyes tingle - he realises that the movements he sees in the window are tricks of his own eyes, tiny flashes of tired nerves in his retinas giving everything an electric blue buzz, bringing everything to life - *I need a proper rest.*

At 10:12 he receives a message from Lucy: *"I'm getting some great information from the guys and from the networks, but I'm struggling to process it all, any chance of some support?"*

"Jez mate, err… issue."

"What's up Alex?" Jez says, rolling over on the bed having almost achieved a half doze.

"It's Lucy; she's having trouble keeping up with the amount of intelligence being generated, she needs help to get it to our people effectively – she wants me to go back to London to help her."

"Well there's not much you can do about it, I can't do without you here now, not with two targets. Maybe if I was a hundred percent, but I'm still not convinced I haven't got a stress fracture."

"I know. I wouldn't leave you with two targets… what if there was just one? Can we insert a decision point for me returning to London based on the second fella disappearing?" Jez thinks it through for a few seconds. Alex goes on, "I could take the majority of today's stag so you can get properly rested, then if he leaves before 17:00 there'll still be a meaningful amount of time for me to go back and help Lucy." Jez still looks as though he needs further convincing. "I can be a real force multiplier back in London; I can double the amount of real time intelligence getting to the guys on the ground, some of which might be vital for the operatives."

Jez scratches the thickening stubble on his right cheek firmly with all four fingers of his right hand, anchoring them with his thumb pressed onto the point of his chin. "Okay, we keep the option open until 17:00. If we're down to a lone target by then, you can go."

"Cool."

"But you're stagging on until then though – deal?"

"No worries." Though Alex had used the word 'stag' for guard duties and watches throughout his Army career, he has never received a definition for 'stagging on'. He figures it is something to do with the usually staggered pattern of over-lapping shifts, he likes the term - but hates stag. He hates it less now with his mind buzzing with thoughts of a clandestine organisation that may or may not be linked to his operation, and which may or may not be actively looking for him and possibly his Lucy. Alex has every faith in Lucy's ability to manage the intelligence for the mission; he has greater concerns for her safety, and greater concerns about seeing her again.

Alex can't put his phone down, with a steady trickle of recce reports coming in over the network. He tallies fourteen 'target not seen' cases once he's taken off the ones that have appeared since initial reports. The mobile traffic is so heavy, that at 13:22 hours he almost misses seeing the door to the flat across the street open - Zafir and his comrade depart, heading west. "Jez, they're leaving, both of them."

"Not carrying anything." Jez notes.

They turn left off Merville Road. "It looks like they might be heading to the Mosque." says Alex. As they disappear around the corner, Jez and Alex both receive messages on their operational mobiles. "*DLD made.*"

"DLD?" Alex asks.

"Dead letter drop. The insulin's been delivered, I'll go and pick it up - I might have a sly look down the road while I'm out."

The dead letter drop, or dead letterbox, is a covert method of passing messages or items which does not require two parties to meet. Mike has demanded drop points from all operatives and has then passed on the comprehensive list of locations and instructions to his drivers.

"Roger, be careful." Jez strips off his overalls and leaves immediately.

Alex watches Jez cross the street and glance past the end of Newland Road before continuing west towards Birmingham, and disappearing from view.

Alex suddenly finds himself feeling alone and isolated once more. He checks his phone, for comfort, more than for any real need. He stares at the end of Newland Road and waits.

Jez is back in the room inside six minutes, clasping a small brown paper bag, soaked in water and beginning to fall apart. "Ten millilitres of insulin and a tube of anaesthetic cream." Jez takes the cream out of the bag and places it on the bed, then scrapes the remains of the paper bag off the plastic container and discards it into a pouch in his duffel bag. He shakes the plastic container lightly; there are still small fragments of ice floating in the water and the syringe bobs amongst them within its casket. "It should be fine in there until tonight. The targets went beyond the Mosque, I saw them disappearing up the road. Any sign of them returning?"

"Not yet."

Alex receives a steady influx of intelligence messages from Lucy, as she copies him in to the updates that she sends out to the operatives for whom they are relevant. No news of the group that Zafir is linked to - maybe that is a good thing, maybe it isn't. He looks up from his phone - "Jez, they're back." It is 13:59. "Zafir and his mate have just come back around the corner of Newland Road and are heading back into the flat."

"So we've still got two." says Jez.

"For now." Alex holds out hope that this unknown character has come to Hodge Hill for a specific purpose, possibly a meeting that they may just have had. If Alex's assumptions and logic are correct, it shouldn't be too long before he bugs out.

14:10 and the flat door opens again. "Jez, the unknown fella is leaving."

"Is he carrying anything?"

"Only a small backpack."

"He's probably just popping out for a bit then."

Alex feels his own conscious bias at work, but considers that departure with a bag points towards him leaving for good. He takes time to strategise his argument.

"I've been thinking about the purpose of this bloke's visit to Zafir's place - I think he's been up from London to do something or meet someone on Zafir's behalf, I reckon that's why they went out for this afternoon, and now that's done I think he's headed home."

"Possibly." Jez responds. "Let's give it until 17:00 like we planned. If he's not back by then – you can go."

"Thanks Jez."

Jez smiles an acknowledgement then rolls back over onto the bed. Alex is now counting the seconds until 17:00; he's got two hours, forty-eight minutes and nineteen seconds before he gets to head back to Lucy.

Zafir goes out for thirty minutes during the afternoon, but there is nothing further to report from the flat. Alex checks train times and notes several intelligence updates sent by Lucy to operators in London – he messages her and Craig to let them know that he is highly likely to return to London that evening. The remaining time passes soon enough, and he is out of his boiler suit with his bag packed ready for 17:00 on the dot.

"Are you sure you can take him down on your own?" Alex asks, as Jez gets off the bed and occupies the stag position.

"Piece of cake. You go and help Lucy, I'll be fine."

24

Hard extraction

Alex boards the 17:30 train from Birmingham New Street after catching the bus from the service he's seen passing between the flats about seventy times over the past fifty hours. He makes himself comfortable in an empty double seat which backs onto the toilets, precluding anybody from gaining a view over his shoulder. His duffel bag on the seat next to him deters anyone from asking for the seat while it is not too busy – it won't hold up much defence if the train approaches its capacity, but will do for some respite in the meantime.

His phone has his undivided attention for the coming hour and a half; he starts catching up with the situation as it is being communicated to him through the digital medium. With Lucy's help and some good initiative, three of the 'targets not seen' have now been tracked to new locations - that brings the outstanding number to eleven, or 167 targets confirmed. The phone buzzes in Alex's hand with a new message: "*The unknown has returned – two targets stand.*"

Alex feels his heart shrink inside him, as he immediately feels the huge risk that he has put on Jez realised.

"*Do you want me to come back? I can get off at the Airport stop and get the next return train?*" he texts back.

"No, you get going on the intel, I'll deal with these two Charlies."

Alex imagines himself faced with the task that Jez now has before him - in Zafir's flat with two targets confronting him, in a dark, hostile environment laced with weapons, explosives and evil. He imagines being there in a weakened state - he physically clasps his arm, feeling Jez's pain. He has come to like Jez immensely, but is now seeing images in his mind of him defeated and in torturous pain, Alex is overcome with guilt and holds his face, and unable to hold back his emotions, he lets go with trembling tears. More than just not being there for Jez - the past week has been supremely stressful and things have come to a head. Alex's thoughts have become boxed off in his mind, stove piped and claustrophobic. Operating in isolation in his own head, he has had no release, not without Lucy there to share his concerns with. He has a moment of realisation that he needs to open his mind – the alternative is a downward spiral of personal turmoil and panic, leading to inevitable mistakes, oversights and poor judgement. He makes a conscious effort to strive for clarity of thought; he mentally grips himself and forces his mind to give him time and space to think.

He can feel people to his right looking at him; he brings himself back to normality, rubs his eyes and his face with his hands and then wipes his sleeve across his eyes and recomposes himself. He puts his mobile phone down for the next twenty minutes and gives himself a break. He thinks about his mum; *is she back from holiday yet? Maybe I'll go and see her once this is over; it'll be done and dusted tomorrow morning.*

Alex takes the Northern Line from Euston. As the tube pulls away from the platform, he books a cab to pick up from the Server Building before he losses phone signal. He exits Charing Cross station and decides to head east on foot and follow the Thames south a few hundred metres to approach the Server Building from an alternative direction. He feels this to be good counter surveillance, but knows in his heart of hearts that if anyone is following him or Lucy, he will have to try a whole lot harder. Craig's additional security is still in place and has been made aware that Alex will be on the scene again from this evening. As he takes a final look at the great river, he turns right onto Horse Guards Avenue and takes his phone from his pocket to message Lucy: *"Outside in two minutes."*

He slows his pace to a dawdle as he heads towards the stone arch entryway.

While he considers faking an incoming phone call to further delay his approach, a black cab swings round the corner and slaloms between the huge, perfectly carved pillars into the courtyard. Alex resumes normal walking speed and follows it up to the doors and gets in.

"Good evening." he says to the cabbie, "One more to come."

"Right you are, Sir."

Alex pulls his phone from his pocket to send Lucy an update that transport is waiting, but the big chrome and glass doors part and Lucy emerges, looking irresistible in her uniform; the neat feminine shirt and skirt combination giving unsubtle clues to the shapely body beneath. Alex smiles and sighs with delight, taking strength just from laying eyes on her.

He opens the cab door, takes her bag, and then takes hold of her in an awkward embrace, half twisted as they both sit back on the firm cab seats. They enjoy a slow, deep kiss and forget about the pressures of the mission and the conundrum of the Interest Group just for an instant.

"Er, where too?" The cabbie asks as politely as possible.

"Sorry mate, The Royal Court Hotel, and take the scenic route please – at least twice over the river."

"No problem."

They are already South of the river, having crossed Lambeth Bridge before they come up for air. Lucy straightens her uniform and they adjust to a more formal posture beside one another, smiling at each other as they receive a mildly embarrassed glance in the rear-view mirror from the driver. His attention is diverted by the roundabout at Elephant & Castle, which he loops around, turning onto the A3 South towards Clapham.

"Did you get anywhere with our group of friends?" Alex asks, doing his best to encode the subject matter.

"Yes, some friends have been working on our bin lorry driver and his bits and bobs – they've linked him to two of our group members."

"Shit." Alex says, taking a look forward to the cabby, who seems oblivious, "So that's a likely indirect link from him to my target then? What with the toys in his bath - this is starting to look well organised. Have they got any more out of him?" He further lowers his voice - "Future targets?"

"Not yet, but they'll be working on it, and our mission guys' findings have helped. They've also ID'd another two of the previously unknown chaps from our group. I collated their information and that of the six of the seven previously identified guys. I reckon we should put tabs on them all and try and pre-empt their next meeting and intercept it."

"Why just six?"

"Your friend from the flat in Birmingham's the seventh; I'm thinking he might not make the next meeting."

"Fair one."

"Now I don't suppose that their next meeting is scheduled for another week or so, looking at the dates of previous meetings, but with tonight's activities – this might trigger an extraordinary meeting, so we need to have over-watch of these guys in place by first thing tomorrow morning."

The cab turns right up Silverthorne Road, heading towards Battersea Power Station. "I'll get on to Craig; it sounds like a Committee level task."

"He might want to get the operatives who have not acquired targets onto it – they can be stood down from current targets now, get an evening's rest, then be good to go in the morning."

"Sounds good."

Lucy puts her arm around Alex and moves close to his ear, "It doesn't have to be the best blokes; all they need to do is keep eyes on and report movement. As soon as they all begin to move together – that's what will signal the meeting, then we only need to tail one or two of them to the meeting place and ensure that a capable strike force is ready to intercept them." she whispers, then kisses him on the cheek.

As the cab crosses back north of the river over Chelsea Bridge, Alex thinks about the clinical analysis and planning that Lucy has executed, and again finds himself feeling like a pawn in her game, rather than she being a partner in his. He is not sure that he likes it all that much, but she inspires him and gives him strength. He thinks back to an hour ago, when he was crying, alone on a train, like some sort of feeble little whelp – he is a changed person from then, and purely because of her.

The driver cuts right on to Ebury Bridge Road, a quiet street. Alex takes the opportunity to check for a tail, but there is no one obviously following them; he maintains watch until they pass Victoria Station.

"Is everything okay up at Hodge Hill?" Lucy asks.

"Not exactly - Jez messaged me once I was on the train, saying that the second target had returned."

"Oh shit, sorry."

"Not your fault. I'm a bit worried about him though, his arm is nowhere near one hundred percent – that is your fault."

"Cheers for that."

"I think the other guy will leave before tonight, but even if he doesn't, Jez is more than capable, and well prepared to get the job done on both of them. I would have probably just got in the way."

"Zafir's friend is one of the ones that we still have no information on, but it would be a bonus to have one less to worry about." says Lucy.

Alex begins to consider the final approach to the hotel as the cab rounds the one-way system. As they turn off onto Victoria Street, he instructs the cabbie; "Don't drop us outside mate, can you run us down Vandon Street and drop us by the sandwich shop at the end please?"

"No problem."

Lucy steps out onto the kerb as Alex pays the driver. As the cab pulls away, they cross the road behind it, meeting the end of the road as they reach the far side and continue round the corner onto the west end of Caxton Street, then cross diagonally to the right, over the road to the hotel façade. As they are greeted by the porter a young man wearing a hoodie puts his hand in his pocket. Alex eyes him with suspicion, but thinks nothing more of it.

The lift doors open on the third floor; Alex and Lucy step out onto the landing and turn right towards their room. Lucy opens the door for Alex, and as he enters he notices immediately that the bedroom window is smashed. He looks left – clear, and as he looks right his head is met with a solid bar – he is unconscious in an instant. Lucy screams, but is dragged into the room over Alex's limp body and hit on the back of the head as she stumbles forward – she too is out like a light.

"Alex, Alex, ALEX."

Alex slowly comes round, groggy and dis-orientated, he has no idea where he is, he can remember his own name, but doesn't recognise the man trying to wake him up. "Who are you? Where's Lucy? Is she okay?"

"I'm here Alex," says Lucy from behind the stranger, "I'm fine, are you all right?"

"What happened? Who are you?" He asks his apparent rescuer.

"I'm Shep, me and my colleague Elves have been watching out for Lucy. We headed you off here on your way back from the Server Building, we spotted the dicker out front, but didn't realise he was reporting to the two already up in the room until they smashed the window. By the time we got up here they'd dropped your stuff out."

"What happened to the two in the room?"

"They're taking a bath. Don't worry about them; we'll clean it up once you're safe." says Shep.

"Where's your mate? Elves?"

"He legged it back downstairs to try and catch up with the third guy and your stuff. I don't hold out much hope; he had a bit of a head start. Are you both okay? We don't need to get any medical help in do we?"

"A Paracetamol would go down a treat." says Alex.

"Ditto." says Lucy.

"Great, we can sort that out. What did they get off you?" Shep asks.

"I'm down my work laptop and my mission phone." says Lucy.

Alex looks around and takes a few seconds to recall what he'd had with him, "I'm down a mission phone, a laptop and my memory stick."

"Is that bad?" Shep asks.

"Only if they break the encryption. It'll take a pro-hacker, with a big enough computer, a month to crack the laptop with a brute-force attack; the pen drive could be done in a few days. The phone security is good enough to keep them off it overnight which is all we're worried about." says Alex.

"My work laptop is pretty much bullet-proof without the encryptor fob; luckily I keep that on my keys, which they didn't take. I'll probably get the sack for losing the asset though. I'll need to stop by the office to pick up another one for tonight, or else we'll be hamstrung."

"We will need replacement phones to get us through the night, they're basic handsets that I can get at the nearest phone shop, the software can be downloaded easily enough, and I backed up my app data to a secure server.

"On the bright side, them thinking that they've got the list might speed-up the time lines for the next meeting of our mysterious group." Lucy says to Alex. They all pause for thought, Lucy and Alex thinking through the configuration management implications of what has just happened, and Shep wondering what they are both talking about.

There is a knock at the door; the three of them look at one another. "That'll be Elves." Shep says, as he stands up and looks through the peep-hole, "It's Elves." he confirms, and then opens the door to let him in.

"No luck, he was gone before I got down there."

"Not so quick on your feet these days are you old man?" Shep says with an evil looking grin.

"Fuck you dip-shit… Sorry Lucy."

Elves is a big man, but no slouch and certainly no fatty – he has 'Rugby Union number eight' written all over him – meaty, sturdy, powerful. "Have you contacted hotel security about the window yet?" he asks.

"No." Shep answers.

Elves crosses the room and picks up the phone on the bedside table and dials reception. "Hello, I'm afraid we've had a little accident in room 311 – I tripped over the corner of my bed and put my briefcase through the window, I'm terribly sorry. All the glass went outwards, so there's no mess up here, but if I could ask you to send someone to fix it after nine o'clock this evening please? My wife and I are getting ready for an evening out at the moment and don't wish to be disturbed just now… thank you." He replaces the handset. "Job done."

Alex assesses Elves and Shep as both very switched on, a trait that has been common to almost all of the handlers and operatives that he has met, but Elves particularly so; he seems to be analysing the room and the way the situation has played out in a strategic context.

"This raid, it was a bit of a strange tactic;" Elves says, "knocking out the window, dropping the loot, using a split team – it scuppered our interception big-style - very clever."

"They're learning." says Alex.

"How so?" says Elves - who seems not to have been given the full detail on the mission history.

"Both contacts we've had with them so far have resulted in them taking losses through underestimating us, John came from nowhere and took down two of them first time, and we ambushed them on the way to finding Lucy the second time.

"Lucy took down her guard and escaped, but I reckon that they'll assume that she was rescued judging by Lucy's aggressive handiwork. So they seem to have developed this clever little manoeuvre to avoid any cavalry that we might have on standby. To be fair – it worked a treat.

"Get these two out of here. I'll prep our friends in the bathroom and wait for the clean-up support." Elves says to Shep.

Shep turns to Alex and Lucy; "You heard the man, let's go."

"Where to?"

"Craig's."

25

Hard day's night

The journey to Craig's is not straight forward; full counter-surveillance is observed. They exit the hotel via the stairs and a service exit that links the kitchen entrance-way to the back of the underground car park - there is a white transit van waiting. The driver gets out as they approach; Shep liaises; "Evening Mitch, all quiet?"

"Aye Shep, all clear, no-one down here but me, the street's clear a hundred yards either way of any potential suspects."

"Thanks Mitch, good work."

"I'll follow you to the destination and keep the tail covered off."

"Roger, we've got a couple of stops to make." Shep gives Mitch the details, "We'll see you at Craig's." Shep guides Alex and Lucy into the back of the van through the already open sliding door, "Sorry it's not more comfortable, but it's safer this way."

"No problem." says Lucy, Alex just smiles. They get in and make themselves comfortable. Alex scopes the decor of the van, he finds the equipment levels reminiscent of the van they used to find Lucy – it's possibly the same vehicle.

Fully kitted up with IT again, and as sure as can be that they are not being followed, Alex and Lucy arrive at Craig's place. The big man greets them at the door in full night-ops black rig. "Alex, Lucy, you pair of heroes. Are you okay?" Craig reaches out and grabs them in one big bear-hug, one under each arm. Alex begins to answer, but Craig is in full welcoming-mode. He turns them on the spot and walks them up his garden path, "Come in. Let's have a nice cup of tea, before things start getting any more exciting.

The group crowd into the dining room. "Mitch - get the kettle on will you please, pal."

"No worries, what's everyone having?" Mitch gets the brews on while everyone else gets comfortable.

Craig completes his welcome; "So this is my gaff, treat it as your own 'mi casa, su casa' as they say. I recommend you set up in the sitting room, the broadband is strongest in there and the sofas are lush. Are you back in comms yet?"

"In and working, but not had a chance to catch up with the message stream yet." Alex gestures towards his new phone.

Craig gives them his perspective on the current operational situation; "It's all going off... in a good way – a few intel feed-backs, a few concerns... nothing the handlers can't manage."

"We'll be back in the game in seconds few, I just need to plug in." Lucy waves her new laptop under Craig's nose and slips past him into the sitting room.

"There's no stopping her, I'm glad she's on our side." says Craig.

"You're not wrong." says Alex, giving a slight shake of his head. "Any news from the hotel? Did Elves get everything sorted out?"

"All done." said Shep, "The other team arrived as we left and had it all cleaned up by the time we were done at the Server Building."

"That's great, thanks Shep." says Alex, "What are your plans for the rest of the night Craig?"

"I've had as much kip as I could fit in this afternoon, I want to be on top form for the blokes during the night – I'll be helping on one of the quick reaction force wagons with Mitch. Hopefully I'll still have plenty in the tank and we can get after these Interest Group Charlies from tomorrow. I've got ten blokes on standby, mostly in and around London, you just say the word and I'll have them stood up."

"As soon as we've got good information on the subjects; we'll start sending out target packs. Have these operatives of yours got secure comms?" Alex asks.

"Yes, they're all existing mission men." Craig says firmly, maintaining a stern expression, "We won't be taking our eye off the ball tonight, but your main effort has to switch to that group once the primary job is done Alex, got it?"

"Roger that," he replies with a solemn nod. "Those bastards have had two goes at me and two goes at Lucy; they're going down."

"Damn right." Craig picks up his freshly filled thermal mug and a weighty looking shoulder bag, "We'll drop Shep off with Elves – remember there are four teams out and about in London if you or any of the operators need us. The other handlers have similar arrangements in their respective areas outside of London too. See you on the other side."

"Good luck." He shakes Craig's hand and gives Mitch a firm pat on the shoulder as they file out to the van.

Alex grabs the two remaining brews from the kitchen sideboard and joins Lucy on the sofa. "Are you in the shit for the lost laptop?"

Lucy glares back at him. "Well I couldn't exactly tell them the full circumstances, could I?"

"Not really... I suppose." Alex says sheepishly.

"Carol will cover for me as much as she can, but it'd be a real bonus if we could recover it when we catch up with these cretins."

"Fingers crossed we get the chance eh?" Alex can't help but laugh at the practical points being applied to a potential mass killing. "Are you in?" He asks looking at the opening windows on her laptop screen.

"Yes, I've had an email from Agent Thew, it looks like she's identified another of our Interest Group unknowns - it's your boy visiting Hodge Hill, identified as one 'Amin Sareedi' - a HUMINT report indicates that he's a money man, or money courier at least." HUMINT – human intelligence, or intelligence which is procured from agents, actors, or simply gleaned from members of the knowing, or unknowing public. She goes on: "The bag he took to Birmingham was probably a large quantity of currency."

"What's Zafir doing with a stack of cash and that much plastic explosive?"

"Nothing if he's brown bread." says Lucy.

"What's this Agent Thew like, can we work with her?"

"Charlie? She's on the ball - from what I've heard from her, she has a similar take on the terrorist front as us – would ideally like to get them convicted and put away for life, but understands that it's not going to happen until after they've murdered a good few people first."

"So you think she'll cooperate?"

"She is so far, not that I've told her that we plan on sending Craig and the boys in."

"What are the implications for Jez, as far as Amin is concerned?"

"That depends on a couple of things; firstly does the Interest Group know that Zafir is on our list? They can't be certain, but if they are – will they plan to warn him, or Amin? The other key consideration is, do they know the planned date-time of our strike? Even if they do plan to warn either or both of them, if they don't know when, then there's not much they can do, other than put them on a heightened level of vigilance."

"They haven't learned anything new from tonight, other than I'm back in London. What would they infer from that?"

"I don't want to make you feel bad, but I think they were waiting for you. It was fairly clear where I was - I suspected that they have been watching me, but they struck as soon as you were on the scene."

"I, I put you in danger again, I'm so sorry."

"Don't worry, I'm up for this, I've judged the level of risk for myself – it's worth it. You're worth it." Lucy slides her laptop onto the arm of the sofa and wraps her arms around Alex's torso, then drags herself on top of him and smothers him with a deep, hard kiss. "Let's not get carried away, we've got work to do." she says, releasing him and getting straight back to her computer.

"So would my appearance and the receipt of our phones and laptops be enough to stimulate any kind of action that we might pick up on?"

"Impromptu meeting? Possibly."

"What's the earliest they're likely to get that organised for?"

"It could be as early as tomorrow morning; it depends on what urgency they place on it. Tonight would probably be a bit of an ask - assuming that they all have lives, and aren't putting themselves on hold for just such a development."

"No, I don't buy it. I think they'll bide their time, if they don't have an immediate crack on the list, and they don't know our mission timeline." says Alex.

"A more immediate trigger might be when they begin receiving reports of their people dropping – assuming that their people are on our list." says Lucy.

"Well Zafir's on there for a start."

Lucy runs through the scenarios of tracking the group members in her head. "Even if we get Charlie Thew in bed with us, I'd still say that we should put our own watch on the group members from right now."

"Okay, I'll message Craig and get him to stand up some of the 'operatives without portfolio' straight away. How many do we need?"

"Eight."

"Have you got targets packs for them ready to go?"

"I have, but they're fairly thin - enough for what we need though; names, addresses and photos for each at least."

"Cool. You need to be putting some time in with Agent Thew, making sure that she's as tuned in with us as we can get her."

"Roger. How are the phones looking?"

"Steady, the handlers seem to have it covered from their ends, there's nothing much coming out of the targets now that the sun's gone down; the only issue I expect to cause us any drama now is this group."

"Hi is that Charlie Thew?"

"Yes, who's this?"

"My name's Lucy Butler, I'm British Army Intelligence, working out of Whitehall. We've had a few messages over the past twenty-four hours. I wondered if we might be able to help each other a little more than we are at the moment."

"Thanks for what you've sent me so far, it's been a big help. Can I ask - what's the nature of your interest in my work? I'm guessing it's not something that we can discuss in detail on this line?"

"Correct. I just thought I'd drop you a line in person as a courtesy."

"To sound me out?"

"If you like. The mission we're running is a little unorthodox, it involves cutting a few official corners to get results, I just wanted to see if that would be the kind of thing that you might get on board with." Lucy imagines Agent Thew's thought processes and knows that she will be extremely cautious.

"Of course not, I'm a consummate professional." she replies.

Lucy reads between the lines and proceeds with political diligence: "I'm sure that you are, as am I." The line goes quiet. Lucy needs to convey urgency, but knows that she cannot offer up too much information - Agent Thew might well be open to cutting some corners, but there is certainly no time to cultivate her into the mission and Lucy knows it. "I have systems in place that could bring your current investigation to a neat and timely conclusion. Are you interested in hearing about it? We're ultimately on the same side." The silence from the other end of the line continues for a few brief seconds.

"Are you in town?" Agent Thew answers eventually.

"London?"

"Ya-ha."

"Yes."

"Meet me, tonight, I'll send you the details." Agent Thew hangs up without giving Lucy a chance to respond.

Alex has been close enough to hear both ends of the conversation. "Interesting." he says.

"It's a hell of an opportunity, I wonder where she is."

Within thirty seconds of Charlie terminating the call, Lucy receives an email to her Skynet work address;

"*2200hrs, The Huntsman, Upper Richmond Rd, Putney, SW15 6TD*"

Lucy points the laptop screen in Alex's direction. He reads it, and then looks at the time on his phone screen, "That's less than three quarters of an hour from now."

"Can you do without me for an hour?" she asks.

"Craig said not to take our eye off the ball tonight, but we can't turn it down really - can we?"

"Like you said – the phones are quiet, and probably will be now until the confirmation reports start coming in."

Alex thinks for a moment - *we need to take these Charlies down.* "Go for it."

Lucy hands Alex the laptop as she stands to gather what she will need for her short-notice expedition.

Alone without Lucy, Alex only has his fears for company. His remaining qualms, regarding the mission's ethicacy, are back in the forefront of his mind and are now magnified by the immediacy of H-Hour. His only distraction from them now is his phone, which has fallen quiet. He busies himself by checking and re-checking the handset for messages, but there is nothing happening - the calm before the storm.

He looks around Craig's living room, it's homely and comfortable, almost like that of an elderly couple's home, not the kind of environment that he would have imagined a man like Craig would have surrounded himself with. He considers that this comfortable environment is what Craig would claim to be defending, but then in what circumstance could anyone put it at risk? *That's not the point,* he tells himself – *the point is having the right to freedom to relax wherever you might be; there should be no fear of walking on any street or visiting any place.*

There is a tapping at the front door, Alex opens it to let Lucy back in. Once more she brings his world back to life.

"How was Agent Thew?"

"Good actually, she's really grateful for the updates on Amin's movements." Lucy seems buoyed after spending time with someone of her own ilk. "She'd really appreciate any other intelligence we might provide if we are able to surveil other members of the Interest Group."

"I bet she would."

"In return she'll keep us in the loop with developments in the identification of the as-yet unidentified members."

"Well you can let her know that Amin is back at Zafir's flat. Did you tell her how important it is to us that we get an early warning on any of them mobilising?"

"No."

"No?" Alex replies, somewhat shocked and disappointed.

"No. She's on side, but not to the point where if we take action against the group, she'll stand by and say nothing. We need to maintain plausible deniability. The neutralisation of the group needs to appear as much of a shock to us as it will be to her. We need a plan to make the attack on the group look like some kind of gang dispute."

"I see." This gives Alex something else to think about other than the mission in hand, another distraction.

"She's not got the resources to track any of the group effectively yet, and as we're getting boots on the ground – I figured that our request for this help has become redundant.

"You're right. I'm guessing that Craig has his blokes in place by now too."

Lucy ignores his rhetorical statement. "Charlie's going to send me over a couple of new pieces of information – I'll add that to the relevant packs and fire updates to the operatives and the big man."

02:00 and something in the region of 160 operatives across the UK mainland are beginning to think about their preliminary moves in full and final detail. Six of them are already held up inside the abodes of their targets, lying under beds, concealed inside disused cupboards, but most are eyeing up the target sites from their stakeouts or hide locations.

Jez is taking his time, still watching through the nasty, decaying net curtains and across the deserted street to the seemingly lifeless flat. Resigned to the fact that he has two targets to face, he has mixed emotions on this count – it may be double the risk to him as an injured operative, but it comes with the potential for double the satisfaction of removing twice the threat. His savouring of this prospect is not entirely founded on patriotism - his innate desire to administer violence, to experience the thrill of action, spurs him on.

He stands from his over-watch position and meanders over to his duffel bag. He takes a knee beside it and sifts its contents, pulling out a litre bottle of paint thinner, a lighter, a glass bottle containing two hundred millilitres of sulphuric acid, and a shallow curved glass bowl big enough to submerge his phone in, but small enough to fit in his right map pocket. He re-checks that the lighter works and has plenty of fuel in its body, then stows it in his chest pocket. He searches the rear left trouser pocket of his suit for his lock-picking tools, he checks the wire is serviceable, no weak points, not about to snap at the first swipe of the lock barrel. Finally he takes the syringe from its box and gently slips it into his left map pocket with the tube of gel.

Jez stands upright, turns back to face the window and then closes his eyes. His mind walks the route to the flat, practices each step of his mission, picking the lock, counting to miss the creaking steps, retrieving the secondary weapon, everything that he has mentally made note of. He war-games through the required actions of this coming hour until he gets to the injection. Jez breaks a sudden cold sweat - *have I got enough insulin for two targets?* He thinks back to Craig's orders as given some five and a half days ago, and tries to imagine the words as spoken by Mike: "Y*ou'll be issued ten millilitres, five should be plenty.*" He is sure those were the exact words. '*Five should be plenty' – is that good enough, what if they both just wake up the next morning feeling a bit sick?* This is not good enough for Jez, *secondary weapon it will be for Amin.*

Lucy picks up her phone to read an update from one of the East London operatives: "*Gained entry to target accommodation, target not present.*"

"Some of these guys aren't the best at surveillance, are they?" Lucy says to Alex as he picks up his phone to read the same message.

"School-boy." Alex says mockingly, then sends a reply to the operative and copies in Mark, who happens to be his handler; "*When was last confirmed sighting?*" It takes a few moments to get a response.

"*Last seen through the curtains at 23:56hrs. Curtains closed, downstairs lights went out, and then upstairs lights went out at 00:12hrs. No lights or movement since.*"

"That doesn't sound like a careless oversight." Alex remarks.

"Fair enough." Lucy acknowledges, "Where'd he go then?" Alex has no answer.

The first confirmation report arrives at 02:08 from Greater Manchester – the operation has not gone to plan: *"Target woke on entering the room, terminated with cosh, clear of location, out."* - 'Out' - the military voice procedure pro-word that is so definite – I've finished talking to you and I don't expect a reply. That particular operative's work is done and he is on his way. His plan has not gone as expected, but his contingency plan has taken effect and the end-state is almost as desired.

"One down." says a downbeat Alex.

"Are you not happy with that?" Lucy asks.

"In terms of the bigger picture, I suppose I am, but it's a life at the end of the day isn't it?"

"Opportunity cost, Alex, how many lives will we save?"

"I know."

Jez sits in his overview position for the last time. He grasps his right upper arm where Lucy struck him and massages his fleshy tricep hard, pushing it around the weakened humerus until it meets with his bicep and then squelches fluidly back past the bone. Even through the thick material of his boiler suit he can feel the toned, but relaxed muscle strands as they slip back between his thumb and the aching bone of his upper arm. All manner of thoughts go through his mind, from the mission in hand, how his injury might affect his performance, to what he might do tomorrow. He gets to his feet, picks up the bottle of accelerant and his duffel bag, and makes his way to the door. As the clock ticks over 03:00, he takes one last look back into the stakeout flat that has served him well over the past couple of days, he leaves it without a trace of his presence, pulling the door closed behind him.

He can feel his excitement and apprehension build as he walks down the stairs; he takes several slow calming breaths as he exits the rear of the building. He places the duffel bag on the ground at the back of his van as he quietly opens one of the back doors. He puts the bag in the van and slips the paint thinner carefully into his left map pocket, ensuring that the syringe is pushed safely against the front seam. A pause, a few more deep breaths, and Jez walks left out onto Shetland Road, taking his time to scope out any presence on the main road – all is quiet. He continues across the dimly lit street, no need to keep to the shadows; with only twenty metres to travel, Jez feels less conspicuous following a natural line down the centre of the pavement towards the flat door. He arrives to face its worn flaky red surface and places his gloved hands on it, as though in a standing press-up position. He takes a moment, and as he feels a sense of gravity pulling him towards the door, he meditates against it, pressing his baseball cap brim awkwardly up against it, seemingly trying to connect with it, asking it to give up the secrets of what might lay in wait for him behind its patchwork of melded planks.

He takes a confirmatory glance up and down the street, then over-emphasises a scoop of his rear left trouser pocket to make sure that he gathers both elements of his lock-picking kit together in his gloved fingers. He prepares himself for a battle with the barrel and sets to work. Click, click, click in quick succession, click, another few seconds, click. *The door is teasing me surely, how long for the last one?* Click, he's in – in less than ten seconds. It's so easy that he nearly forgets himself - he must be silent.

The door closes - Jez pauses at the bottom step to get into a battle-winning frame of mind; he mentally switches off his sense of personal restraint and prepares himself to do what is necessary and to allow his night vision to optimise – no torches tonight. The right corner of his top lip and right side of his nose give the slightest of twitches – his game face is on, he is ready.

Sixty-five confirmation reports in, the mission is progressing smoothly so far. Quick reaction teams have only deployed twice across all regions. "It's going well." Alex ventures.

"We won't hear of any horror stories or failures until the dust settles I shouldn't think." Lucy says without looking up from the laptop screen. Alex makes no come-back, just hopes that there won't be any. Their phones buzz: "*Target not present - disappeared from flat, no rear exit???!*"

"That's two of them." says Lucy.

"The first one was East London, where's this one?"

"Leicester."

"Does it mean anything? Could it just be clumsy operatives?"

Lucy shrugs. "As long as it's only two."

The phones buzz in tandem again – a positive confirmation, followed by another, and another. The phones are like popcorn once critical temperature is reached, the reports keep coming, all positive confirmations. The pair aren't sure whether to be openly gleeful or remain constrained at the prolific loss of life. Alex catches Lucy letting out a vindictive grin as another report is received, "Are you enjoying this?" he asks her.

"Not enjoying it... relishing it. I'd contend that we won't get to do this much good again in our entire careers." The phones buzz again, Lucy reaches for the handset with a more relaxed smile on her face in anticipation, "Uhhh?"

"Put a news channel on. We've lost one – ONE13." comes the message from Blakey, the East region handler.

Alex grapples for the remote control and turns on the television and switches to a news channel, a bulletin is already in progress;

"Firefighters are unsure of what caused the explosion at a house in the Chapeltown area of Leeds, but they confirm that at least one, yet to be identified person, has lost their life."

Alex makes a voice call; "Blakey, what happened?"

"Alex? Fucking hell mate, we can't be sure. Neil had messaged in to say that he was inside the property, but that he couldn't locate the target – he'd just gone, just disappeared. We were about ten miles off him, so headed in his direction, but by the time we got there, there were blue lights everywhere, half the house is gone and the place is on fire, it's like a war zone."

"Fuck." Alex is truly lost for any words of substance or value - the contingency planning had not gone this far.

"What am I going to tell Jill?" says Blakey, with tears in his voice.

"Blakey, don't think about that now. You've still got blokes out there, they might need you. We can't take our eyes off the ball tonight, we need to get the job done, get it seen through, okay."

"Roger, out." and Blakey is gone.

"We're becoming quite the military leader aren't we?" says Lucy without a hint of mockery or sarcasm. Alex takes solace from the compliment, but his mind rests on the thought of 'Jill'.

Having taken the bottle of thinners from his pocket to avoid any unwanted crackling, Jez climbs the stairs missing steps three and eight. He hears noisy breathing as he reaches the top. He places the bottle on the carpet by the doorway to his left as he enters. He surveys the room; the bed is occupied, but a second body is not obviously present, though there are sheets on the floor at the foot of the bed. Amin is a noisy sleeper and is lying on the mattress at the distant end of the room from Jez, but is no more than three metres away from him.

Jez peers into the open bathroom door – empty. He opens the kitchen door with a swift movement, knowing that this will reduce the noise made, knowing that there is nothing hanging on the back of it that might clatter or jangle - *time spent on a recce is never wasted,* one of his favourite military catchphrases. The only thing that it might have hit would have been Zafir if he was to have been there, but the kitchen is as it was during the recce – empty.

Jez experiences a mixture of emotions, some relief that he only has a single target to tackle, some disappointment, that he only has a single target to tackle, but mostly irritation at himself for having lost his primary target – *how is that even possible? I didn't take my eyes off that door.* He takes his phone from his right trouser pocket, it is set to silent - he sees a missed message from Lucy: *"Beware booby-traps, some targets have avoided detection and disappeared – be vigilant."*

Jez looks about him, checking for any subtle changes, *if any target location is going to be booby-trapped, it's this one.* He is somewhat consoled by the fact that he has already conducted a search of the property and knows about one improvised explosive device and a huge mass of plastic explosive. He sends an update to John: *"Primary target not in location, secondary present, about to proceed."* He places his phone back in his pocket, steps into the kitchen and grasps the cutlery drawer handle gently. He pulls it slowly until he is able to see the black handles of the sharp knives in the left-hand section of the drawer and then stops. The biggest knife rests on top of the others; he pinches the end of its handle between his left thumb and fore-finger, and pulls it out carefully. He leaves the drawer open, seeing no benefit, and only risk, in trying to close it. He inspects the knife at close quarters; good quality, heavy, expensive – it looks almost new, or at least not well used. Jez feels the tacky friction between the rubber of his glove and the course, black handle, a rough heavy plastic resin that feels like coal. The blade is matt grey, and so thick that it has vents shaped into it. The triangle of perfectly shaped steel reminds him of a shark's fin.

He removes the anaesthetic gel and syringe from his left map pocket and slides the knife in their place while he prepares himself. He removes the sheath from the needle of the syringe and puts it in his pocket, then places the syringe, needle-up, in his chest pocket. He removes the cap from the gel, and holds the tube by the centre of its mass firmly in his left hand. He draws the knife from his map pocket with an over-hand grip with his right hand. He stares through to the bedroom, his eyes transfixed on the end of the bed where his awaiting victim lies just out of sight. Everything is ready; he takes a long deep breath and raises the knife aloft into its emergency standby position.

The influx of reports has begun to show that insulin administration is not simple, and many kills are being made by secondary weapons. Jez's update arrives between confirmation reports eighty-seven and eighty-eight.

"Another one gone missing." Alex says.

"Zafir… fuck." says Lucy.

"You don't think that the other Interest Group members will be moving too do you?" Alex asks.

Lucy thinks for a second. "Unless they're heading for a meeting right now – I'd doubt it. If they are on to the fact that our mission is executing tonight; I'd say that they would want to move anyone that they want to save who has a criminal record or who they know is being watched for whatever reason."

"But if Zafir was warned and he did know that we were coming for him, then are they deliberately sacrificing Amin?" he asks.

"That's cold." says Lucy.

"It's consistent with what they told me in my flat. They want us to succeed to some level. They're just saving the ones that are strategically important to them by the looks of it."

"Zafir would certainly fit into that category – an experienced and skilled bomb-maker."

"Get hold of Craig and let him know - we need to be sure that those operatives are in place now, and are aware that targets are escaping – we don't want them slipping off the radar."

"Roger. I'll warn Charlie too." says Lucy.

"No. The last thing we need is added Security Service attention if we're going in after them. You said that she didn't have the means to have them properly monitored, so let's just keep that covered off ourselves – there's not much more that she can do for us now."

Jez treads every pace around to the far side of the bed with the grace, precision and silence of a ballerina. As he moves alongside his target he is nervous of every grunt and snore that Amin makes, but the noises have a simultaneously contradictory effect, as Jez feels assured that Amin is fast asleep.

Fortunately for Jez it is warm in the flat, so Amin is not snuggled up tight under the covers. He lies flat on his back with the duvet pushed down past his chest, he wears a thin white vest, which has been pulled tight over his shoulders by his movements in the night. His thin but muscular arms appear remarkably luminescent for an Asian man; Jez recognises this as a trick of the ambient light, which his eyes have adjusted to perfectly.

Jez slowly turns to face his victim; he stands level with his chest, inches away from Zafir's bedside table and drops onto his left knee. Jez's injured right arm is feeling heavy after just a few moments of holding the knife in the attack position; he allows the arm to bend so that the inside of his clenched right hand rests on the side of his head, the blade sticking out over his target like some kind of metallic antenna.

He gives the tube of anaesthetic the slightest of squeezes until he can see the glistening of the clear gel emerging from the mouth of the tube. He places a generous blob of gel onto Amin's neck, where he can see the bulge of a vein amongst the thick growth of beardy stubble - Amin does not move. Jez identifies several other ripe target areas on Amin's arms and left deltoid and applies pea-sized spots of gel to each location. He moves out of the way swiftly, as Amin swats with his right hand at his left arm. Jez realises that he must have caught a sensitive area on the inside of Amin's left elbow. He pauses for a few seconds to make sure that he has not disturbed Amin's slumber.

The gel on the inside of the left elbow has been wiped clear, and the rapid movement of his upper body has made most of the spots of gel slide to varying degrees, dependant on their distance from the right arm and the angle of gradient of the skin to which they had been administered. The spot of gel that was on the left deltoid, which was Jez's favoured site, has slipped off completely and is now numbing a small patch of bedsheet under Amin's shoulder. Jez has five minutes to decide which is his second favourite site - *the neck is the best blob and will be properly numb, but it'll be tricky to inject without pushing into his windpipe. The back of the left hand is okay, but it's not fleshy enough to inject ten millilitres quickly. A bit pissed off about the deltoid, no use trying again; the surface is wet now, it won't stick. Could try the other shoulder, but that means moving around the other side, that means more risk. Fuck it – in the neck.*

As Jez looks from one gradually melting blob of gel to another, his gaze moves to Amin's face, whose eyes are open. It takes as long for him to register this as it takes Amin to respond to an intruder at his bedside.

Jez eventually lunges downwards with the knife, aiming directly for Amin's chest, pushing his weight forward, anticipating some sort of reaction from his target. Amin rolls towards Jez, but instead of trying to push him away he flings his right arm around the back of Jez's legs and pulls Jez over the top of him. Jez is immediately over-balanced, he over-shoots his target, and sees the blade scuff past Amin's back. Jez is catapulted over Amin, and is now focusing on the rapidly approaching far side of the bed. He manages to tuck his head underneath himself to begin a combat roll off into the open bathroom door, but he runs out of bed too soon. His neck hits the mattress, but his shoulders slide off it and his right leg slams into the bathroom doorframe with a smash, and he falls awkwardly into the gap between the bed and the wall, with his left leg ending up in the bathroom. There is instantly a pungent smell in the room, and through the adrenalin Jez feels a searing pain in his right leg.

In the split second that it takes for Jez to deduce what has happened to the bottle of acid in his map pocket, Amin grabs the large, heavy engineers' lamp from the desk table and launches it at him, it smashes against the back of his head and takes his focus. Jez is lucky that Amin is out of effective ammunition and does not have the confidence to attack him unarmed. Instead he turns again to the desk – Jez knows that there isn't anything more dangerous there than a scalpel, but Amin opts for the sturdier soldering iron.

Jez gets to his feet and turns to face his enemy. Unable to put weight on his right leg, he steadies himself and decides to wait for Amin to come to him, doing his best to mask his debilitation. Amin yanks the electrical cord free from the plug socket, raises the iron over his head and charges at Jez, leaping up onto the bed and diving towards him. Jez thrusts his blade forward, Amin's left wrist partially defends the blow, but guides the knife inwards – it enters Amin's neck on his left side, and begins to take its own direction, following the path of least resistance – following the softest path, steered inwards by the clavicle, down into the lung; it creates a significant wound, slicing through the muscles, tendons, blood vessels, lung and a catching the pulmonary artery. Simultaneously, Jez fails to defend against the soldering iron, having focussed on his weakened attacking right arm. Amin's weapon of choice plunges into the top of Jez's left deltoid, inflicting a wound that further incapacitates Jez, making his badly bruised right arm now his strongest. The men's bodies come together, arms entangle, and Jez lets his melting right leg fall away. He pivots round on his left, and uses his remaining strength to steer Amin through the doorway and towards the bath.

Amin slams into the side of the bath unit, landing high on the plastic trim. The impact smashes the right end of the facia into the space under the tub, the left hand end is conversely pushed out – even in the darker room and darker space within it, Jez can see that the plastic explosive is no longer where it was during the recce. Amin comes to rest with his shoulders almost underneath the rim of bath, the knife still sticking out and upwards from his neck. Jez tries for a second time to get to his feet, and makes it half way up, but feels a comprehensive weakness envelop him. He can feel blood streaming out of his leg, while he knows that this is likely the source of his weakness, he is elated by it, as it provides a cooling function to the burning of the acid. The veil of weakness thickens, and Jez collapses back to the floor, slumping back against the inside of the bathroom door frame, in touching distance of his adversary.

Jez feels defeated as he looks across to his nemesis; Amin has plenty of life left in his eyes and pushes with both hands and shuffles himself out the few inches he needs to free himself from under the edge of the bath tub. He straightens his back, wincing as the blade prevents its sheath of flesh from moving around it, catching new nerves, igniting fresh waves of pain. Amin slowly raises his right hand and takes hold of the handle of the knife, all the time with his eyes locked on Jez. He gains strength from observing his attacker in such a sorry condition. He grimaces and braces himself, then yanks the blade free in a single clean movement. Blood instantly spurts from the wound like a garden hose, jetting over the wall to his left, splashing all over his body and legs.

Jez flinches as some of Amin's blood splatters on his face; his attention then turns to the knife once more. Amin still has it firmly in his grasp and is supporting his weight on the closed fist that clasps its handle. Amin leans forward and begins to raise it into the air, but he makes little progress – as the pace of the blood ejecting itself from his body slows, the knife drops to the floor and Amin slumps back onto the bath.

"We're almost there." says Alex, as the 155th confirmation report is received. "Ten targets not found, eight disappeared - that leaves six operators yet to report in."

"Which includes Jez and his additional target." says Lucy with a searching look to Alex, trying to detect any hints of concern from him and sees it is all over his face.

"He'll be fine." he says unconvincingly, "When we did the recce he was telling me that he liked to leave it until late." The phones buzz again – another confirmation report, but alas not from Jez. "Five more."

"What we've achieved is actually amazingly good, considering we've apparently been compromised." says Lucy, "We've had a much higher yield than I would have expected, even if things had gone exactly to plan. And when I say 'we've', I mean 'you've' - you've done this Alex, you've made it happen."

"I'm still not so sure that it's something to be proud of."

"Of course it is. We just need to make sure that we take down this Interest Group and minimise any fall out from it."

"So what do we think about these 'disappearances'? Should we be worried that this group might be stronger than we thought? That they know more than we initially thought?"

"Maybe." Lucy looks back at her laptop screen; she doesn't have a real answer immediately. She quickly realises that she needs to give Alex a more professional response, both for her own sense of professional pride, and to keep Alex's morale up, so she makes her full analysis as positive as she can, while still keeping it in the realms of reality; "Their organisation seems well connected, they have good intel on us, but they are operationally stupid. They demonstrate limited ability to learn from the first three encounters with us, but not enough to prevent sustaining two casualties. I'm confident that they will not have learned enough to prevent us from intercepting their next meeting, recovering our assets, and neutralising their actors."

Alex smiles in appreciation of Lucy's improved response.

Jez and Amin lay in silence in the dark, the acrid smell of burning flesh hanging thick in the air, not that this is high on the list of concerns of either man. The two of them make eye contact; Jez manages to raise a snarl of hatred in Amin's direction. Amin replies with a stern, but equally hate-filled leer. "You have failed my friend." Amin says in the quietest of voices, which takes significant effort.

"My job's done fella, you are ended – I'll die happy."

"Really my friend? I am but a pawn in this game, you came for a bigger fish… and besides, even in this state - I can see that you are shaking. You are terrified of your life ending. Tell me, do you have a God?"

"Do I have an imaginary friend? No, I grew out of that when I was six."

Even though Jez can feel his pulse getting weaker, his heartbeat seems to be getting louder and louder in his ears. "You don't really believe in God do you? You must know that's all made up bullshit?"

"I have faith; I don't care about the details or the interpretations. All I need to know is that I have faith. That is why I am not shaking, I have no fear. No matter how much training and how much skill your people have, you will never have faith like my people."

Jez growls in anger, frustration and pain, as he feels the precious liquid life force flowing out of him from just above the knee.

"The British Empire was built on faith, the World Wars were won on faith – but now you have no faith. Now, you win battles on firepower, not on faith. That's why you couldn't win in Afghanistan – your hearts weren't in it, but the people of faith that you face will never accept defeat, or bow to a godless people." Amin looks at peace, almost glowing. He might have been meditating, not dying, but dying he was.

Jez fights to cling to life and a tear rolls down his cheek and soaks quickly into the breast of his boiler suit alongside the patches of blood. He looks at his adversary with an envy of the glory that he is feeling. He whimpers as he exhales his last breath and gently relaxes into nothing. Amin slips away almost simultaneously, but he passes without movement in solemn calm, and maintains his light smile.

26

Bitter suite

05:00, 159 targets confirmed neutralised, ten not seen, nine disappeared, and no report from Jez regarding Amin, the additional target with no code.

Alex sits on Craig's sofa with Lucy's dozing head on his shoulder. His eyes are transfixed on his phone, willing it to buzz one last time, in his heart knowing that it won't. He hears a key rattle into the front door and the sudden outbreak of noise of Craig and the other members of the London crash-out teams as they make their way back into the house.

"Get the kettle on." are the first audible words he hears from Craig. The other three men divert into the kitchen, Craig joins Alex and Lucy in the living room. Lucy jolts into consciousness. The three look at one another, evaluating each other's mental condition before opening conversation.

"Rough night?" Craig ventures, "Are you okay?" focusing his question firmly towards Alex.

"One friendly forces casualty, one failure to report; we couldn't have hoped for much better than that realistically," says Alex.

"I know, but that doesn't always make it any easier. Have you tried contacting Jez?"

Alex has fallen into a sullen trance and doesn't properly hear the question, Lucy answers for him; "We assumed that if he was on target he'd have his phone on silent, so we texted him at 04:00. We got no reply, so tried calling at 04:30 - again; nothing."

"Shit… but let's not get too down in the mouth about it, there could be any number of reasons for him not to report in, he might have done the job and the report message failed, or he forgot to send it – he might have got carried away and destroyed the phone without thinking. Let's have a nice cup of tea, then get a few hours head down. We'll give him a chance to get clear, or whatever he needs to do, then send out a team tomorrow night to check the target location if he's not surfaced."

"What about these disappearances, any news from colleagues?" Craig asks, softly referencing Lucy's intelligence community contacts.

"We've not engaged any further tonight, we didn't want to attract any attention during the operation. It looks like they might have gone the same way as Tony Blunt." she replies.

"Roger. We need to switch focus to this Interest Group now. I'll pull together some relief for the fellas on the ground, and get a team assembled for when their next meeting takes place. Come on, let's get that brew."

A few minutes after eight in the morning, on the bedside table in Craig's spare room, Lucy's personal phone rings. She checks the caller ID; it's withheld. "Hello."

"Corporal Butler?"

"Yes, who's this? Charlie?" Lucy recognises the distinct regional twang in her voice, though she still can't place where in the North it is from.

"Yes. Good morning Lucy. How was your night?"

"Fine, how was yours?" Lucy says feigning a sense of surprise at the call, and the question.

"Busy; there's been all sorts going off through the night."

"Like what?"

"I take it you've seen the news reports of the explosion in Leeds?"

"Yes, I know, it's terrible. It looked like a gas explosion on the television. Was there more to it?"

Agent Thew senses that she is being played, but knows that there is no way that Lucy can tell her, even if she does know more than she is letting on. "There's a lot more going on, lots of incidents that aren't in the public space, and that I can't discuss on this line… but I thought you might like to know."

"Know what?" Lucy asks in anticipation.

"There's been a sighting of Zafir. He's making his way into Central London."

Lucy pauses for thought. *What can I ask her on insecure means? What can I ask that will not incriminate me?* - "Are you tailing him?"

"No, but I think that he's heading for a meeting. I haven't got the resources to track him or his colleagues, as you know, but if you pick up on anything, I'd appreciate a heads up."

"Of course." says Lucy with a level of appreciative energy. "I don't have much by way of resources myself, but I'll pass on anything I get."

"Good luck." Agent Thew hangs up.

"Did you hear any of that?" Lucy asks a slowly rousing Alex.

"Enough." he says, immediately rising from the bed and grabbing his jeans and heading out of the door in a slow-motion, almost sleep-walking state.

"Craig, Craig, are you up?" Alex says with a whispered shout around his bedroom door.

"I'm down here." Craig calls back to him from the bottom of the stairs. "Couldn't sleep, what do you want, tea or coffee?"

"Craig, The Security Service has spotted Zafir, he's in London and might be on his way for a meet – you need to alert your blokes."

"I'm on it. Get down here and make the brews, there's a good lad."

Craig switches his attention from the kettle to his phone and begins the process of assembling a reliable team. He opens a new message on his mission phone and adds recipients; *John, Mark, Don, Mike… any point including Jez*, he thinks to himself. Craig then considers the time sensitive nature of the task and deletes John and Mike – *too far away*. He adds six of his top London lads from the crash-out crews, who will not have had reason to destroy their mission mobiles, and sends them all the same message;

"Warning order - urgent mission in Central London. RV to be confirmed, get tooled up, into the city and wait out."

Having properly awoken over a strong coffee, Alex and Lucy sit at the kitchen table awaiting a response from any one of the group over-watch team. Craig sits down to join them. "I'm heading out into town; I've got a crew mustering. As soon as we get any movement from the delegates I'll start steering the blokes in the right direction." Craig takes a long slurp of his cup of tea, bangs it back down onto the table, and wipes his mouth on the back of his sleeve.

Alex grabs his other arm as he gets up to leave, "I'll come." he says almost as a demand. He re-evaluates his tone - "I want to come. Lucy can keep us up to speed with anything The Security Service comes up with, but I'm not much use here, and I'm the only one who's seen Zafir in person.

Craig takes a second to consider it. "Come on then, let's get amongst it."

Lucy shoots a look of concern at Alex; he sees it, stands up from the table and walks around to her, cupping her head in his hand, "I'll be alright, Treacle."

She smiles and shakes her head with a grimace. "You take care." she says with fear in her voice. They kiss softly, but briefly, and then Alex is gone, chasing Craig out of the house.

"Where are we heading then?" Alex asks as they stride down the garden path.

"I thought you'd be telling me that."

"We haven't got much information; we need to hear something from one of your guys on stake out."

"Let's just head into the city and grab a coffee and hope we get some good news."

"Roger. Best take the bus so that we don't lose mobile signal."

"Not many buses round this part of town, we'll hail a cab." The two men turn right out of Craig's garden and head for the A205 Circular, hoping to bump into an unoccupied taxi on the way.

"Where have the previous meetings been held?" Craig asks.

"Expensive business conferencing venues, all different locations, but all in Central London. They seem to be well-funded."

Craig decides not to arrange a centralised meeting place for his team members at this point, he figures it is best to have them spread around the city; at least one of them might be near to the final destination. Their phones buzz: "*Farwaz is on the move, heading towards Kilburn Park Tube Station.*"

They check the map using Alex's phone and agree that the current plan is still good. "We'll have to be ready to react; the operative might not have signal on that line until he gets out of the distant end station." says Alex.

"He could be going anywhere on that route, we'll have a better idea when he gets off, or from whatever connection he takes, then we can start directing the blokes effectively." says Craig.

A black cab trundles along Bushwood Road with its yellow light on, signalling that it's available for hire. Alex flags it down. The men jump into the back; "Into the City Centre please boss," says Craig.

They set off towards Kew Bridge, Alex smiles as they pass the boxing gym.

"We'll have to get the gloves on and have a re-match." he says to Craig, who just laughs at him.

The phones buzz again. "It's Ron, he's in Balham." says Craig as he reads the message - *"Aziz is moving, looks like he's going to get on the Central Line, wait-out."*

Within ten minutes, all of the operatives in over-watch have reported in, all group members are moving towards Central London, all using the Tube.

"Farwaz is off at Oxford Circus and onto the Victoria Line."

"North or South?" Craig says, thinking out loud, but it doesn't take a lot of consideration.

"South." they both say in unison.

Craig takes a quick look at the map and gets straight onto the phone to message his strike team;

"Meeting point looks to be somewhere near Westminster, preliminary RV point is western entrance to the Imperial War Museum."

He messages the over-watch operators separately; *"Keep your distance, follow targets to destination, report location, and then fall back."*

Craig taps on the Perspex to get the driver's attention, "Imperial War Museum please boss." The cabbie nods an acknowledgement.

"Farwaz has alighted at Pimlico, now heading on foot east towards the river."

"That's good; we won't be too far from wherever they're meeting." Craig receives several more updates, all supporting his deduction.

"Strange how eight targets can disappear without a trace, but these supposedly 'clued up players' can't lose their tails." Alex says, thinking aloud.

As the cab makes its way along Birdcage Walk a further message refines the possible area that the meeting place might be in; *"Marco has got off at Westminster and is heading south along Millbank."*

"We must be seconds away from the first delegates arriving at the destination." says Craig with growing anticipation. He knocks on the cabby's window again and calls through to the driver; "We'll jump out here thanks, pal." He posts a twenty pound note through the partition window and they jump out onto the kerb to scope their surroundings. The museum dominates the area and Alex identifies the steps where they will meet up with the guys.

Before they make it across to the steps they can already see a few fairly conspicuous military-type characters grouping together. Craig's phone buzzes again with the all-important confirmation of the meeting place; *"Farwaz has entered the Millbank Conference Suite, I'm playing the tourist on the river railings a good 200 metres away through the trees."*

"The necky bastards." Craig says, pulling his personal mobile from his inside jacket pocket.

"What?" asks Alex.

"They're only meeting up about a hundred metres from The Security Service's headquarters." Craig sends a message on his own phone, then puts it away and switches back to his mission phone to message the strike team, for those yet to make it to the museum; *"Target building is Millbank Conference Suite, RV is now the fountain in Victoria Tower Gardens, just North of MI-5 HQ."*

"You're not supposed to have your own phone with you on mission." says Alex, only to be ignored by the boss man.

Craig and Alex walk up the steps to join the four men who have made it there in good time. Alex recognises three of them, two from the crash-out teams, and of course Mark. "Morning fellas, hell of a night." Craig says to his soldiers. They all shake hands, Alex joins in and is particularly pleased to shake the hands of Elves and Shep. He enjoys a strong 'man-hug' with Mark too; it seems an age since he last saw him. "Alex, this is Ben." Alex shakes Ben's hand and they give each other a nod of greeting. "Let's go."

The men walk in a loose huddle, turning left at the bottom of the steps and left again onto George Street. The road is scattered sparsely with pedestrian commuters, which ensures that conversation is kept fairly muted, but Craig gets chatting to Ben about his night's work; "I had a gig in Brixton, it went all right – the needle thing was a bit fiddly though." The group bumps into another member as they turn right onto Abington Street, taking their number to seven. They walk on south for a further 350 metres before entering the Gardens, and then follow the path across, past a large monument, to the river-side walk-way. They enjoy the views across the Thames to Lambeth Palace, and Alex feels like some kind of perverse tourist on his way to create havoc. Soon enough they are at the fountain and are met by Don and another two operatives.

Craig checks his phone; four more of the delegates have entered the meeting place. He looks around the park and can see a few of the tracking team in their fall back positions.

Craig greets the rest of the men as the group converges round the fountain, but he dispenses with full pleasantries. Alex is unsure of what Craig has in mind and wonders how he plans to crack this particular nut.

"Right gents, a good night's work last night, but we've got a group of serious enemy organisers congregating in that building behind me." Craig points a thumb over his right shoulder towards one of the important-looking buildings of Millbank through the trees and across the road.

"We've been kind of lucky in a way; I was in that building about a year ago for a charity function, I can remember most of the layout, but while I was there I bumped into Sandy Shaw."

"Two Para Sandy Shaw?" Don asks.

"The one and the same." Craig replies. "He's running their security team. I've dropped him a line this morning – unfortunately he's in Tenerife with Jenny and the family, but he's hooked me up with his shift manager and sent me a copy of the floor plans. I'll forward it on to you all.

"Now we won't have time for a proper recce, we'll have to go off what we can glean from Sandy's lad inside, but I reckon that with almost even numbers we can walk in there and take them on hand-to-hand without too many dramas. Is there anyone not up for that?"

There were a few chuckles and macho comments affirming their willingness, not a single utterance of discontent.

"Alex – you'll have to stay a tactical bound behind the main force; your face risks giving the game away." Craig isn't sure if Alex will be up for it or not, but doesn't want him in the way of the trained combatants. Craig doesn't give Alex a chance to respond; "You're on comms too. We'll need you to call in the cavalry if it goes tits up. We also need you to link in to The Security Service, through Lucy.

Craig looks back at the latest message from Sandy and delivers more information to the troops; "This group is the only client booked in for the morning at this gaff, so Sandy's organising for a staff meeting at 09:50 – Don you're responsible for making sure that his team get locked in the staff room. Alex you'll be responsible for cutting the CCTV which is managed from an office behind the reception desk. That leaves us with the place to ourselves to put an end to this bunch."

Craig sends the floor plan file to the men; his phone buzzes with a message just as he is putting it back in his pocket: *"Isram has arrived at meeting venue – confirmed Millbank Conference Suite. Not sure if he knew he was being followed – he looked back and smiled at me as he went in. Falling back into the gardens now."*

The message leaves Craig feeling a little cold, but he is too fired up to take notice of this inkling. "That's the last one in." he says, "Any questions on the building?"

"Do we have any idea which room they are using?" Mark asks as he reviews the building floor-plan.

"They've got the entire complex booked, but Sandy's chap will give us a heads up once we're inside. Anyone else?" There are no further questions.

"Right I'll send our trackers for a scout along the front of the building to check for any sentries, then we'll be off. Get your game faces on." Craig messages the ten men who are mostly in the same area of the gardens as they are. Within seconds of the transmission men begin to move in the direction of Abington Street. A few seconds later, after nothing of significance is reported, Craig gives the order to move; "Let's do it men."

Craig leads the team down to the south exit of the Gardens, over the road, hopping up the single large granite entrance step into the grand old building.

The reception is deserted, but for one man, who greets them with vigour; "Craig? I'm Baz, I work for Sandy – he told me to expect you."

"Hi Baz, where are the staff?" Craig replies shaking the stout, balding man's hand.

"I've taken the liberty of locking them in the staff room, I've told them that there's a situation on-going and that it's for their own safety. I've disabled the CCTV too. I believe that the group that you are looking for are in the Grand Crucible Theatre. Well that's where they asked for their refreshments to be served and that's where they were ten minutes ago. I sent the last couple to arrive that way too, that said, they do have the whole place booked, so they may have moved."

"Thanks Baz. How many of them are there?

"A few, eleven or twelve I think."

"Great, thanks mate. Have you served?" Craig asks, wondering if Baz might prove more useful with his knowledge of the building.

"Yes, I was RAF Regiment."

"Wow, you'd better stay here and look after Alex then."

"No problem, he's in good hands."

Craig leads the rest of the men to the right, through the extravagantly decorated lobby and along the central corridor. The building's interior is lined with ancient mahogany panelling, the floors with antique woollen carpets; it is like being in a living museum – not like any other place that Craig has ever done battle in before. Triggered by Craig's motion, the corridor lights come on one at a time in sequence, illuminating the group's path in sectors, revealing more of the beautiful antique panels and classical works of art hanging from them.

Following the corridor to a T-junction, there is a grand double door directly ahead; "Jonah, Woody - you take this door, await my signal." he briefs two of the operatives. He takes the rest of the group down the corridor to the left, turning right at its end. Half way down the next corridor there is another, less elaborate, double door; he details off Don, Stretch and Steely to take position at what is effectively stage left. Craig takes Mark and the two others on down the corridor, turning right onto a longer corridor, running behind the stage, and right again until they find the other set of less elaborate doors that gives entry to stage right.

The men are all in place, Craig does not want to hang around, but needs to achieve as much surprise as he can. He messages the team: *"Enter on the turn of 10:15hrs by this means, acknowledge all stations."* Craig knows that each of their phone handsets are synchronised by the telephone network. He receives two replies in quick succession - it's well into 10:14 hours. His eyes are fixed firmly on the clock on his mobile hand set.

On the turn of 10:15 hours Craig thrusts the doors open and steps back. Mark, Shep and Elves push through into the room. Craig checks beyond them that the other groups have entered on time – they are all there. He then scans the rest of the room – there is no shock or surprise. The twelve men sitting around the table, which is somewhat unusually placed on the open parquet floor of the ground-level stage, all turn calmly outwards to survey their visitors. The man at the head of the table stands, looks at the three individual groups of operatives paying close attention to their faces, he then looks directly at Craig; "Welcome Mr Medhurst and colleagues, do come and join us."

Craig does not answer, he is on the back foot; not knowing his adversary's name, but feeling confident that the fight will still be easily won with his band of trained killers against what looks like a fairly scrawny bunch of men with an even higher average age than his own team. He assumes that the only younger looking member of their group is Zafir, the bomb-maker from Hodge Hill. Craig advances, the men in front of him respond by moving forward, slowly, down the shallow, carpeted steps, past the ends of the rows of seats on their left, the back wall to their right. The other two groups react in kind and move forward, all eyes on the table of targets.

As the men reach the bottom of the steps, they are less than five metres from their enemy. The operatives begin to ready the rudimentary weapons that they have had concealed about their persons, but as the first of them steps onto the room's magnificent floor, three of the men at the table stand and draw hand guns. The strike teams freeze, like a networked group of machines that has simultaneously lost connection - they all revert to default setting and look to Craig.

Craig recognises the guns as Zastava M88s, he has fired them in the Balkans when training the local Special Forces, they are Serbian made, eight rounds in the magazine and fairly reliable if properly serviced and oiled. The room is frozen in a temporary state of indecision on all parts.

In the lobby Alex learns what he can from Baz. "What have they got this place booked for?"

"The booking form just said 'planning conference', no more detail than that."

"Did they email it in or book online?" asks Alex, hoping that he might discover some digital intelligence.

"No, the form was handed in at reception and the booking was paid for in cash at the time; it was only a couple of days ago."

"And then they just turned up here this morning?"

"Yes. The young fella was here first, he was very early. He arrived with his big black holdall - he was lucky I was here ahead of rush-hour, he wouldn't have got in otherwise."

Alex thinks - *why would he have a holdall for this meeting? None of the tailing operatives reported their targets carrying bags on the way here.* The silence in the lobby is suddenly shattered by an uneven series of loud bangs coming from deep inside the building – it is obvious to both men that it is gunfire. "Fuck, it's a trap." Alex tries to envisage what is going on in the room and shouts at Baz – "Can you kill the lights in the theatre?"

"Yes, from the control panel." Baz hesitantly shows Alex down the corridor towards the theatre, the gun fire quells, and then another loud bang as a round comes through the door, sending splinters over Alex and Baz. Baz opens the door on the right before the T-junction, yards away from where the action is going off.

The first firer's opening shots have been aimed at Craig's group, one round hitting Shep in the stomach, the others somehow missing them all. Everyone has hit the deck, taking cover behind the rows of chairs. The armed assailants stop firing as their targets disappear from view - now they consider their options, knowing that the men that they intend to kill are all experts in close quarter combat.

Craig suppresses the urge to call for a situation report from his team, knowing that his men are not in a position to be able to shout out their casualty states. He crawls forward from his relatively secure place in the fourth row to look around the edge of the last chair; he can see the nearest gunman walking towards Shep, the only man exposed, and raise his weapon into the aim bearing down straight at Shep's chest. Craig has a thousand thoughts at once, but the strongest of them, at the fore-front of his mind is *charge him*. It is massively risky, almost certain for him to sustain some level of damage, but he commits to it.

As he begins to lift himself to his feet the lights go out, plunging the room into almost complete darkness. Craig's confusion lasts a split second less than the gunman's – based on spacial memory alone, he bounds over Shep and throws himself at the blurred mass of blackness in the dark that he knows to be the enemy. As soon as their bodies collide Craig fires his head forward and connects with the gunman's face, he tracks him down to the ground, soaking up sensory information with every touch of contact. Already, in mid-flight, he is positioning his body, moving to the left to locate and seize the weapon upon landing. Craig wrenches the gun from its owner's hand, takes a firm grip of it in his right hand, and then fires off two rounds into the chest of the barely conscious foe.

The room is alive with action. Shots flash and ring out in the darkness as the operatives move to attack, the two remaining gunmen panic and fire at any sign of movement, only to be blinded by their own muzzle flashes. The unarmed men of the group stand from their seats at the table and move slowly around into the space behind it. Their leader wants to order them to join the fight, but he knows that it would be futile – he must rely on his armed men. The gunman on the left of the room is taken down from behind, by a phantom unseen, his neck crushed in the crook of Steely's strong arm, his right arm is twisted back on itself and thrust up between his shoulder blades – Steely's grip tightens around the gunman's trigger finger, forcing the shot to be released, it fires in through the gunman's ribs, through his left ventricle and out through the top of his chest. The gun is easily wrestled from him on his way to the floor.

Steely fights the urge to try and see what cannot be seen in barely a millilux of light. *Relax into it, let your eyes go, they're no good for now.* His training kicks in; he reorders his senses, builds a new picture on top of what he is able to recall of the room layout. He has his bearings; he is orientated, now every sound, even smell, will develop the picture in his head. His night vision may improve in the next 30 seconds, but for now his eyes are irrelevant. He takes a knee and focuses. He knows that his colleagues will be moving on the targets, the last thing he wants to do is shoot one of them in the act; he also doesn't want to get shot by one of his mates if they've captured a weapon and assume that he is an enemy gunman. He falls back to the soft cover of the first row of seats, then tries to make things clear; "I've got one of their guns."

Craig replies; "I've got one too."

Four shots are loosed off in rapid succession in Steely's direction, followed by another double tap from Craig at the centre of mass behind the muzzle flash from the centre shooter.

"Steely, are you all right?" Craig calls.

No reply.

The gaggle of men run from behind the table towards the main entrance doors, as best they can in the dark, the first of them trips over the body of the centre gunman, the second is tackled to the ground by Don, who instinctively follows up with a tirade of swinging punches to the area of the face of his prey, as the remaining seven fall over each other in their bids to get away. The operatives sense what is going on and home in on the panic stricken enemy.

Zafir wrestles his way free from the tangle of bodies, finding his way out of the sprawling bunch, and crawls quietly and carefully along row seven of eight towards the left exit; the sound of his movement is covered by the commotion of the multiple beatings that are going on in the centre of the room. He composes himself and stands, takes two steps towards the door, then, at speed, opens it as narrowly as he thinks he can to get away with. He is through and out, with the door closed behind him.

As he launches himself down the corridor he takes a mobile phone from his pocket, he turns left and then right, he selects and then dials a number from the diary as he speeds past Alex, who emerges from the control room door.

"ZAFIR." he shouts. Zafir flicks a look over his shoulder at Alex, but keeps running. Alex gives chase and is five metres behind him as he bursts from the corridor into the lobby.

The blast wave hits Alex from behind, throwing him forward as shards and splinters of the beautiful old double doors dart into him, sending him tumbling into the open space of the lobby, sliding on his face as he goes down. The extreme power of the blast even at Alex's range from it, does not bode well for anyone in the crucible room.

Smoke churns down the corridor as though it were a chimney, engulfing the lobby area. Alex wants to think about his friends in the theatre as he comes to rest face down on the carpet, but knows that he must put every effort into chasing down Zafir. He looks up and sees him getting to his feet with no sign of injury or impediment. Alex hauls himself up into a run, shoving the heavy entrance door, which is now missing its windows, as it springs back from Zafir's exit. Cubes of shattered safety glass are spread from the doorway, as though the building had coughed them out. He crunches over the fragments, leaping down the steps and bearing left onto the pavement after Zafir. He is now twenty metres behind, and the gap continues to increase.

"HE'S THE BOMBER, HE'S THE BOMBER, STOP HIM." Alex bellows. He sees some of his mission men moving instantly, some already on the road, having heard shots fired, some still in the park - all running to intercept Zafir. Alex slows a little to dodge pieces of office furniture and fragments of building infrastructure that have rained down onto the pavement, safe in the knowledge that Zafir is about to get smashed into the pavement by several former elite soldiers. The debris and a shower of scorched paper that is now falling down onto the road adds further to Alex's worry; magnifying his fear for Craig and his team.

Having made it a hundred metres, Zafir is crunched into the wall and then engulfed by seething men, his head is bounced off the concrete and punches start to fly. As Alex catches up, one of the men draws a flick knife and moves to inflict a fatal wound to Zafir's neck.

"NO, STOP!" Alex shouts. "The Police will be here in seconds, MI-5 might even be here before them. If you were working with us last night, you all need to get as far away from here as you can, right now." The men are silent, but clear away from Zafir and allow Alex to take over the goose-neck hold of his undoubtedly broken right arm. "GO". The men melt away.

"You should have let them kill me, Alex." Zafir says, without even trying to look around at him.

Alex is mildly surprised that Zafir knows who he is, but has an immense feeling of closure and sees no threat or reason to be concerned. He replies; "No Zafir, you're going to prison for a long time."

"I don't care about prison; I'll be coming for you. You will be one of the first of many when I am freed, but not before Corporal Butler."

Alex feels rage come over him, but restrains himself from striking his enemy; a crowd is beginning to form. Instead Alex pushes down on the back of Zafir's right hand, adding significant strain onto the arm lock. Alex can feel the loose ends of snapped bones grinding against each other and catching on tendons and muscle strands, every twang eliciting a shudder of pain from his captive. He then pushes on the wrist, wrenching it almost up to the top of Zafir's head. Zafir's body convulses with the magnitude of pain, but he somehow manages to resist acknowledging it vocally.

Sirens can be heard - within seconds the scene is awash with blue lights. Alex is relieved of detaining Zafir by several officers, who handcuff the terrorist and take him away.

"What happened?" One of the cops asks Alex.

"It sounded like a bomb went off down there." Alex points back down the path. "This guy came running along and someone shouted 'stop him, he's the bomber', so I shoved him into the wall as he came past and put him in an arm lock."

"Good work young man. We'll need to take a statement."

"Of course, yes. Can I just phone my girlfriend? I'm supposed to be meeting her."

"No problem, come and see me when you've finished, we'll take you somewhere more comfortable."

"Cheers." Alex says as he pulls out his phone and begins to dial Lucy. He walks across the road and into the gardens, wandering northwards as he speaks; "Lucy, they're all dead, all of them, Craig, Mark, all of them." he says through his tears. He hangs up the phone and then increases the speed of his walk to a gentle run, he comes out of the north end of the park where he had entered it earlier that morning and hails the first cab that he sees.

27

Epilogue

Sky News, Wednesday 21 June, a week on:

"As the security services pore over the scene of the Millbank bombing, in which forty-one people are now known to have died, there are theories developing that the blast could be linked to the killing of over one hundred and fifty suspects from the UK terror watch list.

"Several killings made the headlines over the last week, but the Home Secretary has said in a press conference this morning that those deaths are highly likely to be connected to the explosion in Central London. He added that 'many more individuals also listed on the Government's terror watch list appear to have died under suspicious circumstances'.

"A source close to the investigation said that 'it has taken nearly a week for this to come to light, as whoever is responsible used covert and almost undetectable methods'. The investigation continues."

The coverage made no specific mention of the deaths of the ten former Servicemen, nor did Alex expect it to. The conference building had suffered irreparable damage to its fine heritage. It required a structural rebuild of most of the ground floor, and the two levels directly above the blast area had been completely destroyed, leaving only the heavy beams in the roof. Twenty of the dead were working in the upper floors, employed by the outsourcing company which had leased them.

Jez's body had been discovered by John minutes after the bomb was detonated in London. He had let Alex know by text, who in turn had warned him to get clear of Zafir's house after his arrest – John had refused to leave Jez's body behind.

Alex had held out hope that some of the strike team might have made it out alive from Millbank, but this hope was extinguished when he made contact with Sandy Shaw who confirmed that this was not the case.

Alex had returned to the hotel from Millbank, and Lucy had been a source of strength once more. They comforted one another in the room for a while, but Lucy had news that Alex did not want to hear. She had told him that they needed to put distance between themselves, that it was too risky for them to be associated with each other, at least until things had settled down - 'It is for your own good' she had told him. She was right; she would be easy to connect to the mission, through digital footprints, and from what Agent Thew knew – linking the two of them might unlock what had happened, and that would not end well for anyone involved. Nevertheless, it still hurt him intensely for them not to be together.

Zafir had denied being at the Conferencing Suite, though there was clear CCTV footage of him entering the building long before it had been switched off. He had Amin's body in his flat to explain; he fairly claimed not to have known anything about his death, or who the other blood left in his flat might have belonged to, but it gave ammunition to the Police to ensure his further detention while investigations were ongoing. There was plenty of evidence to link him to the Millbank bomb and deeper into the investigation The Security Service would find solid links to the Birmingham Gardens bomb too. Alex would not need to worry about Zafir for a long time, but worry he would.

Alex returned to his mum's house, unsure whether elements of the Interest Group might still remain. He took precautions, and having a different surname would make it difficult for anyone to find him there. He decided to sell his flat through an agent and had asked for his possessions to be put into storage temporarily - Lucy would do the same with her beloved house.

The mission had been a success, but the outcome in terms of rate of terror activity on the UK mainland, would not be known for years to come. The investigation rumbled on, with new findings being announced in the press on a daily basis. Craig's involvement and subsequent death eventually came to light and the hunt for the remnants of a vigilante gang ensued. Alex's insistence on strict rules of communications ensured that none of the operatives faced any charges. Those who were questioned were released - there were so many victims that even without alibis, the authorities had little hope of linking any of the men to a specific target.

The revelations in the press about the suspicious deaths of terror suspects made the time right for the mission's press release; Alex hit send on his draft to the Sky News mailbox:

"A week ago 178 individuals that posed a threat to the security of the UK, were targeted by a group individuals with no agenda other than to keep the general population of this country safe – 159 were successfully neutralised permanently.

A further eleven fundamentalist leaders were killed in the Millbank bomb which was initiated by them. We hope that the country is safer in light of our action and that we might be forgiven."

Friday 23 June: Having his eighth consecutive lazy day, Alex decides that he needs some fresh air to clear his head in order to start planning for the future. He walks from his mother's house, around the block and into a comfortable family-run coffee shop.

"Morning Alex, cappuccino?" asks the lady owner of the establishment.

"Yes please Myra."

He pulls out his mobile phone and contemplates messaging Dickie to see about some new work. He senses someone moving towards him. He looks up to see John closing in on him.

"Alex, are you all right fella?"

Alex is shocked to see him, and totally unsure of what his motive for seeking him out might be, but John seems to be in a friendly mood. Alex stands to greet him, they shake hands, and John pats him on the back, strong and firm, just like Mark and Jez had done.

"Myra, can you make that two cappuccinos please."

"Don't be soft. I'll have a white tea please Myra, two sugars." John smiles to himself, looking down at the table. He raises his eyes to Alex's, "How have you been?" he asks solemnly.

"Pretty shit." Alex replies.

"It's a tough one. I wish I could have been there."

"There was nothing that you could have done. No one could have known that Zafir was going to blow the place. You'd have just been another one dead."

"Yeah, but it would have made me feel better." They both chuckle at the sick irony.

"I still can't believe it, what the hell did they think was going to happen? That they were going to win a fight against our guys with a few pistols?" Alex says angrily.

"Maybe. Maybe they used themselves to lure us there, planned to shoot us all, and then blow the building once it was full of Police and investigators?"

"Fuckers." Alex snaps, as Myra appears by their side with two large mugs, "Sorry Myra." Alex says sheepishly.

"Don't worry." she smiles, knowing him as a soldier; she is forgiving in the same way that his mother is. She places the drinks on the table and walks back to the kitchen.

"It was too easy; it must have been a trap from the start. Apart from Zafir; there was nothing real on any of the group men in that room, but they took our boss and ten other good men - and nearly me. Where are the ten targets that disappeared? Zafir's in prison, but all the others have gone without a trace. Where's Tony Blunt? I can't help feeling that we were bluffed from the off."

"Maybe. What are you going to do with yourself now?" John asks.

"Back on the IT circuit I suppose; I could do with some pocket money until my house sells – I spunked most of my cash on mobile phones and never got the money back."

"Fucking blokes." John laughs. "Why don't you come and work with me?"

"Doing what?" Alex asks, with muted intrigue.

"That's where it gets interesting…"

End

Review?

Did You Enjoy This Book? If so, you can make a HUGE difference in helping me get it to more people by leaving a review.

As an indie author, it's impossible for me to compete with big publishing houses, but something just as powerful as heavy advertising and promotion is a collection of well-written and honest reviews, penned by a committed and loyal bunch of readers - it's something that those big publishers would kill to get their hands on.

Honest reviews of my book help bring it to the attention of other readers. If you've enjoyed 'The Watch List'; I would be really grateful if you could spend just a couple of minutes leaving a review (it can be as short as you like) on the Amazon page or on your favourite readers' website. Thank you so much—you're a legend!

Follow my Amazon Author's page for news of forth-coming the sequel – search 'Joseph Mitcham' on Amazon.

About the Author

Joseph Mitcham served with the British military in elite and technical units for over 16 years. His service not only gave him a thorough tactical and technical understanding of some of the techniques and processes employed in his first novel, it also provided him with the opportunity to develop himself, earning a first class honours degree in business leadership by the end of his service.

The inspiration for writing 'The Watch List' was taken from personal experiences from the roles that he has served in, and characteristics from some of the people that he has served with. Joseph has written an incredible, yet compellingly credible story that plays out in our world as he sees it today.

Printed in Great Britain
by Amazon

49778905R00180